# The Other Husband

Kathryn Croft is the bestselling author of seven psychological thrillers and to date she has sold over one million copies of her books. Her third book, *The Girl With No Past* spent over four weeks at number one in the Amazon UK chart, and she has also appeared on the *Wall Street Journal*'s bestsellers list. With publishing deals in fifteen different countries, Kathryn has just finished writing her eighth and ninth novels and is now working on book ten. After twelve years living in London, she now lives in Guildford, Surrey, the place she grew up, with her husband and two children.

D0388505

# Also by Kathryn Croft

*The Lying Wife*
*The Mother's Secret*

# *The* Other Husband

## KATHRYN CROFT

San Diego, California

Canelo US
An imprint of Printers Row Publishing Group
9717 Pacific Heights Blvd, San Diego, CA 92121
www.canelobooksus.com

Printers Row Publishing Group is a division of Readerlink Distribution Services, LLC. Canelo US is a registered trademark of Readerlink Distribution Services, LLC.

This edition originally published in the United Kingdom in 2021 by Canelo.

Published in partnership with Canelo.

Correspondence regarding the content of this book should be sent to Canelo US, Editorial Department, at the above address. Author inquiries should be sent to Canelo, Unit 9, 5th Floor, Cargo Works, 1–2 Hatfields, London SE1 9PG, United Kingdom, www.canelo.co.

Publisher: Peter Norton • Associate Publisher: Ana Parker
Art Director: Charles McStravick
Senior Developmental Editor: April Graham
Editor: Angela Garcia
Production Team: Beno Chan, Julie Greene

Design: Brianna Lewis

Library of Congress Control Number: 2022941412

ISBN: 978-1-6672-0381-2

Printed in India

27 26 25 24 23   1 2 3 4 5

*For Leela*

# PROLOGUE

*Abby*

July

The pounding on the door forces her up. She's still half asleep, her senses blunt, maybe she's imagined it?

No, there it is again. And someone banging on your door at three a.m. is never a good thing.

Beside her, Rob remains asleep, in spite of the racket going on outside. He wasn't joking all those times he's claimed he'd be able to sleep through a hurricane.

Although Abby isn't scared – surely nobody wishing to do them harm would draw attention to themselves in this way – her stomach twists into a tight knot.

Rushing to the window, she peers through the blinds, although from upstairs it's impossible to see who is standing on the doorstep. Sienna's car is parked haphazardly across the drive. It almost looks as if it would have taken more effort to get it at that angle than if she'd kept it straight. No need to wake Rob, then. Sienna has come for her.

With the hallway bathed in darkness, she almost loses her footing on the stairs in her effort to get to the door before the hammering begins again. Everything about this is wrong; Sienna isn't the kind of person who asks for help with anything, and she isn't the kind of person who ever *needs* help with anything. Abby knows without a doubt that this is something to do with her. There will be no more hiding.

Shock numbs her when she flings open the door and takes in the state of Sienna: smeared make-up under her eyes, damp hair plastered to her flushed cheeks. Despite the rain, she's wearing only a pyjama shorts set under a long, thin cardigan, slippers on her feet, which are already soaked through. Abby manages to take in all these details, despite the rapidly spreading apprehension she feels.

Outside, rain hammers against the ground, an almost soothing distraction, the weather matching the situation as though they are characters in a literary novel.

Tick, tick, tick. Seconds pass before Sienna opens her mouth to speak, even though it's clear she is desperate to spill what she's come here to say. Then her words finally come.

'Where is he?'

'I don't... Sienna, what's going on? Come inside. You're getting soaked.' Abby beckons her in.

'No, I won't set foot in your house.' Sienna's eyes become slits. 'Just tell me where he is.'

'Greg? Are you talking about Greg?' Of course Abby knows that she is.

'Where is he?' Sienna repeats, spitting her words at Abby.

'I don't know where Greg is. Why would I? Look, just tell me what's happened.' Again, Abby attempts to coax her inside.

The shake of Sienna's head is so violent that droplets of water fly from her hair, like a dog shaking itself after a bath. 'Don't!' she screams. 'Don't you do that. Haven't you already lied enough?'

'Sienna, you're not making any sense. Please, just come inside and tell me what's going on.' It's worth trying to calm her down, even though Abby knows that this is the end of them, the end of everything. There is no way back.

Rob appears at Abby's side – she hasn't heard him come down – and places his hand on her shoulder as he squints into the night. 'Sienna? What's going on?'

She turns to him, and her ghost-like face softens a tiny fraction. Of course, it isn't Rob her venom is aimed at.

'Ask your wife,' she says. 'She knows exactly what's going on. And soon the police will too.'

And then she's gone, leaving the screech of her car tyres burning in Abby's ears.

*PART ONE*

# ONE

## *Abby*

Late April

'Are you happy here?' Rob asks, handing her a glass of Prosecco.

They've been living in their house in Winchmore Hill for three weeks and four days now, and this is the first time he's asked Abby anything like this. She takes her glass and places it on the carpet beside her. It's an accident waiting to happen, but she keeps it there anyway. They're sitting on the floor – the new sofa hasn't yet arrived, and they sold the old one on eBay before leaving Ipswich. A tatty old thing, faded, colourless, yet now Abby misses it. It had been Rob's when he'd lived with his old flatmate, and it reminds her of when they'd first met. What different people they were then, even though only a short time has passed between then and now.

'Of course I'm happy,' she says. 'How could I not be? This is the dream, isn't it? A four-bed house in London.' She gestures around, still not quite able to believe they own this place. Do her words sound as hollow as they feel? She hopes not. She's determined not to ruin this for Rob – he's worked so hard for promotion at his law firm, and neither of them could have known it would entail a huge move to a city she's only ever been to once, and that was as a child. They are closer to Rob's parents in Reading now, though, and for him that is another bonus.

There is no way she can tell Rob about the crushing loneliness, how it has her in a vice grip from morning until night.

Rob leans across and kisses the top of her head. 'I know you're finding it hard not having a job here yet. A school will snap you up in no time, though.'

His smile demonstrates that he really believes this, and she wants to have his faith, but every day she checks online, her positivity evaporates when she finds no vacancies within commuting distance for a primary school deputy head. The summer term is nearly over, most of the positions for September having already been filled, and long, empty weeks loom before her. Abby doesn't point out to Rob that it might be a whole year before a suitable position comes up. The truth is, her only option might be to take a step down and apply for a class teacher role instead, meaning all the work she's put into her role at Box Hill School will be wasted.

Abby will never express her fears aloud to Rob. He is living his dream, and she will just have to put her own on hold for a while. Isn't that what marriage is about? Sacrifices. Give and take. *And all the other things people don't talk about.*

'You're right,' she says to Rob. 'I'll find something soon. I'll just have to make the most of this free time and get this house sorted.' The thought fills her with anxiety. This is not what she wants to be doing: she should be planning for the autumn term.

They are eating Thai food – the usual Friday takeaway that has become a routine since moving house – and Rob offers her the last spring roll. 'You've done loads here already,' he says. And it's true: Abby has painted every room and scrubbed every surface, eradicating all visible traces of the previous owners, but there is still plenty more to do. 'You can't do everything, Abby. I'll get some free time soon so I can get stuck in too. It's just a bit crazy at the moment while I'm finding my feet at the office. I'll get used to this city life eventually, though.'

She has no doubt that he will; Rob seems able to adapt to pretty much anything, and his living in London as a student means this isn't completely unfamiliar territory. Still, the late nights are taking their toll. On both of them.

'Don't worry about the house. I'll get it sorted,' Abby says. 'You do whatever you have to do.' She smiles. 'Remember?'

Rob chuckles. Five years ago, at the beginning of their relationship, the two of them made a pact that neither would hold the other back from achieving their career goals. They would support and understand each other's drive and determination, even though they are in different professions. Abby had only just turned thirty then and Rob had been a year older, so it was easy to focus on just their work and each other. It never crossed her mind to wonder whether this would ever change.

'I'm sorry it's all a bit one-sided at the moment.' Rob reaches for her hand. 'We moved here for my job – at the expense of yours – and I—'

'Nothing in the pact said it would be equal at all times. So stop worrying. Let me get this house sorted because when I'm back, working all hours in a school, I won't even have time to make beans on toast for dinner. And as for laundry and cleaning – well, forget it!'

Rob laughs. She's glad she's eased his worry. He already carries enough guilt about this move to London, and she hates seeing him worry about her. He's already done enough of that, looking after her when her mum died two years ago. Never again will Abby let him carry a burden for her.

Later that night, while Rob sleeps, his laptop still open on the bed, she walks through the house in darkness, the torch on her phone guiding her way. It feels like wandering around a stranger's house. She never tells Rob that her heart is still in their two-bed rented flat in Ipswich. They could have bought somewhere years ago, but she couldn't bear the thought of leaving it, even though it meant throwing money away on rent.

She needs to get a grip. This will be a beautiful home once they've finished doing it up, and she'll be back working in the job she loves soon enough. But no matter how much she tries to force it, she can't escape the feeling that she's left so much more behind than just memories of her mum.

Abby doesn't know it, but she's less than twenty-four hours away from meeting Sienna Wells. Her life is going to change beyond recognition, making her wish all she has to worry about is adjusting to their new life.

Sienna Wells.

Abby will come to wish she'd never laid eyes on you.

# TWO

## Sienna

There are two sides to every story, aren't there? But not this one. This one has far more. For Sienna, everything starts and ends with Abby. There is nothing unusual about how their paths cross – not really. A chance meeting, much like any other, no different from the way anyone enters another person's life. There is nothing sinister or premeditated about any of it, even Abby will have to admit that much. Random. Somehow, that makes what happens even worse.

'Are you feeling okay?' Greg asks in the morning. 'You seem a bit... I don't know... not yourself.'

He doesn't look at Sienna as he speaks, and she wishes that he would, that there is something behind his words, something to show her that he means it, that he can actually *see* her. Instead, he is preoccupied with his phone, and swipes and jabs at the screen, a thin smile on his face, as he sips his usual strong black coffee. It's hard to tell what he's looking at, but Sienna's convinced it isn't the news or anything work-related.

As usual, Greg looks immaculate this morning: a crisp white shirt and navy tie, his trousers neatly ironed with a sharp crease. It's the same every morning when he goes to work – he has to look the part, inspire confidence in the patients he'll be seeing. They literally have their lives in his hands; she wonders how it's never occurred to her that he might actually enjoy playing God.

'I'm going to do it,' she says, pushing aside her plate. Although Greg is definitely not a breakfast person, she can't function without it, and this morning she's already found room for scrambled eggs, hash browns, toast and a baby avocado.

'Where do you put all that?' Greg asks, his eyes still fixed on his phone. At least his question demonstrates that he's somehow been paying attention, in his Greg way.

'I must burn it off with nervous energy or something,' she replies, even though she has no idea what that means, or if it really is a thing. 'Did you hear me? I said I'm going to do it.'

'Do what?'

Of course Greg will have no idea what she's talking about. He struggles to see her as anything other than a medical secretary, because that's what she'd been when he'd met her. And that's who she'd been the first time he leaned across the sofa they were sitting on and kissed her, taking her by surprise. She hadn't known at the time whether she'd wanted him to or not, but it had felt right, so she'd gone with it and never looked back. Some things do change, though, and that job title no longer fits her, or she no longer fits *it*. Either way, Sienna is determined to do something about the crossroads she's reached.

'I think this redundancy happened for a reason, to force me to make a change. A *big* change,' she explains to Greg.

She waits for him to challenge her statement and, sure enough, it doesn't take long.

'But you'll find something else – you're damn good at your job and you interview well. And there's no rush, is there? You can take your time and make sure you find the right place.' He's talking to her as though he's a teacher and she's the student. This doesn't sit well with her and fuels her determination. She is his equal: their jobs shouldn't define anything in their relationship.

She rests her elbows on the table. 'If I don't do it now, I never will. I'm thirty-eight, Greg. And what have I got to show for my thirties?'

He looks straight at her then, his eyes widening. This must be obscure to him; she's not usually one for complaining. She just gets on with things. 'You've got all this,' he says, looking around the kitchen. 'You practically designed this whole house. I wouldn't have had a clue what to do with it.' He smiles, no doubt hoping this is enough to appease her.

However, Sienna's on a roll now, there's no way she's giving in. 'And that's exactly when I realised what I want to do with the rest of my life.' She's read all about how most businesses fail within their first year, but it hasn't put her off. She's determined to start her own interior design company, never mind the statistics. She explains this to Greg, seconds ticking by while she once again anticipates his response. What she wants is for him to probe her more, to ask her if she's done her research, if she's thought everything through in detail. Surely, at least he will ask how she'll go about it when she has no business experience.

Instead, with his eyes fixed on his phone, he says, 'Well, it sounds like you've got it all figured out. Anyway, remember we've got that dinner tonight? Seven o'clock.'

The dinner. Greg's work colleagues and their partners, none of whom ever want to give Sienna the time of day. It's not Marty, Reuben or Harry who are the problem – it's their wives. She can't be sure but Sienna suspects that they look down on her. She's not like them, not one of them, and certainly not good enough for Greg. Unlike Holly.

'And you remembered that Jackson's coming over after school?' Greg continues. 'Holly has that work meeting, but she's promised she'll be home by six, so I can get him back for then. I'll make sure I leave work as early as I can; otherwise I'll hardly see him.'

Jackson. Greg's son. A thirteen-year-old boy who can barely find a word to say to Sienna, even though she had nothing to do with the break-up of his parents' marriage. What irks her the most is that Holly was the one who left Greg, so it's not as though Greg deserted *them*. When Sienna came along later, all she did was pick up the pieces, try to help Greg put himself back together again. There is no reason for Jackson to resent her.

'He's a hormonal teenager,' Greg is always pointing out. Yet Jackson had only been nine when she'd met Greg – a long way from the teenage years. Greg never has an answer for this. She admires the way he jumps to his son's defence though – that's exactly how it should be.

'He's been having some trouble at school,' Greg says, 'fighting with some boys in his class who've been bullying him.'

'Oh? You never mentioned that.' This shouldn't surprise Sienna. Greg rarely volunteers information about his son: she is always the one pushing him for details.

Greg frowns. 'Didn't I? I thought I had. Holly's dealt with it all, though, so best not to bring it up unless Jackson mentions it. Anyway, I'll be home before we have to leave for dinner,' he says. 'It might be a bit tight, though, so we'll have to leave straight away.'

'It will be fine,' Sienna says, because that's her nature – always trying to focus on the positive.

–

It's nearly half past five and Jackson sits on the sofa, hunched over his iPad, flicking his long fringe from his eyes. Sienna has no idea what he's doing on it and contemplates checking to make sure whatever he's looking at is suitable, but from the little she knows of Holly, she's confident parental controls will be in place.

She tries to hide from Jackson that she's anxious, but it's been boiling in her stomach since Greg called five minutes ago. He'll be late, he's stuck in horrendous commuter traffic, so he's had to ask Holly to pick up Jackson instead. It's Sienna's instant reaction to offer to make her own way to the restaurant, so that at least one of them is there on time.

She does this even though she's dreading the dinner as it is, let alone having to walk into that place without Greg, to face the questioning glances of the other wives. She tells herself she can do it, that she's managed many times before so it's no problem to do it again. After all, wasn't she adept at putting on a show, a pretence that everything was perfect? Greg isn't running late on purpose – it can't be helped. He'd been about to leave when he'd had to take over a colleague's operation – an emergency hysterectomy. The surgeon's wife had collapsed at home and was rushed to a hospital near their home in Surrey. Being married to a consultant gynaecologist, Sienna is used to Greg being on call, having to deal with emergencies that keep him away from home, but lately, more often than not, he seems to take every opportunity to stay away as late as possible.

This isn't one of those times, she convinces herself as she sits in silence with Jackson; Greg has been looking forward to this dinner. He always does.

Yet it's impossible for doubts not to creep in. Sienna might try her best to focus on the positive, but her mind wrestles with itself. Are Greg's late nights only because he cares about his patients? Yes, he is passionate about his job, there is no disputing that, but is this all too convenient? She tries to recall if it had been any different when he'd been married to Holly, and Sienna had been a secretary to another doctor at his hospital. It is easy to misremember things given the passage of time, so she can't be sure. She'd hardly known him then. And when she had become part of his life, all she learned was what he'd let her see from a distance.

'Why isn't Dad back yet?' Jackson asks again, staring at his iPad rather than looking at her. *Like father like son.* Sienna has already explained the situation to him, yet every few minutes he repeats his question.

She expels a deep breath. 'Like I said, Jackson, he's at work. Operating. But your mum's picking you up instead, and you'll see your dad again soon. I'm sorry you missed him this time. I know he's really disappointed not to have seen you.' She stops talking, not even sure Jackson's listening.

The silence in the room is excruciating. 'How's school?' she asks to fill the void. Yet as soon as she says it, she's aware that if he's being bullied and getting into fights, then this is the last thing he will want to discuss. Still, it is an opening for him to talk to her about it if he wants to, although she doubts this will be the case.

What Sienna also wants to ask him about is Holly. For four years she's been intrigued to know more about her husband's ex-wife – Greg only ever serving her snippets of information. It's understandable after Holly had left him in shreds, yet Sienna longs to know more about the woman Greg had loved so much. The woman before. Unfortunately, Greg is a closed book, his lips tightening whenever she ventures Holly's name. Sienna knows this yearning for information isn't healthy, but she needs to fill in the missing pieces of her husband.

You'd think that because of Jackson, and the amount of time he spends at Sienna's house, she'd have got to know Holly fairly well by now, but this is far from the case. It's Greg who usually does the pick-ups and drop-offs, and even when Holly does have to come and get him, like this evening, Holly will wait in the car, offering only a quick wave in Sienna's direction.

There's only been one time when Sienna's seen her close enough to study her features, and that's when she came to see Greg at the hospital, long before he and Sienna were anything. Sienna can still recall Holly's face lighting up in the corridor as Greg walked towards her, the way she wrapped her arms around him as if there was nobody watching them. Or as if she didn't care if there had been. Neither of them had noticed Sienna pass right by them, and she'd smiled to herself to witness such an unrestrained display of affection. Of course, this was long before she had any feelings for Greg, long before that kiss. But it had shocked her how soon after this Holly had left him.

'School's okay,' Jackson says, still not gracing her with eye contact.

It's clear that she won't get much more from him, so she gives up. 'Do you want to watch Netflix while you wait for your mum?' This isn't much better than his iPad, but at least there'll be some noise in the room, drowning out the excruciating silence.

Jackson answers with no hesitation. 'Yes, please.'

At least he's always polite.

–

In the end, Greg is forty-five minutes late to the restaurant. Sienna sits at the bar of The Ivy in Covent Garden and does her usual thing. She's unable to recognise that her loquaciousness is masking nerves. Anxiety even. She has convinced herself that her confidence is finally genuine, coming only from strength of character that she's fought hard to develop. In this moment, she would never believe for a second that soon all of that is about to change.

Marty sits beside her; he's the only one of Greg's friends who bothers to engage her in conversation beyond a polite but forced greeting, and Sienna is fond of him, despite his wife.

'So, how's life treating you?' he asks. The smile that follows is warm and friendly. The other two – Reuben and Harry – have already greeted her and are now standing next to them, leaning over the bar engaged in a heated debate about something medical she won't even try to make sense of.

Marty is a cardiothoracic surgeon and Greg's closest friend at work. She had no idea what cardiothoracic meant when she first applied for a job at St. Thomas', but she'd made sure she did her research, spending hours filling herself up with medical information that wouldn't ever come up in the interview. Although she'd had plenty of admin experience, none of it was in the medical field, so she needed an advantage to make her interviewers believe she was the only person for the job. It was never intended to be a career, just something interesting to delve into while she waited for inspiration to hit.

'Very well thanks, Marty.' She pats his arm. 'How about you? How are *you* doing?'

He points to his wife who, as usual, is keeping her distance, huddled at the bar with Eva and Nikki. Sienna likens it to the huddles of mothers in a school playground, forming a clique and deliberately excluding others, although, having no children, Sienna's never experienced this. The three women have barely acknowledged her since she got there, and the little they have said has been only to ask where Greg is. She knows, without having witnessed it, that Holly would never have had this issue.

'Jo and the kids always keep me busy,' Marty says. 'Oh, and the surgeries, of course.' He laughs.

This is something else she likes about Marty – he's a top surgeon in his field, and works just as hard as Greg, yet his wife and children always come first. They are what make him truly content and fulfilled, this is clear for anyone to see. And even now, after being married for far longer than she and Greg, he still can't keep his eyes off Joanna.

'So, how's Jackson?' Marty asks.

'He's great. Doing well at school.' She makes it sound like she knows this first-hand, yet all she's doing is relaying what Greg passes on. 'He was with me after school this afternoon, as Holly had something she needed to do.' This makes it sound as though she knows Holly well, as if they are friends who are aware of each other's movements. Sienna hopes that by mentioning her, Marty might reveal something – anything – about the woman. He'd known her well when she and Greg were married, so it stands to reason that he'd be someone who could share some information. Sienna just has to be careful how she approaches it; everyone knows that Greg is reluctant to talk about his previous marriage.

'Ah, Holly,' he mutters. 'How is she?'

'She's well. You're not in touch then? Only, I thought you were good friends?'

Marty rolls his eyes. 'Yes, we were actually. And I know it was hard on Jo, but it was best we kept out of it. It's always awkward when a marriage falls apart and you have mutual friends. Difficult choices have to be made.' His eyes shift to the door; he's nervous talking to her about Greg's ex-wife. 'Still, Jackson's a great kid, isn't he?'

'Yes,' she agrees, even though she's got little to base this on. Maybe he is, maybe he isn't – in the four years she's been with Greg she's never quite worked this out. He's just Jackson. A boy who keeps as far away from her as he can, despite her best efforts to bond with him. He's never rude to her, though, she has to at least give him that.

'I expect you and Greg will have children soon enough.' It isn't really a question and, coming from anyone else, she might take offence, but Marty's eyes are still glued to his wife, who is now talking animatedly to the other two women. Sienna's sure he's just making small talk to keep her company. She notices, though, that every so often Jo glances in their direction, prob-ably desperate to stop Marty having a cosy chat with her, but equally unable to pull herself away from the gossip her friends will be sharing.

Jo doesn't need to worry about Sienna, though. She wouldn't so much as flirt with another man, let alone another woman's husband. She can't say the same for Nikki, Reuben's wife, though; the woman takes every opportunity to fawn over Greg, touching his arm, her voice turning gentler, more feminine, when she talks to him. It turns Sienna's stomach. She should laugh about it really – Greg would never respond to someone so obvious. Nikki is a commanding woman, though, a managing director for a technology company, and with the exception of Eva and Jo, she treats everyone like one of her employees.

'No children for us,' Sienna tells Marty. She has no desire to have a baby and is certain it will never burn within her. It doesn't worry her that she's leaving it late. It has nothing to do with not being maternal or caring – nobody could accuse her of that – it's just that she's happy with what she has. She and Greg in their own world, a new career path to focus on. There isn't room for anything else. And even though he's never said it, she's certain that Greg feels his baby days are behind him. At least they are on the same page with that.

Marty seems shocked by her response. 'Oh, I thought—'

'Sorry I'm late.' Greg appears, pulling at his tie. 'So what have I missed?'

After this, the rest of the night proceeds exactly as she knows it will – the men discussing the latest medical advances or surgeries while Joanna, Nikki and Eva exclude her as much as possible. She deliberately makes this difficult for them, taking every opportunity to insert herself into their conversation, but eventually she tires of this game and is left feeling dejected. They want her to feel like an outsider; their judgement of her screams from their pores. She's not on their career level; therefore, she's not worthy of their company.

It's not like her to give in to them, to anything.

But she can't stop wondering what Marty was about to say before Greg turned up.

–

Later, as she lies in bed, she watches Greg through the open door of the en-suite bathroom, listening to the hum of his electric toothbrush as he meticulously brushes his teeth. Four years together have done nothing to lessen the attraction she feels for him, and she longs to feel the warmth of his skin against hers. She can't remember the last time he touched her – has it been weeks? Surely not months? Things always seem to get in the way. Tonight, she is determined to change this.

When Greg finishes in the bathroom and climbs under the duvet, Sienna slides her arm across his chest, surprised by how cold his skin feels. Placing his hand on hers, he prevents her moving any further along his body. 'Sienna, I'm really tired.

I'm sorry. Today was… let's just say it was a very long, difficult one.'

Will tomorrow be the day he finally runs out of excuses?

# THREE

## *Abby*

She is restless today, has been since she woke up in the morning to the sound of Rob showering. Normally she's up before him, even during this time between jobs. That's how she likes to think of it; she's not unemployed as such, devoid of a job – her life has simply hit pause. It's temporary; she will soon be back on her feet, holding her head high. Abby loves to get a head start on the day, to be awake before most people stir and have a moment to catch her breath. Old habits die hard.

Perhaps it's a sixth sense she doesn't realise she's in tune with, but there's definitely something in the air, even though she's barely conscious of it. There's no way she can know that within hours things will be set in motion that will change her life forever.

'It's still weird that you've gone,' Mel says, her sigh a static blast down the phone.

Rob has left for work, and the whole day stretches before Abby like a vast ocean. There are a thousand things she could get stuck into; none she actually wants to. Right in that moment she can't plan beyond talking to her closest friend on the phone, relishing the comforting familiarity of her voice.

'I've got the whole Easter holidays ahead of me,' Mel continues, 'and no one to spend it with. What am I going to do?'

Abby laughs – this couldn't be further from the truth. Mel is a social butterfly; her evenings will be spent seeing family and friends, while her days will be filled with lesson planning. She can't relax until she's organised for the next term. Unlike Abby. Rob always teases her about how she can be so effective at her job when she lives in chaos.

'I wish I was there,' Abby says. 'I miss Box Hill. And you, of course.'

'We've still got each other,' Mel assures her. 'Distance won't change that, will it?'

She doubts this but won't let Mel know her fears. Life has changed beyond all recognition and, aside from Rob, Mel is the only thread linking her to her old existence. Before Abby left Ipswich, they both made promises to stay in touch, swearing to message constantly and visit every school holiday. Now, Abby wonders for how long they'll be able to maintain this. Life will eventually get in the way, stop them from doing all the things that in that moment feel essential. She doesn't want years to go by where she and Mel might become just two people who once knew each other well.

''Course it won't,' Abby replies. 'Nothing will change.' This is more for her benefit than Mel's.

'Anyway, I wanted to check in with you to make sure you're okay?'

Abby immediately knows what Mel's talking about. 'I miss Mum every day. It's not always painful when I talk or think about her now, but other times it bowls me over and I wonder how I'm ever going to breathe again.'

'That's totally natural. Grief is a bitch. You just have to ride the waves.' Mel sounds like an unconventional therapist of some kind, and Abby can't help smiling. Until her friend speaks again. 'What about all the other stuff, though?'

She doesn't want Mel bringing this up, doesn't even want to think about it: that will make it real. 'It's all fine,' she says. 'Everything's fine.' And then she launches into her spiel about how much she's enjoying doing up the house, how exciting it is to be in London, how she and Rob are living their dream.

She doesn't think of herself as a liar – these things she's telling Mel, she says only to protect her. Her statements are a glossing over, like painting a picture of how she wants everything to be. How she's sure they *could* be if she tries a little harder. She just needs a bit more time.

'You're a strong person, Abby. You've been through so much and look at you now. I'd have totally fallen apart.'

Mel is just being kind – she would have dealt with everything a whole lot better than Abby did. Than she still is. She appreciates her friend's words, though. Sometimes it's easy to lose sight of yourself, and it's nice to have a reminder from someone who knows you well.

'No, you wouldn't,' Abby replies. She's about to ask her how Fergus is, but Mel jumps in again. 'So how does it feel to be a married woman?'

A question that is easy to answer. 'It feels… really good. Like we're a team.' This is true, yet she and Rob were together for three years before they said their vows, so not much is different. They'd lived together for two of those years, knew each other inside and out before they stood in that church. Sometimes Abby loves that about them; other times she wonders if it's good to know someone as intimately as you knew yourself.

'Ah, you two make me sick!' Mel jokes. 'Do you realise you've set a dangerously high bar here for everyone else?' She laughs, and Abby can picture her face, how sweet she looks when she smiles.

'How's Fergus?' she finally has the chance to ask. He and Mel met during their teacher training but had only got together a few months ago. Mel, only a couple of years younger than Abby, has never had a long-term relationship. It isn't a deliberate choice; things just never seem to work out for her. She's never bitter, though, and Abby never feels awkward discussing Rob with her. Not that she does this any more – not since they got married; it feels disrespectful discussing intimate details of her marriage with anyone else, even Mel. This is one change being married has brought about.

'Oh, Fergus is fine. It's early days, though, so I'm not reading too much into it. It's funny, but now I'm thirty-three I almost don't care if I end up single. There's more to life, isn't there? And I really can't be bothered with dating apps; all of that feels like too much trouble. As long as I've got my friends and Benji I'll be fine.'

'How is the pup?'

'High-maintenance, but that's guys for you.' Right on cue, her Labrador barks in the background.

We always want what we don't have. Hearing Mel talk about single life makes Abby yearn for something she can't identify. She has so much: a loving husband, a home they can grow into, a career – once she finds a school. It's like a to-do list and she's ticking things off one by one, only to find there's nothing left, only to feel bereft.

'Anyway, what are your plans for today?' Mel asks.

She mentions the Pilates class she's reluctantly booked, just for something to get her out of the house, to rehabilitate her mind.

'Ooh, Pilates? That sounds... interesting.'

No, it doesn't. It sounds like exactly what it is: a desperate attempt for Abby to create a new life here in London. 'Well, I'll let you know how it goes. It may not be for me. I'll have to see.'

The Pilates class. Soon enough there will never be a moment when Abby doesn't curse herself for booking it. There are so many alternative options she could consider: a book club at the library, art classes – anything else that would mean she doesn't get involved in Sienna Wells's life.

The call to Mel ends with the usual promises of speaking soon, and the minute they've said goodbye, Abby is back within her void.

–

When evening comes, she almost doesn't go to the Pilates class. She's about to email the fitness centre with some excuse or other for not showing, but before she gets a chance, Rob texts to say he has a meeting and won't be home until late. This decides it for her. She's already spent the day at home alone, attempting to unpack and organise things that are still in boxes. She needs to get out and see other human beings, not just for her sanity but because she owes it to Rob to make this effort, to be happy in their new life.

Fate has a way of steering you in a direction, making sure you're right where you're supposed to be for whatever's meant to come next. Sometimes this is a comforting thought, and at other times it's terrifying.

Pulling up outside the fitness centre in Southgate, once again Abby is a hair's breadth away from changing her mind. It isn't as though she'll make friends here – everyone will be consumed with the class and then rushing home to whatever awaits them. This is London, a place where nobody seems to want to get to know anyone else. She's learned this already in her short time here.

Inside the building, nobody mans the reception desk and there's hardly a soul around. The registration email advised her to go to the yoga studio, so she follows the signs up the stairs, finding the room empty when she gets there, and peers through the glass doors. It's two minutes to seven now, so it's strange that she's the first one here. Surely the instructor should be here already, or at least some other participants.

She hears a voice before she sees who's speaking.

'Hi, are they not in yet? I thought I was late!'

Swivelling around, she finds herself face to face with the woman who's addressing her. She looks around the same age as Abby, but this is where any similarity ends. While Abby is dressed in basic black leggings and an oversized T-shirt she's borrowed from Rob, this woman wears bright patterned leggings and a yoga vest, both of which do a good job of showing off her toned, slim figure. Her face is fully made up, and her glossy dark hair is tied in a ponytail that seems to dance as she moves.

Abby makes an immediate judgement, something that is out of character for her. This must be an arrogant woman who stands before her, someone who comes here only to show off how fit and active she is. She can probably be found in the gym at least five times a week as well, and expertly looks after a brood of perfect children at home. All of this enters Abby's head without her even thinking about it. It's just there: a projected image with no foundation.

She will quickly come to realise that she's got Sienna completely wrong, yet it is a mistake Abby will keep making, fuelled by her need to stamp out her loneliness.

'There's nobody in there,' Abby points out. 'Are you here for Pilates?'

'Yep, and usually everyone's in there by now.' The woman pauses. 'Is this your first class?'

Abby smiles, not wanting her to see that she's nervous, that she feels like a small child in an imposing new school. 'Yes, am I that obvious?'

'No, I just haven't seen you before. Oh, you'll love it.' The woman pats Abby's arm. 'And Gwen's a brilliant instructor. She's actually a trained physiotherapist too, so she knows what she's doing.'

Abby nods. 'That's good. How long have you been doing it?'

'Hmm. About six months. I had an accident about a year ago and it gave me the most horrendous back pain known to man! Anyway, after intensive physio, they told me to try Pilates.' She leans forward and lowers her voice, even though there's no one else around. 'To be honest, I was sceptical at first and didn't take it seriously. I thought Pilates was what pensioners did in their spare time, but then after about six sessions, my back stopped hurting.' She rolled her eyes. 'That will teach me to make assumptions, won't it?'

'Really?' Abby is intrigued now. This woman is turning out to be nothing like she's imagined.

She peers through the glass then pushes through the door. 'Better than standing out here, isn't it?'

Abby follows her in, and they both stand in the vast, empty hall, peering into it as though they might be missing something.

'Okay, something's going on here.' The woman's voice echoes through the room. 'It should be set up ready with mats. Maybe they've changed the room?' She studies Abby for a moment. 'How about you wait here in case anyone does come and I'll check with reception?'

'That sounds like a good plan.' There's no point telling her there was nobody there when Abby came in; she will have seen that for herself. Instead, she watches her hurry off.

It's less than a minute before she's back. 'Apparently the class was cancelled tonight, and we should have all had an email. I definitely didn't get one, did you? Actually, you couldn't have; otherwise you wouldn't be here and I'd be alone feeling like a complete idiot! Which I am anyway.' She pulls out her mobile and begins tapping, and Abby watches as slowly her eyes widen. 'Oh, crap. Here it is. How did I miss that one?' She's talking to herself, and Abby can't help but smile. Sienna is beginning to strike her as just one of those people it's impossible not to like.

Checking her own phone, there's no email. From the Pilates instructor or anyone else. 'I didn't get one,' Abby says. 'Maybe because I only just registered?'

She rolls her eyes. 'Yep, sounds about right. This place is great but useless as far as admin goes. Unless it involves taking your money, of course. They're very skilled at that!'

They both laugh, and this is the moment Abby realises she really likes this woman. Yes, she's a stranger, and she doesn't even know her name, but it's the aura people project that attracts you to them, makes you feel like this is someone you'd like to have in your life. Also, if they've caught you at the right moment – when you're vulnerable – then they are impossible to resist.

28

'I'm Sienna, by the way,' she says, holding out her hand. The formality of it is both strange and comforting to Abby. 'And if you're actually going to give this another go, then you'll definitely see me again.'

'Abby. And yeah, I think I'll be back next week.'

This is it. Abby's first encounter with Sienna. Completely innocuous, just an ordinary crossing of paths for two strangers. No hint of the dreadful things to come.

–

'So how was your day?' Rob asks.

They're lying in bed, Abby sitting propped up against her pillow reading. She hasn't picked up a book since they moved, despite having so much more time on her hands, yet tonight she feels the urge to get lost in a story.

'It's been good,' she tells Rob. It is true in a sense. Meeting Sienna, however briefly, has given her hope that she can make a go of things in London. Perhaps it will take time, but she can do it. There's nothing in particular Sienna has said to inspire this positivity in her. It must have just been something about *her*. How she made Abby feel just being in her presence.

Rob reaches under the duvet and strokes her arm. 'I'm glad to hear that,' he whispers. He's not being patronising – that just isn't Rob. 'I'm excited about the future,' he continues. 'Our future.' And as Abby studies the smile on her husband's face, the way his hazel eyes are alight, she vows to herself that this will be enough. That she will make sure it is.

# FOUR

*Sienna*

A few weeks have passed since Sienna met Abby and, in that time, she hasn't given her much thought. They smile or wave to one another at the fitness centre, but no more than that.

Sienna considers Abby to be nice enough, but she's too consumed with her decaying marriage to have space in her head for a new friendship. Decaying. That's how she's come to feel about her marriage, and she's fully aware that once decay sets in there's little that can be done to stop it.

Pilates has come to be an effective distraction for her, a space she can be free of worry; after all, none of the other participants know a thing about her. She is who she appears to be: it's as simple as that when no one knows otherwise. How things look on the outside does matter; sometimes it's all there is.

Abby approaches Sienna this evening when everyone's packing up to leave. 'Can I pick your brain about something?' she asks.

It feels good to be needed for something, no matter how small it may be, and besides that, she is intrigued. She suggests they grab a coffee. It's gone eight p.m. and what she wants to do is get home to Greg, to try to coax some discussion out of him, but she senses Abby needs to talk.

There's a coffee shop on the ground floor of the fitness centre, which Sienna knows stays open late. 'I've never seen it busy before, so we can give it a go,' she tells Abby. 'I just need to make a quick call first, so I'll meet you there?'

Abby's face brightens, making Sienna wonder if she'd expected her to say no. She's pleased she's doing something small to make someone feel good.

'Great,' Abby says. 'I'll get the coffees; what would you like?'

'I'm a latte girl,' Sienna tells her, before heading to the changing rooms to make her call.

Greg's voice sounds odd when he answers. Not cold, but definitely distant, his tone certainly not the one he reserves for everyone else. Has it always been this way? It certainly wasn't in the beginning; otherwise she never would have fallen for him, and he is the one who did the pursuing. Perhaps that grates on her now: the fact that she wasn't even interested to begin with, yet now she feels like she will never be able to walk away. To Sienna, love is both a blessing and a curse.

'I'll be a bit late back this evening,' she explains.

'Uh, huh. I've got a lot to do anyway so don't worry.'

That's it. No asking why, no wondering what she is doing. She used to tell herself that this was a good thing, that Greg just isn't the jealous type; he trusts her and has faith in their relationship. Lately, though, she's started to wonder whether her determination to be optimistic is clouding her judgement, blinding her from reality. If she's honest with herself, part of her wants him to be disappointed that she's not there; they share so little time together as it is.

'I'll see you later then,' she says.

'Yep. No doubt I'll still be up.'

Downstairs, the coffee shop is busier than she's ever known it. Abby sits at a table in the corner, engrossed in something on her phone. Catching sight of Sienna, she looks up and gives a vigorous wave. Sienna does what she always does: waves back, giving all her attention, a clown's smile plastered on her face, even though she's crumbling inside.

'So, you must be wondering why I wanted to talk to you?' Abby begins as soon as Sienna sits. She is bubbling with excitement, unable to remain still, like a toddler who's about to be

31

given a new toy. Sienna can't imagine what it is Abby wants to talk about.

'Well, I was talking to Gwen,' Abby continues, 'and she mentioned you were an interior designer and—'

'Hold on.' Sienna holds up her hand. 'In the interests of full disclosure, I'm not *yet*, I'm just taking a business course so I can hopefully set up my own small business.' Saying it out loud to someone other than Greg makes it feel real, as if she is actually doing this. The course only started a week ago, so it still hasn't sunk in, but Abby's words fuel her with adrenalin.

Abby leans forward, undeterred. 'You must be good at design, though, right? And I could really do with some help.' She launches into an explanation of how she and her husband have recently moved to London and need to do up their house. 'I've made a start and done some painting upstairs, but I don't have a clue what to do with the downstairs,' she admits. 'The kitchen's a mess and I can't even pick a colour to paint it.' She rolls her eyes, and Sienna likes the fact that Abby can laugh at herself.

'It's not as easy as people think,' Sienna explains. 'There are so many things to consider.' She pauses. 'So how would you like me to help?' She's already decided she will help Abby; it will look good for her to have some work, other than her own house, to show prospective clients.

The barista brings over their drinks and she notices Abby has chosen the same as her. 'I'm a latte girl too,' Abby says, and they both chuckle.

The two of them are still sitting in the cafe when the barista begins cleaning up. Everyone else has already left; something Sienna only now realises.

'I think that's our cue to leave,' Abby whispers. 'I can't believe I've kept you here this long. I'm so sorry.'

But she has nothing to apologise for; at least not yet. In those two hours, Sienna has really warmed to her and enjoyed their conversation so much that she's barely given any thought to going home. They're vastly different people, that much is clear. Abby strikes her as sensible and down to earth, while she always has her head in the sky. That's what her mother used to say, before she left.

As well as this, Abby really *listens* to her. This is a novelty, given that she's used to being around Greg and his colleagues, and it makes a refreshing change to feel that someone is valuing her words.

They spend two hours in this coffee shop, and by the end of it, Sienna has agreed to go to Abby's house the following Monday. She needs to get a feel for her place and exactly what she wants to do with it.

–

Sienna is buzzing when she gets home that night, the possibilities that lie ahead are a drug infused in her body. She's landed a design job, something that will help her kick-start her business, and she's excited to let Greg know. She's not going to be a negative statistic – with her career or her marriage. She's going to make everything work.

As he said he would be, Greg is still up, sitting at the kitchen island, staring at his laptop screen. He hasn't heard Sienna approach, and she hovers by the door, watching him. If she could freeze this silent moment, then she would; as soon as either of them speaks then it will all be ruined.

After a moment she breaks the silence. 'Guess what? I've got a job!' She heads over to him and plants a kiss on his cheek. He smells nice, she thinks. He always does, no matter what time of day it is.

A look of relief crosses Greg's face. She's not sure whether it's about her having a job or because she's not asking him what he was doing. 'That's brilliant,' he says, and the smile appearing on his face reminds her of the man he was when they first got together. The effort he used to put in. He'd made her feel as though she was important to him, that he didn't want to be without her. 'Which hospital?' he asks.

She frowns. 'No, it's not a hospital job, it's a freelance design job for a woman in my Pilates class.'

Greg's smile quickly vanishes, and the disappointment emanating from him feels like knives piercing her skin. 'Oh. Okay.'

She pulls out one of the bar stools and sits beside him. 'It's proper paid work, Greg. And this is good for my business. Something to show prospective clients. I've got to start somewhere, haven't I?'

He stares at her, silently, for too long. 'I know. You're right. I'm sorry. I don't want you to think I'm not supporting you.'

Yet this is exactly what she does think. She's about to say so until Greg speaks again. 'Tell me about this woman. What is it she wants you to do?'

She tells him all about Abby, how friendly she'd been and how badly she seemed to want Sienna to help make her new house feel like a home. Greg appears to be listening, saying all the right things: a flashback to the way they were before something she can't explain happened to them. Still, it's not enough to convince Sienna he believes his own words.

'This is great in lots of ways,' she continues. 'It gives me experience of doing the interior of a home other than ours, and I get to spend time with a woman who I really get on with.' Perhaps even a friend, she wonders. Until now, she hasn't let herself consider that this might be something she wants – needs, even – from Abby. Sienna knows a lot of people but slowly, almost imperceptibly, contact with people always fizzles out.

Finally, Greg gives her a genuine smile, one that might demonstrate that he's pleased for her. 'I'm happy for you, Sienna.' He pulls her towards him and kisses the top of her head. It isn't the passionate kiss she wants from him, but it's something at least. Proof there is still something there.

'What were you up to before I came back anyway?' She can't hold back from asking.

34

'Just writing up some notes on a patient.' There is no hesitation, nothing to suggest he's lying. Yet she'd been convinced he was reading an email when she'd first walked in. Now she isn't sure; it's possible he could have been emailing notes to himself. Sienna briefly considers probing him further, but she lets it go. It's all about choosing her battles carefully.

She remembers there's a bottle of Prosecco in the wine cooler and she pulls it out, holding it up. 'I know it's not champagne, but how about we celebrate my new job?' She laughs, because that's what she always does – taking herself too seriously is dangerous ground and has never worked out well for her.

'Not sure I feel like a drink tonight,' Greg says. He taps his head. 'Got a bugger of a headache. I might just head upstairs.'

This is unusual; on most of the nights Greg doesn't have to work too late they at least have a drink together before bed – an alcoholic one or otherwise. It's how they catch up with each other, even if only briefly. It wouldn't be fair to Greg to show her disappointment, so she smothers it, as she does everything else.

'Don't feel like you have to come up too,' Greg says, packing away his laptop. 'It's still quite early, isn't it?'

And in that moment, all the euphoria she felt at landing a design job crumbles away.

# FIVE

*Abby*

What Abby quickly realises about Sienna is that she doesn't have many friends. She knows a slew of people, and is outgoing and confident, yet, other than Greg, there doesn't appear to be anyone who is a big part of her life, a permanent fixture. A person who will be there for her no matter what.

'This really is a beautiful home,' Sienna says one morning at Abby's house.

It's been a couple of months since the two of them first met, and each passing week has further cemented a bond between them. To Abby it feels natural and strong, like a plant that grows only in its own time, nothing forcing it, urging it on. It's surprised Abby how much she has taken to Sienna, when she'd been convinced she wouldn't meet anyone in London, at least until she started working. Even then it takes time to form attachments to work colleagues. This friendship – that's what she now considers it – has grown so organically that she never stops to question just how little time they've actually known each other, how much more there is that they don't know. It's the biggest of clichés, but to Abby the feeling is there in her bones that they've known each other for years.

'I'm sure it will be beautiful,' Abby responds, 'when you've finished with it!' From the work Sienna has already done, Abby has the utmost confidence in her. Everything she's suggested so far is perfect: a brightly coloured feature wall to contrast with more muted, paler tones; a mixture of old character decorative accessories alongside modern pieces. Most of it, Abby never would have thought of trying.

Sienna smiles. 'Well, let's just say you inspire me.'

Abby knows this can't be true. Sienna's natural confidence suggests she has no trouble finding inspiration from within.

'Seriously – I mean it,' Sienna continues. 'People have a... let's say, aura... that they project without even realising it, and it's all around your home. This is a truly positive space and I love being here. It's almost like... no, never mind.'

'Go on, say it. You won't offend me.'

'Well, it's almost like I can feel the love you and Rob have for each other. Does that sound cheesy?'

Abby laughs, even though what Sienna's said surprises her. 'Yes, definitely cheesy, but it's nice too.' Sienna has met Rob several times now, and they've spoken at length on those occasions. She is a master at getting people to open up, even someone as shy as Rob.

'So is Rob on board with it all?' Sienna asks.

'With what?' Rob stands in the doorway; neither woman has heard him come in. It's only eleven a.m. and he should be at work.

Abby frowns. 'You're home! Is everything okay?' It's always a battle not to assume the worst.

She needn't worry, though. Rob explains that he left his USB stick in his computer upstairs and needs it for work. He isn't usually a forgetful person – in fact, Abby can't remember a time when he's ever left anything important behind.

'Well, it's a good job we weren't talking about you – can you give us some warning next time, please?' Sienna laughs, and they all join in. She heads over to Rob and gives him a hug.

'Yeah,' Rob agrees. 'Not sure I'd want to hear that conversation.'

'Oh, believe me, you've got nothing to worry about. Greg, on the other hand... I'm just kidding!'

'So you forgot your USB?' Abby asks.

'Yep.'

'Isn't it backed up to the cloud?' Sienna asks, smiling.

Rob frowns. 'I thought it was, but I can't find it. Anyway, don't let me stop you from whatever you were doing.'

'We were just going through the final plans for the kitchen,' Abby explains.

'You should have a look,' Sienna urges. 'Make sure you're happy with it.'

'Oh, I trust Abby.' Rob turns to her, smiling. 'I don't have a clue about stuff like that, I'm afraid.'

Sienna gently nudges him. 'You men are terrible. Anyway, it will just have to be a nice surprise for you then.'

Rob gives Abby a quick kiss, and from the corner of her eye she notices Sienna watching.

'Nice to see you, Sienna,' he says, rushing off.

Once he's gone, Sienna seems quieter, as though she's a sparkling drink that's been left out too long and is losing its fizz.

'Are you okay?' Abby asks.

'I'm fine. Just a bit of a stomach-ache. I'll be okay, though, don't worry.'

'We don't have to do this now,' Abby is quick to say. 'You should go home and rest.'

'I can rest when I'm dead,' Sienna says, and even though Abby forces a laugh, her thoughts dart straight to her mother. It's exactly what she used to say.

'How long have you and Rob been married?' Sienna asks before taking a sip of the coffee Abby's made.

Even though Abby is certain she's told her before, she doesn't expect Sienna to remember every detail of her life. 'Just over a year.'

Sienna raises her eyebrows. 'Newlyweds. I thought so. You've got that... freshness about you both when you're together. You know, that excitement of it all being new.'

Abby frowns. 'We're not really newlyweds. Well, I suppose technically we are, but we lived together for a couple of years before that, so it doesn't really feel new.'

'Really? It's still such a short time, though, isn't it?'

Abby doesn't want to admit this, but Sienna is right. Being married only this amount of time shouldn't feel like so long.

'It's all so fresh and exciting in the early days, isn't it?' Sienna muses.

It doesn't occur to Abby to wonder why Sienna is so interested in her marriage; she's more concerned with changing the subject because the picture Sienna is painting is not Abby's reality. 'How about you and Greg?' Abby's met Greg a couple of times, and Sienna's always talking about him, but she's never thought to enquire about their relationship.

'Greg and I have been together for five years. Married for four. I'm actually his second wife.' She pauses. 'From the look on your face I'm guessing I haven't mentioned that before?'

She's right that Abby is shocked. Not that it matters. 'Oh, no, I don't think you have.'

'Yep, he was married before, and he has a thirteen-year-old son – Jackson. Who hates me, by the way.'

'I'm sure he doesn't,' Abby says. It's hard to imagine anyone disliking Sienna.

'Well, he hardly says a word to me, yet with his dad he's Mr Chatterbox.' She shrugs. 'I try, though, I really do.' Then she looks at Abby and laughs. 'Oh, I know exactly what you're thinking right now. You think I'm the reason his marriage broke up?'

'No, I—'

'I'm just kidding. In all seriousness, though, that's definitely not what happened. I would never have an affair with a married man. It goes against everything I believe in. I'm not judging anyone, but for me that's a big no-no. I got together with Greg long after his wife left him.'

'I wouldn't judge you even if you had,' Abby says, and she means every word of this.

39

'That's good to know, but it really isn't something I'd do.'

'Do you honestly think someone can say for sure they would never do something?' Abby asks. Her question isn't meant to antagonise Sienna – she would never do that – she's interested only in her thoughts.

Sienna takes no offence. 'You're right. We can't really know for sure what we'd do in any situation until we're facing it, can we? That's why I try not to judge people.'

In this moment it would be easy for Abby to open up to her, to lay herself bare and tell her everything that's been eating away at her, but of course she doesn't. Can't. There is too much at stake, too much to protect. 'Having high moral standards is important,' she says. 'What have we got without that?'

They spend the rest of the morning going over Sienna's design plans until Sienna has to leave. 'I've got a doctor's appointment,' she informs Abby. 'Hey, I've had an idea – we're having a barbeque next Saturday – it will just be a few of Greg's work friends and their wives – you and Rob should come. Yes, definitely come. It's about time Greg and Rob met – I think they'll really get along.' She doesn't give Abby the chance to say no.

–

She doesn't know it at the time, but Abby will remember the first time Rob and Greg are introduced. She will eventually realise that everything hinges on this moment, and it could so easily have gone a different way. A better way, for all of them.

They're late for the barbeque – hours late, and when they finally arrive at Sienna's, everyone's already eaten.

'I'm so sorry,' Abby says. She's already messaged Sienna to explain how they were held up in Reading and then got stuck in traffic that didn't move. It was only as they finally started to crawl along that they realised there'd been an accident. A burning car. Ambulances. Police. Fatalities, Abby is sure of that.

Sienna gives them both a hug then grabs Abby's hand. 'Not your fault. Please don't apologise – you're here now.' She leans closer, her voice almost a whisper. 'And I can't tell you how glad I am that you are. I'll explain later.' She turns to Rob and loops her arm through his. 'First, I need to introduce you to Greg – I've been dying for you both to meet.'

As Sienna leads them through the house, Abby realises she's nervous. What if Greg doesn't like Rob, or vice versa? She enjoys Sienna's friendship, has come to depend on it, and can't bear the thought of anything placing a dent in it. If she forces herself to be logical, then she knows that their husbands not liking each other shouldn't affect their own friendship, yet she feels anxious as they head out into the garden.

Greg's standing by the gazebo, huddled together, deep in conversation with three other men, who Abby assumes are also doctors. Sitting down close by them are three women, who all turn and stare as they approach. Sienna grabs Greg's arm. 'This is Rob. Finally, you get to meet!'

Greg stops talking and smiles, reaching out his hand to Rob. 'I feel like I already know you,' he laughs.

'Same here,' Rob says, shaking his hand.

Greg leans down and kisses Abby on the cheek. 'Lovely to see you again. Let's get you both something to eat and drink.'

–

Later, when everyone except Rob and her have left, Abby sits in the kitchen with Sienna, finishing another bottle of wine, as Rob and Greg chat in the garden.

'What were you just thinking about?' Sienna asks. 'You looked contemplative?'

'Did I? I was just… no, it doesn't matter.'

'Well, now I'm intrigued. Go on.'

'I was just thinking how stupid I was. I've been worrying about Rob meeting Greg, and whether they'd get along. Silly, isn't it?'

Sienna looks out to the garden. 'No, not at all. I've been doing exactly the same!'

'Really?'

Sienna nods. Even if she's just trying to make her feel comfortable, Abby is grateful. 'But just look at them out there. I have no idea what they're talking about but they're certainly getting along. Just like I knew deep down they would.'

'You're not close to those women, are you?' Abby says, turning back to Sienna. 'Sorry, I can't remember their names. I blame this!' She holds up her glass.

'Is it that obvious? Let's just say they're not in my fan club.' Sienna laughs, but behind it, Abby senses there is sadness. 'That's why I'm so glad you could come here today. You saved me from an excruciating afternoon. I usually just flap around playing host while they all enjoy themselves. That suits me fine, though. It's too much effort to talk to them sometimes. Kind of like I'm fighting a losing battle. I do try, though, and they love me for that!' She chuckles, and it's loud and infectious, wrapping around Abby until she's laughing just as hard.

It's some time before Abby notices how late it's getting. 'I'll just use your bathroom, and then we'd better head home,' she says when she's finished her drink. 'Otherwise we'll be here all night.'

'That's fine with me,' Sienna calls after her.

When Abby steps out of the downstairs toilet, she walks straight into Greg. 'Oops, sorry,' she says.

'No, it was my fault.' He smiles. 'Thanks, by the way.'

'What for?'

'For being there for Sienna. I think your friendship is just what she needs.'

'Well, that's mutual,' Abby says.

'Anyway, I'll say goodbye now, I've got to make a call. Work. Can't get away from it! Hope to see you both soon.' Greg squeezes her arm as he walks past, and as Abby heads back to Rob, she can feel herself flushing.

And there it begins. The first of several get-togethers the four of them will have over the next couple of months, none of which are anything other than an ordinary gathering of four people who enjoy each other's company.

Until, at the height of summer, everything changes.

# SIX

## Sienna

July

Sienna will never deny that it was all her idea. Later her motivation will be questioned, speculation over why she wanted it to happen spreading like a disease. She will be blamed. But to Sienna, it is just meant to be harmless fun, something to help them all escape from whatever they're all running from. And they all are running from something, even if they won't admit it to themselves.

'What are you both talking about?' Sienna asks.

They've finished dinner – gunpowder lamb, which turns out surprisingly well considering she's never made it before – and Greg and Rob are deep in conversation in the gazebo at the bottom of the garden. The fairy lights hang over their heads, small sparkles of light, making her feel like she's anywhere other than London. Sienna is aware of how beautiful the evening is – there's still a hint of evening sun, which wraps its warmth around them, and the sky is a mixture of purple and orange, like an abstract painting.

It's been a while since Abby trotted off to the bathroom, and Sienna wonders if she's being sick; they've all been a bit overzealous with the wine this evening. She doesn't care; she wants to live in this moment for far longer than she knows it will last.

'Can you believe we're talking about reality TV?' Rob says. 'How dreadful it is. I mean, what kind of person do you have to be to want to put yourself out there on one of those shows?'

Beside him, Greg snorts. 'Although, the ones where they at least have to have some sort of talent aren't quite as bad. For example, there's that cooking one, isn't there? I forget what it's called.'

Sienna wonders how on earth this conversation came up but she's grateful everyone seems to be enjoying themselves. Except where is Abby? Perhaps she should go and check in a minute.

Greg is lying back on the garden sofa, one hand behind his head and the other clutching his beer, which rests on his stomach. She rarely sees him this relaxed – mostly his body language gives away the fact that he is stressed or uptight – but whenever he's around Rob and Abby all the tension within him seems to evaporate. Perhaps even more so than when he's with Marty and the others. Her theory is that maybe there's less pressure when he's not around other surgeons.

'*The Great British Bake Off?*' Sienna suggests.

'Yep, that's the one. I don't mind that, not that I watch it.'

'What are we talking about?' Abby asks. Sienna is so engrossed in their conversation, and marvelling at how relaxed Greg is, that she hasn't noticed Abby has returned from the bathroom and is sliding into the chair Rob sits in. Although he shuffles up, they are still squeezed together, their bodies merging into one. Neither of them seems to mind. Sienna can't imagine Greg being comfortable like this. He would make some excuse and get up. Being protective of his personal space, he'd call it, but she would know otherwise.

'Reality TV,' she informs Abby. 'Not sure why or how this came up, but I do love a good debate.'

Abby raises her eyebrows. 'Are you saying you like it?'

'I'm just saying live and let live – if people want to flaunt themselves on TV, then that's up to them.'

Rob frowns. 'But is it good for young people to grow up watching it and being influenced by this stuff? Just wanting a shortcut to fame and money?' He shudders. 'I definitely don't want my future children to be any part of anything like that. And didn't I hear something about that love show? People have committed suicide after being contestants on it.'

His words should be an omen, a warning for them all, but none of them will heed it.

Sienna studies Rob for a moment. What you see is what you get with Rob, and she had quickly realised that he's straightforward to work out. He has opinions, yes, but he is never out to cause conflict. Like she's told Abby many times – a good man.

'I totally agree that people's mental health needs to be considered first and foremost, before entertainment value,' Sienna says. 'And, of course, you wouldn't want your kids to be so desperate for fame that they would put their lives out there, but they'll end up being their own people and you can't control that.'

Rob is quick to make sure Sienna hasn't misunderstood him. 'No, course not. I didn't mean it like that. I just meant I won't be encouraging them to sit down and watch that stuff.'

Greg leans forward and takes a gulp of beer. 'It's about educating them to see it all for what it is, isn't it? Thank God Jackson's not into those kind of programmes. It's all about gaming for him. Actually, I don't know if that's a good or bad thing. Anyway, like I said, if the people on these shows actually have a talent, then it's fairly harmless. A bit like the talent shows of the old days.'

'Now you're making us sound old, Greg,' Sienna says. Although he is forty-two, she still has a couple of years to go before she reaches his decade. Given that Abby has only just turned thirty-five and Rob is only a year older, she's sure they won't be offended by her statement.

Rob nudges Greg. 'Does anyone remember that TV show where the husbands swapped wives – how on earth did they get away with that one?'

'It wasn't like that.' Abby tuts. 'I think the wives just had to be in charge of the other husband's home and kids or something

46

like that. Run the household? Although it was called *Wife Swap*, and don't get me started on everything that's wrong with that title!'

Sienna only has a vague recollection of this show, but suddenly she's intrigued. 'So how did it work exactly?'

As Abby explains the format, the seed of an idea plants itself in Sienna's mind. She and Greg need to live a little, to have experiences together that they can talk about as they grow older. Isn't this what life is about? They need to do things they can laugh about, things they'll wonder how they ever got away with. Maybe this is what's missing from their marriage.

This is what floats around Sienna's head, everything her mind allows her to believe. 'We should do it!' she blurts out, placing down her glass.

Silence follows and all three of them turn and stare at her.

'No, no, I don't mean like *that*, but how funny would it be if, say, we spent the night in each other's homes with each other's partners – just for fun? Just to live a different life for a few hours. That's all it would be.'

Greg is the first to object. 'That's ridiculous, Sienna!'

But now that she's come out with the idea, she won't be deterred. She's determined to talk them all around, to see it through, not only because she doesn't want to look like a fool for suggesting such a wild idea, but because she's already convinced herself that this is something they all need to do.

Now they're all turning to each other and Rob smiles nervously. 'I don't know,' he says. 'It sounds a bit... wild?'

But Sienna is on a roll. 'Wait, just hear me out. I'm definitely not suggesting anyone... you know, is unfaithful. This isn't about sex. Or cheating. Look, you're all mocking those people who do those reality TV shows, but at least they're living their lives. They're not scared, stuck in their comfort zones, afraid to be adventurous, break free of conventions.'

Silence again, but this time it feels different, as though her words are seeping in, planting themselves in their minds, growing despite resistance.

47

Finally, Abby breaks the silence. 'You know, it might actually be quite fun.' She giggles. Sienna knows that she would never have agreed without the help of alcohol.

Beside her, Rob frowns. 'But... really?' He turns to Greg. 'I think our wives might have just lost the plot.'

Sienna waits for Greg to agree with Rob, to put forward his objection, because there is little chance of him going for this. He remains silent for a moment, lifting his glass to his mouth and putting it straight back down again. He misses the side table and the glass crashes to the lawn, beer pooling across the grass. 'Shit,' Greg says, leaning down to retrieve his glass. 'Better get another one.'

It crosses Sienna's mind to follow him, to push him for an answer, because she fears that once he comes back the momentum of the conversation will be lost. They will move on to other topics, her idea trampled on and abandoned, and if anyone remembers it in the morning, then they'll put it down to too much alcohol.

She takes a tentative step forward, to follow Greg, but thinks better of it. She can't conjure up a good enough excuse to go after him, so instead she turns back to Abby and Rob, who are animatedly discussing the show they've been speaking of.

'No, nobody cheated on anyone,' Abby insists. 'It really wasn't like that. I think they used to put completely incompatible families together – to cause conflict. It's all about the conflict, isn't it?'

'But I bet someone must have done. Behind the cameras,' Rob says. 'I'm sure the cameramen weren't there all night.'

'No, but I think they all had kids. Seriously, it was more about families.' When Abby says this, her last word comes out as *fam-leees*, and Sienna starts laughing.

'Well, luckily none of us have any kids living with us,' she says.

Rob chuckles. Is he coming around to the idea? 'Ah, but you could just google how to entertain kids, couldn't you? You can learn how to do anything online.'

Sienna only half listens as they continue this discussion. All her focus is on watching the house, where through the bi-fold doors she can see Greg in the kitchen, pouring himself another drink. It's hard to tell from this distance, but his head leans to the side, as if he's balancing his phone on his shoulder.

When he finally wanders back to them, her eyes fix on him as he approaches, a dark silhouette against the warm golden glow of the kitchen lights. The bi-fold doors are still open, and she envisages the swarm of moths and other insects they'll find once they head back inside.

'Let's do it,' Greg says, easing himself back in his chair. 'I'm up for a laugh. And Rob, I totally trust you to be a gentleman around my wife.' There are chuckles all around.

'Okay,' Abby says. 'You only live once, right?' She holds up her glass.

Rob's eyes widen, but eventually he nods. 'Looks like I'm outvoted then.'

'Cheers!' Greg says, clinking his glass against Abby's.

This should feel good. Sienna has got her own way, just like one of the jurors in her favourite film who manages to convince all the others to change their verdict. This outlandish suggestion is hers and now they're all agreeing to do it. She is wielding power over all of them.

Instead, she feels cold. Detached. It doesn't feel real. But in her usual style, she easily forces out a '*cheers*'.

'There have to be strict ground rules, though,' she warns them. 'No sleeping in the same beds, of course.'

'Oh, no, that would be weird,' Abby says. 'No offence, Greg.'

He holds up his hands. 'None taken.'

'And it goes without saying,' Sienna continues, 'no physical contact of any kind. We are just house guests in each other's homes for one night, nothing more.'

Everyone murmurs their assent.

'Also, I don't like the idea of it being a *wife* swap. I think it should be the husbands who go into the wives' homes.'

Abby giggles. 'A husband swap is much more twenty-first century.'

While the three of them all speak at once, their animated voices blurring into each other, Sienna's whole body begins to buzz, melting the numbness she feels and filling it with something else. Satisfaction?

'One more thing,' she says. 'We need to live a little. We do it tonight before any of us has a chance to change our minds. It's now or never. A one-time only offer. Agreed?'

One by one she studies each of them, attempting to read their faces. Apprehension? Excitement? A mixture of both? It's hard to tell, until she turns to Rob and sees clearly what is scrawled across his face.

Fear.

# SEVEN

## Abby

'Well, this is weird,' Abby says to Greg as she watches him make himself comfortable on her sofa. He's been in her house before – with Sienna, of course – yet now he is gazing around, studying every framed picture, every ornament, as though he's a visitor in a museum.

He nods. 'It feels nice, though.' He picks up a magazine from the coffee table – one of the interior design ones Sienna has left here – and puts it straight back down again. 'Good to have some different company.'

She doesn't know what to say to this. She feels like laughing because the situation is just so bizarre. She's here alone with her friend's husband and they'll be spending the whole night together. Even though everyone is aware of what they are doing, it still somehow feels illicit.

'What's so funny?' Greg asks.

She hasn't even realised that she's laughing. 'Nothing. Just ignore me.'

He looks around. 'It's peaceful here. It doesn't feel the same as my house.'

'Well, they're two different houses, aren't they?' Again, she wants to laugh, but she has no idea why.

'Ha, yes, you're right. But it's more than that. Here it's calm. Quiet, but in a nice way. My house is just… empty.'

'Oh, I find that hard to believe with someone as lively as Sienna living in it. I've never met anyone so…' She searches for the right word. 'Full of life?'

'Vivacious?' Greg says. 'Yes, she's certainly that.'

'So how can your house feel empty?'

He ignores her question. 'I think another drink is in order. I've got this.' He reaches down to the rucksack he's brought with him and pulls out a bottle of wine.

'I thought you had pyjamas in that bag,' Abby says, chuckling again. Even in her drunken state she's aware that she's acting like a schoolgirl.

'It's all about priorities,' Greg says, smiling and holding the bottle towards her. 'Do you want to pour it or shall I?'

When she comes back from the kitchen, Greg is looking at the photos on the mantelpiece. 'Here you go,' Abby says, handing him a glass. 'Shall we sit?' She doesn't want him asking who's in the photos, doesn't want to think about her mum. She's still grieving, and it only takes the mention of her mother to set her off again. 'You're right, actually,' she says, quickly.

Greg smiles. 'Well, I usually am, but what exactly am I right about?'

'About this house being peaceful. It really is. I can't explain why, but I do feel calm here. At least since Sienna worked her magic.'

'Houses are like people,' Greg says, holding up his glass and staring at it. 'They all have a story to tell. And maybe happy things happened in here.'

She thinks about the previous owners – a middle-aged couple with three children – she forgets their names. Carolina and Doug, was it? Something like that. Or was it Stephanie and Mike? She can't remember. They'd seemed happy enough every time she and Rob viewed the house. They'd sold so they could move to Ireland to be closer to the wife's – whatever her name was – parents.

'I've never really thought about it,' she tells Greg.

'Well, make the most of this peace because it will all change if you have kids, which according to Rob won't be too long from now.' He winks, but somehow, coming from Greg it isn't creepy.

Abby blushes. 'Is that what he told you? We haven't really spoken about it. There's been a lot going on.' She and Rob often make references to future kids, but neither of them has actually suggested trying for a baby. It's as if they've thrown a ball in the air that neither one of them is waiting to catch.

Greg's eyes widen. 'A lot going on? Like what? Anything you want to talk about?'

'What, are you a counsellor now or something?'

'No, just happy to chat about anything.' He looks at his watch. 'And there's still time to fill. The night is pretty young, I'd say.'

If she didn't know it before, Abby decides she likes Greg. When she'd first met him, he'd struck her as serious, but now she's seeing that when you break through his surface, as she's doing now, there lies a sharp sense of humour, even if it is understated.

'I just meant moving house was stressful. Leaving my hometown behind. It's... lonely. A crushing kind of loneliness. Until I met Sienna.' She's had far too much to drink. She needs to be careful what she reveals to Greg. Some avenues should never be explored. She needs to change the subject. 'I feel so lucky to have met her. She's become a really good friend. And she's definitely a lot of fun.'

Greg nods. 'Yes, and what could be more fun than swapping partners for a night?' He raises his glass and she clinks hers against his, both of them bursting into laughter when they realise their glasses are empty.

'How about another?' Greg says. 'I'm beginning to feel like I'm sobering up.'

It's bizarre to see Greg like this when he's usually so guarded. 'Shouldn't doctors be above all that?'

'Probably. But we're human too. We might also have things we need to block out.'

If she hadn't been drinking, she'd have deliberately ignored his statement. It feels too personal, too much like interfering in his marriage with Sienna, even though she can't be sure this is what he's referring to. Since getting to know Sienna, Abby has had a picture in her head that she and Greg fit together like jigsaw pieces, and she doesn't want that image to crumble before her – what would that mean for the rest of them? But despite this, the alcohol gets the better of her.

'What would that be then?' she asks, her words so slurred that they barely make sense, even to her own ears.

'Oh nothing.' He smiles. 'This is all getting a bit serious, isn't it? Shouldn't we be talking about lighter things?'

She wags her finger. 'That's very true. Hang on and I'll hunt down something else to drink. This one won't last long, will it?' Even though there is plenty left in the bottle Greg brought, she's at that stage now where she doesn't want the buzz to wear off. She hasn't had this feeling since her twenties when she'd spend her nights clubbing until the early morning. This is an escape for Abby, and she doesn't know when another chance will come along.

She stands up and teeters, falling straight back to the sofa. 'Oops!'

'Let me go,' Greg offers. 'I think I can find my way around your kitchen.'

He begins to stand, but Abby beats him to it – this time able to steady herself. 'No, I insist. You just stay here and… make yourself at home. I mean, that is what we're supposed to do, isn't it? But not too much at home, right?' More laughter, from her, or both of them, she no longer knows.

'I already feel at home,' Greg says, smiling and resting his head back against the sofa.

A frisson of excitement passes through her in that moment; it's not that she's attracted to Greg – although he is a good-looking man – but it feels nice to have his company for a few hours. Different company. Rob doesn't even cross her mind.

All that's in the cupboards is an opened bottle of gin. There's nothing to mix it with and no way she's going to burn her throat with that stuff, but she hopes Greg won't mind it.

'Straight gin,' he says, when she hands him a glass and takes a sip. 'We can pretend we're young again with no standards! I might need a coffee after this.'

Abby agrees that they should definitely have coffee afterwards, yet she's disappointed there's no more alcohol.

There's nothing unusual about the next couple of hours; they're just two people having a drink together, talking without restraint. It surprises Abby when Greg opens up about his divorce; Sienna always mentions how much of a closed book he is, and that she feels she knows little about his life before they were together, so it feels like a compliment that he's discussing these things with Abby. She wonders how a marriage can maintain itself in this way, with two people not truly knowing each other inside and out, but then she thinks of Rob and decides that Sienna and Greg probably do have it right after all.

'It must have been hard,' she says. 'Your divorce.'

He nods, a slow, methodical movement. 'Yes, it was hard. Harder than you could ever know.'

It occurs to her that maybe he still loves his ex-wife, but not even alcohol prompts her to go there. 'I can imagine—'

'I really hope you can't. I hope you never have to know what it's like. What a mess it makes of everything.' He stares at her and his eyes glaze over. 'You and Rob seem solid, though.'

Solid. Yes, that's what they are. Or what Rob is, at least. She feels anything but that; more like a wave on the ocean, no foundation, never knowing quite where it belongs, or where it will end up. 'Yes,' she agrees. 'We were friends for a while before we got together. I think that helps. We already knew each other's faults.'

Greg ponders this. 'Friends. Interesting. Sienna and I weren't, not really. And probably still aren't.' He looks at her as he takes a sip of gin.

If they were having this conversation under any other circumstances, she might feel uncomfortable, almost as if she is betraying Sienna by absorbing Greg's words, allowing them to flood into her and make a permanent home inside her. But she decides that their agreement to do this in the first place means social norms have taken a back seat.

'Friends talk openly to each other, don't they?' Greg continues when she can't find an answer.

She has to defend Sienna. 'Yes, but she's a very private person, despite being so, well, open. I might not have known her that long, but I've worked that much out.'

'To the outside world, she is, sure. But I'm on the inside. It's a very different thing to be on the inside.'

The thread of the conversation is lost on her; if Greg is saying that he knows Sienna *too* well, then that contradicts his assertion that they aren't friends. She's confused now. 'All I know is that Sienna's been a brilliant friend to me,' Abby says. 'I don't know what I would have done without her these last few months.'

Greg looks her directly in the eyes, piercing her with his intense dark stare. He's an attractive man – the sort of attractiveness that creeps up on you, that you don't know is there until it's bowling you over, chiselling away at your control. Above anything, it's his personality. Even after drinking all evening, he's somehow still in control of himself. Dignified. 'Whatever it is that you've gone through, you'd have been fine without Sienna. You're a strong woman, Abby, I can tell that about you. You don't need anyone but yourself.'

Delighted as she is by his compliment, she wants him to understand. Some of it, at least. This is what compels her to tell Greg about her mum's death. How her stage four bowel cancer had gone undetected until it was too late. How Abby never got the chance to say goodbye because she'd chosen that exact moment to leave the hospital for a break. She'd been there every day, all day, for a whole week, watching her mum die, yet Val had chosen her daughter's short absence as her time to go. 'It was only eight months ago,' she tells Greg. 'Before we moved here. She was only sixty. I've been a mess ever since.' Abby feels purged saying all this, allowing it to leave her body. Some of it she's never even told Sienna.

Greg grabs her hand and the warmth of him sends a jolt through her body. It's the alcohol. Nothing more. She has no desire to be unfaithful to Rob, and she's positive, despite Greg's comments about Sienna, that this isn't on his agenda either.

'Cancer is a cruel and heartless beast,' he says. 'And there's nothing I can say that will make you feel better about losing your mum, except that, believe me, it does somehow get easier to live with. Just give yourself time.'

And what about everything else that's wrong in her life? Will that just take time too? She wants to ask this, but of course she won't. Greg doesn't have those answers and, even if he did, she can never speak aloud things she won't even admit to herself. Not to her friend's husband. Not to anyone.

For over an hour Greg listens as she talks about her mother. He lost both of his parents years ago, so he understands and, being a surgeon, he will be accustomed to dealing with grief. This is exactly what she needs. And then he is making her laugh, so that she feels lighter, as though her pain is beginning to seep from her pores.

How is it possible that this man – who she's known such a short time – is able to help her like this when the closest person in her life can't?

Abby will often wonder whether her opening up to Greg so candidly prompts what happens next. It will play out in her mind like a scene from a film she's seen a thousand times. Only she won't be able to rewind or erase it – as much as she'll want to.

The next morning, when she wakes up, the dread hanging over her tells her that nothing will ever be the same.

# EIGHT

*Sienna*

As soon as Abby and Greg leave, Sienna sees a change in Rob. The alcohol is beginning to wear off, and there's nothing left to drink. Sienna is sure there was one more bottle of red, but she's searched everywhere and can't locate it.

'Sorry, we've run out,' she tells Rob.

'Don't worry. I've probably had enough anyway.' His eyes dart to the door then to his phone.

'She'll be fine,' Sienna says. 'Stop worrying.'

Rob's face reddens. 'I'm not. I'm just—'

'Wondering why we did this, now that it's actually happened?'

'Something like that,' he admits. 'Sorry. No offence to you.'

'Oh, none taken.'

'It's just that I'm not the kind of person who… does things like this.'

Sienna knows this is inevitable – one of them was bound to get cold feet. She's surprised, though, that so far Greg hasn't. The fact that he left with barely a glance back chills her, cements in her mind that she needs to do something to fix the cracks before they are beyond repair.

'I'll make coffee and we can chat a bit if you like?'

Rob follows her into the kitchen and stares through the doors where, outside, the gazebo lights are still on, dotted against the black sky, highlighting the mess she'll have to clean up tomorrow. She tries to focus on this moment; she wants

Rob to enjoy himself, so it's important she puts him at ease. 'Greg's really fond of you,' she says, spooning too much coffee into two cups.

'That's good to know. I like him a lot. How long have you two been married?'

'Four years.' She smiles and wonders if Rob would prefer to hear that they've been married for ten or more. Would that make their marriage appear more solid? Or would that make either one of them more susceptible to cheating? 'Not as long as he was married to Holly.'

'So that's the ex-wife then.'

'Yep.' Sienna chuckles. 'She who must not be mentioned.' More laughter.

Rob's face is blank.

'It's from Harry Potter,' she explains. 'Don't tell me you've never read it, or at least seen the films? How is that possible?'

'I thought that was for kids,' Rob explains, but at least he's smiling now.

'Not at all. Anyway, we've all got an inner child in us some-where, haven't we?'

'You're probably right,' he says.

'Here,' Sienna says, handing him his coffee. 'Drink this and sober up. We don't want you embarrassing yourself, do we?'

They take their coffee outside and sit at the patio table. The air is still muggy, even though it's past eleven p.m., and she wishes she could stay in this moment, pause it until she's ready to face Greg. Being around Rob feels easy, natural, as though she doesn't have to keep up the show. She can just be who she is. She feels this way with Abby too, although to a lesser extent. Abby is more on guard than Rob, more aware of what she says.

'You and Abby,' she says, 'have really got something special.' She's not trying to pry; she just knows that talking about Abby will help Rob feel better about what they're doing.

'I think so,' he says. 'I'm a lucky man.'

'And she's a lucky woman.'

He blushes. 'Oh, I'm not sure about that.'

Sienna leans forward, intrigued. She abhors gossip but wonders if Rob is about to reveal something about himself. 'What do you mean? Of course she is.'

He takes a sip of coffee. 'An ex-girlfriend said something once that still sticks in my head – I think it always will. At the time I didn't pay it much attention, but now I think she had it spot on. She claimed that in every relationship one person always loves the other more. There's no perfect balance as we all want to believe. That just doesn't exist. For example, there's always one person who would cope better if the other left.'

Rob's words cement themselves in Sienna's head. All this time she's been desperate for her relationship with Greg to be equal, when most likely there's been no chance of this happening. She will always be the one who loves more. With a different man, had she made other choices, it might have been the opposite, but this is the way it is with Greg.

'I think you're right,' Sienna says. 'So who is it in your relationship?'

His answer comes without hesitation. 'Oh, definitely me,' he says, shocking Sienna with his candour. 'When I first met Abby, I never dreamed she would be interested in me. I mean, we were friends so I knew she liked me as a person, but I just never thought I could be... good enough for her, I suppose.'

'Why on earth would you think that?' Sienna says. 'You're an attractive man. You're intelligent and work hard. I don't understand.'

Rob shakes his head, stares at his shoes. 'It's not about that, though, is it? I can't explain what it is, it's just a *feeling*. Please don't tell Abby I've said all this.'

'Does Abby make you feel this way?' Sienna can't believe this is true. Abby is so down to earth, so unassuming.

He ignores her question. 'So what about you then?' Clearly, he's ready for this conversation to change direction. She can't blame him for that.

'Greg,' she lies, without hesitation, because telling the truth is not an option. 'Maybe it's always the men who love larger? Now isn't that funny?'

'Can I ask you something?' Rob says.

'Go ahead.'

'Why did you suggest this?'

She looks at Rob and knows that she will never be able to tell anyone the truth. 'Because I want to feel alive.'

—

It's to be expected that she'll be a physical wreck the next morning. Those days when she could party all night, waking up bright and fresh after only a few hours' sleep, have long since gone. Somehow, she manages to clean up the mess in the garden, and with every bottle or glass she transfers to the recycling bin or dishwasher, she marvels at how only four people could produce such a gargantuan mess.

Rob has already left, having the excuse that he was desperate to shower and get into clean clothes. He'd declined her offer of something of Greg's to sleep in, saying he'd make do.

Being in the kitchen with the sun streaming through the doors, it's hard to believe this is the same place where last night everyone had gone along with her suggestion. It's too late to be undone, but now she fears things might be different between her and Abby. They have seen each other's husbands in a way that they never would have normally, and there will always be those missing hours in their marriages, long moments shared between their partners and someone else. Something they will never be part of, even if they recount every detail.

Greg has already left Abby's to go to the hospital; Sienna found this out when she texted him the moment she woke up. He needed to catch up on paperwork, he'd said, even though it is a Saturday.

It feels strange that she hasn't seen him since he left last night with Abby, and that she isn't the first person he saw when he woke this morning.

She can still picture him walking out of the door last night with Abby, with barely a glance back, as if what they were all doing was the most natural thing in the world.

She's tried calling him several times already, only to find his phone switched off. She's also sent Abby a text, but she's yet to reply. It's nothing to worry about; they're not avoiding her. This is just paranoia, and she must control it. Greg will be home eventually and then she'll see that everything is normal. A normal that she knows has to change.

–

It's well into the afternoon before she hears Greg's key turn in the door. She remains in the kitchen – she doesn't want to show him that she's worried – and calls out a greeting.

'How was everything?' she asks when he appears in the doorway.

'I feel a lot better now I've caught up on work. Do you want a coffee?' He doesn't wait for her to answer but busies himself at the coffee machine, clanging about, making too much noise.

'I meant how was last night. How was it with Abby? I hope you two weren't talking about me!' This is a stupid thing to say, and Greg will see right through it. But she's nervous, unsure how to speak to Greg about what they've all done.

How different things look in the cold light of day.

Greg shrugs. 'She's nice. How did your night go?'

She tells him about chatting to Rob in the garden, and that he started yawning before too long, so she'd taken pity on him and made up the guest bed. Greg isn't listening. 'That's good,' he says, focusing on the coffee. 'I like Rob.'

She shakes her head even though Greg isn't looking at her. 'I'll call Abby in a bit, see if she wants to meet up for a walk or something later. I'm sure we could both do with some fresh air, and Rob mentioned he's got a load of work to do at home today.'

This catches Greg's attention. 'Is that a good idea? I mean, we've just spent a whole evening – and night – with them. Shouldn't we just give them some space?'

Sienna senses it immediately – there's something there, something she should worry about – but she lets it drift away like a balloon, out of reach and then out of sight. She refuses to be that paranoid person.

'Maybe you're right,' she agrees. 'I'm sure I'll catch up with her in the week. Make sure you didn't bore her to death.' She forces a laugh.

Again, Greg doesn't respond. 'Here you go.' He hands her a mug. 'Do you mind if I take this upstairs? My head's aching from staring at the computer all morning. I just need to relax.' This will mean music on his headphones and lying back in his reclining chair, something Greg always does after stressful days at work. As desperate as Sienna is to get out of the house, she's not about to force him.

–

It is much later when Abby's reply finally comes. Sienna is throwing some random food together for dinner that evening, hoping it will turn into something she can pass off as a meal. She doubts Greg will care; he's too distracted today to notice anything.

Abandoning the food, she sits down to read Abby's message.

> Thanks for a such a fun evening! Hope you're feeling ok after our overindulgence. Just planning a takeaway and Netflix this eve – can't agree what to watch though. Hope Greg's ok.

There is nothing out of the ordinary in her message, yet when Sienna replies, asking Abby to let her know when she's free to meet up, all she gets in response is a smiley face and a kiss.

The food turns into an inedible jumbled mess in the end, so Sienna convinces Greg to go out for dinner. She can tell he's reluctant, but he gives in when he realises there's nothing she can rustle up for them.

'Let's walk somewhere, though,' he suggests. 'We can try that new Greek place on the high street.'

Their house is only a five-minute walk there, so they make their way, Sienna grabbing Greg's hand as they walk. Neither of them speaks, and Sienna laps up the silence. Sometimes it's easier not to say anything. Instead, she makes a point of being mindful, taking in everything they pass, letting the scenery imprint on her mind. People walking past will assume they are a normal couple in love, and she relishes this idea; sometimes the surface is what matters.

'I don't think we should mention what we did last night to any of our friends,' Greg says, letting go of her hand. Sienna freezes.

'I wasn't planning to.' She slows down, even though Greg doesn't. If anything, his pace quickens.

He nods and finally slows his walking speed. 'It's just that... well, it wouldn't look good, would it? I'm a doctor. I shouldn't—'

'Shouldn't what? None of us did anything, did we? It was just a bit of fun. What's the big deal?'

'*We* know that, but you can see how it would look to others?' Greg persists. 'They wouldn't believe that it was all innocent.'

Sienna concedes that he has a point. Now that they are away from the situation – no alcohol masking their inhibitions – it does seem unlikely that people would believe them. And Greg's friends don't know Abby and Rob. Only she and Greg know that they aren't the type of people who spend their weekends swapping partners. 'Okay. My lips are sealed.' She reaches for his hand to reassure him. It's felt comforting walking together hand in hand and she's not ready for it to end.

Then it happens – the first clear sign that something is wrong; one that Sienna can't ignore.

'Do you trust Abby?' Greg says. His question comes out of nowhere, hurtling around her head, refusing to still.

'What do you mean?'

'I don't know. It's just that spending that time alone with her made me see things I wouldn't have otherwise noticed.'

Sienna feels clammy, even though she's wearing a thin top and the evening air is cooler tonight. 'You'll need to give me more than that, Greg.'

He doesn't reply.

'What did you talk about?'

'She spoke about herself mostly. And Rob. I just got the impression that maybe they're not as close as they seem.'

What Greg is telling her makes no sense; Sienna has always had the opposite impression – that Abby and Rob are as solid as steel. Then she remembers Rob's declaration about loving Abby more than she loves him. Sienna tries to press Greg on what has led him to this conclusion, but he remains vague.

'It's hard to remember, Sienna. I'd had so much to drink. It's more of a feeling I got, which I still recall now, even though I can't remember every detail of what she said.'

Again, she tries to coax more detail out of him, which only leads to Greg shutting down. This is what he always does.

'Can we talk about something else?' he says.

They're outside the restaurant now, and Sienna's appetite has vanished.

If she didn't before, now she knows she has something to worry about.

# NINE

### Abby

When she wakes up on the morning after the dinner party, Greg has gone. For a fleeting moment, none of it seems real. She reaches across the bed for Rob, but of course he isn't there. On her phone there's a notification from Sienna; she can't bring herself to open it.

Abby needs to speak to Greg.

She recollects from the dinner party that he was planning to go to the hospital the next morning, despite it being a Saturday. Something about dealing with paperwork. He'd mentioned it to Rob, and she'd paid little attention at the time. Now it feels as though nothing could be more important; it might be her only chance to catch Greg alone.

In the shower, Abby leaves her hair unwashed – she needs to be out before Rob gets home. She has no idea what she'll say to him if she sees him now, or what she will do. Will she be able to act normally? It's likely that Rob will see straight through her. But this isn't the first time she's had to hold back from him; she just never thought she'd be facing it again so soon.

She's too late. Rob's standing there in the bedroom, peeling himself out of yesterday's clothes. She stops in the doorway, wrapped in her towel.

'The morning after, eh?' Rob says, smiling. 'So how was your night?'

'Yeah, fine. Greg's nice. How was it with Sienna?'

'She's certainly easy to talk to,' Rob says. 'I feel a bit bad though – I was shattered and just wanted to crash out. In their spare room, of course.' He winks. 'I see Greg's already gone.'

'He needed to get to the hospital early.'

Abby always gets dressed in front of Rob, never hiding any part of her body from him, but right now she can't seem to manage it. Instead, she wraps the towel tighter around her, conscious suddenly of her body, of her whole self.

Rob pulls on a clean T-shirt and jeans. 'I'd better get straight to Mum and Dad's.'

Lillian and Eric. She's forgotten he promised them he'd help them sort out their garden this weekend. Now she won't have to explain where she's going. The fewer lies the better. 'Okay, do you mind if I stay here? I've got a few things I need to do.' This much, at least, is the truth.

''Course not. I'll probably have lunch there, though.'

This gives her more time. Still in her towel, she begins applying her make-up, even though she always gets dressed first, while Rob says goodbye.

As soon as the front door shuts, she lets the towel drop to the floor and hunts through her underwear drawer, pulling out the first thing she finds. Another sweltering day is forecast for today, so she grabs a white summer dress and pulls it over her head. She usually feels good in this dress, confident; right now, though, she doesn't feel a thing. It doesn't matter – she has to find Greg before he goes home to Sienna.

–

St Thomas' Hospital looms before her, large and imposing. On the other side of those walls is death and life, and she's powerless to prevent images of her mother playing through her head. It's a different hospital, yes, but she knows stepping inside will be reliving the pain. There is too much at stake to turn back, though, so she continues. She has no choice.

If she had Greg's mobile number, she would have called him instead, but she only has Sienna's; until now there's been no reason for her to have Greg's. Still, what she needs to say is better done in person.

Inside, she realises she has no idea where to begin looking for him. She knows he is a gynaecologist, but this place is so vast that she's afraid she'll never track him down. And surely there are rules about the public wandering around hospitals when they have no reason to be there? She has no choice but to ask someone at the front desk.

'I'm a friend,' she explains. 'I've lost all the numbers on my phone so I couldn't call his mobile. I really need to speak to him, though. Is there any chance you could contact him for me?'

The young woman she's speaking to silently scrutinises her, and Abby's cheeks flush with warmth. She must be wearing her guilt like brightly coloured clothes, there for everyone to see. The woman's eyes narrow and there's an almost imperceptible shake of her head. 'Can I have your name?' she asks.

There's no point lying. If Greg refuses to see her, then she'll wait here until he leaves. A pointless vow when there are probably more exits to this building. 'Abby Nichols. Can you please tell him it's urgent?'

She waits while the young woman speaks into the phone, relaying Abby's message with a frown creasing her forehead. Whatever happens next, Greg won't be happy that she's turned up here.

The receptionist hangs up the phone. 'He's coming down to see you. You can wait in the seating area over there.'

It's nearly twenty minutes before Greg appears, flanked by several people as he steps out of the lift. For a moment it looks as though he's brought them with him, and it's only when they head off in different directions that she realises she's mistaken. He scans the hospital entrance, squinting until he spots her by the window. He's smiling as walks over to her, and this surprises her. He must know why she's here. The cynic in her believes it is just to keep up appearances; they're in a busy hospital and he'll know a lot of the staff here: he won't want anyone to witness him having any type of altercation.

'Abby? What's going on?' he says as he reaches her. He stops at least two metres away. 'Is everything okay? Did I leave something behind?'

'We need to talk, Greg.'

He looks around and smiles at someone passing by. 'Of course. I'm a bit snowed under at the moment, though, can we catch up another time? Maybe we can all go out for dinner or something?'

This reaction is something she's unprepared for. Is he going to pretend last night hasn't happened? That everything has been concocted by her imagination? She lowers her voice. 'This can't wait, and we both know it.'

His smile vanishes. Now she knows it's real. It takes Greg a moment to answer. 'Let's sit in the coffee shop over there.' He walks off and she follows, yet still he keeps his distance.

As soon as they're inside she knows why he's suggested this place. It's far noisier than the lobby, with little chance of them being overheard above the clinking of cups and rumble of chatter, even though the tables are crammed together. It's the perfect place to hide.

'I'd offer to get coffees, but I really am short of time,' Greg says, making a point of looking at his watch. His initial confidence has waned, and Abby hopes now he might be ready to deal with the consequences of last night.

'Look,' he begins, before she says a word, 'I apologise for my drunken state last night. It's all a bit of a blur to be honest.' He searches her face. Is he trying to work out exactly what she remembers? Is he hoping that she won't recall enough of it? 'And I'm sorry I left without saying anything,' he continues. 'You were still asleep, and I had to get here as early as I could. You won't believe how hectic it is at the moment.'

She doesn't know how true this is; it seems more likely that he's running. Hiding. 'You need to talk to Sienna,' she says. Twenty-four hours ago she would never have believed she'd be talking to Sienna's husband this way, making demands of him. All lines have been blurred. She doesn't add anything further; discussing details isn't necessary. She just needs Greg to be honest with her friend.

He frowns and leans back in his chair. 'Talk to her about what exactly?'

So this is the game he wants to play. 'You know what I'm talking about, Greg. Please don't make me repeat it. We need to tell her.'

'Abby, I'm not sure why you've come all this way here, but I really don't understand.' He is so believable, so genuinely flummoxed that doubt creeps in.

'Tell Sienna the truth,' she says. She decides she must soften her tone; perhaps this is how she'll get through to him. 'Please, Greg, you have to. She needs to know everything.'

'You shouldn't have come here, Abby.' There is no acknowledgement of anything. No guilt or shame.

She needs to try harder; there's got to be a way to get through to him. Greg has always seemed reasonable, although that was before she really knew him. 'I came here because I care about Sienna,' she tells him. Her friend needs to know, even if it means causing her pain. 'There's no way I can live with myself, keeping this a secret. I won't do it, Greg.'

Greg stands. 'Abby, I really think you should stay away from us. Okay? Just stay away.'

As he leaves, she calls after him, no longer caring that people will hear. 'If you don't do it then I will!'

He doesn't even turn around.

-

That night, lying in bed with Rob, sleep eludes her. It's nearly midnight and Rob is on his laptop, browsing Amazon. She doesn't know what he's looking for and can't muster up the effort to ask. Right now there are no words she can manage to speak; with every ticking second, it's become harder to carry on as normal.

'Do you think Greg's okay?' Rob suddenly asks, catching her off guard.

She pulls herself up, forces herself to look at him. 'What do you mean?'

'Oh, it's probably nothing, but I messaged him earlier to see if he wants to go for a drink next weekend and he hasn't replied.'

This is news to her. Rob hasn't mentioned anything about this plan of his.

'He's probably just busy.'

'Yeah, you're right.' He turns back to his laptop. 'It's just that he seemed really keen when we talked about it last night. Before... you know.'

Before they all made a huge mistake.

Abby tries to sound nonchalant, even though her heart is thumping in her chest. 'When did you text him?'

'This afternoon. When I was at Mum and Dad's.'

'Give him a chance. Some people don't reply the second they get a message.' She doesn't point out that just because Rob does this, not everyone else will.

'Yeah, you're right. I just hope I haven't offended him. To be honest, I can't even remember a lot of last night.'

If only this was true for her, as if the night was a chalk drawing that could be wiped away, permanently erased.

Rob's concern about Greg highlights to Abby that she can't keep ignoring Sienna or fobbing her off. There's no clearer sign that something is wrong, and Sienna is intuitive. Although Abby has replied to her messages, keeping the words she chooses light-hearted, as normal as possible, she can't avoid seeing Sienna for long. She has to give it time, though, and give Greg a chance to do the right thing. It is down to him.

At two a.m., just as she's managed to drift off, her phone pings with a text. There's no name, only a number, and she knows before she reads that it is Greg.

> Just give me a week to talk to Sienna. Please. I promise I'll do it.

The clock is ticking.

# TEN

## Sienna

From the moment she wakes, Sienna feels that something is wrong, out of place.

It's been a week since the dinner party with Abby and Rob, and none of them have seen each other since. This in itself isn't unusual – they all have busy lives, so seven days is not long in the scheme of things – it's what Greg has said about Abby that Sienna can't ignore. He didn't explicitly state that he doesn't trust her friend, but that's what lies beneath his comments, she's sure of it.

Whenever she reminds him that he'd planned to go for drinks with Rob, Greg brushes it off with excuses about having too much work to do. 'I just can't spare the time at the moment. We'll do it soon,' he says before shutting himself in his study.

Yesterday evening, his study door had been slightly ajar when she'd walked past. She walked in without knocking – that's what they always did unless a door was shut – and he quickly slammed his laptop shut when he noticed her, his eyes wide with surprise. 'No more work for me,' he'd said, standing up, smiling at her. 'Shall we have coffee then?'

Sienna tries to piece things together, her mind constantly whirring, playing out every detail she can remember of the dinner party and the days that have followed. It always comes back to one thing. Greg and Abby.

She pores over the few texts Abby has sent her, yet there's nothing concrete she can grab hold of, other than the fact that these messages have been few and far between this week.

But there is something, and she needs to know what it is.

Normally Sienna resists pushing Greg, even when he is being infuriatingly cagey, but this is too important to ignore. Something is happening which is out of her control, and she's not used to that. As well as this, it brings home how much Sienna has come to value Abby's friendship. She misses her.

'I need to speak to Abby,' she announces in the morning. 'I think something might be wrong; she barely replies to my messages.'

Sienna is watching Greg while he sits on the bed, leaning down to tie his shoelaces. 'Aren't you being a bit melodramatic? We only saw them last week. I'm sure she's fine.'

She's expected him to say this, and she's prepared. 'I just need to know that we're still okay. After me practically forcing everyone to go along with my idea. Maybe she regrets it.' Just as Sienna does.

'I'm sure nobody's even thinking about it,' Greg assures her. His nonchalance puts her on edge, especially given how stressed he's been for so long now. 'They're just living their lives and we need to do the same. Nobody did anything wrong; we just spent time in each other's company. So stop worrying.'

She stares at him, noticing the way he's so intently focused on something as simple as tying his shoelaces, and it strikes her that she no longer knows him. 'You're probably right. I'll go over there this morning, though, just to make sure she's okay.'

Greg stands up, his cheeks burning red. Yet when he speaks his voice is controlled, almost soft. 'What's wrong with you? You're just so... intense all the time. What if – and I know you don't want to hear this – but what if Abby just wants some space?' He shakes his head. 'You're blowing this all out of proportion.'

'So that's what you think of me? That I'm intense?' Like him, she manages to speak calmly, even though she's raging inside. The shock of his words has numbed her; he's never said anything like this before. Perhaps it's what he's always thought, though.

She can deal with criticism – she is her own biggest critic – but she's becoming aware that Greg is lying to her, and with each passing second, she knows it even more.

'I am who I am, Greg. If you don't like it then why did you marry me?'

He stares at her, his mouth hanging open. An argument like this is unusual for them; she suspects they're both too good at keeping uncomfortable thoughts hidden. 'What kind of question is that, Sienna?'

'I don't think it needs explaining. It's very straightforward. Why did you marry me?' She is measured, in control, at least on the surface.

He shakes his head, turns away from her to focus on retying his tie, even though there was nothing wrong with his first attempt. 'I really don't need this,' he mumbles.

In hindsight she will wish she'd let this go. She can walk away, avoid the confrontation that has been brewing all morning, but there's no way back for her now. Everything that's been troubling her for months – or is it years? – has amalgamated into a storm of tension that's run out of space in her head. So many times she's tried to talk to Greg about their marriage, and it's all come to this.

'So you don't know why you married me?' She is pushing him, desperate for honesty, and she won't let him leave this house until she has answers.

'You're being unreasonable, Sienna. Do you really expect me to answer that?'

'Yes. Why don't you answer? It's a fair question, isn't it?'

'It's a ridiculous question.' He avoids eye contact; he's never been one for confrontation.

Sienna's never known rage like this. It starts as a dot and rapidly expands until it's seconds away from erupting. 'Just tell the truth,' she says. 'Why are you with me?'

'I'm not doing this, Sienna. I just... can't.' He stands up, walks towards the door and out into the hall.

'You're a liar,' she shouts after him. 'What are you lying about, Greg?'

It's a few seconds before the front door slams.

She knows that the second Greg gets to work she – and this argument – will be out of his head. He will focus on what he has to do, and she won't be a factor in the rest of his day.

She won't accept it. This needs to change, and it needs to change now.

# ELEVEN

## Abby

For a week Abby hears nothing from Greg. She's done what she promised and given him this time but judging from Sienna's texts — her attempts to arrange get-togethers with words as friendly as they've always been — he definitely hasn't kept his promise to talk to her. Now it's up to her — the guilt is Abby's to bear too — and she has to put things right.

The thought of wrecking Sienna's life cripples her, but there's no way she will live this lie and cause her friend even more pain. A week already feels too long, and slowly she's begun to regret allowing Greg this time.

And what of her own marriage? Despite her best efforts, she withdraws from Rob in minuscule ways that he is too busy, or too trusting, to notice. For now.

On the final day, late at night, Greg's text comes. *I'm going to tell her,* he says. *But can we please meet first?* Abby softens — maybe because he's added a please — despite how angry she is that he's left it until the last possible moment.

Assuming Greg wasn't going to keep his promise, she's already arranged to see Sienna the next day — a morning coffee in a cafe on Palmers Green High Street, somewhere public, and safe. Now she'll have to find an excuse to cancel. The two women haven't seen each other since that night, so Sienna will know something's wrong, but it's only right that Abby lets Greg speak to her first.

*Okay,* she texts back. *When and where?*

hen no reply comes, Abby wonders whether his text has just been a ploy to buy himself more time. It makes her uneasy, but still she waits. She will give him until morning.

It's two a.m. when her phone pings. She's been drifting in and out of a restless sleep, and now she's fully awake.

> Six p.m. tomorrow. At the park near the library.

Her stomach somersaults. She doesn't realise this is her body alerting her to the fact that something is wrong. So she agrees to meet Greg.

–

He is there before her, standing by the park gates with his hands in his pockets, dressed casually in jeans, trainers and a navy hooded top, the silver zip glimmering as it catches sunlight. In time to come, this image of Greg will remain with her, so vividly it will be like looking at a photo of him, which she'll see even when he's not in her thoughts.

'Thanks for coming,' he says when she reaches him. Unlike their last meeting, she senses no animosity and he's smiling at her. Everything will be okay, she thinks.

Still, Abby questions him. 'I have to say I'm surprised. When I saw you at the hospital, you made it clear that there was nothing to talk about.'

He nods. 'Well, you gave me an ultimatum, didn't you? And everything's changed now.'

The confidence in his tone puts her on edge; it's almost insidious. 'What do you mean?'

'Let's walk,' he says. 'I don't like standing still for too long. I've never been able to.'

Several people wander about as they walk. Abby's willing to bet their lives are simple, unlike hers. All because of one mistake. She wonders if anyone assumes she and Greg are a couple. She moves further apart from him, even though there's already a large space between them. 'So you're going to talk to Sienna tonight?' she asks. And once he has, Abby will have her own conversation with Rob.

Greg ignores her. 'I'm not a bad person, Abby. I mean, I don't like to hurt people. But sometimes… well, we're just up against a wall.' He stares straight at her. 'Aren't we?'

A shiver runs through her, despite the warmth of evening. 'What are you talking about?'

'I'm talking about you, Abby. Forcing me into a corner. Leaving me little option. I hate what I'm about to say to you, but you've brought this on yourself. I'm so sorry.'

She stops walking, quickly turns to him. There's no anger on his face, just resignation. And somehow that frightens her more.

'I'm a surgeon, Abby,' Greg continues. 'A respected one, and I've worked too hard to lose everything in my life now. Reputation is everything, you see. And Sienna won't understand. She's not like you.'

Abby's not sure what he means, only knows this isn't a compliment. 'I…'

'What happened between us that night can never be spoken about. To anyone. Can you understand that? I'm desperate here, Abby, so I've had to take precautions to protect myself and my family. I have a *son*.'

'That's exactly why you—'

'You have things you might not want people to know about, haven't you, Abby?'

His words penetrate her body like a bullet ripping through her skin. Now she's burning up and the heat threatens to burn her alive. 'What are you talking about?' she manages to ask.

Greg heads to a bench and sits down. 'I think you might want to reconsider talking about what happened the other night. To anyone.'

She can't answer. Doesn't want to or know how to. Slowly, she joins him on the bench.

79

'And with all this in mind, I don't think you should be forcing me to talk to my wife. And if it all comes out, maybe Rob might understand about the night of our dinner party, but I'm sure he wouldn't understand everything else, would he? That's something quite different altogether I believe.'

Now she understands Greg's words about being backed into a corner; this is exactly what he's done to her, so the next sentence out of her mouth is a lie.

'I don't know what you're talking about.'

'I'm going to do you a favour right now and spare you any more lies.' He pulls his phone from his pocket and scrolls though it, passing it to her when he's found what he's looking for. 'There you go.'

For a second the words don't make sense, swimming before her eyes until one by one they all come into sharp focus. The words she's staring are her own. Words that Greg should never have been able to see. She stops reading and shoves his phone away. He swipes it from her before it can fall to the ground.

'You really should be more careful to delete your emails,' he says.

'How... did you get that?'

'As I said, Abby, you backed me into a corner and forced me to do things I never normally would. With a bit of help, I got access to your emails. Then I just forwarded this one to myself. It wasn't difficult.' This is why he needed this extra time, she realises too late.

'I can't let you talk to Sienna,' he continues, 'and this is the only way I can stop you.'

She remains silent. Now she is the one whose back is against the wall. She can't let him show Rob – it would destroy him. He doesn't deserve that; all he's done is love Abby – too much probably – so she owes it to him to protect him from it.

'Well, that tells me I'm right,' Greg says when she can't reply. 'It turns out we all have skeletons in our closet, don't we?'

Abby stands, somehow managing to pull herself from the bench. There is nothing more to say. He doesn't call after her when she walks away, yet she can feel his eyes on her. He knows he has won.

But no matter what, she can't let Greg get away with this.

# TWELVE

*Sienna*

Sienna lies in an empty bed, staring at the ceiling. Greg would be at work now; she's glad she's slept through the time he'd have been getting ready. Nothing is right now, and she knows it's only a matter of time before everything implodes.

She only gets out of bed when Abby's text comes through, cancelling the coffee they've planned this morning. Abby. What is she playing at?

Sienna gives no thought to what she does next, going through the motions of dressing, brushing her hair, applying make-up with so little effort that it's pointless. Her body is taking over, on some sort of autopilot, until she finds herself standing on Abby's doorstep.

Perhaps she will appear crazy turning up like this when Abby clearly doesn't want to see her. Sienna doesn't care, though, she just needs to know what's been going on.

Rob answers the door, his eyes widening when he sees her. 'Sienna, hi! This is a nice surprise. Abby's not here, though.'

'Oh.' She hasn't considered this might be a possibility. Hasn't thought beyond coming here. 'It's my fault, I should have called first. I was just out and thought I'd pop in and surprise her. I haven't seen her since the dinner party.'

It's barely perceptible but Rob's face reddens slightly.

'Yeah, it's been a bit of a hectic week. Abby's been desperately searching for jobs and, you know, getting her CV up to date.' He's fumbling and nervous, unsure what to say to her. Why?

'Well, I don't want to interfere with all that.' She peers past him, into the house. 'Are you happy with how the house looks so far?' She wants to keep him talking.

'Oh yeah, it's great. Thanks so much for all your help. We really couldn't have done it without you.'

He's nervous, she can sense it. They talked for hours that night, discussed things she promised not to share, yet now he's acting as though she's a stranger. Sienna smiles. 'Happy to help. It's not finished yet, though. There's the upstairs still to do.'

Rob bites his lip. 'Yeah, we're thinking that might have to go on hold for a while. We need to watch our finances until Abby finds a new teaching job.'

It is a plausible excuse, but she senses there's far more to this. 'Well, I'm here whenever you're ready to resume,' she says, still smiling. 'I'll get going then. Will you tell Abby I came by?'

The relief on Rob's face is palpable. 'Shall I tell her to call you?'

'Yes, you do that.' She waves as she walks away, her legs like lead weights. Something makes her turn and glance up at their bedroom window, where the silhouette of someone quickly disappears, and the countdown begins.

—

Greg doesn't come home in the evening. He is angry with her, deliberately staying late at the hospital. All day she's refrained from messaging him, but now it's important that she does.

No alarm bells ring. Greg is avoiding further conflict, staying away until he's certain Sienna won't push him any more. He should realise that this will only make things worse. There's another alternative, of course, one that she would never have considered him capable of before: he's punishing her, deliberately avoiding her because she pushed him too far: to a place he didn't want to go. He's already acted out of character, and given the magnitude of their argument, it makes complete sense that he is making her suffer, even though he's never been that type

83

of person before. It wouldn't be the only unprecedented thing to happen in the last week.

Sienna doesn't panic. Even when she climbs into bed just before ten p.m., staring at the empty space beside her.

—

It's only when she wakes the next morning – Greg's side of the bed cold and uncreased – that she knows something is wrong. He might have avoided her for a while, but he would never have been so cruel as to stay away the whole night.

The house is silent, emptiness filling the walls, but she checks every room; it's possible he's decided to sleep in the spare room, or downstairs. There's no sign of him. His mobile is still off when she tries calling again, and now anxiety seeps through her veins, spreading throughout her body, crippling her.

She should call Abby. She doesn't know why, when Abby hasn't even called her back, but she needs her friend. She is the only person Sienna can talk to, the only one who will understand her fear, even if something has shifted between them.

'Greg didn't come home last night,' she says after the beep. She knew before she tapped Abby's name that she'd have to leave a message, that Abby wouldn't answer. She takes a deep breath. 'I'm really worried. Can you call me when you get this?'

It takes a minute and a half for Abby to call back, ninety long seconds in which Sienna's panic expands and grips her in a chokehold. Hearing Abby's voice, it's as if nothing's changed. She is the same woman she's been all these months, firing urgent questions at Sienna, her voice fuelled with concern: *When was the last time you saw him? What had he been doing yesterday? Did he say anything unusual?*

'I'll come straight over,' she says when Sienna's filled her in on everything she knows. 'Give me half an hour.'

Only when she stands by the window, waiting for Abby, does Sienna pause to question what lies behind Abby's apparent concern. Is it Greg she's worried about, or herself?

–

As soon as Sienna opens the door, Abby throws her arms around her. Beyond the apparent warmth of it there is something different. It's too brief, both of them pulling away almost as soon as they've embraced. Still, she's glad Abby is here.

Inside, Abby slips off her denim jacket. 'I'm assuming you've called the hospital?'

She shakes her head. 'He's not there. He had some annual leave saved up, so he took this week off work. Rosa, his secretary, has no idea where he might be.'

Abby's brow furrows. 'What about his friends? Maybe one of them knows where he is?'

She wants to tell Abby that of course she's called them all, that there's nothing she hasn't thought of, but she can't take her frustration out on her friend. 'I just got off the phone with one of them. Marty. He says he hasn't heard from him. He's been away at a conference all last week so hasn't even seen Greg at work. This is just so…' She struggles to find the right word. She wants to tell Abby the truth; what is the point of her being here otherwise? If Abby knows, then there's a chance it might encourage her to be open in return.

'We had a huge fight.' She studies Abby's reaction. Does this come as a shock or something she's not surprised to hear? Her face is poker straight, though, so Sienna learns nothing. 'I'm so ashamed of how I acted. I think… do you think… he's left? Left me?' She can barely say it.

Something shifts in Abby's demeanour, as if everything is now clear. 'Oh. I'm sorry. Maybe he just wants some space?' She pauses. 'What did you fight about?'

'I wouldn't call it a fight. That implies something physical, doesn't it? It was more a clearing of the air. I said things that I've kept bottled up for years, and I couldn't stop myself.'

'Oh, Sienna.' Abby leans forward. 'Look, you don't have to tell me any details. It's between you and Greg.'

Sienna nods, relieved that Abby has said this; it is personal after all – something to be kept between Greg and her.

She waits for Abby to say something else, but she doesn't speak, she only stares at Sienna, making her regret opening up. 'You don't know the half of it, Abby. What it's like to be in our marriage.'

Abby places her arm on Sienna's. It's hard not to pull away. 'Maybe so, but I do know that what people present to the outside world isn't always what's happening behind closed doors.'

Sienna should question her about this, ask her if she's talking about her own marriage, but she's too consumed with worry over where Greg might be.

'He's never stopped loving his ex-wife,' Sienna says. 'I feel it in my bones. And I've spent all these years trying to be the best wife I can be, trying to help him get over her, but it's futile, isn't it? The heart wants what it wants, and nothing can change that.'

Abby frowns. 'You think he still loves his ex-wife?'

Sienna loathes every second of this. Laying her soul bare like this doesn't sit well with her; it's usually she who listens to everyone else's troubles while keeping her own locked away. She doesn't want to be a victim of anything. But Abby needs to hear all this 'I *know* he does.'

Abby passes her a tissue from the coffee table. 'I'm sorry, Sienna. About all of this. I just… don't know what to say. I don't know Greg well enough to—'

'I'm sorry to ask this but I need to. That night of the dinner party – did he say anything at all about our marriage or Holly? You spent all that time together, so I was wondering if anything came up. He was acting strangely after that, and alcohol does tend to loosen our tongues.' She knows she's coming across as accusatory; she needs to tread carefully in case Abby clams up.

Abby's answer comes too quickly; she is too eager to assure Sienna that nothing had been wrong. 'Not at all. He was... full of praise for you. Told me how proud he was of you for taking a leap and starting your own business.'

That's when Sienna knows Abby is lying. Greg hasn't wanted her to start her business; they've had enough discussions about it for her to know that he's worried it will fail, that Sienna is wasting her time. Even finishing the downstairs of Abby and Rob's house hadn't changed his mind, and he'd still warned her not to get her hopes up.

'Greg said that?' she asks Abby. 'Well, that's good to hear.' For now, Sienna doesn't want to confront Abby. She will bide her time and find out exactly why she is lying.

Abby pulls out her phone. 'Look, I hate to leave you, but I really need to get back. I promised Rob's parents I'd do some shopping for them.'

'That's kind of you,' Sienna says, not believing a word of it.

At the door Abby gives her another brief hug. 'He'll come home, Sienna. He's probably just angry and needs time to cool off. Will you let me know as soon as you hear anything? I'll call you later to see how you are.'

And then she hurries off, turning to wave before she drives away.

-

Sienna fills the rest of the day calling and emailing everyone she can think of who knows Greg, even those he hasn't corresponded with for years. It's hard to hold it together as she speaks or writes, her pain growing more intense as she repeats her explanation. *She doesn't know where Greg is. Have they heard from him by any chance? Can they give her a call if they do?* Nobody knows anything, and the flicker of hope she feels with each contact with a new person quickly diminishes.

If he's not back in the morning, then she'll call the police. There's no other option now. She wants to believe that Greg is punishing her, that he's left her even, but in her gut – despite the state of their marriage – she knows he would never want her worrying about him. It's not that, she knows it like she knows the sun will set this evening.

It's one a.m. when she finally falls into bed, exhausted, her frazzled thoughts drifting back to Abby. A woman she's put her trust in, opened herself up to. Yet now Abby has avoided Sienna, and lied to her, and it's all been since the night of the dinner party.

What the hell has Sienna done?

Sienna tries to convince herself she is being irrational, that none of this is evidence of anything, yet she can't shake the feeling that Abby is hiding something.

# THIRTEEN

*Abby*

Knowing that she is responsible for the pain Sienna is in, Abby couldn't have spent another second inside her house yesterday. She tried to convince her that Greg is just taking some time out. He isn't missing: he's taking a break, hitting pause on his life. People walk out on their spouses all the time, and it isn't unheard of to do it without any explanation.

'Are you okay?' Rob is watching her, curious. She has to be careful; he knows her well enough to sense when something is wrong. 'You were staring into space,' he continues. 'It worries me when you do that.' Going blank, he calls it.

'I wasn't thinking about Mum,' she assures him, although telling him that she was would be the easiest way to explain her distant behaviour. She won't lie about her mum though; the memories Abby has of her have no place in the mess her life has quickly become. 'I'm worried about Sienna.' It's as close to the truth as she can get.

It's Monday and they're sitting down to a rare weekday breakfast together, which normally she would appreciate. Rob usually grabs something at work, and she can't recall the last time he's sat down to eat before leaving. But this morning she needs to be alone.

'It's weird that Greg just left like that, isn't it?' Rob says, biting into his toast.

Sienna messaged Abby the second she woke up to update her. Still no Greg. No message even. Nothing. 'I guess you just never know what's going on in a marriage, do you?' Abby says.

89

Rob shakes his head. 'It doesn't make sense, though. Why wouldn't he just tell her he's leaving her? Why disappear like that? It just doesn't seem like him.'

'You're acting as though we knew him really well,' she snaps. 'We didn't, not really.' This feels like an interrogation, and she's sure her cheeks are flushing. There's no way Rob could know her connection to Greg – it's impossible.

Rob ignores her snipe. 'I like to think I'm a pretty good judge of character. He just always seems genuine and, well, decent.'

This is exactly how Abby thought of Greg before she knew better. Sienna's never said anything to the contrary, at least not until she'd mentioned his feelings for his ex-wife. Abby knows this can't be true, that it's not Greg's ex-wife Sienna should be worried about.

'I don't know,' she tells Rob. 'Maybe he can't face telling Sienna their marriage is over. Maybe he's a coward.' It's hard to keep animosity from her voice.

'I get it. You're protecting your friend. And that's what Sienna needs.' Rob always tries to see the best in her.

She stands up, begins clearing away the plates. Rob doesn't mention the untouched toast on hers.

'Still, he doesn't strike me as a coward,' Rob says. He won't let this go. 'Did he take things with him? Pack a suitcase or anything?'

With her back to Rob, she loads the dishwasher, explaining that according to Sienna he hasn't. There was nothing missing, not even his toothbrush.

'I don't know, Abby. Greg just upping and leaving without taking a thing seems a bit weird. What about work? Surely he's still going in? He's a surgeon: he wouldn't let his patients down.'

'That's the thing. He's on leave, so Sienna's worried the police won't take this seriously until he doesn't show up for work. That's a whole week away.'

'The police? So she thinks—'

'She's going to call them today. She really thinks something might have happened to him.' The messages she's sent Abby this morning are a testament to that. 'I tried to tell her that's not likely, but she's convinced he wouldn't have left her without a word.'

Rob scratches his cheek. 'Well, she does know him better than anyone.'

Nausea swirls around her body. He is wrong. Sienna doesn't know Greg better than anyone.

'Aren't you going to be late?' She needs to stop Rob talking about this.

He checks his phone. 'Yeah. I'd better go.' He rushes over and kisses her. She can taste the coffee on his lips. 'I nearly forgot – would you mind popping something over to Mum and Dad's for me? It's the hard drive for their computer. I took it last week to fix for Dad and he needs it back. I completely forgot this weekend. Sorry. Is that okay?'

This is her payback from the universe for telling Sienna she had to do shopping for Lillian and Eric yesterday. At the best of times she dreads visits to their house, especially alone, but right now the thought is unbearable.

She can't resent Rob for asking her to run this errand. It's not his fault that he's unaware of the tension that exists between her and Lillian. His mother is a skilled actress: a loving and doting mother-in-law while in company, hoarding her venom to spit at Abby when no one's around to hear her vicious words.

Abby puts up with this for Rob's sake; she refuses to damage his relationship with his mother by revealing her true colours to him. Especially when to him she is nothing but a kind, loving mother. A clash of personalities, she considers it, and she's never dwelt on it. This was easy to do when her mum was alive, but now Lillian's callousness is getting harder to ignore.

'Of course I will.' Abby forces a smile.

'Great, thanks. See you later.'

She stands by the window and watches him leave, a suffocating panic rising within her. What the hell is she going to do?

When she traces things back, Abby will see that everyone has a part to play in this, and Rob's parents are no exception. Lillian and Eric are so far removed from Sienna that it is impossible for Abby to see her mother-in-law as anything other than a frustrating cross she has to bear. Yet Lillian is about to become instrumental in what happens.

After Rob leaves for work, Abby makes the drive to Reading. She needs to get it over with, so she can focus on dealing with the mess she's created. This is how she's begun to look at it; she could have been the one to put a stop to it. She should never have gone along with Sienna's idea that night, and then she would never have been alone with Greg.

'Oh,' Lillian says as she opens the door. She lifts her glasses and peers past her. 'Where's Rob?'

Despite the weight on her mind, Abby can't resist sarcasm. 'Well, it's a Monday morning so my guess is… work?'

Lillian rolls her eyes before glancing at the plastic bag Abby holds. 'He said he'd bring that himself.'

This woman won't get to her today, no matter how hard she tries; there is far worse for Abby to contend with. She should hand Lillian the bag and leave, offer some excuse, but she can't pull herself away. She is drawn inside by the promise of finally having it out with Lillian and unleashing everything she's kept bottled up for years. This is what gives her the confidence to walk straight past her, into the house as if it were her own.

'Oh, it's no trouble.' Abby smiles. 'How's Eric?'

'He's not here.'

Eric is nothing like Lillian; he's a calm and peaceful man who's not interested in getting involved in anyone else's business. It's unfathomable that he ended up married to a controlling woman like Lillian, and years of knowing them both has left no clues. Abby has often joked to Mel that maybe she'd used a mind control tactic to lure him.

'Oh, I was hoping he'd be here. I'm sorry to have missed him,' Abby says, knowing it will rile Lillian. She feels out of control, unable to stop provoking her. It's payback for the years of snide comments.

Lillian's lipsticked mouth is a straight line, her thin lips barely visible. She would have been an attractive woman when she was younger, but now any hint of beauty she possessed is masked by a permanent frown or scowl. Unless, of course, Rob is around.

'Well, don't let me keep you,' she says. She hasn't moved from the front door and is holding it open. 'I'm sure you have a million things to do. Found a job yet, have you?' She smiles as she asks this.

'Soon enough,' Abby says.

Lillian snorts. 'It's lucky Rob works so hard and got his promotion then, isn't it? And how is it that you're doing up the house? How can you afford that when you're not working at the moment?' The battle has begun.

'It was hardly doing up the house. A friend of mine just helped choose paint colours.' She doesn't need to give any details to Lillian.

'That all costs money, though. Really Abby, you need to be more careful.' She shakes her head, and Abby feels the swell of anger she's been trying to suppress. She has that same over-whelming feeling she had when she met Greg in the park, when she realised what he'd done.

Lillian continues. 'I told Rob…' She stops and stares at Abby, shakes her head again.

'Told him what?' What she wants to do is shout, but somehow, she manages to keep her voice level.

'Nothing.'

This is all it takes for Abby to snap. 'You've never liked me, have you, Lillian?'

Her mother-in-law looks away, unable to meet Abby's eyes. 'I don't know what you're talking about.'

Abby has always thought that if she ever confronted Lillian, then the woman would fight back, stand her ground. Now

93

she knows different. 'I've never been good enough for your son, isn't that right?' She doesn't wait for an answer. 'You're one of those mothers, aren't you? The ones who can't let go of their sons, even when they're grown men? It kills you to see him happy with someone, doesn't it?' Confronting Lillian like this feels like her soul is being cleansed. The fact that she isn't fighting back convinces Abby that it's only ever been passive-aggressive behaviour she's demonstrated – never healthy assertiveness.

And then everything changes.

Lillian throws back her head and laughs, a billowing banshee shriek that's so at odds with her usual stoic manner that all Abby can do is stare open-mouthed.

'Oh, you couldn't be more wrong,' Lillian hisses, once more in control of herself. 'There's nothing I want more than to see my son happy with someone. In fact, I did. But you put a stop to that, didn't you?'

Without her elaborating, Abby knows exactly what she's talking about. Or rather, who.

Tamara. Someone she hasn't thought of for a long time now.

'I did nothing wrong, Lillian. Rob…'

'He was happy until you came along. And now look. He'd probably have started a family by now, but look at you, in no rush to even try. All you do is worry about your career.'

The bullets Lillian fires keep coming. Abby needs to deflect them. Stay calm. Hold it together. 'That's my business, Lillian.'

'Rob's my son. He'll always be my business.'

'And I'm his wife. So I guess that means you're stuck with me, aren't you?'

Lillian lowers her voice, back to being calm, her head held high. 'Not if I've got anything to do with it. Rob needs to see that you're no good for him, and it's only a matter of time before he opens his eyes.'

It's only because she's afraid of what she might say that Abby turns and leaves. If she stays to continue this fight, there really will be no going back. Rob will be devastated to learn of the tension between her and his mother, let alone a full-blown fight.

If only his mother knew that she doesn't have to do a thing to blow apart Abby's marriage to Rob. That is already happening.

# FOURTEEN

*Abby*

The last thing Abby expects when she gets home on Monday evening is to find Sienna in her living room, drinking coffee with Rob.

Her morning encounter with Lillian hit her hard, so on a whim she drove to Ipswich; Mel would help her escape for a few hours, even if she couldn't know what was happening in Abby's life.

But her friend had been rushing to an optician appointment when she arrived, so for an hour and a half Abby had sat alone in her flat, using her phone to scan the internet for everything she could find on Greg Wells. She'd expected there to be nothing other than his work at the hospital, yet still the disappointment was crushing. She needed something. Anything. When Mel came back, Abby hadn't mentioned anything, made sure Mel mostly talked about herself; for two hours at least, she could pretend that Greg and Sienna didn't exist.

And now Sienna is sitting in her house, and who knows what she and Rob have been talking about. She has to face it; most likely Sienna is here because she knows. Abby's legs weaken beneath her, as if they won't bear her weight for much longer.

'Sienna's here,' Rob says, as if she won't have noticed. 'She came by to give me this.' He holds up his driving licence. 'I must have dropped it the night of the party.'

'I know it was a while ago,' Sienna adds, 'but I only just found it buried under the sofa cushions.' She says this too quickly, as if she is expecting Abby to question it. 'Rob said you'd be back soon, so I wanted to wait for you.'

How long has she been here? An hour? Longer? Abby will check with Rob later. He seems relaxed enough, so even if Sienna does know something, it's unlikely she's mentioned it.

'Is there any news?' Abby asks, knowing there can't be.

'No. I've reported him missing to the police, though. They've searched the house too and said they'll be talking to everyone he knows.' She stares at Abby. 'I've just been to see his friend, Marty, too, to let him know. I found out from Greg's secretary that he had two weeks annual leave booked, not one. So that means he hasn't walked out on his job, or at least we don't know that yet. Marty didn't even know Greg had any leave booked.' Sienna shakes her head. 'I could tell he was thinking what everyone else is – that Greg's left me. But I know he hasn't. We've always promised each other that we'd be honest if our feelings ever changed; this was so important to him, especially after Holly.' Her eyes stay fixed on Abby. 'It's funny, but I was just saying to Rob that it feels like he's been gone for weeks rather than two days. And the dinner party, well that feels like a lifetime ago.'

Why is she mentioning that? Guilt swarms around Abby. 'Can I do anything?' Her words feel traitorous.

Sienna shakes her head. 'Thanks, but I don't think there is anything. I've been out just driving around, hoping I'll catch sight of him. That's ridiculous, isn't it? I mean, he's not a missing child, is he? He's a grown man who can go wherever he likes and do whatever he wants. Why would he be wandering the streets? It helps me just to look around, though.'

'That's understandable.' Despite everything, Abby wants to comfort her.

'The next thing I have to do is contact Greg's ex-wife.'

'Why? Surely he—'

'Jackson needs to know, doesn't he?'

Abby hasn't thought of this. She's never met Jackson and hasn't stopped to think that Greg has a son this will impact. 'Oh, yes,' she agrees.

'I've tried to call his mobile, but I must have an old number for him. And I don't have Holly's. I've never had to call her myself, and I can't find it anywhere in the house. I have no choice but to tell her in person. I've put it off long enough.'

She knows she should offer to go with Sienna, but she doesn't have it in her. She is already sinking in Greg's life, moments away from drowning, so there's no way she can survive throwing herself further in. 'When will you go?'

'Tomorrow morning. Unless, of course, he comes back before then.' Sienna throws a glance at her now – her eyes boring into Abby's – and that's when she knows that her friend doesn't trust her.

–

'How long was Sienna here before I got home?' she asks Rob when they're in bed that night. She hasn't had a chance to speak to him before now; he's been buried in work until this moment.

'Not sure. An hour maybe. I didn't think you'd be that long. How was Mel? Was she surprised to see you?'

But Abby doesn't want to talk about her impromptu trip to Ipswich. She needs to know exactly what Sienna has said to Rob, and she can only hope it doesn't raise any suspicions when she asks.

'She's fine.' Abby pauses. 'How did Sienna seem tonight?'

Rob frowns. 'Well, not good. She's always been so... bubbly?'

Abby despises this word but it's an accurate description, at least for how Sienna *was*. Now it's as though all the life has been sucked out of her, leaving behind a hollow shell. 'She's worried about Greg,' Abby says. 'But I don't think she wants to admit that maybe he has actually left her.'

Rob nods. 'I hate jumping to conclusions but you're probably right. I mean, if he'd had an accident or something then someone would have found him by now.'

'Unless he's done this on purpose? Maybe he wants people to think he's disappeared so he can start a new life somewhere. You hear about people doing that, don't you?'

Rob's face creases. 'Yeah, I suppose. But it wouldn't be easy to just... erase all traces of yourself, would it?' He takes Abby's hand, gently kisses it. 'Do you think you've been reading too many crime novels?' He smiles, and she knows it's to show he doesn't mean this to be patronising.

She turns onto her side. 'Ignore me. I'm just worried about Sienna.'

Rob switches off his bedside lamp. 'Let's see what tomorrow brings.'

And this is exactly what she fears.

–

When she's certain Rob is asleep, she creeps out of bed, tiptoeing out of the bedroom. There's no need for her to take such precautions; Rob is a heavy sleeper, so she's unlikely to wake him just by slipping out of the bedroom. Still, there's something she needs to do, and she doesn't want to have to explain herself.

In the spare room she crosses to the chest of drawers and pulls her laptop from the bottom drawer. She sits on the bed while she waits for it to load. They still haven't decorated this room; now she doubts they ever will. Sorting out the house is no longer important.

What she's doing can easily be done on her phone, but she makes the choice to hide away in here; she needs to read those words again, larger than her phone screen would allow them to be.

*I'm sorry*, he writes.

I know what we did was wrong, I've been telling myself that ever since it happened. But it was impossible to keep my hands off you. I needed you, Abby, and I think you needed me too. Can we talk? Please. Properly this time. I'm ashamed of how I acted, and what I did, when we last saw each other and I want to make it up to you. Please reply to this.

She reads it again, and then a third time, until the words begin swimming before her, a jumbled pattern, something frightening, yet she wants desperately to bring them to life.

She makes invisible circles with the mouse, watching the cursor spin around until it lands on the reply button. Of course she doesn't click on it, instead shutting the laptop down and placing it back in the drawer.

The chance to reply has passed. It is far too late for that now.

# FIFTEEN

## Sienna

Day three. With each passing hour it gets harder to deal with. There's a bomb beneath her, and the threat that she'll set it off is there with every step she takes.

In a few moments she'll be face to face with Holly, the woman Greg loved, and she can't quite grasp that this is real. She's rarely been within a metre of her. Whenever she's dropped Jackson off, or picked him up, all she glimpses of Holly is her tall frame in the doorway. There's always a friendly nod from her before Sienna closes the door, but Holly has never felt the need to speak to her. Holly has moved on from Greg; it's clear that she couldn't care less what he does with his personal life. This should have made it easier for Sienna to deal with, but it hasn't. Greg didn't want his marriage to end. Sienna is his second choice.

It's late morning, and she's taken a gamble that Holly will be at work. She's a mortgage broker, her office nestled between a florist shop and a bakery on Richmond High Street. Sienna pushes through the doors with every ounce of confidence she can muster. Will Holly even speak to her? She can't see why not when there's been no animosity between them, and Holly's always happy for Jackson to spend time with Sienna.

Before she can approach anyone to ask for her, Holly appears, walking towards Sienna with a warm smile on her face. Then recognition hits, and a frown replaces her smile.

'Sienna? What's going on?'

'Is there somewhere we can talk?' She looks around the open-plan office. It can't be here. 'In private?'

Holly stares at her, taking her in. Perhaps she feels just as strange being up close to her husband's new wife as Sienna does. Despite the urgent reason why she's here, Sienna can't help wondering what she's thinking. As an ex-wife, is she making comparisons between them? Scrutinising Greg's choice of a second wife? They look nothing alike; Holly's curly red locks are nothing like Sienna's dark, poker-straight hair. Sienna reminds herself that Holly was the one who left Greg, and she'd had plenty of time to change her mind before she came along.

'Okay,' Holly says. 'Let's go to my office. It's this way.'

Sienna follows her as she weaves in between her colleague's desks, finally stopping outside a closed door. 'Here we are. We shouldn't be disturbed.'

Inside, the space is neat and organised, minimal for an office; it's exactly what Sienna has imagined. Greg would have found it hard to live with someone who surrounded themselves with clutter.

'I'm sorry we haven't met properly before,' Holly says, gesturing for Sienna to take a seat. 'I just didn't want to interfere in Greg's life in any way. Plus, I know from Jackson that you're a good person.'

She raises her eyebrows. 'Really? Jackson said that?'

She nods. 'Maybe not in those words, but from everything he's ever said it's clear that he likes you. Why does that surprise you?'

Sienna tries her best to be tactful. 'I don't know, he just doesn't...'

'Talk much?' Holly smiles, picks up a pen but does nothing with it. 'Yep, that's Jackson for you. He's always been a quiet child, but I think it hit him really hard when I left Greg.' She sighs. 'I'll forever feel guilty about that.'

'Mum guilt,' Sienna offers. 'But it's not your fault – you did what you had to do.'

Holly nods. 'Yes. Thanks for saying that. I'm not proud of myself for the way I left Greg, though.'

Despite coming here only to tell her about Greg, to find out if Jackson has heard from him, this is the most information she's had about Greg's previous marriage and she's desperate for more. 'If you no longer love someone, then that's not your fault. You did the right thing. How many people stay in loveless marriages and miss the chance for everyone to be happy?'

'I suppose you're right.' Holly glances at her door then lowers her voice. 'The truth is I met someone else as well. Oh, does that make me a bad person? Probably. But we're still together now so, yes, I definitely did the right thing.'

This is unexpected. 'Greg's never mentioned that.' Before he disappeared, Sienna would never have admitted this to Holly. In fact, she would have done everything she could to show her how close she and Greg are, to prove that he tells her everything, that they have something above and beyond his first marriage.

'That doesn't surprise me.' Holly rolls her eyes. 'He still keeps things close to his chest then?'

Sienna nods.

'It's not a bad thing, it's just… well, Greg. Tell me then, what's going on? How come you're here?'

And she begins, unfolds only the parts of the story she can let Holly be privy to: Greg has been missing for two days, and she's here because she needs to know if Jackson's heard from him.

Holly leans forward. 'Missing? That's awful. He called Jackson on… let me see… Friday, I think. Yes, definitely Friday after school.'

The day she and Greg argued. Sienna didn't see him on Saturday; she'd assumed he'd slept in the spare room before heading straight to work without waking her.

'What happened?' Holly continues. 'Sorry to ask this but did you have some sort of argument?'

Rather than being annoyed by it, Sienna respects the fact that Holly gets straight to the point. 'No,' she says, because telling the truth to this woman is too difficult. In the short time she's spent in this office, she already senses that Holly likes her, that if nothing else she might believe Greg has done okay for himself. Sienna can't let her believe that she's a disaster, that it's no wonder Greg has left. Too many people already believe this, and just for once she wants someone to be on her side.

'And what have the police said?'

'They've got all his details, and they've assured me they're looking into it.'

Holly pops the pen in her desk tidy and places her hands on the desk. 'I'm sure they can check if he's used his credit card, can't they? It's amazing what they can do to find people now. You should demand that they do that.'

'I know they'll be doing all they can. It's difficult when he hasn't even missed work or anything.'

Holly frowns.

'He took a couple of weeks leave,' she explains.

'I see. That's bad timing, isn't it? Greg would never miss work, so if he was supposed to be in then the police would know for sure something's very wrong.'

Sienna agrees. 'What will you tell Jackson?'

Holly exhales deeply. 'I don't know, Sienna. I'll have to let him know, but maybe I'll just wait a day or two more? He'll be devastated, and if Greg's about to stroll in at any minute, which I'm sure he is, then maybe it's best not to upset him until we know more?'

Sienna's not sure she agrees with this – isn't it better that Jackson knows straight away? She can't insist on this, though, when he is Holly's son. 'Whatever you think.'

'Oh I don't know. I'll probably change my mind in an hour. It's so hard knowing the right thing to do as a parent. And I definitely don't always get it right.' She picks up a business card from the small pile on her desk and hands it to Sienna. 'Here's my number. I can let you know if Jackson hears from him.'

'Thank you. I'll call you so you can save mine in your phone.'

When she stands to leave, Holly places her hand on Sienna's arm. 'Please try not to worry. Greg can take good care of himself.'

Walking back to her car, she tries to believe this, but her jumbled thoughts keep coming back to one thing: Abby is lying to her about something. And what would make her friend do that?

# SIXTEEN

## *Abby*

Sleeping at night is impossible. She should shut this all down, block out these intrusive thoughts of Greg, convince herself she'll never have to face Sienna if she just steps away. But the guilt won't allow her to do that – both her mind and body are ruled by it. No matter what she does, the shadow of Greg hangs over her, and Rob, although he doesn't know it.

It is something Rob says on Wednesday morning that plants the seed in her head.

'Hey, imagine if she did something to Greg.' Rob is buttering his toast. It almost makes her angry that he's oblivious, able to do something so normal like preparing breakfast without anything weighing him down, making his actions feel purposeless.

'What are you talking about?' But Abby knows, of course she does.

'Sienna. You said they'd had an argument. What if she…' He stops when he registers her expression. 'Hey, sorry. I was only joking. I'd never think Sienna could harm anyone, let alone her husband.'

Abby changes the topic, but Rob's words remain in her head.

Later, when she's alone, she pictures the argument she had with Greg in the park, how she's never felt anger like that before. How easy it is to snap.

Just as she's buried deep in these murky thoughts, Sienna texts, and Abby almost forgets to breathe.

It's been four days and I'm really scared now.
Can I come over? Could do with my friend right
now.

She stares at her phone, willing the message to disappear, for it to have been something her imagination has conjured up out of her paranoia. She closes her eyes, opens them again – a futile action – and Sienna's words are there, as clear as glass.

It would make her a callous person to ignore Sienna's plea for help. She taps a reply, trying to be supportive without addressing the request to come over. It's awful of her, probably passive-aggressive in some way – she is no better than Lillian – yet she can't be around her friend.

I'm so sorry, Sienna. Have the police said
anything else? Can I do anything?

When no reply comes, Abby begins to believe that Sienna has understood her silent message to keep a distance between them.

It's hours before Rob will be home from work, and she'll at least have the task of cooking dinner to immerse herself in. Time stretches before her, endless while simultaneously ticking louder and louder, reminding her that she can't stay safely in the bubble of her home forever. Sooner or later, she will have to confront what she's done.

Heading upstairs, she finds her laptop, placing it on her lap as she sits on the floor. This time she doesn't check that email again. She's only on here for an internet search. Another hunt for information on Greg, even though nothing will have changed since she last looked. It's all about algorithms; she knows that much, even though she can't explain in any detail exactly what they are. There might just be something here that hasn't appeared before.

Finding nothing new, she loses herself in copying links to every page that mentions his name, pasting them into a blank Word document. She names it 'Summer Term', and safely buries it in one of her teaching folders.

There's no denying that she's become obsessed, no different to a stalker, even though she believes she's justified in what she's doing. Greg had that email evidence, and there's no way to know what he's done with it. Will the police check his computer? Then the link to her will be right there for anyone to piece together.

It rains in the evening when she goes to her Pilates class. Warmth and drizzle, a combination that makes her skin uncomfortable. Rob has been held up at work, so she's left the dinner she's made wrapped in foil in the oven. She knows Sienna won't be here; she stopped going weeks ago, saying that evenings were the only quality time she could spend with Greg. So many of them were spent working at home, so she had to make the most of any time she could grab with him. Oh, Sienna. She has no idea she was fighting a battle she'd never be able to win.

Abby has got used to her not being in the class, but this evening she feels her presence, feels Sienna right beside her, her movements adroit and precise, mocking her, blaming her. It's hard to concentrate, and less than halfway through the class it's more than she can bear. She explains to Gwen that she isn't feeling well, and rushes home.

Rob is in the hallway when she opens the door. 'Oh, you're back early. Everything okay?'

'I just feel a bit rough. Wasn't feeling up to it tonight.'

He walks to her and gives her a kiss. It's only when he pulls away that she sees he's holding two coffee mugs. 'Oh, thanks,' she says. 'But how—'

'Sienna's here,' he whispers, nodding towards the living room. 'She's not in a good way, so I told her it was okay to wait for you.'

Again. What is she doing? Abby's stomach plummets, her whole body heating up. She almost screams at Rob, but it isn't his fault. He knows nothing about the deep trouble that is brewing. 'Okay,' she manages to say.

He leans forward, so close she can feel his breath on her skin. 'She asked if she can stay the night. She can't handle being in the house just hoping Greg will turn up any second. I said of course you won't mind.' He takes Abby's hand. 'She's lucky to have you as a friend.'

This should floor her, learning that Rob has agreed Sienna can stay, but somehow instead she feels only anger, ready to fight this and deal with it head on. Sienna is playing some kind of game in which only she knows the rules, but Abby is determined to win.

When she follows Rob into the living room, she expects Sienna to be a mess, but what greets her is a woman who looks exactly as she always has: hair freshly washed and styled, make-up flawless, a smart knee-length skirt and blouse which look brand new. Her husband is missing, yet she's managed to go to all this effort. Abby can't let go of this thought as Sienna begins to speak.

'Hi, Abby. I'm sorry to intrude like this. It's so awful being stuck at home alone. I feel like I'm going insane.'

Abby studies her face, searching for hints of insincerity. Although her words are soaked with emotion, her eyes remain dry as sand. 'I… I'm sorry you're going through all this.'

Beside her, Rob hands her a mug. 'I was just telling Sienna that we're here for her, whatever she needs.'

'Of course,' Abby agrees. 'So do the police have any ideas?'

Her heart thuds in her chest, reminding her of a poem she studied in school where the protagonist is so overwhelmed with guilt about a crime he's committed that he thinks he can hear his dead victim's heart beating in the room.

'They're not doing anything,' Sienna tells her. 'I know they think he's left me. Is that what you think, Abby?'

Abby doesn't know why she turns to Rob; she's not even sure what his opinion is. 'I, um—'

'We both think you know him best,' Rob says, stepping in. 'And we trust what your instinct's telling you.'

Sienna smiles. 'Thanks, Rob. That means a lot to me.'

When she turns back to Abby, she has no choice but to agree.

'If you don't mind,' Rob says, 'I need to catch up on some work upstairs.'

'Thanks so much for your kindness, Rob.' Sienna stands and gives him a hug, which Abby can tell takes him by surprise.

Before he's even left the room, dread envelops her. She forces herself to sit next to Sienna, to smile and comfort her by holding her hand for a moment.

'Okay,' Sienna says, letting go of her hand, 'now it's just the two of us you can tell me the truth.'

Abby's breath feels like it's being sucked out of her. 'What do you mean?'

'I know what you're doing. You're humouring me, but what you really think is that Greg's left me, isn't that right?' She reaches for Abby's hand. 'I really appreciate that you're just trying to be a good friend, and you are – you're the closest person in the world to me right now – but please just be honest. You think he's left me, don't you?'

It's an understatement to say that Abby feels relieved hearing this. She lets out a deep breath. 'I'm so sorry but it does kind of look that way.'

Sienna slowly nods and tears pool in the corners of her eyes. 'Well, thank you for being honest at least. That's all we can ever hope for, isn't it? Honesty.'

Abby nods, tries to ignore her nausea. It's not late, barely past nine p.m., but she offers to go and make up the bed in the spare room.

Sienna grabs her arm. 'Can we just talk for a minute first?' she asks, her eyes pleading. 'It's nice to have some company.'

Abby can't refuse her this, even though she's on edge having her in the house. She owes it to Sienna. Maybe she's been wrong about her. Looking at her now, curled up on the sofa, childlike and torn, it's hard to believe she's capable of manipulation, or worse.

'Is it strange seeing me like this?' Sienna asks, as if she can read Abby's thoughts. 'I'm nothing like the woman you first met, am I?'

Abby considers how to answer this. 'I think we all have different sides to us,' she says. 'And they probably present at different times.'

Sienna frowns. 'That makes it sound like a personality disorder. That's not me, Abby.'

Her defensiveness catches Abby off guard; she hasn't accused her of anything. 'I know. I just meant that—'

'You know, when I was in school, I was so desperate to fit in. I've never told you this, but my mum was having an affair for years and she left my dad to be with this other man. I know what you're thinking – this kind of thing happens all the time, right? But can you believe she actually left me with my dad and went to live in France with Mike?' She pauses for a moment, perhaps picturing it in her mind, reliving that time. 'I got to spend school holidays there, until that phased out and then I only saw her about once a year when I was older. I missed her, of course, but do you know what was sometimes even harder to deal with? Being at school and feeling like some abnormal freak because my mum had run off. Nothing like that had happened to anyone else.'

'I'm so sorry – I had no idea.'

'Well, it's not something I advertise. I just wanted you to understand me a bit more. That I'm not just this frivolous woman who doesn't have a care in the world. I don't just exist for people's amusement, to help them live a bit.'

Guilt grasps hold of Abby, squeezing her tightly. 'I would never have put you in a box like that. I know there's so much more to you.' But isn't that exactly what Abby *has* done? Hasn't she come to depend on Sienna and enjoy being around her for just that reason? Before the dinner party she'd barely even tried to get to know her on a deeper level than just enjoying her company. It hadn't been a calculated thing, just something subconscious she'd given no thought to. What did that say about her?

'I suppose it's my fault,' Sienna continues. 'I don't really let people get to know me beyond what's on the surface, so I can't blame you.' She takes a sip of her coffee. It must be cold by now. 'Anyway, I made a conscious effort to become this person who fitted in. I learned to make people laugh, to lift them up, and it overshadowed all the pain I felt.'

'Sienna, it's great that you can see all this, that you have such self-awareness.' Why is she telling Abby this? Why now?

Sienna's eyes flick to the ceiling. 'Oh, I can't take credit for that. I've had a lot of counselling in my life.'

Despite what Abby is now learning about Sienna, it shocks her to hear this. She still struggles to see her as needing anyone for anything, even though her being here in Abby's house is evidence that she does. 'Because of your mum leaving?' she asks. Talking about Sienna's past means Greg's name shouldn't be mentioned, for now at least, and that's one small comfort.

Sienna ignores her question. 'The problem is, I really believed that it didn't actually matter what was going on in my life, it only mattered what things looked like on the outside.' She rolls her eyes. 'That's so messed up, isn't it?'

'You were young,' Abby says, to make her feel better, while inside wondering if Sienna still feels this way, if she is so determined to ignore the trouble in her marriage because she's afraid of how it looks. Or worse still, what she is prepared to do to maintain the façade.

'Greg was a broken man when I first started getting close to him,' she continues, the sudden change in conversation once again throwing Abby off guard. 'That's why it took so long for me to get involved with him physically. I wanted to make sure he was over his ex-wife. Holly. I don't just jump into things. I think them through, carefully, make sure I know what I'm doing.'

Abby can't help but wonder if this is what Sienna did with the dinner party. The way Sienna's eyes fix on her makes her shudder. She is already on edge, and this only heightens her guilt and shame. She nods, unable to answer with words.

'What about you?' Sienna asks. 'I don't think you've ever told me how you and Rob got together.'

'Oh, you don't want to hear about that now. It's not that exciting.'

'Go on, humour me. Please. I need something to take my mind off Greg.'

Abby wishes she could believe that this is Sienna's only motivation for asking. A conversation to distract herself. But there's no getting past how strange it is that she's picked now to share so much.

Despite her misgivings, Abby begins. She explains the shaky start she had with Rob, something she often forgets about; it is so far from the life they now have together. So unimportant. But it's far from irrelevant, Abby knows that, even though she tries hard not to acknowledge it.

'Rob was with someone else when I met him,' she says.

Sienna's eyes widen.

'No, wait a minute before you jump to conclusions. It wasn't like that.'

'Tell me, I'm intrigued.' Sienna puts down her cup and leans forward.

'Her name was Tamara and they'd been together since university.' She catches Sienna's surprise. 'Yes, a long time. Anyway, I met Rob when I was on a night out with a friend of mine. I'd just split up with an ex and wasn't in a good place. So when Mel started talking to Rob's friend in the bar, we all just amalgamated. Spent the evening drinking and chatting. Nothing else.' She glances at Sienna, checks her expression, surprised to find herself desperate to be believed. For all the other things Abby may have done, getting involved physically with Rob when he was with someone else isn't one of them. Sienna's face is impassive, but it's clear that she's listening intently, eager to hear more.

Abby continues. 'Have you ever had that feeling that you're talking to someone familiar, even though you've only just met them?'

Sienna nods silently.

'Well, that's how I felt talking to Rob that night. I felt like he was someone who was meant to be in my life.'

'When you know, you know,' Sienna says. Abby immediately senses that she's talking about Greg as much as about her and Rob.

'That's just it, though,' she continues. 'I didn't know anything, not like that. I just saw him as a friend.'

Sienna's eyes narrow. 'Really? Just a friend?'

'I really wasn't looking for any kind of relationship, and he'd told me about his girlfriend. But we exchanged numbers and kept in touch. We ended up texting every day and meeting up sometimes. Nothing ever happened, though. Then one day Rob told me he had feelings for me and said it was crushing him because he didn't want to hurt his girlfriend. They'd been together for so long, and even his mum referred to her as her daughter-in-law. She was part of the family.'

'Had your feelings for Rob grown at this point?' Sienna asks.

This is something Abby has already asked herself over the years. 'No,' she says, surprising herself with her answer. 'Not in that way. Not then.'

Sienna is nodding, sucking in all this information. Will she use it against Abby? It doesn't matter, though; this is nothing Rob doesn't already know.

'Then what happened?' Sienna asks.

'I tried to put him off. I'd never met Tamara, but it was clear, from everything he'd said, how much she loved Rob. I knew I could never love him in that same way, so I had to make him see that we shouldn't be together.'

Sienna's face crinkles. 'How?'

'I told him there was no way I could do anything with him while he was seeing someone else. He said he understood, and I thought that was it. Then a week later he turned up on my doorstep telling me he'd ended his relationship.' Abby doesn't add that Rob's declaration completely threw her, unsettled her. That it hadn't been what she'd wanted; all she'd been trying to do was maintain the status quo, keep their friendship as it was.

'And you lived happily ever after,' Sienna says more to herself than to Abby.

A shiver runs through Abby. She should be keeping Sienna at a distance, not drawing her closer into her life. But Sienna speaking so candidly, showing such trust, has silently encouraged her to do the same. Now, though, the regret creeps in. This is exactly what Sienna wants. 'Yes,' she replies. 'So far so good.'

'Do you mind if I get some sleep now?' Sienna says, suddenly shutting down the conversation. 'I haven't had much over the last few days and it's taking its toll. Look at me, I'm a mess.'

This is so far from the truth that again Abby wonders what Sienna is doing. 'Let me go and make up your bed,' she says.

–

There is little sleep for Abby that night. The spare bedroom, where Sienna lies, is right next to hers, the two of them separated only by a thin wall. Abby replays their conversation in her mind, trying to work out what it means. Did Sienna just need an escape from worrying about Greg, or is there more to it? Abby can't be sure, but somehow convinces herself that nothing she's said is dangerous.

It's an hour later, when she's beginning to drift into sleep, that she remembers something. Her laptop is in the spare room, nestled in a pile of her clothes in the chest of drawers.

And now she can't be sure she's logged out of her email.

# SEVENTEEN

*Sienna*

She's done it. She's an overnight guest in Abby's house and she won't leave until she's found what she's come for. Sienna has no idea that this will happen sooner than she imagines.

She still hopes she's wrong, that Abby – a woman she's trusted – wouldn't lie to her, that it's nothing but a coincidence that Greg began acting strangely so soon after he spent the night alone with Abby. She doesn't want to believe that his disappearance is anything to do with her friend. Perhaps life has hardened Sienna, but this is preferable to being gullible, having the truth right there in front of her yet being unable to grasp it.

Everything she told Abby last night was the truth; she bared her soul in order to achieve her purpose and it worked, just as she'd known it would. To get people feeling comfortable all you have to do is open up yourself, share part of you – even if you'd rather not – in order that they'll be willing to do the same. It's never worked with Greg, of course.

Now she knows the foundation of Abby and Rob's marriage is fragile, and this doesn't make her feel good. She already knows from Rob that the love in their relationship is unequal, and Abby has proved this is true. But what does it mean?

With nothing concrete to go on, she will try to be around Abby as much as possible. Secrets and lies can't stay hidden forever and, sooner or later, if Abby is hiding something then it's bound to appear.

Last night it was clear from Abby's body language that she hadn't wanted Sienna there. She'd tried her best to hide it, but she'd been on edge, too careful of what she was saying to begin with. Rob, on the other hand, had been the complete opposite: natural and accommodating. Trusting. He is Sienna's only chance.

In the morning, Sienna gets her opportunity. She is sitting in the kitchen, listening to the sound of running water from the bathroom upstairs when Rob joins her. It's Abby in the shower, then. She'd wanted to know who it was but hadn't wanted to snoop around upstairs to find out. If she's patient, then things will fall into place.

It's a Thursday, so Rob is dressed in a suit for work. She becomes conscious that she's wearing one of his old dressing gowns; even though Abby has given it to her, she has no idea whether or not Rob minds.

'Ah, that old thing,' Rob says, pointing to it. 'Haven't seen that for a while.'

'Thanks for letting me stay,' Sienna says, relieved about the dressing gown. The last thing she wants is to antagonise Rob. She points to the coffee machine. 'It's fresh, if you want some.'

'Did you sleep okay?' he asks, pouring himself a cup. 'Actually, sorry, that's probably a stupid question. Of course you won't have.'

'Actually, I slept quite well compared to the last few days. It really helps being somewhere else.' Anywhere other than in the bed she shares with Greg.

Rob nods, takes a sip of coffee. 'No need to thank us. Look, I feel a bit useless, like I should be doing something to help you find Greg. Is there anything at all I can do?'

She stands up and gives him a hug, noticing how different his body feels to her husband's. Rob is thinner, less sturdy somehow. She can't remember what it feels like to be so close to any man other than Greg. 'Actually, Rob, there is something,' she says, pulling away. 'You know the night of the dinner party?'

Rob's face reddens. 'Um, yeah. What about it?'

'I know you didn't see him after that, but did Greg text you or anything?'

'No,' he says, frowning. 'I don't think so. I would have told you. Why?'

'I'm just trying to work out if there was something bothering him. He didn't seem the same after that night. He was… distracted. Distant.'

She studies Rob's face, waiting for him to piece together what she might be suggesting. She has no intention of screwing with his marriage – he doesn't deserve that – she only wants him to look at Abby, to turn in her direction and see everything he needs to see. That way he might end up helping Sienna, albeit unwittingly. 'He seemed fine that night,' Rob says, after a moment. 'In really good spirits actually. To be honest, I wasn't expecting him to go along with the whole thing. I thought that if anyone would scupper your idea it would be Greg.'

This thought has been bothering her too. It should have been Greg who refused, drunk or not. Up until now, she's blamed the alcohol, but now she must face the possibility that she might have given Greg exactly what he wanted.

'Then don't you think it's strange that he would just leave me a few days later?' she asks Rob.

Once again, his face turns a shade of puce. 'I…'

'It's okay. It's a possibility I have to consider, as much as I don't want to believe he could leave in such a heartless way.' She finishes her coffee. 'It's better than the alternative, though, isn't it?' She doesn't wait for an answer. She can tell Rob's beginning to feel uneasy, and that's the last thing she wants. 'According to Abby he didn't say anything unusual to her, and she'd have no reason to hold anything back, would she? I mean, she's such a great friend but I know she wants to protect my feelings at all costs.' She lets this hang in the air for a moment, willing it to leave an imprint in Rob's mind.

'She'd definitely tell you everything,' Rob says. 'If Greg had given her any hint that he wasn't happy, or was about to leave, then she'd have told you way before he actually left.'

'Or went missing,' Sienna reminds him.

'Yeah, sorry.' He lowers his eyes.

She smiles, even though he's not looking at her. 'I know. Abby always does the right thing; I've learned that much about her.'

This seems to put Rob at ease once more. She has to be careful; if Abby isn't on her side, then she at least needs Rob to be.

'What are your plans for today?' he asks.

She shrugs. She might just stay around the house, make some calls to see if anyone's heard anything in the last couple of days. This is what she tells him.

'Okay, that's good. Our house is your house.' Rob finishes his coffee and places his cup in the dishwasher.

'Thank you.' She feels bad intruding into their lives in this way, but if she leaves now, she might never get another opportunity. Abby is already trying to shut her out of her life. One day she hopes he will understand, and Abby too – providing she is innocent.

Neither of them hears Abby coming downstairs, but now she is standing there, framed in the doorway, watching them. Even though she is dressed and wearing make-up, her hair is still damp. 'Good morning,' she says, not looking at either of them. She heads over to Rob, kissing his cheek before turning to Sienna. 'I hope you slept well?'

'Thanks for all this, Abby. I don't know what I'd do without you.'

'You'd be fine because you always are. Remember that.' Abby smiles at her.

It's forced, Sienna is sure of that.

'I'll get going,' Rob says, placing his cup in the dishwasher. He's mindful of tidying up after himself, Sienna has noticed. 'See you ladies later.'

She catches it then: the hint of confusion on Abby's face. She throws Sienna a quick glance before following Rob out of the kitchen. Sienna doesn't need to be in the hallway to know what's happening out there.

'So,' Abby says when she comes back, 'Rob mentioned that you're planning on hanging around here today?'

'I hope you don't mind? Being at home is so... difficult at the moment.'

There's a brief hesitation, barely discernible, before Abby answers. 'I have a doctor's appointment this morning, though. It's at ten past ten. Then I promised I'd go shopping with Rob's mum, which, knowing her, will probably take all day and most of the evening too. I wouldn't mind you being here, but we don't have a spare key in case you needed to go out. The front door only locks if you use the key.' Abby is piling it on thick, throwing so many excuses at Sienna, which convinces Sienna even more that Abby doesn't want her here.

There's not much Sienna can do; trying to persuade Abby otherwise will only give her more reason not to want her in the house. 'Of course, that's no problem. I suppose I need to face home eventually. Home.' She repeats the word, trying it out for size. 'It's funny how it no longer feels that way.' She stands and reties the cord on her dressing gown. 'Do you mind if I have a quick shower before I go?'

'Okay.' Abby pulls at her wet hair. 'I'll go and sort this out and then we can leave together?'

Upstairs, Sienna waits until she hears Abby's hairdryer and then makes her way back down. She's often seen Abby open her back door with a key from her main keyring, and she's sees it now on the phone table by the door. Comforted by the continuing hum of the hairdryer upstairs, she grabs the bunch from the phone table and takes them to the kitchen. It doesn't take long to work out which one is for the back door, and she quickly unlocks it, checking that she has definitely unlocked it before she closes the door again. It shouldn't be hard to keep Abby distracted so that she won't think of checking the back door before they leave; Sienna's never seen her do it before, so the odds are in her favour.

Her shower will have to be quick; she can't risk Abby going downstairs and checking the back door. In the end, though, she has nothing to worry about – Abby's thick, curly hair needs a lot of attention, so she's still not ready when Sienna comes out.

'We'd better get going,' she says, standing in her bedroom doorway, 'or you'll be late for your appointment. I hope everything's all right?'

Abby unplugs her hairdryer and stares at her. 'It's just routine. My cervical screening is way overdue.'

'I'm glad it's nothing serious,' Sienna responds.

By the time they leave the house, Abby hasn't checked the back door. One thing floats through Sienna's mind as they say goodbye and head off in different directions, with Abby promising to text later: Sienna will always win. When it comes to her marriage, and her husband, Abby has no chance against her.

–

Sienna knows Abby is telling the truth about her hospital appointment – she'd noticed a letter on the phone table when she'd grabbed her keys – so this gives her a small window, at least. It's risky, but she makes the decision to go home first. She's desperate to put on clean clothes, and it will also buy her some time in case Abby forgets something and returns to the house.

While the hospital appointment might be legitimate, Sienna knows that shopping with her mother-in-law could still be a lie. She will need to be in and out as quickly as possible. If she's caught there, there will be no way to explain her presence, no way back.

When she's finished at home, she makes her way back to Abby's house, fully aware that what she's embarking on is reckless. She has no idea what she's hoping to achieve. What evidence could there possibly be to prove that Abby is lying to her? Yet still she is compelled to go through with this, desperate enough to try anything, no matter how futile it seems, or how risky.

At least twice she almost turns back. There is an alternative – she can just come out with it and confront Abby directly, tell her about her suspicions. There must be something left of their friendship. Maybe they'd even laugh about it later, when Greg comes back, and all of this is behind them.

But her feet keep moving in the direction of Abby's house, and before long she is turning the handle of the back door, opening it wide enough to slip inside.

That's when she hears a voice, somewhere upstairs.

Abby's voice.

There's only a split second to make a decision, but what sways it for Sienna is that this is proof of Abby's deceit. It's ten o'clock now, so if there was an appointment then it certainly wasn't at ten. But does this prove anything more than Abby wanting her out of the house? A harmless white lie because she can't bear to be around Sienna. She can even understand this; she is drenched in grief, it oozes from her pores, and nobody, no matter how saintly they are, can deal with that for too long.

She turns back to the door when something Abby says causes her to freeze.

'It was a mistake, Mel. Rob can't find out. He'll never forgive me. Our marriage will be over. It was just one stupid night and now it's haunting me.' There is a silent pause before Abby speaks again. 'I know, I know.'

She's on the phone, then. Before Sienna has a chance to consider who she might be talking to, she hears Abby's footsteps coming down the stairs.

Sienna has to leave before Abby finds her here. At least she got what she came for.

—

At home, she paces the living room, every emotion flooding through her body. Sadness, anger, fear. They all mingle into one, turning into something even more deadly and horrific. Something happened between Greg and Abby; she's known something is wrong but hoped it wasn't this. And now Abby revealing to whoever was on the phone what she'd done is further evidence. Sienna wanted proof of something when she'd gone back to Abby's house — but the shock of what she's heard has shattered her world.

Now it all makes sense: Greg's behaviour after the dinner party, Abby distancing herself. It's been right there in front of her all along. But she'd wanted to see the best in her husband, to believe that her marriage has been worth all the time she's put in, all the time they've both put in.

So Greg has left her. For Abby? Are they planning to be together somehow, and Abby is biding her time, finding a way to tell Rob? There must be more to it. She's still convinced Greg wouldn't hide away from this, even if he has committed adultery. He's not a coward; he would face Sienna, no matter what.

She stops in front of the hallway mirror and stares at her reflection. She barely recognises the woman staring back. The eyes looking back at her, glass balls of hatred, don't belong to her.

She knows what she has to do.

*PART TWO*

# EIGHTEEN

*Abby*

The pounding on the door forces her up. She's still half asleep, her senses blunt, maybe she's imagined it?

No, there it is again. And someone banging on your door at 3 a.m. is never a good thing.

Beside her, Rob remains asleep, in spite of the racket going on outside. He wasn't joking all those times he's claimed he'd be able to sleep through a hurricane.

Although Abby isn't scared – surely nobody wishing to do them harm would draw attention to themselves in this way – her stomach twists into a tight knot.

Rushing to the window, she peers through the blinds, although from upstairs it's impossible to see who is standing on the doorstep. Sienna's car is parked haphazardly across the drive. It almost looks as if it would have taken more effort to get it at that angle than if she'd kept it straight. No need to wake Rob, then. Sienna has come for her.

With the hallway bathed in darkness, she almost loses her footing on the stairs in her effort to get to the door before the hammering begins again. Everything about this is wrong; Sienna isn't the kind of person who asks for help with anything and isn't the kind of person who ever *needs* help with anything. Abby knows without a doubt that this is something to do with her. There will be no more hiding.

Shock numbs her when she flings open the door and takes in the state of Sienna: smeared make-up under her eyes, damp hair plastered to her flushed cheeks. Despite the rain, she's wearing only a pyjama shorts set under a long, thin cardigan, slippers on her feet, which are already soaked through. Abby manages to take in all these details, despite the rapidly spreading apprehension she feels.

Outside, rain hammers against the ground, an almost soothing distraction, the weather matching the situation as though they are characters in a literary novel.

Tick, tick, tick. Seconds pass before Sienna opens her mouth to speak, even though it's clear she is desperate to spill what she's come here to say. Then her words finally come.

'Where is he?'

'I don't... Sienna, what's going on? Come inside. You're getting soaked.' Abby beckons her in.

'No, I won't set foot in your house.' Sienna's eyes became slits. 'Just tell me where he is.'

'Greg? Are you talking about Greg?' Of course, Abby knows that she is.

'Where is he?' Sienna repeats, spitting her words at Abby.

'I don't know where Greg is. Why would I? Look, just tell me what's happened.' Again, Abby attempts to coax her inside.

The shake of Sienna's head is so violent that droplets of water fly from her hair, like a dog shaking itself after a bath. 'Don't!' she screams. 'Don't you do that. Haven't you already lied enough?'

'Sienna, you're not making any sense. Please, just come inside and tell me what's going on.' It's worth trying to calm her down, even though Abby knows that this is the end of them, the end of everything. There is no way back.

Rob appears at Abby's side – she didn't hear him come down – and places his hand on her shoulder as he squints into the night. 'Sienna? What's going on?'

She turns to him, and her ghost-like face softens a tiny fraction. Of course, it isn't Rob her venom is aimed at.

'Ask your wife,' she says. 'She knows exactly what's going on. And soon the police will too.'

And then she's gone, leaving the screech of her car tyres burning in Abby's ears.

Rob shuts the door and turns to her. He's staring at her, his eyes questioning. There's accusation there too, she's sure of it.

'What the hell was that?' He takes a step back, as though she is brandishing a knife.

'I… I don't know. Sienna's just… I don't know what's wrong with her.' Because it's a lie, every word is a struggle. She knows exactly what's wrong, but there's no way she can tell Rob and unleash a flood that will result in the end of her marriage.

Rob isn't buying her answer. 'Why did she tell me to ask you about it? And why did she mention the police?' His voice is calm, considering the bomb Sienna has just detonated.

Abby shakes her head, feigning shock. 'I've been really worried about her, Rob. I don't think she's handling Greg leaving very well.'

Rob frowns, but it's confusion more than disbelief. 'That's strange. She seemed fine yesterday morning when she was here. I know she thinks he's missing but… this is just weird. Why would she turn up in the middle of the night like that?'

Abby's ashamed of how easily she provides him with a plausible explanation. They'd had a disagreement after Rob had left for work, she explains. 'She said I wasn't being supportive, and that she knows I don't believe Greg is missing. She accused me of helping him to leave her.' The words lodge themselves in her throat.

'That's ridiculous. You'd never do something like that.'

Although this is true, Abby can't bear to listen to Rob defending her; she doesn't deserve it. 'I'm so tired. Can we just go back to bed and deal with this in the morning?' What Abby really wants to do is grab hold of him and pull him into her, tell him everything will be fine as long as they both want it to be. She doesn't, though. It would only make things worse in the long run.

Rob nods. 'Okay.'

They're halfway up the stairs when he stops. 'Actually, I might just have a decaf coffee. I'm wide awake now. I'll be up in a bit.'

This is when Abby knows she's about to sink.

–

Despite coming to bed so late, Rob is up before her the next morning, staring at his untouched bowl of muesli. 'Hey,' he says. 'Did you sleep okay?'

'Not really. You?'

'I had about an hour in the end, after, you know... Sienna.'

'It's horrible, isn't it? She must be feeling really lost right now.' In saying this, Abby isn't lying; she still feels compassion for Sienna. The woman is in pain and lashing out; of course, she's choosing to take it out on Abby. Greg's not here, so all she's left with is unanswered questions. And now, Abby needs to find out exactly what Sienna knows, and why she hasn't come out with it to Rob. She has something else planned, that's the only reason she's kept quiet, only dropped hints. And underlying this is the question of how Sienna found out.

Sienna's declaration about going to the police surprises her, and Abby stews over this, only coming up with one answer that makes any sense: Sienna believes Abby has something to do with Greg's disappearance.

'I think I should go and see her,' Abby says to Rob. 'After breakfast. I need to make sure she's okay.'

'That's probably a good idea. I tried calling her this morning, but she didn't answer. I feel bad that we didn't invite her in last night. We shouldn't have let her drive home in that state.'

She hasn't considered that Rob might contact Sienna himself. All this time she's been so consumed with what happened with her and Greg that night, that she's given no thought to any bond that might have developed between Rob and Sienna. 'I'll go now,' she says. Breakfast is the last thing she wants.

Pulling up at Sienna's house, it strikes Abby that she hasn't been here since the night of the party. Although it was two weeks ago, it feels like an ocean of time has spread between then and now. That night had taken her mind off everything: Mum, finding a new job, the life she's left behind. None of it mattered when she'd been in the company of Sienna, none of it was *her* life. Then Greg happened. And now here she is, about to knock on the door of a woman who has every right to despise her.

Even though the doorbell is one you can't hear from outside, Abby presses it several times, sweat coating her palms. Sienna's car isn't parked in the driveway, but there's still a chance she's at home.

The house stares back at her, imposing and silent. Only then does it occur to her that Sienna might refuse to open the door. Perhaps she believes she's said her piece, and now she only plans to take action. The police. The thought of this terrifies Abby.

She pulls out her phone and tries both the landline and Sienna's mobile, neither of which she answers.

There is no choice but to go home, her body heavy with dread; she knows Sienna will never let this go.

# NINETEEN

## Sienna

She feels nervous sitting in her living room with DC Roberts. His presence here is all wrong, a scene from a film, not something she should be part of.

Only when he smiles at her does she relax, grateful for his warmth. These last few days she's wondered if the police have been taking this seriously, assuming they've already made judgements about her, about Greg, decided that he is a man who's grown bored of his marriage, someone who doesn't want to be found.

Now, though, she knows that something has changed. She's no longer dealing with uniformed officers. This both comforts and terrifies her.

'Are you sure I can't get you anything to drink?' She's already asked him, but she almost wants to stall the moment he will begin talking, even though she is desperate for all the information he can give her.

'I'm fine, thanks.' He flicks through the file he's been holding. 'As I mentioned on the phone, I'll be overseeing this case now. We're concerned that there's been no action on any of your husband's cards, and no activity on his bank account. And it's been six days now.'

Sienna feels like her insides are being crushed. 'How can he still be okay, then? Wherever he is he'll need money, won't he?' She's fully aware that she's asking questions nobody yet has an answer to, but she needs to let them out.

'I know this is difficult, but it's important not to assume the worst. We're looking at every detail of his life, and we'll keep you fully informed.'

She stares at him, fights the urge to scream out that he needs to be doing more, that he shouldn't just be sitting in her living room talking when something might have happened to Greg. She knows this is highly irrational and smothers these intrusive thoughts.

'You said there was something else you wanted to inform us of?'

Despite the fact that DC Roberts has taken over the investigation – a sure sign that they will be doing everything they can to find Greg – she can't help seeing herself through everyone else's lens. She is a betrayed wife, out for revenge, or overdramatising everything for attention. But she *knows* she is right, that there's more to this, and in these last few days she's had to learn to pay no mind to how she looks to others.

She takes a deep breath. 'I've just found out that a friend of mine – Abby Nichols – was having an affair with my husband before he went missing.'

DC Roberts's eyes widen. 'I see. Go on.'

'I overheard her on the phone, admitting it to someone. She didn't know I could hear.' Sienna knows exactly how this sounds, like she's a teenager gossiping about someone. But this is her marriage. Her life.

DC Roberts jots something down on a blank sheet of paper. 'I see. She's not someone we've spoken to about your husband, is she? She wasn't on the list of his friends you provided us with.'

'No, I... she's not really a friend of his; they only know each other through me.' There are other reasons Sienna hasn't mentioned Abby before, but of course she won't explain this to DC Roberts; he can't know about what they did the night of the dinner party. She can't have them knowing about the role she has played in this.

'And have you spoken to her about this?'

133

Sienna recalls the last time she saw Abby; how her expression had been so flat, and calm, despite the fact that Sienna had been screaming at her on her doorstep in the middle of the night. 'Not yet,' she tells DC Roberts. 'I wanted to report it first.'

She watches him, but there's no way to guess what he's thinking. 'I know my husband's affair doesn't seem like a police matter, I get that, I really do. I know by itself that it isn't, but I also know Greg, and he would never have run away from this. He would have stayed to face the music, to tell me to my face.'

'Mrs Wells, with all due respect, people do all sorts of things out of character when they're in a new or tricky situation. We can't second-guess people. You're right to inform us about any detail to do with him, though. We'll definitely be contacting Abby Nichols to see if she might know anything about your husband's last movements.'

Sienna has thought about this all night, and still isn't sure what Abby's exact involvement might be. 'Thank you. And I'm sorry I didn't give you her name before. I didn't think I had reason to.'

DC Roberts stands. 'I'll keep in touch,' he says, handing her his card. 'And if you think of anything else then please call.'

At the door, Sienna asks him to wait. 'I'm not bitter about Greg having an affair,' she says. 'I need you to know that. I'm not out for revenge or anything like that – all I want to do is find him, so I know he's okay. I can handle the truth. I'm just not good with the unknown.'

DC Roberts appraises her; Sienna knows he will be having trouble figuring her out. She is a jigsaw piece with all the wrong edges.

–

In times of crisis Sienna has always been a loner, never wanting to turn to other people for help, preferring – or needing – to deal with things herself. To prove that she is strong and capable. Nothing can knock her down, and life has tried its best. So in a way, as much as it causes her pain, it comes as a relief that she no longer has Abby to depend on. From the beginning, their friendship has taken her by surprise. Normally she keeps people at a distance by talking openly and confidently, yet at the same time keeping part of herself hidden. Abby changed that; her defences had caved in. She became open to trusting someone.

And now Abby has done this to her.

Desperate for fresh air, as soon as DC Roberts leaves, Sienna is in her car, heading towards the North Circular towards Hanger Lane. The traffic is almost at a standstill, but she doesn't care. It's better than facing her empty house.

She has no idea that, at this moment, Abby is knocking on her door.

It's long after lunchtime when she arrives back home, and she stays in her car, still with her seat belt on, dreading stepping inside to be confronted with the helplessness and loneliness that waits for her. One thing is clear – inaction will floor her; she has to keep moving.

She reaches for her phone and texts Abby.

> I've just spoken to the police. Are you ready to tell me the truth?

Although she's certain Abby won't reply, part of her hopes she might agree to meet, that they will discuss everything, and by the end of the day she might be closer to knowing where Greg is.

A reply comes within minutes.

> Sienna, I really don't know what you're talking about. Please let me help you, or get it from someone else if you prefer, but don't do this to yourself.

And that's when she explodes, her scream filling the car.

–

Sienna's mobile rings in the late afternoon, and she rushes to answer it without checking who's calling. In the first silent millisecond she can almost hear Greg's voice greeting her, telling her that he is sorry, begging her forgiveness.

'Sienna? Hi, it's Holly. How are you doing?'

She snaps alert. A friendly voice at least. 'I'm… okay.'

'It's okay not to be,' Holly replies. 'I'd be in pieces if it were my partner who was missing. Look, I know I stopped loving Greg a long time ago, but he's Jackson's father, so I do care what happens to him.'

Her voice is different over the phone, deep and soothing. Had she sounded that way when Sienna turned up at her office? It's hard to recall. 'Thanks, Holly.' She's unable to fully express how much this woman's words mean to her.

'Anyway, I wanted to let you know that I've told Jackson.' She lowers her voice. 'As you'd expect, he's not taken it well at all. He burst into tears and has barely said a word since. I knew this would be hard on him, so I tried to tell him his dad was just taking a break by himself, but Jackson can't be fooled. He knew immediately that something was wrong. He said Greg would never leave without telling him.'

Holly's words penetrate through her. This is true, so why hasn't it occurred to her before? No matter what, Greg would never leave Jackson.

'I'm so sorry he has to go through all this,' Sienna says.

'This isn't your fault, Sienna.' Her voice is firm, and in the background, Sienna hears the sound of a fridge opening. 'Can I do anything?'

'The police are saying he hasn't used any of his bank cards or taken any money out. Nothing. If he had, that might have told us something.' *Us.* Because of Jackson, she and Holly are equally invested in finding Greg. She is not totally alone.

136

'It's possible he had enough money on him to last a while. I hope the police will keep checking his account,' Holly says. She doesn't need to explain why; if more time goes by without any activity, then Sienna's worst fears will be realised. Unless, of course, Greg doesn't want to be found. In which case he'd have had to draw out a lot of money to live on, taking it out in small instalments so it didn't look suspicious. Either way, Sienna might soon have an answer.

'Can I help with Jackson in any way?' she offers. She needs to focus on him now; this isn't just about her. 'I know I'm not exactly—'

'That's really kind of you. I think he just needs time, but I'll keep you updated. Please just look after yourself. And call me if you need to talk.'

Once they've ended the call, Sienna sits in the garden with her laptop, researching husbands who have gone missing. She needs to read stories of hope, to know that men who vanish do sometimes come back. She also wants to learn the reasons why they disappear in the first place.

Usually, feeling the warmth of the sun on her skin is a tonic, able to obliterate anything negative from her mind, but as she reads, there are no happy endings, and deep in her gut she fears that this will also be true for her. She may as well be sitting in a snowstorm.

She doesn't plan what happens next – it all just falls into place, born from her need to find Greg. Whatever he's done, she wants to hear it from him, to know that he at least values her enough to talk to her, that their years of marriage haven't been worthless. Only then will she be able to move on; how could she without having the full story? All she has now are her assumptions, and an overwhelming fear that what little she does know is only just the surface.

But she is conflicted in her thoughts. The small chance that Greg hasn't left her eats away at her. What if he didn't want to disappear? Everything comes back to one thing: Greg would never leave Jackson.

Abby is the person standing between her and the truth, and it's clear from her earlier message that she won't talk to Sienna. That leaves only one option: Sienna will make sure Abby has no choice but to tell the truth.

# TWENTY

## Abby

Rob is looking at her differently. Everything he says seems normal enough, there's just something in his actions, in the way he throws too many silent glances her way. Since he got home from work, it feels as though he's keeping a physical distance between them. She hopes it's only guilt and paranoia forcing her to read too deeply into everything.

She hasn't told him about Sienna's text this morning, has somehow managed to avoid mentioning her at all. This has been easy enough now that she has some news to distract them both.

'I've got a job interview,' she declares, watching him pull off his suit jacket and loosen his tie.

'That's great. Where is it?'

'Palmers Green. It's so close.'

'That's fantastic.' Rob smiles but doesn't come over to kiss her as he usually would have; instead he roots around in his briefcase.

'The only thing is it's not a deputy head position, it's for a Year Six teacher. But I can't wait forever for something to come up. I need to get back into a school, at least, then I can keep looking for something else.' Abby doesn't add that the other reason she's going for this post is because she's desperate to be busy again, for something normal to fill up her days and overshadow what's hanging over her.

She waits for Rob to ask why she's changed her mind so suddenly, but thankfully his thoughts lie elsewhere.

'Are you ready for dinner at Mum and Dad's?' he asks.

For once, the thought of spending the evening with Lillian and Eric doesn't fill her with anxiety. It means that Sienna's name won't come up for a few hours. 'Give me ten minutes,' she says, and as she heads upstairs, she can feel Rob's eyes on her.

–

'Oh, how lovely; you didn't need to bring anything,' Lillian declares, taking the bottle of red wine Rob has bought for them. 'We're your parents, we don't expect anything.'

Rob laughs. 'Every time, Mum. Maybe one day you'll just take it without saying that.'

Lillian chuckles and nudges his arm before turning to Abby. 'How lovely to see you, Abby.' She leans forward and places her arms around her, her touch so light Abby can barely feel it. 'Well, come in, dinner's almost ready.'

Abby can't fault the food – slow-roasted pork – which has been cooked to perfection; it is as though Lillian has spent weeks planning what to cook, when it's only the four of them, not a formal dinner party. Has she done this to show Abby up? To prove to Rob that he can do better? Her dinners would never live up to Lillian's. But if the woman believes for one second that Rob cares about how well his wife can cook, then she doesn't know her son at all.

Although Lillian is on her best behaviour as they eat, it's clear that Rob is distracted, his mind elsewhere. Abby needs to talk to him, yet that opportunity won't come for at least a couple more hours.

They've just finished eating when Lillian clears her throat. 'We've got something we wanted to run by you,' she declares, smiling at Eric. 'To see what you think.'

Rob raises his eyebrows. 'I'm intrigued.'

'We know you've both worked hard to get the new house, and that things are a bit of a struggle at the moment with Abby not working, so—'

'Actually, Abby's got a job interview next week.' Rob turns to her and smiles, grabbing her hand under the table.

Lillian is taken aback and stares at Abby in silence for a moment. 'Oh, well, that's great news,' she manages to say. 'We wish you the best of luck with it.' She places her hand on Abby's shoulder. 'And if you don't get it, there'll be plenty more, won't there?'

Eric congratulates her. 'I've never doubted you'd find something quickly,' he says, 'Good luck. Not that you'll need it.'

'What were you about to say?' Abby asks, unsure how to take Lillian's comments. Perhaps she is genuinely pleased; after all, if she gets this teaching post it will mean that Rob's no longer the main provider, which he has been for months now. No doubt this won't be sitting comfortably with Lillian, despite her antiquated ideas.

'Oh, yes.' Lillian turns to Rob, focuses only on him. 'Your father and I had an idea, and there's even more reason now as Abby might be back at work soon.' She smiles, pleased with herself, even though she's told them nothing yet. 'A friend of ours has a villa in Portugal, and he's offered it to us for next week. You remember the Porters, don't you, Rob?'

Rob nods vaguely.

'Anyway, how would you like to come with us? Our treat, of course; you won't have to spend a thing.'

*No*, Abby's mind silently screams. *No way*. Spending an evening with Rob's mother is hard enough, let alone a whole week. It would be the end of any pretence the two women have both kept up.

'That's so kind of you, Mum, Dad,' Rob begins. 'I'm not sure I could take a week off work at the moment, though.'

'We understand,' Eric says. 'Shame, though. We don't see you often enough, or for long enough.'

'How about a few days then?' Lillian offers. 'I'm sure you'll be able to find a last-minute flight. You can even work out there if you have to.'

Abby stares at Rob, silently praying for him to say no, to not be talked into this by Lillian. She was good at doing that. 'Um, we'll see,' he said. 'I do have some leave stored up from before the promotion, so maybe I can take a few days. You're not paying for us, though.'

Lillian smiles. She's a fraction away from getting her own way, just as she always does with Rob. Not being with Abby is the one thing she's never been able to convince him of. 'It will be lovely. We always took you away on holiday as a child, even if it was somewhere in the UK. It's important to recharge the batteries, isn't it?' She turns to Abby when she says this.

Rob nods. 'We'll have a chat about it and get back to you.'

'Don't take too long, will you?' Lillian warns. 'Now, who'd like dessert?'

–

'Are you okay?' Abby asks Rob when they're driving home. He's been quiet since they set off and it's not hard to guess where his mind is.

He pats her leg, keeps his eyes fixed on the road. 'Yeah, I was just thinking about Sienna. And Greg. We should check she's okay, shouldn't we? I can't get the vision of her turning up at three a.m. like that out of my head. And her mentioning the police. I know you tried earlier, but why don't we stop off there on the way home and see if she's in now? It's not that late. She's not replying to either of us. What if she's... done something to herself? You hear about it all the time, don't you? She was pretty desperate, wasn't she?'

'I think she's probably just taking time away from everyone to sort things out in her head.'

'I don't mind dropping you home and going by myself, if you're tired?'

There is no way she can let Rob go by himself and pushing reasons not to go will only arouse his suspicion, so Abby is forced to agree. If Sienna answers this time, then she will just maintain that she doesn't know what Sienna's talking about. Abby is on fragile ground, but until she knows for sure what Greg has said, denial is the safest option.

Still, her panic doesn't subside, even when they reach Sienna's house and see no sign of her car. There's every chance she's still at home.

'Her car's not in the drive. She must be out.' Rob seems almost disappointed. Abby doesn't want to acknowledge what this means.

'I'll go to the door and check,' she tells Rob. 'If she is in, it might be too overwhelming for her if we're both standing on her doorstep. We don't want her to think this is an ambush.' Abby doesn't believe there's any chance of Sienna feeling this way; she is too confident, too calculated, even since Greg's disappearance.

'Okay,' Rob concedes. 'Maybe you're right.'

Heading to her front door feels like walking the plank. If she's home, then there's nothing to stop her spurting out all those things about Greg again. Abby takes a deep breath and presses the doorbell, glancing back at Rob in the car before standing back to wait.

There's no answer, and Abby can't decide how she feels about this. Perhaps it would be better to get it over with, because one thing she's sure of is that her judgement day is coming.

She waits another minute before making her way back to the car, shaking her head. 'I don't know where she could be,' she tells Rob, and it's the truth. Even though she and Sienna have been in each other's lives for months now, Abby really has little idea about her life outside of their friendship, and outside of her marriage.

'We can try again tomorrow,' Rob says as she gets in the car and clicks on her seat belt.

Abby realises she might be powerless to convince him otherwise.

# TWENTY-ONE

### Sienna

Saturday. A week since she laid eyes on her husband, and she's learned that people are wrong when they say that time heals. Nothing about this gets easier with each passing day. Not one thing.

Sometimes she talks to him as if he is there in the house with her and can hear her words as they echo through the empty rooms. She asks him where he is. How he has found it so easy to hurt her. Or if he is hurt himself. She organises his clothes, washing them and hanging them in the wardrobe just as he does, cooks smaller portions of his favourite dinners and barely touches them.

Another thing she's learned is that sometimes we don't even know ourselves; we can't know what we're capable of until we're pushed to our limits.

Yesterday evening she went to Abby's house. She'd gone there as a warning, to show Abby that she is prepared to do anything to find Greg. Of course, it would be much simpler if she'd just tell Rob what she knows, but there are several reasons why this isn't a good idea. If she comes straight out with it then there is every chance Abby will deny it: it will be her word against Sienna's. She knows enough about Rob's feelings for Abby to believe he would so easily be blinded to the truth, without something more concrete to convince him of Abby's guilt.

As well as this, even if Rob did do the right thing and leave his cheating wife, then confronting Abby would leave Sienna with no leverage. There'd be no reason for Abby to tell her where Greg is because she'd have nothing left to protect. Her marriage would be over. Her life wrecked. This isn't what Sienna wants. She just needs to find her husband.

If Abby won't be honest with her, and Sienna has tried to get the truth, then she has no option but to push Abby to her limit. She is bound to crack eventually and see that talking to Sienna is her best option if she wants to preserve the life she has.

So this is why she is now standing outside Rob's parents' house, ready to plant a seed in their heads and see how it will grow. Another warning for Abby. A different one. More effective, she hopes.

Abby and Rob had been getting into their car when she'd turned up yesterday, so without any idea why she was doing it, she followed them. Before long it was clear that they were heading to Reading, and she knew Rob's parents lived there. She hadn't known last night what she'd do with this information; it is only now that she knows.

'Can I help you?' Lillian asks. This woman has to be Rob's mother, the resemblance is clear. Sienna is pleased she took the trouble to put on full make-up this morning, and that her hair is freshly washed. She needs to make a good impression; this is one thing she's good at.

'Hi, I'm a friend of Rob and Abby's and I was just wondering if you could spare a minute to chat?'

She holds her breath, waits for Rob's mother to frown and tell Sienna she is busy. She couldn't blame her if she does this; Sienna is fully aware that turning up on her doorstep like this is nothing short of strange.

The woman's eyes narrow, suspicion clouding her expression, even though she appears friendly. 'Oh? What's happened? Is Rob okay?' She flattens her hand against her chest.

'Oh, yes, sorry, it's nothing like that. I'm so sorry. Are you okay?'

She manages a nod. 'Yes, I just... for a minute there I thought something had happened to Rob.' She straightens up. 'What's your name?'

It doesn't escape Sienna's notice that she hasn't mentioned Abby, that her only concern is for her son. She holds out her hand. 'Sienna Wells.' She waits for recognition to dawn; surely Abby would have mentioned her after all the time they've spent together since she moved to London.

Rob's mother reaches forward, her handshake firm. 'Oh. Rob's never mentioned you.'

'I'm more a friend of Abby's actually.'

This is when it happens; all the warmth drains from her face and her eyes harden. There's something there, something off between Rob's mother and Abby. If she's right, then this can only help her. 'So something's happened to Abby?' the woman is saying. She frowns. 'Rob would have told me.' There is no concern in her voice, just curiosity.

'It's not that. It's... a bit complicated actually.'

'You're going to have to give me more than that,' she says.

Standing here in front of this woman, Sienna can tell she is fierce, and that to get her to listen she will have to be bold. No nonsense, no games. 'My husband Greg's gone missing, and I think Abby might have something to do with it.' There. She's said it now. There is no going back. 'Let me show you something. To prove I know Rob and Abby.' She pulls out her phone and scrolls through her photos until she finds one of the four of them together. A selfie, taken at Abby's house one evening. Sienna remembers how nobody had been thrilled to have it taken; now she's glad she persisted. She holds the phone up for Rob's mother to see.

She only looks at it for a second. 'I think you'd better come in. I'm Lillian by the way.'

This is all it takes to get through Lillian Nichols's door, and moments later Sienna is led out to the back garden. 'It's too nice out to sit inside,' Lillian says.

147

'Can I get you something to drink?' she offers as they sit at her large garden table. Everything out here is tidy, the garden beautifully landscaped, reinforcing the idea Sienna has already formed that Lillian is a perfectionist. Someone who needs to be in control. All of this can only help her.

'No, thank you. You're already giving me your time, please don't go to any more trouble.'

'It's no trouble. I'm intrigued to hear what you've come here to say.'

'Really, I'm okay.'

'Well, I'm getting myself some water, so I'll be back in a moment.'

Sienna turns to watch Lillian in the kitchen where she's filling two glasses with water. Clearly this is a woman who doesn't like to be argued with.

'You said your husband's missing?' she says when she comes back out. 'I'm sorry.'

'Greg disappeared a week ago. Took nothing with him, only his wallet. At least, he always had it on him, so I assume he took it.'

'How awful. I can't even imagine what you're going through. So what's Abby got to do with this?'

Sienna has to be careful here; if she reveals that Abby has had some sort of affair with Greg, then there'll be nothing to stop Lillian getting straight on the phone to Rob and telling him everything. There is nothing for it but to tell a lie beyond anything she's thought herself capable of. Needs must.

'Before he left, my husband told me that he felt Abby might be fixated on him.'

'What do you mean?'

'Greg said she'd been texting him, showing up at his work for no good reason, always trying to see him or talk to him. He said it made him feel uncomfortable. And right before he went missing, he told me that he doesn't trust her.'

Lillian stares at her, silent. Has Sienna read this all wrong? Perhaps she is about to jump to Abby's defence.

148

'Well, that doesn't surprise me at all,' Lillian says finally, and this is more than Sienna could have hoped for.

'Really? Do you know something? Has she done anything like this before?' She tries to tone down her eagerness: her words and actions need to come across only as concern.

'This sounds like exactly what she did to Rob. He was in another relationship when they met. A lovely girl called Tamara. We couldn't have wished for a nicer daughter-in-law, but Abby put paid to that.' Lillian flicks her eyes in disgust. 'She fixated on Rob, made sure she got him no matter the cost. And I'm sorry to say this but it sounds identical to what she was doing to your husband.'

Sienna digests these words, tries to make sense of them. This is a very different story to the one Abby presented her with the night Sienna stayed at her house. The one where she wasn't interested in Rob as more than a friend. And Rob's admission that he is the one in their relationship who loves more backs this up. It's clear that Lillian dislikes Abby, and Sienna senses that the woman wants to believe this is what happened in her son's relationship. To Sienna, though, it's not important. All she needs is for Lillian to believe her.

'I just don't know what to do. Abby denies everything, of course, and Rob will naturally want to believe his wife over me. Without Greg here, I just don't have anything to prove it.'

Lillian's eyes narrow. 'Don't get me wrong, I appreciate you telling me this, but why are you here? What is it you think I can do?'

'I truly believe Abby knows something about Greg's disappearance, but I can't get the truth out of her. I just have to hope the police can find him. I'm here so that you're aware, and maybe you might have more success convincing Rob that Abby can't be trusted. He won't listen to me. They just think Greg's left me.'

'Hmm. And you're sure he hasn't? Sorry, but I have to ask.'

'I can't be sure of anything; I only know what Greg told me before he left. And that Rob deserves better than this. He deserves the truth.'

Lillian takes a small sip of water, ponders Sienna's words. 'Well, there's little chance of him listening to me. He's a grown man and makes his own mind up about things. But I can try and work on him.' And then she smiles. 'Actually, I'll have the perfect opportunity to do this. He's coming away with us on Monday to a friend's villa in Portugal. They were both invited, but Rob texted this morning to say Abby won't be coming. I'm not losing any sleep over that.'

Sienna stores this information away; it is bound to be useful. She'll do whatever leads her to Greg. 'Well, I'll leave that to you, I just wanted you to know.' She stands. The longer she stays here, the more chance her story will come crashing down.

They make their way back through the house. 'Let me give you my number,' Lillian says. 'And I'll take yours. I hope you find your husband.'

Sienna walks to her car, relieved that this appeared to go well. She feels sorry for Abby as she drives away, and recalls the times they've laughed together, shared moments that have filled Sienna with happiness.

Then she pictures Greg and Abby together, her hands all over him, and she is blinded by rage. And fear.

# TWENTY-TWO

### Abby

The weekend passes uneventfully, a lull in the tension she's felt over the last couple of weeks, even though it's still there, underlying all she does. Once again Sienna didn't answer when she and Rob went to her house on Saturday, her car still missing from the driveway. For Abby this was a relief.

Abby would be worried about Sienna if the neighbour hadn't seen them knocking and rushed over to tell them he'd just seen Sienna drive off. She was okay, then.

It's also a relief that Rob is going away for a few days; it means Sienna can't get to him, and it will buy Abby more time to sort this out as best she can.

With no texts or calls from Sienna either, Abby is lulled into a false sense of security. She knows Sienna won't let this go, but she pushes that thought away, focusing instead on preparing for her interview.

'Good luck today,' Rob says as he grabs a hooded top from the coat hook. It's Monday morning and the taxi has arrived early, ready to take him to the airport. 'I feel a bit like I'm playing truant,' he says. 'Running off to Portugal.' She sees the doubt in his face; he is seconds away from changing his mind.

'Work were fine about it, though, weren't they? They encouraged you to go. And you needed to use up that leave.'

He nods. 'You don't mind me going on my own?'

'"Course not. It's good that you'll get to spend time with your parents without me there. You've been working so hard lately that they hardly see you.'

This, she knows, will convince him, even though he's still hesitant as he picks up his suitcase and wheels it out, doubt scrawled across his face. She watches him get into the taxi, and just for a moment there is a brief flicker of regret. She owes it to Rob to fix this mess, no matter the consequences.

–

She hasn't dressed in a trouser suit, or any smart clothes, for so long that it feels alien to Abby as she walks to the school. She could have driven, but she's so anxious that she can't sit still in the house, she needs to keep moving, and the walk will do her good. So much depends on this job, things far more important than just earning a living. She needs this to escape the nightmare she's in.

As she reaches the school, she takes a deep breath. She's fully prepared for this, has gone over every possible question they might ask, and she is prepared to bend the truth. She will explain that she wants to take a step back from being a deputy head to focus on being in the classroom with the children, which is what, she will tell them, she has missed.

The L-shaped school building is welcoming; a mixture of decades old brickwork contrasting with a newly built extension. This amalgamation of old and new shouldn't work, yet somehow it does. She can picture herself here.

'I'm here for an interview,' she tells the school receptionist. 'Abby Nichols. Sorry, I'm a bit early.'

The woman smiles, putting Abby at ease whether it's intentional or not. 'Let me just check my list.' She shuffles papers around, finding what she wants and squinting at it. 'Did you say Abby Nichols?'

She nods.

'I can't find that on here. That's strange. Hold on a moment, I'll just find out what's happened.' Behind the reception desk is a small office, and she disappears inside, closing the door and picking up the phone.

Abby can't make out what she's saying: she only hears muffled sounds. It's a couple of minutes before the receptionist returns, her lips thin and her forehead creased. 'I'm sorry, the Head says you sent an email at the weekend to withdraw your application?'

Abby is confused. 'There must be a mistake. I didn't cancel at all; otherwise why would I be here? It must be one of the other candidates who emailed. Could you just check again for me, please?' She tries to keep the frustration from her voice.

'I'll check,' the woman says, sighing.

She's longer this time, and while she's waiting Abby tries to focus on her upcoming interview. She is convinced they'll sort this mistake out, and she can imagine laughing about it in time to come.

'Here you go,' the receptionist says, handing her a piece of paper. 'I've printed out your email.' The smile on her face is self-satisfied, as though she has won a fight.

Abby's hand shakes as she reaches for the sheet. What is this? And as she reads the words, their meaning sinking in, it's all she can do to stop herself throwing up.

There's no point telling the woman that she hasn't written this email, that the address it's been sent from isn't hers. It's similar, yes, but not hers.

The woman is staring at her, waiting for an explanation. Abby needs to think quickly, to save her reputation. Ordinarily, she would point out that this isn't her email address, insist that she didn't cancel the interview, but how would it look to the school that Abby clearly has enemies? 'Ah, yes, I'm so sorry – I meant to cancel a different interview I had, not this one. I don't know how I could have got it mixed up. Please accept my apologies.'

'Ah, I see. These things happen. I have been known to send emails without attachments.' She smiles, as though they are members of the same club.

'So, is it okay to still have my interview today?'

But as soon as she's asked it, Abby knows what her answer will be: it is written all over the woman's face. 'I'm sorry but they've already contacted another candidate to fill your slot and we're limited as to how many we can shortlist. But the Head said she will keep your application on file, in case we don't end up recruiting from this round.'

Again, under any other circumstances, Abby would stay right there and argue her case, try to reason with them, but she doesn't know how much longer she'll be able to hold down the nausea churning in her stomach. Turning away, she thanks the woman and leaves as quickly as she can, swiping away tears before anyone has a chance to notice them.

–

That evening she sits alone in the house, still unable to shake off what happened at the school. It's not even the disappointment of losing out on that job that crushes her – there are bound to be others – it's that she knows this is only the beginning of something.

It has to be Sienna. But no matter how much she goes over it, Abby can't work out how she would have known about the interview. She'd only heard about it last week and she and Sienna have barely exchanged a word. She can't have hacked into Abby's emails as Greg managed to; otherwise she would have sent the email directly, rather than from a fake account.

Rob is the only person who knew about it. Lillian and Eric were aware that she had an interview, but they'd never asked which school it was with. Besides, Lillian made it clear that she wasn't happy about Rob earning all the money at the moment, so she wouldn't have done this.

All of this thunders through her head. Sienna is punishing her, and Abby doubts she will stop here. She needs to find out exactly what Sienna wants from her; this has gone far enough. She picks up her mobile, ready to confront what she must.

There's no answer, but she keeps the phone pressed to her ear, her heart beating faster as she anticipates the possibility of hearing Sienna's voice.

The second she ends the call, Rob's name flashes on the screen.

'Hey,' he says, when she answers. 'Are you okay? You sound a bit strange.'

She's tried to keep her greeting normal, but perhaps she no longer knows what that is. 'Yeah, all fine here,' she says.

'We just arrived at the villa. How did the interview go?'

She doesn't want to lie to him, but he will only worry if she tells him now, when he's so far away. She also doesn't want his thoughts turning to Sienna. 'There's no way I've got the job,' she says, instead. It's not the full story but neither is it a lie.

'Oh no. It didn't go well? They must realise you're overqualified. Maybe you should wait and hold out for a deputy head position after all.' He's being supportive, just as he always is, and this is too much to bear. It would be easier if he would turn on her.

'Maybe I should,' she agrees.

In the background she hears Lillian's voice, hurling commands at Eric. Something about unpacking straight away. Not being there herself is one small mercy, at least.

'Anything from Sienna?' Rob asks.

She tells him no, yet this is not the truth. Sienna has sent her a silent message today, a warning.

'I'd better go and help Mum,' Rob says.

The second the call ends, she misses his voice breaking the silence of the empty house.

–

Sienna hasn't returned her call by the time Abby goes to bed. She tries again now, and this time leaves a message. Anger has bubbled inside her all evening, and it's only grown stronger as each hour passes with nothing but silence from Sienna. She knows it's not healthy to feel this way, not good for her or anyone else, yet she's struggling to keep it under control.

'We need to talk,' she hisses into the phone. 'I don't know what you think you're doing but this has gone far enough.'

Still there is no reply by the time she falls asleep.

Sometime in the night her eyes snap open. She knows she's heard something, but she can't work out the sound. Turning on the bedside light, she climbs out of bed and checks the bedroom. There's nothing out of place, nothing has fallen and the windows are firmly closed.

In the hallway, she flicks the light switch and checks the other rooms. Again, there is nothing out of place. She relaxes a fraction now while she makes her way downstairs. There's nobody here, she tells herself, a mantra she repeats until she's peered into every room. This isn't the first time she's missed their old flat; being on the first floor of the building, she'd rarely worried about intruders. Now, though, she shudders to think what she'd do if she found someone in here; she hasn't even grabbed anything to defend herself with.

All the lights are on now, the house lit up like an amusement arcade. She will leave them on tonight. Just for reassurance.

Back upstairs she's making her way back to bed when she hears it again. A thud. Something smacking against the back wall of the house. She rushes to the spare room and peers through the blind. There's someone out there, standing in the back garden; a dark shadow.

Sienna.

Abby knows it's her, even though she can't make out any of her features. She rushes downstairs and unlocks the back door, rushing outside in her bare feet. She's had enough of this.

But she's outside alone.

'I know it's you, Sienna,' she yells, her voice seeming to swirl around her. 'This needs to stop.' Softer now. 'Please. We need to talk.'

Only silence answers her back.

# TWENTY-THREE

*Sienna*

Each morning she wakes, there's a fleeting moment of time where she forgets. Maybe forgets is the wrong word, it's more that she's unaware of it. She wishes she could stretch these moments, manipulate them into lasting longer, so that even for this short time she can believe that Greg is downstairs. He's woken before her and is making them coffee and toast, almost burnt, just how she likes it.

Inevitably, reality hits, and the pain in her chest intensifies so greatly with each day that she's convinced it will be the end of her.

Beside her on the bedside table her phone rings. She checks the caller ID and sees that it's safe to answer.

'Hey, how are you doing? Any news?' Holly's calm voice is a tonic.

Sienna pulls herself up, embarrassed that she's still in bed when it's past ten a.m., even though there's no way Holly will know this. 'Nothing,' she says.

'I knew it but every time I call you there's a glimmer of hope.' She sighs. 'Jackson keeps asking when his dad will be back. It's strange because he knows I don't know – I think he just needs to ask so he's got something to cling on to.'

'This must be really hard for him.'

'And for you. Sorry, I wasn't trying to make out that this is all about Jackson.'

This thought hasn't crossed Sienna's mind; of course Jackson is more important in all this. Greg's his father. She reassures Holly of this.

'There's another reason why I've called,' Holly says. 'I was wondering if you'd like to come for dinner? Tonight, if you don't have any other plans. Tuesdays seem to be the only evenings Jackson doesn't have something going on at the moment. Not that he's been in the frame of mind for anything lately.'

Sienna is touched by this woman's kindness. 'That would be nice. Are you sure Jackson won't mind?'

'Mind? It will do him good to see you. You're his stepmum, after all, and married to his dad. Maybe it will also help you to see Jackson?'

She nods, forgetting Holly can't see her. 'Yes, thank you. Tell me what time and I'll be there.'

–

As soon as she steps into Holly's house, she is struck by how starkly it contrasts to her own. There are bold prints and colours everywhere, the décor a mixture of styles that shouldn't work together yet somehow do. It would be Greg's idea of hell. The reason Sienna hasn't experimented with more colour is because Greg always insisted on neutral shades and a minimalist feel. He abhors clutter.

'Thanks for coming,' Holly says, ushering her through to the kitchen. 'Jackson's just finishing off some homework. I only just realised he has some that's due in tomorrow, so I told him he needs to finish it before dinner.'

Holly steps forward and gives her a hug. 'This is weird, isn't it? Unconventional or something? But I'm not one for following stupid rules. We're in this together as far as I'm concerned.'

Sienna is comforted by this woman's hug – human contact has been rare since Greg disappeared.

'Now, before we go any further, in the interests of full disclosure, I have to admit that I'm no master chef, and I apologise now for the food you're about to have.' She peers into the oven. 'It's supposed to be paella but, um, we'll see. No doubt Jackson will moan that it's not chicken nuggets.' She pulls on an oven glove. 'Actually, he's not too fussy with food, so I guess I'm lucky really.'

Despite the situation, and how odd it feels being in this house, which she's only glimpsed from the car before, Sienna laughs. 'I'm sure it will be lovely. And to be honest, any food will do right now. I haven't had much of an appetite.'

Holly smiles. 'They'll find him,' she says. 'We have to just keep believing that.' She reaches into a cupboard and pulls out some plates. They're fuchsia coloured and don't match anything Sienna can see in the kitchen. 'Listen, before Jackson comes down, I just wanted to ask you about the police investigation without him hearing. How's it all going?'

'The problem is, it's all happening behind the scenes. To me it feels as though nothing is happening, but I know DC Roberts is fully invested in finding him.'

'Well, that's good. I suppose they can't update you on every detail of what they're doing. You'll know when something important happens.'

'Are you talking about Dad?'

Sienna swivels round and sees Jackson standing in the doorway.

Holly rushes over to him. 'Yes, we are, Jax, but it's nothing to worry about. Okay?'

He nods before turning to Sienna. 'Hi.'

'Hi, Jackson. How are you doing?' It surprises her how pleased she is to see him, and she wonders if she's ever felt that before. Now, though, she feels a flood of emotion for Greg's son, for what this must be doing to him. Sienna is tempted to hug him, but she stops herself; he's still a teenage boy and it's probably the last thing he wants.

'Did you finish your homework?' Holly asks.

'Yeah. It didn't take me long. It was easy.'

Greg is always talking about how academic Jackson is, and she can picture his face now, the way he beams with pride whenever he mentions something Jackson has done. Sienna's taken it all for granted before, these snippets of conversation about Greg's son. She hasn't tried hard enough to bond with Jackson. She needs to put that right.

They don't speak about Greg while they're eating, and Sienna senses this is what Holly wants in order to protect her son. When his name does come up, it is Jackson who mentions him.

'I miss Dad,' he says, placing down his fork. His plate is still full; all he's done is shovel food from one side to another.

Holly opens her mouth to speak but Sienna beats her to it. 'I know it's so hard right now, Jackson. And I miss him so much too.' Even though Greg has betrayed her, this is the truth. 'Isn't that funny, we've got something in common now, haven't we?'

He shrugs, glances at her for a second before staring at his plate once more.

'I promise you one thing. I'm going to do everything I can to find him. Okay?' And she means this with every fibre of her being.

Later she sits with Holly in the living room while Jackson is upstairs in his room. She knows she'll have to leave soon – it's nearly nine p.m. – but she's in no rush. Being here, she is in a protective bubble where nothing on the outside can reach her. She's almost forgotten that Holly is Greg's ex-wife, and Sienna is surprised to find herself so relaxed in her company.

'Does your partner live here with you?' Sienna asks.

'Andrew? Oh, no – as much as I love him, I like it being just me and Jackson. I did my time of living with someone – sorry, no offence to Greg – but I prefer things this way.'

'No, I understand. It's not always easy to live with people, is it? Even when we love them.'

Holly looks at her. 'You really love him, don't you? I'm glad.'

Sienna finds herself wanting to open up to Holly, to share stories about Greg, even though it's Abby she would have spoken to before. 'For a long time, it was as though it was Greg and me against the world. Does that make sense? That's how I thought of us. As a team.' She doesn't add that it all changed, and she doesn't know why, or exactly when. Something just slipped through her fingers.

Holly nods. 'That's exactly how it should be. And Greg deserves that after being with me. I just… couldn't give him all of me. Or any of me, really.'

Even though it's clear that Holly is consumed with guilt, Sienna is pleased that she ultimately didn't love Greg – how can she not feel good about this when she and Greg would never have happened if Holly hadn't left him? 'We can't force feelings, can we?' she tells Holly.

'No, and, believe me, I did try. Anyway, it all worked out well because he found you. And now I don't have to feel guilty.'

Sienna wants to be comforted by this, but how can she be when her marriage is just as much of a sham, only in reverse? Greg is the one who couldn't give all of himself. She's spent all this time believing that he still loves Holly – and maybe it's true – but Holly has never been the one she has to worry about. No, it's Abby she should have been watching. Her friend. The woman she should be sitting with right now, the woman she should be leaning on, sharing a bottle of wine, and her pain, with.

Perhaps it is thinking of Abby now – and feeling her betrayal like a fresh cut in her skin – that spurs Sienna to mention her.

'There is something I haven't talked about,' she says. 'It's been… difficult to get my head around.' She glances at Holly. The words she wants to say are right there, yet they seem to take an eternity to leave her mouth. 'I think Greg cheated on me. Well, actually, I know he did.'

Holly's eyes widen. 'Are you… are you sure? That doesn't sound like something Greg would do.'

Sienna nods, takes a deep breath and tells Holly what she heard, and how Greg and Abby both acted after that night. She doesn't realise she's going to reveal every detail, including swapping husbands for the night, until she's saying it aloud, her voice low so that Jackson can't overhear.

'Please don't judge me. It wasn't supposed to be like that. Nobody was meant to cross any lines.'

Holly, although it's clear she's taken aback, holds up her hand. 'Please, you'll get no judgement from me. I'm just shocked that Greg would go for something like that. I guess I don't know him any more, though; it's been years since we were together. People change, don't they? But still. Greg doing that?'

'Maybe Abby was the reason he went for it. Maybe that's what he wanted all along.' Sienna doesn't want to believe this, would rather think that Greg gave in to something on the spur of the moment. That is a far easier pill to swallow.

Holly frowns. 'I really don't think Greg would—'

'I don't know what to think. I just don't want Jackson to find out either. Other than you I've told no one.'

'Jackson will never hear anything like that from me. He adores his father, and I wouldn't ever want him to think badly of him.' She shakes her head. 'Have you spoken to your friend? Abby. What does she have to say about it?'

'When I tried to contact her and asked her to tell me the truth, she claimed to not know what I was talking about. She also said she doesn't know where Greg is.' Sienna stops short of telling Holly she's been trying to get the truth out of Abby in other ways. She's not a monster: she's just desperate to find her husband and get to the truth. No matter how comfortable she feels with Holly, though, there are some things she needs to keep to herself.

'Please don't think I'm taking sides or anything, but maybe she's telling the truth? About not knowing where he is, I mean. The two things might not necessarily be related.'

'It's a strong coincidence if they aren't, though, isn't it? I'm not sure I believe in coincidences.'

'You need to try talking to her again. If you were good friends before, then maybe there's a way to get through to her?'

Before Sienna can answer, Holly's mobile rings. She checks the screen. 'Sorry, I really need to take this call quickly – do you mind?'

'Not at all. I'll just use your bathroom.'

'You'll have to use the upstairs one. We're having the downstairs one refitted at the moment, so everything's been ripped out.'

Holly answers her call, and Sienna slips away. Upstairs, she finds the bathroom but stops short of entering it when she hears the sound of crying; it's coming from the room next to the bathroom and can only be Jackson.

She knocks on the door, unsure whether she should be intruding like this. It feels too personal. This is his space, something she's never been part of.

'Yeah,' he says from the other side of the door. His voice shakes.

She opens the door and finds Jackson sitting on his bed, wiping his eyes on his sleeve.

'Hey, can I come in?'

He shrugs.

'Your mum's just on the phone, and I needed the bathroom.' She still does, but her bladder can wait; Jackson's more important.

Walking over to his bed, she sits down next to him. 'I know this is hard, and you miss him so much. We have to just keep hoping, and never let go of it.'

He nods, gives her a brief glance.

'We'll find him.'

'I... I miss him so much.'

Sienna knows this too, but she has to protect Jackson. Until this moment she has never felt maternal. 'Sometimes people do things they wouldn't normally do. Maybe because they're upset or angry.'

Tears erupt from his eyes and trickle down his flushed cheeks.

Acting on instinct, Sienna leans towards him and folds her arms around him. If he pulls away, so be it. At least she is doing what she can to offer comfort while he's in distress. Surprisingly, he doesn't pull away, doesn't even flinch. Instead, he leans his head on her shoulder, his tears soaking her top. They stay that way for a moment, until Holly's footsteps can be heard on the stairs.

Jackson sits up. 'Thanks,' he says. 'For being nice to me.'

'Anytime,' Sienna says. 'Remember that.'

Holly comes into the room, picking up some clothes from the floor. 'Jax, are you okay?' She mouths a *sorry* to Sienna.

'Just a wobble,' Sienna says. And they are all entitled to those.

Later, when she's at home, Sienna thinks about Holly's advice to speak to Abby.

Come what may, she believes it's time to confront her friend.

# TWENTY-FOUR

*Abby*

She's tired, her sleep last night cut short by Sienna's appearance in her garden, and she's never functioned well without a full night of sleep. It's time to put an end to this, which is why she's standing outside Sienna's house at seven a.m. She hasn't showered this morning; she needed to get here before Sienna had a chance to leave the house.

Her car's in the driveway, parked next to Greg's BMW; a tableau of normality that doesn't reflect what's going on inside the house. For a second, Abby pictures Greg opening the door, dressed for work in one of his suits. In her mind he walks to his car, waving goodbye to Sienna who stands by the door. A time before all of their lives were turned upside down.

A flick switches in her mind, turns off those thoughts, and now she's staring at the front door, waiting. When it opens, she struggles to take in what she's seeing. Sienna's not dressed yet, and it looks like she's wearing Greg's dressing gown – it's black and far too big for her.

'We need to talk,' Abby says, and it's as simple as that. She's through the door, wondering how it can feel so cold in Sienna's house when it's already twenty degrees outside. Perhaps it's always been chilly in here; it's funny what you notice when normality is stripped away.

Sienna says nothing until they're in the kitchen. She stands by the bi-fold doors, staring out at the garden. 'Are you finally going to tell the truth?'

Abby has expected this question. 'If you're willing to do the same,' she replies.

Sienna turns, her eyes fixing on Abby. 'I've got nothing to hide. I'm not guilty of anything.'

Abby steps towards her; she needs to prove that she's not afraid. When she speaks, her words are slow and precise. 'I don't know where Greg is. I have nothing to do with him disappearing and I know nothing about it. I'm sorry he's gone, but I can't tell you anything.'

Sienna sighs. 'You see, this is exactly why we have a problem, because you're not being honest, are you, Abby?'

'How about you be honest with me? Why did you cancel my job interview from that fake email account? You know how much I need a new teaching job. Actually, don't bother answering that. I know why you did it, and it's despicable.'

Sienna places her finger on the glass, rubs away a smear.

'So too is sleeping with other people's husbands, isn't it?'

This is when Abby knows she has to leave. Sienna knows too much and there's no way she'll listen to anything Abby has to say, not like this. There has to be another way. 'It was a mistake coming here. I should have known that. Just stay away from me and Rob or it will be me going to the police.'

She turns and walks back to the front door, Sienna following closely behind her.

'You're not denying it then? I never had you down as that kind of person. If I'd known what you were like, I would never have let myself think you were a decent friend.'

Abby almost stops. She wants to defend herself, to help Sienna understand, but she knows it's futile; ultimately there is no defence. It's only when the door slams behind her that she realises she's lost the chance to put things right.

—

She's making a cup of coffee when the doorbell rings that afternoon. Her first thought is that it's Sienna, but when she opens the door, sees the man holding up his badge, Abby knows this is much worse.

'Abby Nichols? I'm DC Roberts. Do you have a minute?'

Her body heats up. She doesn't want to let him in. Does she have to? She's not sure what her rights are.

'Can I come in?'

'Um, yes. Has something happened?' She sounds defensive – surely that's a sign of guilt – yet she doesn't know how to stop it.

DC Roberts smiles. He must be used to this. 'I'll explain everything inside.'

'Of course.' She has no choice. All she can do is hope he believes her.

In the living room, Abby gestures to the sofa. She half expects him to decline, to insist on standing; he seems as though he'd prefer to be anywhere but here.

'Okay, I'll get straight to the point. We're looking into the disappearance of Greg Wells and we're speaking to friends of his, anyone who might be able to help us work out what's happened.'

It's no surprise that Sienna has given them her name; Abby has known this moment was coming. She's only relieved that Rob isn't here. 'Okay. I'm happy to help.' She forces a smile while inside her stomach twists.

'I'm just trying to get a feel for his movements, and his state of mind, before he disappeared. Can you remember the last time you saw him?'

A vision of Greg the day they met in the park flashes through her mind. Quickly she dismisses it, focuses on the story she needs to tell. It's likely that Sienna mentioned the dinner party, but she doubts she would have told him what happened afterwards. It would only give the wrong impression, and Abby knows that Sienna is all about appearances. 'I last saw him at a dinner party they had at their house. About a week before he went missing.'

'And who was there?'

'Just my husband and I.'

DC Roberts doesn't write anything down, he only nods, and she takes this as a good sign. 'And how long have you known Greg Wells?'

'I met Sienna first, in April. We became good friends, and I met Greg soon after. My husband and I often had dinner with them.'

Again, he nods. It's hard not to feel intimidated; there is something unsettling about being in the presence of a person who holds so much authority, so much power. One wrong step and her life will be finished.

'Can you think of any reason at all why Greg might be missing?'

She shakes her head. 'No, not at all. He was happily married. It doesn't make any sense that he'd just leave without a word.'

DC Roberts stares at her. 'Happily married. I see.'

Abby feels herself flush.

'You see, sometimes people might give the appearance that they are, but in reality... well, who knows what they could be up to?'

Abby needs to get a hold of herself. 'Yes, you're right. I suppose all I can say is that it *seemed* as though he was happily married.'

DC Roberts nods. Too slowly. He knows something.

'And how did you get on with him?' he asks.

Abby struggles for breath. 'Fine,' she says. 'He was... easy to talk to.' She almost winces.

'Is there anything else you can tell us that might help our investigation? Anything at all?'

She shakes her head.

'Let us know if you do think of anything.' He glances around the room before fixing his eyes on her once more. 'You'd be surprised what people remember given a bit of time. Things that might not seem important, then suddenly are.' He smiles. It's not a comforting or friendly gesture.

Abby half expects him to confront her right then and there until DC Roberts suddenly stands. 'Well, thank you for your time. We'll be in touch if we need to ask you anything else.'

Once he's gone, she closes the front door and leans back against it, her breathing rapid and shallow. What kind of game is Sienna playing?

–

'I went to see her,' Abby tells Rob when he calls later that evening. She's not going to keep from him that the police paid her a visit; she just won't tell him over the phone when he's in another country.

'And how is she?' His voice sounds different, although she can't figure out in what way. Quieter perhaps. Subdued.

'Well, she seems to think I know where Greg is.' She has to tell Rob at least this much; she hates keeping this from him.

'It doesn't make sense,' he says. 'Why would she think that?'

'I think she's just getting paranoid because he stayed the night here. She assumes he must have told me that he was planning to leave her. Something like that. It's nonsense, Rob – he said nothing about leaving her.'

Rob falls silent, weighing up her words. What sense is he making of them?

'Are you having a good time there?' she asks when he doesn't reply. She needs to steer him away from the conversation they've been having.

'Actually, yes, it's been good to spend time with my parents,' he says, quickly falling silent again.

When it becomes clear he won't say anything else, Abby speaks. 'What have you been doing?'

'Mum and I have been going for long walks, just talking about… everything.'

She doesn't like the sound of this; there's no telling what poison Lillian is infecting him with. 'Just you and your mum? Doesn't your dad go with you?'

'He's done something to his ankle and can't do too much at the moment. He's mostly been sitting by the pool reading. He's fine, though. Look, I'd better go. I'll see you on Friday. Flight's at twelve so I should be back around dinner time.'

Two more nights; that's all she has to get through. Daytimes are fine, but when darkness falls it brings with it the intense feeling that she's not safe.

# TWENTY-FIVE

## Sienna

She's counting the days now; they have taken on a new meaning. She will no longer let herself believe that something awful has happened to him, and now, rather than being terrified of each new twenty-four-hour period, she welcomes it, because it's edging her nearer to the truth. She hasn't been able to think about it too much before – it seemed so long away, and she was convinced Greg would be home before Monday came – but now it's all she can focus on.

It's Thursday now – four more days until Greg is due back at work. On Monday morning, by nine a.m., she will know whether he left on purpose. If he turns up, then she will confront him; if he doesn't, then it means only one thing.

She can't dwell on what that is, so she forces it out of her mind; instead, convincing herself that she will be seeing Greg soon enough.

Spurred on by what Monday will bring, Sienna feels lighter today, as though she can deal with anything that's thrown her way. Spending the other evening with Holly and Jackson has helped; she isn't alone in this – there are others who want Greg home as much as she does.

Her phone's ringing. She reaches over to the bedside table and stares at the screen. No caller ID. Not Greg, then. Nor is it Abby.

'Mrs Wells? It's DC Roberts.'

She pulls herself up, struggles to take a breath. 'Have you found him?'

'No, sorry. But I do have some news. Hopefully, it will set your mind at rest.' He's not speaking fast enough; she needs to know *now*. 'There's been some activity on his debit card.'

'Where?'

'In Brighton. At a coffee shop.'

Brighton. What is Greg doing there? He's never mentioned the place before, and as far as she's aware hasn't even been there.

'Mrs Wells? Did you hear me?'

'Yes, sorry. I'm listening.'

'This gives us something to go on. Does he know anyone in Brighton?'

'Not that I'm aware.' She's still in shock, her mind scrabbling to make sense of what she's hearing. 'Is there CCTV? Did you actually see him on camera?'

'We're still going through all the CCTV in that area. Unfortunately, there wasn't any in the coffee shop. We'll keep you informed but I just wanted to let you know.'

'Thank you.'

'He's due in at work on Monday, isn't he?'

'Yes.' And she fully intends to be there.

After she ends the call, Sienna sits with the information she's just learned. It offers her little comfort; until she's facing Greg, getting some answers directly from his mouth, nothing will ease her mind.

–

Once she's showered and dressed, she calls Holly to let her know what she's found out.

'Well, that's good news, isn't it? I'll tell Jackson straight away. He's at a friend's house today.'

'He's not at school then?'

Holly chuckles. 'It's the summer holidays.'

'Oh, yes. I've lost all track of time.' She pauses. 'Do you know if Greg had any connection to Brighton when you were married? I'm trying to think of reasons he might have gone there and I'm coming up blank.'

'I don't think so. We certainly never went together, and I can't think of a time when he mentioned the place. But that doesn't—'

'I know. He could have picked anywhere to get away from me, couldn't he? And now it looks like that's exactly what he's doing.'

'Sienna, don't think like that. There could be any number of reasons he's done this. It's not necessarily anything to do with you or your marriage. And remember, it's not just you he's walked away from – it's Jackson too.'

She knows this, tries to squeeze some comfort from it. 'If you think of anything later, will you call me?'

'Of course I will. And I'll ask Jackson if he's ever heard his dad mention Brighton.'

Sienna thanks her before ending the call.

There are tasks she needs to do today; her online business course starts in a few weeks, and she's got reading to do in preparation, as well as designing some business cards. She sits on the sofa, her legs curled under her, and opens one of her books. She tries to immerse herself in the words, but ends up re-reading the same sentences, forgetting what they say as soon as she's read them.

Giving up, she reaches for her phone and texts Rob, asking him if Abby has any connection to Brighton.

His reply is immediate.

No, why?

She doesn't respond, pushes her phone to the other side of the sofa, even though she feels bad about not replying. She doesn't want to hurt Rob; there will be enough pain for him once everything is out in the open.

On Friday evening, when she's forcing herself to clean the house – something she's never been a fan of at the best of times – someone rings her doorbell. She leans the mop against the wall, wondering if it's Abby, if she's come to tell the truth this time.

She's so shocked to see Rob standing at her door that she's momentarily speechless.

'I'm sorry,' he says. 'Is this a bad time?'

Her hand reaches for her hair; it's tied up in a messy, sweat-soaked bun and she's embarrassed that anyone is seeing her like this. 'No, come in.'

He steps inside and she shuts the door behind him. 'Does Abby know you're here?'

'No. I came straight from the airport. I've been in Portugal with my parents.' He looks away, stares past her.

She already knows Rob's been away but admitting this serves no purpose other than to make him feel uncomfortable, so she keeps it to herself. He is already ill at ease. 'Can I get you anything?'

'No, thanks.' He follows her into the kitchen. 'I haven't been here since the dinner party. It feels… odd.'

She freezes; she doubts there will ever be a time when she can think of that night without it sending shooting pains into her chest. 'A lot seems to have happened since then.'

Rob sits on the sofa, rests his elbows on his knees. She can tell he's about to say something important. 'I'm not good at a lot of things,' he begins.

'That's not true. You're brilliant at your job.' She can't help interrupting him; she likes Rob, wants to build him up, help him find the confidence to realise he is worth so much more than Abby.

'Thanks, but I mean other than work. I don't have any special talents or anything, but one thing I've always thought is that

I'm a pretty good judge of character. And that's why I'm here. I don't believe for a second that you came to our house that night demanding to know where Greg is with no good reason. I don't think you're that kind of person.'

His words float across to her, lifting her up, validating her. 'I'm not. I don't hurt people or mess with them. I truly believe Abby knows something about Greg.'

'Can you tell me why you think that? I feel like I'm the only person who doesn't know what's going on, even though it's clear *something* is.'

Rob is here because of his mother; Sienna doesn't know what she's said to him, but Lillian will have spent the last few days planting subtle seeds in his mind, causing him to doubt what he's taken for granted. And now Sienna faces a dilemma. She should tell him exactly what she heard Abby admit to on the phone that day, but she already knows he won't believe her. He won't want to. The glasses he sees Abby through are distorted, and he'll never take Sienna's word for it, not without evidence. He'll just go home to Abby, who will deny it, and they'll both dismiss Sienna as mentally unstable. She can see it all so clearly now. No, she needs to be in control of this narrative, to remain someone who Rob will see as rational and logical. Strong. When Greg comes back and it's all out in the open, she and Rob will have to navigate through the mess together.

'I'm in the dark about so much too, Rob. I don't know where Greg is, or why he left. All I know is that he became distant after the dinner party. He's never been the most affectionate man, especially in public, but this was something else. And right before he went missing, he told me that he doesn't trust Abby, that he'd seen a different side to her after being alone with her that night.'

Rob stares at her; this will be a shock to him, something new to digest along with all the doubt already in his mind. It takes him a minute to speak. 'What did he mean?'

'That's the thing, I don't know. He wouldn't explain himself, and it's impossible getting information out of Greg at the best of times.'

Again, Rob is silent, digesting this new information. 'What do you think he meant?'

At the time she hadn't known, but now it is clear, even though it makes Greg a hypocrite. Abby may have shown herself to be untrustworthy by cheating on Rob, but Greg did exactly the same. So why had he turned it all on Abby? Something else must have happened between them.

'Maybe they had some sort of argument?' she tells Rob, omitting the rest of what's weighing her down. 'I've tried to talk to her, but she won't explain anything.'

'I'll talk to her,' Rob says. 'There's another thing I don't understand. When you came to our house that night, you mentioned going to the police about Abby. What did you mean?'

'If she wasn't going to be honest with me, then I thought maybe the police could get the truth out of her.'

'About where Greg is?'

She nods.

'But we can't be sure that Abby knows anything about that, can we?' Rob is already talking himself out of believing Sienna. She needs to try harder. 'And what's this about Brighton?'

Sienna tells him about the police tracing Greg's debit card.

'Well, that's good news, isn't it? It means he's—'

'Alive? Yes. Unless someone stole his wallet.' That doesn't seem likely, though, when they've only used it to buy a coffee. 'And he's still not home, is he?' she continues. 'He still left without a word, without taking anything.'

Rob nods.

'Anyway, I'm ready to confront him on Monday, and maybe then we'll both have some answers.'

'Yes,' Rob says. 'That's what we all need.'

When he leaves a short time later, Sienna can't be sure where Rob's mind is.

This is okay, though. Maybe it's good that he will have these last few days before his world crashes down around him. She will be there to pick up the pieces.

## TWENTY-SIX

*Abby*

She's fallen asleep on the sofa when Rob gets home, the meal she's prepared for them lying cold in the oven. She opens her eyes and he's sitting beside her, watching her.

'I just got back,' he says. 'Found you asleep here.'

'Sorry, I must have just dozed off.' She pulls herself up. 'I only sat down for a minute. Well, that was the plan at least.'

'What's happened to the walls?' Rob asks.

'Oh, I repainted them. I didn't like the colour.' She says this casually, even though they both know that what underlies her action is something serious.

'But we've only just done it.'

She may as well come out with it; this is one thing, at least, she can be honest about, despite what it may lead Rob to think. 'It reminded me of Sienna. Everywhere I went down here just felt like she was here. Her stamp is everywhere, and after the way she's been acting, I just needed her out of this house.'

Rob frowns. 'That's a bit harsh, isn't it? She's just worried about Greg.' Abby knows this, hates herself for saying it all, but she can't tell Rob the truth: that she fears Sienna.

'Since when do you care about the décor?' She's defensive now, even though she's on shaky ground.

Rob stares at her. 'You're right,' he says. 'Whatever you want is fine. It's only paint, isn't it?'

'I didn't mean it like that,' she insists. 'It's your house too, so it's not just up to me how we decorate it. It's just that you've never cared before.'

His eyes fix on the walls, and he stays silent.

'That's all I've done, Rob. I haven't changed anything else.' Not yet at least. 'Anyway, tell me about Portugal.'

'Can we catch up on that tomorrow? I couldn't get much work done with Mum wanting to fill every minute with quality time, so I have a huge backlog. I'll just go up and see what I can get done before tomorrow.'

'Okay. I'll bring your dinner up.'

'Not hungry actually. Sorry. I was starving so grabbed a burger at the airport.'

She watches him head upstairs. Even though he didn't say it, she knows that something is very wrong.

–

It's after midnight when he comes to bed, climbing in beside her. She's not asleep yet but is turned on her side with her eyes closed. She could stay like this, and he'd never know she's awake; it's clear from the amount of noise he's making that he's hoping to wake her, and she senses that if they talk now, the outcome won't be good for either of them.

'I've been thinking about Greg,' he says.

She turns over; there's no point keeping up a pretence of sleep.

'What about him?' she asks, her stomach twisting into knots.

'I just think it's strange that he didn't want to go for a drink that week, like we'd talked about. He never replied to my messages, did he?'

'He was probably busy. And clearly he had a lot on his mind if he was about to walk out on Sienna.'

'While I've been in Portugal, I've been going over and over it and I can't get my head around why he would leave her.'

'People leave their partners all the time,' she says. She wants to shut this conversation down before it leads somewhere there will be no return from.

'Tell me again what happened the night he spent here. What did you talk about?'

'I told you, there was nothing he said that was unusual.'

'So he didn't mention anything about planning to leave? Nothing like that?'

'Rob, if I knew anything, I would have told Sienna. Why wouldn't I?'

'And you and him got on? You didn't argue or anything?'

'No! Of course not. If we had, then I would have mentioned it. We had a nice conversation.'

Rob stares at her for too long, makes her want to shrink away from his glare. 'Okay. Let's get some sleep.'

It's hours before Abby manages to drift off. Things are going from bad to worse.

# TWENTY-SEVEN

*Sienna*

She stares at her reflection in the bathroom mirror, appraising what she sees. She's always tried to make the best of herself, yet she's never been hung up on how attractive she may or may not be. One thing she's learned is that it doesn't matter how beautiful you are – attraction is subjective, and your partner can still cheat on you no matter what you look like.

Despite this, she has washed her hair this morning, wrapped it around her curling tongs so that it falls in soft waves. She's taken extra time with her make-up too, applying it carefully when normally she does it on autopilot. She's not doing any of this for Greg – it's her armour, something to strengthen her against what is to come.

The sky is already cloudless, and she's wearing a vest top and maxi skirt. The Tube will be stifling. It always is, even during cooler months.

She glances in the mirror one last time, smooths her left eyebrow. Now she is ready.

–

Sienna knows her way around this hospital without needing any signs. She walks along the corridors, relishing their familiarity, focusing on the tap of her shoes on the floor. The faces of some of the people she passes are also familiar, and she nods and smiles at everyone she recognises, making every pretence of normality.

Greg's office is on the fourth floor and, as she steps out of the lift, she isn't prepared for the surge of panic, the heaviness in her stomach, the conviction she feels that she won't be able to take a single step further.

'Sienna?'

She spins around and Marty is walking towards her. He's carrying a briefcase and holds a takeaway coffee cup in his other hand. He's just arrived, then. No surprise given that it's only just gone seven thirty. 'Is everything okay? Is he back? Are you with him?'

She shakes her head. 'No, I'm just here hoping to see him.'

Marty sighs. 'I still can't get my head around it.'

Sienna tells him about Greg's debit card being used in Brighton.

'So, he could be in today then,' Marty says. 'Greg won't miss work for anything. Come on, I'll walk with you.'

They head through the corridor. 'You know Rosa won't be here yet? She doesn't start until eight thirty.'

Sienna knows this; she just wants to wait by herself, to have a few moments without having to explain her presence to Rosa. She is hoping Greg will be in early, just as he always is. Not everything has to change, does it? His work life is a separate entity. 'It doesn't matter,' she tells Marty. 'I'll just wait for him.'

A look passes over Marty's face — is it pity? Sienna doesn't need or want that.

'What will be, will be,' she says. 'I'm just here to talk. If our marriage is over, then I'll deal with that, but I need to at least close this chapter properly.'

Marty nods. 'Why don't you come and wait in my office? Greg's will be locked. I can keep checking for you. Actually, he usually pops his head in to see me before he gets started for the day, so…'

'Yes, and I'm sure he will today. I imagine you've got a lot to catch up on.' Maybe this is a better plan; Greg won't be expecting her to be here, so finding her in Marty's office will ensure he has no time to contrive excuses.

By eight thirty there is no sign of Greg. Sienna heads to his office, where she finds Rosa sitting at her desk.

'Hi, he's not in yet then?' Sienna keeps her tone light, even though inside she's crumbling.

Rosa shakes her head. 'No, I'm sorry.' She frowns. 'The police searched his office the other day, but I still thought he'd turn up today. I can't think of a single time when he's been in later than me.'

'So there's no message from him anywhere? Nothing about cancelling appointments or surgeries?'

'No, nothing. Sienna, I'm so sorry. I just—'

'Okay. I think I'll hang around for a couple more hours, just in case. I'll be in the coffee shop downstairs. Would you mind calling me if he turns up?' Sienna has to cut her off. She can't deal with any sympathy right now.

'Of course.' Rosa looks like she wants to say more than this, but she doesn't.

And as she walks away, Sienna feels Rosa's eyes on her, and knows without turning around that they will be full of pity, just as Marty's were earlier.

Downstairs, she sits by the main doors and sips a lukewarm latte. She barely looks away from the door; she wants to cling on to the morsel of hope still within her. She finds her phone in her bag and texts Rob.

He hasn't shown up for work.

There's no need to add anything more. Surely, Rob will see that he needs to talk to Abby now.

–

Everything has changed. Since she got back from the hospital this afternoon, Sienna has spent the day on the phone, hours disappearing as she relays the new information that Greg hasn't shown up for work. It's as though he's only been gone since this morning, even though it's been over two weeks.

DC Roberts has already spoken to the hospital, was aware at the same time as Sienna that things have taken a sinister turn. Greg is being treated as high risk now. The fact that his debit card has only been used once is troubling, DC Roberts has told her.

Next was Holly, who for several moments was stunned into silence. She would tell Jackson, she'd said; he'd known Greg was meant to be back at work today.

Marty has called her, offered to come round and keep her company for a bit, but she hasn't accepted. As much as she likes him, it would just be uncomfortable.

Rob is different, though, and when he texts back and says he will come over, she gratefully accepts.

She needs to keep busy while she waits for him, needs for her mind to be consumed only with the mundane act of cleaning out the fridge. Greg is always the one who does it. For some reason it's one of those things that barely registers on her radar. Superficially it looks clean: that sums her up completely.

She's halfway through this task when the doorbell rings. Rob is quicker than she's expected. She hurries to the door and flings it open, ready to unleash all the pain she's kept trapped inside her since Greg didn't turn up for work.

'I'm sorry,' he says, reaching for her and pulling her into a hug. It is brief and tentative, but she knows he's not a tactile person; at least not with anyone other than Abby.

'Does she know?' Sienna asks.

He nods. 'I told her we've been texting. I don't like lies. Other people seem to be comfortable telling them, but I'm not.'

'And what did she have to say about it?'

Rob looks past her, into the kitchen. 'Can we talk in there? It's making me a bit nervous standing in the hallway like this.'

'I'm sorry. Yes, come on.'

'Actually, can we go out to the garden? It's peaceful sitting out there and I think I need that right now.'

She doesn't ask why, just silently leads him out to the garden, where they sit on the same chairs the four of them sat on that night. It's eerie, the ghosts of two people present with them while they talk.

'Abby seemed upset that Greg didn't show up for work,' Rob says. 'I think this whole time she just assumed he'd left you, and now this is something else entirely.'

Of course it is; Sienna has always been aware of this, even amidst everyone else's doubt. 'Now do you believe he hasn't just left me? I mean, that might be part of it too, but he's left his whole life, hasn't he? His son, his job.'

'Poor kid,' Rob mutters. 'I can't imagine how he's feeling.'

'I've been talking to Greg's ex-wife actually,' Sienna announces.

'Oh? I suppose under the circumstances you have no choice.'

'She's nothing like I expected. Well, in a way she is – she's a strong, capable woman who takes no nonsense.'

Rob looks at her. 'That sounds like someone I know.'

Sienna manages a thin smile, despite the circumstances. 'I know Jackson's got his mum, but I'm going to be there for him too. I have to be. I'm Greg's wife.' It feels funny to call herself that, when right now it's a label that no longer seems to fit her. She may as well be a stranger to him.

'You're a good person, Sienna.' Rob's voice is tinged with sadness. Is he unsure that his wife is? She doesn't want to push him.

'Rob, I need to —'

'I tried to talk to Abby about the night she spent with Greg.'

He's interrupted her, but what she needs to say can wait. She will do it tonight, though, before he leaves; she has no choice now. 'What did she say?'

'She said they had a nice time just talking. She said they didn't have anything even remotely like an argument.'

'Do you believe her?'

He stares at the ground, rubs his trainers against the patio. 'Yes,' he says. 'She's my wife and I trust her.'

Sienna doesn't blame him for this. Some people are too afraid of the truth; living in denial is safer. 'Rob, I need to tell you something. I know I should have said something before, but I... I just wanted to speak to Greg first.'

He shakes his head. 'Don't,' he says, holding up his hand. 'Whatever you're going to say, please don't.'

'You already know, don't you?'

He stares across the lawn to the house. Sienna imagines he's picturing that night, how comfortable they all were, how content. She thinks he nods, but she can't be sure.

'They slept together, Rob.' She throws it out there. After all, this is their burden to share together; Sienna should never have kept it from him just so she'd have something to hold over Abby. She should have put Rob first.

He doesn't say anything, but she notices his hands are curled into fists.

'I have to go,' he says.

Sienna stares after him, calls his name several times, but he doesn't turn around.

She needs to let him go for now. What's done is done.

# TWENTY-EIGHT

*Abby*

She doesn't know where Rob is and has barely heard from him all day. Although they spent the whole weekend at home together, no meaningful words passed between them. There was no hostility, just a mound of excuses on Rob's part to be in any room other than the one she was in.

Then this afternoon a text from him came, telling her that Greg didn't turn up for work. She'd immediately called him, needing more than just written words, wanting to hear a voice telling it to her. It didn't change anything, though. Greg is missing and the chance of him having deliberately walked out is minuscule.

Her hands shook so much when Rob filled her in that she had to make excuses to get off the phone. And even when her legs threatened to give way beneath her, she couldn't bring herself to sit down. The problem is she knows too much, but it's all trapped in her head, locked up. She cannot say a word.

Rob came home after work before heading straight out again. 'Meeting a friend,' he'd said, closing the door before she'd had a chance to ask who.

Now she's sitting on the sofa with her laptop, looking through job vacancies. At least she can try to sort out one issue in her life while all the others pile up around her. They will bury her eventually.

She's typing an application letter when she hears his key turn in the lock. The school is on the other side of London, but she's going for it anyway – a long commute is the least of her worries.

'You're still up,' he says. 'I thought you'd be in bed by now.'

Normally she would be, but normality no longer exists.

'Did you have a good evening?' What she really wants to ask is where he's been, but she knows she has no right.

'Sorry I rushed off like that,' he says. 'Work was tough today and I just needed to get out. Clear my head.'

'Where did you go in the end?'

'To Mum and Dad's. Some of Dad's things ended up in my case. Not sure how that happened. Shall we go to bed? I could do with an early night.'

There is so much more she wants to ask him, yet she needs to give him his mental space. That's what she needs from him, so the least she can do is reciprocate.

She is surprised when, after a while of scrolling through his phone in bed, Rob strokes her arm. What shocks her even more, though, is the frisson of excitement which passes through her body. It feels different, yet she can't explain how or why.

Afterwards, while Rob sleeps, she goes downstairs where she's left her laptop. She logs onto her email and reads his one again, letting the words soak into her.

> I needed you, Abby, and I think you needed me too. Can we talk? Please.

Her finger hovers over the mouse button, and then she is applying pressure, moving the cursor to the reply button.

> Yes. I think we need to meet.

That's all she writes. The rest is now up to him.

–

She never thought she'd be the type of person to sneak out of her house in the middle of the night, like a teenager escaping from a curfew. Yet two days after she's sent her reply, this is

188

exactly what she's doing. Rob could wake up and find her missing, but that's a chance she'll have to take; she needs to do this.

It's nearly midnight when she gets to Richmond Park – the other side of London. She told him she'd wait in the car; there's no way she'll step foot outside. He'll think it's because she's worried about it being so late, so dark. He doesn't need to know the real reason she won't step foot outside the car.

Someone taps on the passenger window, and her body freezes. She can't tell whether it's him, and no car has pulled up anywhere nearby. Then he is peering in, and despite her determination not to feel anything, it's there surging through her veins. She rolls the window down.

'Are you going to let me in?' he asks.

'This was a bad idea,' she replies, forcing herself to look away.

'We're here now. Let's just talk. Please.'

She's torn now, even though she is the one who said they should meet. Now she's here, she's consumed with guilt. She should drive away now, leave him staring after her, but she doesn't. She unlocks the door and stares through the windshield while he climbs in beside her.

'I'm sorry,' he begins, reaching for her hand.

Abby pulls away. He has to know that she doesn't want him touching her. That's not why she's here. 'Don't. I don't want to hear it.'

'But you came.'

'Where have you been? You disappeared off the face of the earth. Why?'

'You know why.'

'Because you regretted it. And you couldn't face up to what you'd done. That's the only thing I know.' She should try not to sound bitter; he is already wielding power over her because she's agreed to be here, despite what he did.

'You just didn't have the guts to tell her the truth, did you? That's what it comes down to. That makes you a coward.'

'And were you going to tell Rob?'

This was the plan, even though she knew it would crush him. She couldn't keep living a lie. That wasn't fair to him either. 'Yes. It was up to both of us to tell the truth, wasn't it?'

He sighs, and Abby warms slightly; this can't be easy for him.

'Don't you think that by not telling her the truth you're hurting her even more? But you never loved her, did you, so I'm guessing you don't care about that.'

When he smiles, it looks to Abby like more of a wince, full of pain. 'We don't choose who we give our hearts to, Abby. It is what it is, and that's actually a beautiful thing. Everything in this world is so planned and calculated, don't you think it's special that love doesn't follow any rules? As much as we want to, we don't control it.' He takes her hand and, despite everything, it feels right. She doesn't want it to: it's Rob who should feel this way, who she should feel like she belongs with.

She pulls away. Too late, though, because the warmth of his skin has already infected her. Again. 'You need to go. Leave me alone. What's done is done and we can't undo it, but this stops now.'

He's shaking his head. 'No, Abby. No way. We're not done.'

And that's when she knows that she needs to put an end to this before it's too late.

# TWENTY-NINE

*Sienna*

She hasn't heard from Rob since he came to her house on Monday evening. Three days have passed, hours in which she's barely existed. Sienna wonders if there's any such thing as an *un*person, because that's what she feels like. She might still exist in her physical form, but inside she's hollowed out.

DC Roberts has been the only one in regular contact with her; each time he calls there's no news, and she's begun to wish he wouldn't bother. Not until he's found Greg. Even Marty's only texted a couple of times since she saw him that morning at the hospital. She understands this. There's not much anyone can say.

She's in her bedroom, looking out of the window, when a silver Audi pulls into her drive. Rob's car. She's opened the front door before he even steps out, and waits on her doorstep, the pavement sending a chill through her bare feet.

'Are you okay?' she asks as he walks towards her. It's Friday morning, and he should be at work by now.

'It's me who should be asking you that.' The thin smile on his face as he says this makes her want to hug him. She knows how much this man loves Abby. Is it more than she loves Greg? Different, perhaps.

'I'm… doing okay. Shouldn't you be at work?'

'Yes. I called in sick. I've never done that before.'

This doesn't surprise her; the second she met Rob she could tell he wasn't one for flouting rules.

'You'd better come in, then.'

'I've got to stop coming round like this,' Rob says once they're inside. 'The neighbours will think something's going on.'

Sienna smiles. 'And how ironic that we're actually the ones who aren't guilty of that.' She heads to the kitchen, déjà vu coursing through her head, and flicks on the kettle. 'Is this a coffee kind of chat or do you want something stronger?'

'Coffee's fine, thanks.' He sits down while she makes it.

She asks him if he's talked to Abby about Greg. She has to. Whether anyone likes it or not, she and Rob are in this together.

'Actually, you know you said just now that we're the only ones who aren't guilty of anything? Well, I'm not sure that's true.'

Leaving the coffee cups on the worktop, she joins Rob at the table. 'What do you mean?' She is already wondering if she'll regret asking this, but Sienna dislikes being kept in the dark.

'When I got home last night, Abby was still up. I was ready to confront her and have it out… but then, I couldn't do it. Actually, that's wrong. I could have done it – I just didn't want to.'

'Listen, Rob, I totally understand that, and it's not for me to tell you how to deal with your marriage.'

'No, it's not like that. I'm not being weak and ignoring what she's done.'

'Then what?'

He falls silent, shrugs. 'I don't know. Maybe I'm punishing her? Because this way I've got something that she doesn't know about, and I can decide how and when to use it.' His head falls back against the chair, and he stares at the ceiling. 'Oh, God, that makes me a bad person, doesn't it?'

Sienna reaches across the table and places her hand on his arm. 'No, it makes you someone who's hurt and needs time to process how to deal with it all.'

He seems relieved that she's said this. 'What about you? If Greg was here right now, what would you say to him?'

'After I thump the hell out of him?'

That elicits a chuckle from Rob.

'I don't know. I'd definitely confront him, though. But my marriage is different to yours. Very different. Greg and I had other issues, long before Abby.'

Rob raises his eyebrows. 'He's done this before?'

She shakes her head. 'Not that I know of. I just mean... I can't deny that there have been things we've needed to talk about that Greg refused to discuss. And that's not healthy, is it?' She won't share all the personal details with Rob; she still believes in maintaining the privacy of her marriage to Greg, as far as this is possible. 'I think you should talk to Abby. And I'm not just saying that because I need to find out if she knows where Greg is. I'm saying it because it's the right thing to do.'

'I know,' he says, hanging his head. 'I know you're right.'

Sienna stands up. 'I was about to go somewhere before you came. Will you come with me?'

He looks up, surprised. 'Where?'

'I need to go to Brighton. I need to feel like I'm doing something to find Greg.'

'But—'

'I know what you're going to say – that it will be pointless, and I need to leave it to the police to find him – and I know you're probably right, but this is something I need to do.'

Without saying anything, Rob stands. 'Come on – I'm driving.'

–

She's never visited Brighton before, and walking along the pebbled beach now with the vast ocean floating in front of her, enveloping her in serenity, she wonders why she hasn't. Rob is walking beside her, yet it almost feels like she's the only person here. She can picture Greg feeling at peace in this place, escaping from whatever he's run from.

'Look at this view,' Rob says, transfixed by the sea, just as she is. 'My parents brought me here as a kid. I don't really remember it, though.' He turns to her. 'So what's your plan?'

Sienna doesn't want to admit that she doesn't have one, that all she needed to do was feel closer to Greg. And closer to the truth. 'The coffee shop he used his card in is right near the cinema.' She's already looked this up on one of her restless nights.

Rob looks as though he's about to say something to put her off, so she's surprised when he tells her it's a good place to start.

Inside the coffee shop, Sienna feels nothing. She's expected to somehow sense that Greg has been here, as implausible as that seems. Yet it's just an ordinary place, bustling with people, even on a weekday afternoon. It's no wonder the police got nowhere with the staff. The queue is nearly to the door, so how can anyone be expected to remember Greg buying a coffee once? It was a normal coffee, the police had found out. No cappuccino or latte, nothing like that. Just plain: how Greg always has it.

'I guess it was stupid coming here,' she says. 'I don't know what I expected to get from it.'

Rob takes her arm. 'Do you want to go?'

'I never did make you that coffee at my house. Shall we grab one and go and sit on the beach? Unless you need to get home?'

'No, I don't. Not yet. Abby thinks I'm at work, so I can't go back yet anyway. I don't relish the idea of explaining that I called in sick.'

Sitting on the beach, Sienna stares at the waves, wonders fleetingly what it would feel like to be pulled away by them, to close her eyes and surrender to it. She would never do it, of course, she has too much passion for life. Usually. Did Greg have thoughts like this? She can't imagine he would ever feel that low. He loved his work too much; it's what he lived for. And Jackson.

'So do you think you'll talk to Abby?' Sienna asks Rob.

'Yes.' His answer is forceful, yet she wonders if he has the determination to see it through, or even the will.

'Will you let me know what she says about Greg?'

He nods, makes her this promise.

For a while longer they sit on the beach together, neither of them mentioning Greg or Abby again. It's refreshing to talk about other things, about the people they are individually rather than as part of their respective couples, and Sienna doesn't want it to end.

'We'd better get back,' she says to Rob eventually. 'Traffic won't be great at this time.'

He seems as reluctant to leave as she is, and they walk slowly back to the car, alone with their own thoughts.

–

Only a few minutes have passed since Rob dropped her home. She's in the kitchen, staring out of the window, when the doorbell rings. He must have forgotten something. She's pleased he's come back; there's something she wants to explain to him that she should have said earlier.

It's not Rob standing in front of her, though, when she pulls open the door. DC Roberts leans forward. 'Can I come in?'

It only takes one glance at him for her to know why he's here. She pictures herself stepping back, slamming the door in his face.

Standing aside, she lets him in. 'Just tell me,' she says. Is her voice shaking? It sounds to her as though it is, even though she wants to appear calm.

'Shall we sit down?'

'No. No, I don't want to sit down.' She clutches her stomach, doubles over to ease the nausea.

DC Roberts glances through the hall. 'I'm afraid... we've found a body.' Another pause. 'Your husband's wallet was with it, so we have to assume it's him. I'm so sorry, Sienna.'

DC Roberts reaches out, but he's too late to catch her when she falls.

*PART THREE*

# THIRTY

*Abby*

Sienna looks beautiful in black. This is the first thing Abby thinks when she and Rob slip into the back of the church. They're late. She hadn't wanted to come, it hadn't felt appropriate, yet she'd eventually given in to Rob's insistence. She could tell he needed to be here, even though he and Greg didn't know each other that well. She suspects he wants to be here for Sienna. Abby has no right to take issue with that.

The minister is talking about Greg as if he knew him well, when in reality he'll never have laid eyes on him. Everything he says will be from Sienna's own mouth, her own thoughts, which can't be objective. But it's only right to only focus on the good in someone when they die. That's what people desperately need to cling on to. Never mind the truth.

*A talented surgeon and loving father and husband.* She almost wants to scream out that it's all lies.

In one of the front rows, a boy she can only assume is Jackson sits with his mother. He's nestled into her shoulder while her arm is placed protectively around him. It's a heartbreaking image; nobody should have to lose a parent so young, especially in the way Greg was taken. Even from the distance Abby sits, she can see Jackson's body shudder as he cries into his mother.

Holly is nothing like she's imagined, nothing like Sienna. It shouldn't surprise her that Greg didn't have a type.

Sienna is making her way to the front of the church; her movements slow yet deliberate. It feels rehearsed somehow.

199

Abby wonders if she's feeling nervous about addressing so many people – Greg wasn't short of friends and acquaintances, and it seems as though the whole hospital has turned up to say their goodbyes. They don't know what Abby knows. Perhaps they wouldn't have flocked here otherwise.

Beside Abby, Rob sits silently, staring straight ahead at Sienna. The two of them don't hold hands as they would have before. Too much has changed in the last few weeks.

Afterwards, there is a wake at a hotel around the corner. 'We shouldn't go,' Abby whispers to Rob. 'It's not right when Sienna hates me so much.'

'We're her friends,' he says. 'We need to be there for her.' This stubborn streak in Rob is new to her, cementing in her mind just how much has changed in such a short time.

Abby doesn't mention that she doubts Sienna would care whether they showed their faces. She hadn't acknowledged them after the church service, even though they'd stood with everyone else to offer their condolences. It was all too much to bear so Abby had walked around the churchyard, trying to focus on the beautiful displays of flowers. Sienna had asked for family flowers only, but people don't listen; they can't help themselves at times like these.

–

Abby's standing in the hotel lobby, trying to take a moment to breathe, when a hand touches her shoulder.

'You came,' Sienna says. 'I didn't think you would.'

Abby struggles to speak. It's been a long time since she's been this close to her friend. There are so many things she wants to say. Needs to say. Where can she possibly start?

'I… I'm so sorry, Sienna.'

'I imagine you are,' she says. 'But let's not do this now. All of this,' she gestures around, 'is for Greg, and his memory. I don't want to fight here.'

Sienna is right. 'Can we talk later, though? We need to, don't we? There are things I need to tell you.'

Sienna sighs. 'I know there are.'

'Tonight?' Abby is probably pushing things, but this has waited long enough. She can feel the weight of Sienna's gaze on her while seconds tick by.

'Okay. Tonight. But not at my house. I'll come to you.'

This will work. Rob has already told her that he's going to stay with his parents for a few days, so he won't be there. It's better that way. He's avoiding her, of course, but she needs to deal with Sienna first before she can turn to the state of her marriage. 'Yes,' she says.

Rob appears and reaches for Sienna, wrapping his arms around her. It's a gesture that takes Abby by surprise, even though she's aware of how close they've become. 'I'm so sorry,' he says.

She nods, and for the first time since seeing her in the church, Abby notices the desperate pain etched on her face. 'Rob, can I borrow you for a minute?' she asks.

He doesn't hesitate, turning to Abby. 'I'll be back in a minute.'

She watches them walk away together, to the other side of the lobby, where they sit down at an empty table, their heads buried together.

Abby knows she deserves this.

# THIRTY-ONE

## *Sienna*

She can see Abby watching them, but she's too raw to feel smug. It's not as though there's anything going on between her and Rob; at least nothing beyond friendship.

'Thanks for coming,' Sienna says.

'I'm sorry for bringing Abby. I just thought she should be here, to face up to what she's done.'

'Has she admitted it then?' Sienna asks this even though she's no longer sure she cares. What does it matter now that Greg is dead?

'No, she hasn't said a word about Greg other than when we first found out.' He looks around. 'I can't imagine how you're feeling right now.'

'To be honest, I'm just numb. It will hit me again when I get home and I'm alone. Being surrounded by so many people like this is kind of like a protective layer. A shield stopping me feeling anything.'

He thinks about this for a moment. 'That makes sense.' There is a pause. 'I'd better go, there are so many people wanting to talk to you.'

'Let them wait,' she says.

He stays another few minutes, just long enough for her to steel herself to carry on.

It's Holly she speaks to next, and just as Rob has done, she wraps Sienna in a hug. Jackson is right beside his mother, his eyes red-rimmed and swollen.

'Come here,' Sienna says, and reaches down to hug him. He's almost as tall as she is, and she imagines he'll easily reach six foot like his dad. 'You're so brave,' she says softly. 'Remember that.'

'Is that your friend over there?' Holly says, nodding her head in Abby's direction.

'Yes, that's her.'

'Are you still sure something happened between them?'

Sienna nods.

'I'm sorry, I shouldn't be talking about this now. Can I do anything for you? Anything at all?'

It takes Holly's kindness to open the floodgates, and now she is overcome with sadness. This is what it's come to – finding solace in Greg's ex-wife.

'No, you're already looking after Jackson. Poor boy. But do you think you could both come back to the house for a bit after this? You don't have to stay long; it would just be nice to have some company.'

Holly doesn't hesitate. 'Of course we will. Just come and grab me when you're ready to leave. Did you drive here?'

'No, I got a cab. Not that I'm drinking or anything. I just didn't want to drive home alone afterwards.'

'Then I'll drive you home,' she says.

–

Back at the house, Holly fusses around her, insisting she sit down and rest while she makes some food. There was food at the wake, but Sienna couldn't touch it.

'I really don't need to rest,' she says, standing up and rearranging the cushions on the sofa. 'I'm not ill.'

Holly laughs. 'You're right, I'm sorry. I'm not good at this kind of thing. I can just about manage to look after my son, so haven't a clue how to help other people.'

Sienna doesn't believe this, but she appreciates what Holly is doing. 'I can make up some sandwiches,' she says. It's her house, so the least she can do is provide food for her guests.

'Actually, I could really go for a sandwich. And Jackson never says no to a plain cheese one.' She points to her son, who's sitting cross-legged on the floor with his iPad resting on his knees. 'That okay with you, Jax?'

'Thanks, Sienna,' he says. It's still strange for her to hear him address her by name when all she used to get was mumbles.

They leave Jackson to it and go to the kitchen, both of them preparing the food, even though Sienna has said she'd do it.

'I know you think I'm helping you,' Holly says, 'but actually it's the other way around. You see, I'm so torn up with guilt over the way I left Greg and, by helping you, I think I'm trying to make up for it. Does that make sense?'

'It does. So you being here is good for both of us, then.'

Holly smiles. 'The police will find who did that to him,' she says.

Sienna shudders. She has tried to push from her mind the details of Greg's death. His murder. But now the image of someone smashing his skull from behind forces its way into her head and lodges there. She can't shake it. And the worst thing of all is that Greg wouldn't have seen it coming. This, above all else, is what she struggles to deal with.

'I keep telling myself that,' Sienna says. She doesn't add that she won't be able to breathe until they do. She doesn't expect it will eradicate her pain, but it will be something.

'They dumped his body in that canal, Holly. I just can't stop thinking about how he lay there for weeks. And it means any possible DNA evidence got washed away.'

'It's amazing what they can do these days. Don't give up hope. We'll know what happened to him sooner or later.'

All three of them eat their food, and while they're clearing away, Holly turns to Sienna. 'Jackson hasn't eaten properly for days. This has been so good for him, thank you.'

It is good for Sienna too, having a small part of Greg here. She watches Jackson at the kitchen table, scrolling through his iPad. 'I know this might seem strange,' she says to Holly, 'but if Jackson ever wanted to come over, any time, then he's more than welcome. If it will help him to feel closer to Greg.' His presence is everywhere, and maybe Jackson feels it as much as Sienna does.

'You're a good person, Sienna, thank you. I'll let Jackson know.'

Sienna tries not to get her hopes up. Perhaps Jackson will disappear from her life, just as Greg has done, leaving no trace of her marriage. She still wants to be his stepmother, still *is*, as far as she's concerned, and she needs Jackson to know this.

'Well, we'd better get going,' Holly is saying as she finishes loading the dishwasher.

'Thank you for everything,' Sienna says. 'You and Jackson.' She wishes she could express how much they've come to mean to her over the last few weeks.

Holly smiles, grabs her hand. 'Don't even mention it. Will you be okay this evening? What will you do?'

'I'll be okay. I just want to think about Greg tonight. It still feels like this day is his, even though the funeral's over.'

'Oh, I totally get that,' Holly says.

Sienna doesn't mention that there's something else she needs to do to finally get the answers she needs.

# THIRTY-TWO

## *Abby*

Rob is packing a bag upstairs while Abby waits in the living room, watching through the window. She needs Rob to leave before Sienna gets here; there's no way he'll leave if he knows she's here. He never talks about his conversations with Sienna, but it's clear that he's protective of her. Somehow, she has managed to creep under his skin, and it frightens Abby what she could be saying to him. She's sure Rob doesn't know the truth, though. There's no way they'd still be living under this roof together if he did.

She has no idea what time Sienna will come tonight, or if she'll actually turn up. And if she does, there is still the fear of what might happen when the two of them face each other. Alone.

She hears Rob coming downstairs, dropping his bag on the floor, calling her.

'I'm in the living room,' she says.

'I'll head off in a minute. Are you sure you're okay with me staying at Mum and Dad's for a few days? I'll drive straight to work from theirs on Monday, so I'll see you in the evening.'

Today is Friday. She has a whole weekend to deal with Sienna. 'It's fine,' she says. 'I'll carry on with the redecorating.'

'Removing every trace of Sienna.'

'If you want to see it that way.'

'I don't *want* to, that's just how it looks.'

She doesn't have the energy to argue with Rob right now; she needs every ounce of what she has to handle Sienna when she comes.

'What I don't understand is,' he says, 'why you hate her so much.'

'I don't hate her at all.' There's no point explaining that Sienna is the one who turned on Abby. It will all become clear to Rob soon enough.

'What did you talk about, anyway? At the funeral?'

They haven't mentioned the funeral since they got home. It's not as though Abby has avoided talking about it – Rob is the one who changed the subject when she tried.

'She's not out to get you, Abby. I wish you could see that.' He walks over to her and gives her a brief kiss. 'I'll see you later.'

–

It's another hour before Sienna turns up. Abby knew she would feel nervous, but she hadn't expected her stomach to somersault just witnessing her stepping out of her car. She's still dressed in black, although her clothes are different: leggings and a floaty, long, sleeveless top. The only colour on her is the dark red hair clip holding her fringe back from her face.

'Thanks for coming,' Abby says when they're inside.

'Don't thank me. I haven't come for you. I've come here for me.'

'Well, all that matters is you're here.'

'Where's Rob?' Sienna asks. 'Surely he's not working this late?'

'He's gone to his parents'. I thought it would be better to talk alone.'

Sienna walks through the hall, gazing around at the freshly painted walls. 'Something you weren't happy with?' she asks.

'It just felt like the right thing to do. Sorry if you're offended.'

'Actually, that's the least offensive thing you've done, isn't it?'

Sienna is right, but Abby needs to extinguish her hostility. 'I know, and I'm sorry, but I'll get to that. Please, will you just sit, and we can talk about everything?'

Sienna does as Abby asks, folds her arms across her body and waits silently for her to continue.

'I need to tell you something, and this is probably the most difficult thing I've ever had to say to anyone.' A lump forms in her throat as she looks at Sienna. She's about to destroy this grieving woman's life even more than it already has been. She almost can't do it; perhaps it's better to let it lie, to bury it along with Greg. After all, she is the only other person left who knows. It never has to come out. They can all live in oblivion; surely, it's better that way?

She's started now, though, and Sienna's eyes are a melting pot of fear, sadness and hatred.

'I already know,' Sienna says. 'I've known for a long time.'

Abby is confused. There's no way. Is it possible that Greg told her after all? But then why hasn't Sienna already confronted her?

'You know? How?'

'That doesn't matter. But I want to hear it from you. Go on, then – tell me how exactly you ended up sleeping with my husband?'

Abby feels sick; she hadn't expected this, and it's thrown her off course. For a moment she can't speak. 'No, Sienna,' she manages to say. 'No, you've got it all wrong.'

Sienna shakes her head, stands up.

'So, even now, even after Greg is found murdered, you can't be honest! You're a despicable woman, Abby, and I wish I'd never laid eyes on you. I'd do anything to go back and erase meeting you… you're just—'

'Sienna, just stop! Please, I'm trying to tell you something and you need to listen.' Abby doesn't wait for a response; she needs to say it now and stop Sienna leaving. 'That night of the husband swap, Greg told me something he's never told anyone. I don't think he meant to, he was so drunk it just came out, and then it was too late for him to take it back.'

Sienna stares at her. 'What are you talking about? You're not making sense.'

'Sienna, listen to me. Greg told me that he killed someone.'

# THIRTY-THREE

*Sienna*

Sienna stares at Abby and, for a moment, it's as though her friend is speaking a language she's not familiar with. Then her words come sharply into focus, like knife blades slicing her skin. Why is Abby saying this? 'What are you talking about?' she manages to ask.

'He killed someone, Sienna. He admitted it. There's no way it was a misunderstanding; you'll see that when I tell you the whole story.'

Sienna says nothing, fights the urge to run from this house. Whatever she's got to say, Sienna needs to hear it.

'Everything was going well that night. We... talked. A lot. Opened up to each other and shared things. I told him about my mum, and he really listened. He just got it. He understood.'

This doesn't surprise Sienna; it sounds similar to how she and Rob seemed to bond. A flicker of something – is it jealousy? – trickles through her. She should have been the one Greg was opening up to.

'But then... he told me he had things he was running from.'

Sienna leans forward. 'And how did that come up? How did you get to that point?'

'I'm not sure – I can't remember every word in the order they were spoken. We were drunk, remember? Anyway, he kind of broke down. Buried his head in his hands and started wailing. Terrifying animal noises. That's the best way I can describe it. I didn't know what to do. I tried to comfort him, tell him it couldn't be that bad, and he looked straight at me and said that it was worse than I could possibly imagine.'

Sienna's heart rate quickens, she can feel it. She wants to throw up because even though every part of her wants to believe that Abby is lying, something about the way she's talking about Greg feels *right*. As if she's just been given a missing jigsaw piece that she knows fits before she's slotted it into place.

'Then he just said it. "Abby, I hurt someone, and watched her die."'

'No... no, you've got it wrong. He's a surgeon, Abby. He meant one of his patients died and there was nothing he could do to save her.' Yes, this is it. This is the only thing that makes sense. 'That was the part of his job he found the hardest. But it happens to all surgeons.'

Abby stares at her as though she's a teacher feeling sorry for a student who just can't grasp something, no matter how many different ways it's explained. 'No, Sienna. That's what I assumed, so I asked him. I even talked about Mum, and how I didn't hold any of the doctors responsible for missing her cancer. But he said it wasn't like that.' Abby looks up to the ceiling, takes a deep breath. 'He was having an affair with one of his patients. He didn't tell me her name or when it was.'

Any second now Sienna will wake from this nightmare. She will open her eyes and realise she is in her own house, not Abby's, that she's fallen asleep on her sofa after the funeral and none of this is real.

'He tried to break it off,' Abby is saying. 'It went on for months, but he realised it was wrong, so he wanted to put an end to it. The girl threatened to report him to the hospital, because she was one of his patients and there'd been many times they'd slept together while he was at work.'

Sienna can no longer listen. She rushes from the room and shuts herself in the downstairs toilet, only just making it before she throws up the little food she's eaten today.

It's only seconds before Abby knocks on the door. 'Are you okay? Please come out. I know hearing this is awful, especially today. I wanted to tell you before but… I feel dreadful keeping this from you for so long. I know it was wrong. I'm so sorry.'

Sienna throws open the door. 'Tell me the rest. All of it. And then you can explain why you kept it to yourself.' She heads to Abby's kitchen, hears her following.

'He said it all came to a head one night when she begged him to come over just one last time. He went. He didn't want to, but he felt that he owed it to her. He told me that's when it happened. When he… killed her. At her flat.'

'No,' Sienna says. She can't digest these words. It can't be Greg that Abby is talking about.

'I told him he must be mistaken, that it must have been an accident, and he said no, that he'd never done anything more deliberate in his life.' There are tears in Abby's eyes as she says this. 'I pressed him for more detail, and he just shut down.'

Sienna shakes her head. She doesn't want to believe this. How is it possible for her mind to grasp the enormity of this?

Abby walks closer to her, tries to take her arm, but Sienna pushes her off.

'He wouldn't. This is a lie. You're lying.'

'No, I'm not. I've never been more honest about anything in my life.'

'Does Holly know any of this?' It's impossible.

'No. Greg said I was the only person alive who knew. He said he's had to live with what he did every second of every day. That's exactly how he put it. He said there was already this huge wedge between you because he was scared to let you in and let himself love you like you deserved. He was terrified of you finding out and leaving him.'

Sienna wants to believe at least this last part – that the whole reason Greg was so distant was because he was carrying around this huge, terrible part of himself.

A bomb has exploded in her life, and she has no idea how to deal with it. All of this information is too much. She needs to pick it apart and reassemble it to make sense of it. There has to be another reason why Abby is saying all of this.

'Why now? If it's true, then why didn't you tell me any of this before? We were supposed to be friends, but clearly your loyalties lay with Greg, a man you hardly even knew.' She wipes tears away. 'You slept with him, didn't you? Even after he said all this! Was it your way of comforting him?'

'No! I swear to you nothing like that happened. Yes, it was a kind of intimacy that he was telling me all this, but it wasn't physical in any way. I wouldn't do that to you.'

Rob, though. Why hasn't she mentioned that she wouldn't do that to Rob? Sienna stares at her, tries to assimilate all of this information. 'What did you say to Greg when he said all this?'

'I told him to tell you, and that you could work it out together. He just kept crying, saying his work could never find out, and that he'd lose everything. He was terrified of losing Jackson. He made me promise not to say anything.' She pauses. 'I made him that promise because I could see how much pain he was in.'

Sienna feels sick again.

'He said that he'd tell you, Sienna. And I believed him. I made up the spare bed for him, and he went to sleep. If I hadn't drunk so much, I wouldn't have managed to get to sleep myself. I don't know how, but I did. And then when I woke up in the morning he'd already left. Without a word.'

This is too much. She doesn't want to hear any more, but she needs to know all of it. She's confused – torn between not wanting to believe Abby, and the minute possibility that maybe Abby is telling the truth.

'And did you speak to him again?' Sienna asks.

'Yes. The next day I went to the hospital to confront him about what he'd told me, and he acted as though nothing had happened. I told him he had to tell you; otherwise I would. Then he texted to ask if I'd give him a week to talk to you. I allowed him that time and, on the last day, he asked if he could meet me before he spoke to you. I really thought he just wanted my advice about how to tell you, or just to go through everything in his mind. I never thought for one second he'd—'

'And you didn't stop to think that the police would need to know about this?'

'Yes, yes, of course I did. I told him that, but I wanted him to talk to you first and then you could deal with it together.'

Sienna reaches for a kitchen chair and sinks into it. Her legs can't seem to take her weight any more. 'He never told me, though. Why? If you were putting pressure on him to tell the truth, then explain why he didn't.'

Abby falls silent. Sienna's convinced she won't have an answer to this. There's more to it, she knows it. Much more.

'He blackmailed me,' Abby says, just when Sienna's about to accuse her of lying. 'He told me that if I told you, he'd tell you I'd tried to sleep with him, and that I was jealous and rejected, trying to get back at him. And right after that he went missing.'

This is too much information to digest, no matter how hard Sienna tries to make sense of it. She needs to know if this is true, to find out with certainty, but she's at a loss at how to do that. Probing Abby further in the hope of catching her out is the only option right now. 'What day was it you met up?'

Abby's answer comes with no hesitation. 'The day he disappeared.'

Sienna stands. 'Does Rob know any of this?'

'No. It's you I wanted to tell. It wasn't for Rob to know, and I wish I didn't know. After Greg died—'

'Was murdered, you mean.'

'I wondered whether to let it go because of the pain it would cause you, but I couldn't let you go on thinking something had happened between me and him.'

'So you're really trying to tell me that Rob knows nothing about this?' Sienna asks.

'No. I told you, I haven't said a word. And I won't, not unless you want me to.'

She's relieved to hear this; she actually trusts Rob and hates to think that he could have held something like this back from her. 'No. Don't say anything. I need to get my head around everything you've said.'

Abby nods. 'Of course. I'm here if you need me for anything.'

Sienna looks at her, she can't smile or thank her; she has nothing left to give. 'There is something you can do for me.'

'Of course. Anything.'

'You can stay the hell out of my life.'

Much later, when she's at home, away from Abby's and free from all the words she was spewing, Sienna feels as though she's losing her mind, that as soon as she tries to cling to something concrete, it vanishes in her grasp. She knows she can no longer trust her own instincts, so all she can do is focus on what she knows for certain: Abby might have been one of the last people to see Greg alive. He was blackmailing her, so what lengths would she go to in order to protect her marriage?

The only other thing Sienna is convinced of is that nothing points to Greg's murder being a random attack. Wrong place at the wrong time. It's too much of a coincidence. His wallet hadn't been taken, and the police had found seventy pounds in there, so it wasn't a mugging.

If Greg did do what Abby claims, why would he so recklessly expose himself after so many years of keeping it carefully hidden? There has to be more to this. Abby must be lying, covering up for something else. Sienna can't get sucked into any more lies; she's had enough. All she wants is to lay Greg to rest now, to work towards finding some peace, yet now this is impossible.

She could call DC Roberts – he would surely be able to find out if there's any truth in what Abby claims Greg admitted to. Before she even thinks about speaking to the police, she needs to verify what Abby has said for herself. And there's one thing making her doubt Abby's confession.

Sienna heard Abby admitting to having an affair. So what game is she playing?

# THIRTY-FOUR

*Abby*

She'd been driving around aimlessly since Sienna left, needing to be out of the house, moving. Until she realised that it was futile; nothing will help. Now she sits in the car outside her house, the engine still running because she can't bear the silence turning it off will bring. She pulls her hand from the steering wheel and sees it's shaking. She tries to steady it, but it's out of her control. Speaking to Sienna tonight has shaken her to her core, and this, she knows, is only just the beginning.

Abby wishes Rob was at home tonight, that she could share this all with him, but she knows that's not fair to him. It's been this way all along, his friendship the thing she's needed most from him, the element that's bonded her to him, at least on her part.

At first, Abby was convinced that Sienna believed her tonight, but something changed; being ordered to leave her alone in that cold manner is evidence of this. She knows Sienna is grieving and would have been in shock after what Abby revealed, yet there was something there that didn't feel right. Sienna was emotional, of course she was, but underlying that was something calculated, and it worries Abby.

She turns off the engine and heads towards the front door, stopping on the doorstep to look up at the house. Nothing will ever be the same again, no matter how much she's tried to put things right.

Greg is dead. Murdered. Almost everything is out in the open. She can't lose sight of this.

She's only been inside for ten minutes when she picks up her mobile and calls Rob. She needs to see him, to try and save what's left of her marriage, to know if there's any chance it can be salvaged. Being away from him for the next few days will only make things worse.

'Hey.' He sounds drowsy and it's clear that she's woken him. It's only now she checks the time and sees that it's past ten p.m.

'I was thinking I'd drive over to Reading and stay there with you? I could help you with the jobs your parents need doing.'

'Oh.' He's alert now. 'When?'

'How about now?'

A long pause. 'Abby, it's late. It would be way past midnight by the time you got here.'

'It's not like it's a school night, is it?' She forces a laugh. 'I'll just throw some things in a bag, then I'll be ready to leave.'

More hesitation. 'Actually, I don't think it's a good idea. Just get some rest. I'm taking Mum and Dad out tomorrow, so we'll be gone most of the day.'

Abby could question him, get more details about where exactly they're going, but it's pointless. Rob doesn't want her to come, and she's not going to push it. Sienna has got to him.

'Okay,' she says.

'Don't worry if you can't get hold of me much tomorrow – we've got a busy day planned.'

She says goodbye and stares at her phone. She should feel bad that Rob doesn't want to be around her, but instead she's seeing the positive within it: she will use this time alone to fix the mess she's in.

# THIRTY-FIVE

*Sienna*

Abby is lying, she's convinced of it. She's had a week to get her head around what she was told, and she's come to this conclusion: there is no way Greg would have taken someone's life. He was a doctor; it goes against everything he stood for, the oath he took to do no harm.

Abby's account might be believable enough, but she's unaware that Sienna knows she slept with Greg, heard it from her own mouth, saw that there was an empty draft email from him to her on his computer, dated the day after the dinner party, even though it had yet to be filled out. Abby could argue that he was emailing her to make sure she didn't say anything. It's a minefield and Sienna doesn't know what to believe.

She needs to fact check Abby's story, just to make sure. She's on her laptop, still in bed. Greg and Holly were married in 2007, so Greg seeing one of his patients would have to have been before that. The whole time she's typing into Google, she tells herself it's just so she can know with certainty. And then she will deal with Abby and her lies.

If this woman was a patient of Greg's, then it's likely she at least lived in London. That barely narrows it down, but it's something to go on. She types in *murders of women in 2007*, then works backwards for a few years. Any longer than that and Greg would have still been a medical student. Just reading the accounts of all the women, whose faces smile at her as though they're still alive, makes her shudder. It feels as though she is violating these women's privacy, their right to be left at peace.

There aren't as many as she assumed there'd be, at least not ones that she can find information on. It's futile, this search. She's not a police officer or a medical professional who might be able to access this information, and she can't find anyone who seems to fit into the right age group.

Because it's not true.

Sienna needs to talk to Holly, but she doesn't want to mention all of this to her. She can't. At the very least she might be able to determine if Holly knows anything about Greg's past. She needs to be careful how she does this; she's grown fond of Holly and doesn't want anything damaging their relationship, especially for Jackson's sake.

Even though it's early, she sends Holly a text.

> Would you and Jackson like to come for dinner tonight? I'll try and do better than sandwiches this time.

She ends her message with a smiley face, even though smiling is the last thing she feels able to do.

While she's waiting for Holly to reply, she scrolls through her photos. It surprises her that they're mostly of Greg – she hadn't realised she took so many photos of him. She can barely recall taking them. It was always an instinctual act, something done without forethought. Out of needing to capture him at different moments.

She stares at one of him smiling and holding out his hands, trying to stop her taking the photo. *Are you a murderer? Did you get what you deserved?* She's hoping something in his eyes will answer her back, but of course there is nothing but silence from a fleeting moment of time.

Her phone beeps with Holly's reply.

We'd love to – but no cooking. I'll treat us all to a takeaway x

In the shower, Sienna confronts something she's tried to avoid dealing with. It's too much of a coincidence that Greg went missing after spending that night with Abby. When it first happened, her instinct told her that Abby knew where Greg was. What if this is still true? That can only mean one thing: Abby knows what happened to Greg. Or worse. Abby is responsible.

Marty is the next person she contacts. He's known Greg for a long time, since before he married Holly, so if anyone might know anything about him seeing one of his patients then it's him. She assumes it won't be easy to get much out of him – his loyalty to Greg won't have been extinguished by Greg's death.

–

They meet in a cafe in Waterloo. It had to be somewhere near the hospital; Marty has to be at work in a few hours. On the phone he'd sounded reluctant, even though he was trying his best to hide it. He's only accommodating her out of duty to his friend.

'How are you holding up?' he asks.

He's already asked this on the phone, and she gives the same response. 'I can't even describe how I feel. It's one thing losing someone, but the way Greg died...'

Marty reaches for her hand. 'I know. I still can't wrap my head around it. Why would anyone do that to Greg? He was a kind, hardworking man, and I've never known anyone to harbour any ill feeling towards him.' He hesitates. 'I'm sorry, this is probably too hard for you to talk about.'

'No, it's exactly what I need. I don't want people to tiptoe around me and be afraid to mention his name. It's not like I can even try to move on when there's a huge, awful question mark hanging over it all.'

'Do the police have any suspects?'

She shakes her head. 'He didn't drown in that canal. He was already dead when someone… dumped him in there.' She surprises herself with how she can be so detached when she's talking about this. It's born out of necessity, out of her desire to get to the truth. She wants to prove that Abby is a liar, even though it's clear that Greg betrayed her. Being an adulterer is far different from being a murderer.

'Oh, Jesus. I didn't know that,' Marty says, wiping his brow. The heat in here is stifling.

'It means that the chances of it being random are slim. This was someone who knew him and didn't want his body to be discovered.' DC Roberts has told her this, even though it's all supposition. 'There's no DNA evidence on him, though. It was all wiped away in the water.' The image of Greg floating lifeless in the water chokes her up. She fights back tears.

'They'll find out who did it, Sienna.'

She manages a nod. 'Marty, I need to ask you something and I need you to promise me that you'll be honest, no matter how hard it might be.'

He looks anxious as he puts down his cup. 'I will,' he says. 'What is it?'

'You've known Greg for a long time.' She corrects herself. 'Knew, I mean. Do you know if he was ever involved with one of his patients?'

Marty's eyes widen. 'No, of course not. He was too focused on his career to risk jeopardising it. Why do you ask?'

'I'm… just starting to piece some things together and I need to try and make sense of them.' Her answer is vague, but she can't give Marty more detail than this.

'What about having an affair while he was married?'

'Greg cheat on you? No, of course not. Greg loved you, Sienna.'

'That doesn't always stop people doing it, does it? Anyway, I didn't mean recently. What about before? When he was married to Holly? Do you know anything about an affair he might have had?' She feels bad asking this when she hasn't even spoken to Holly, but she needs to be sure.

There is no hesitation when Marty's reply comes. 'No, definitely not. He wouldn't have had the time. Greg was always working, and in those days, he didn't know how to balance his work and home life. That's probably why Holly got fed up.'

'So he never mentioned anything about another woman?'

'Sienna, where is this coming from? I know you're grieving and it's such a lot to deal with, but what's going on?'

'I just want to understand him,' she says. 'Because I'm not sure I ever did. I thought I did, but… now I'm questioning everything.' This is as close as she can get to telling the truth to Marty.

'I can assure you that if Greg was seeing a patient or had an affair when he was married, then I'd know about it. Not sure I could say the same for Holly, though. As much as I like her.'

Sienna stares at him. 'What do you mean?'

'I just mean that she was the one who left him, and Greg was in pieces. He never explicitly said that she'd left him for someone else, but I got that impression.'

Whether or not this is true, for Sienna it has no relevance. She's not going to judge Holly – the woman has already admitted she couldn't give Greg the love he needed.

'Okay. I just needed to be sure. There is just one other thing I wanted to ask you. Do you remember when we all met for dinner that last time? And Greg was late?'

He nods. 'Yes. I didn't know that would be one of the last times I'd see him.'

She ignores this. 'You'd asked me about having kids, and when I said Greg and I weren't planning to, you were about to say something, but we got interrupted when Greg turned up. What were you about to say?'

Marty frowns, and she expects he'll say he can't remember. 'I was just surprised, I think, as Greg had recently been saying he could see himself being a dad again.' He pats her arm. 'I'm sorry, Sienna.'

Hearing this, Sienna almost struggles to breathe. She can't find any words to say, instead lifting her coffee and forcing herself to drink.

Marty, too, is silent now and, whatever he's thought of her in the past, she's quite certain that this will be the last time she sees him. Without Greg, there is no reason for them to be in contact. Before they leave this place, he will give her assurances that he's there for her if ever she needs him – he'll say 'they', meaning Jo and him, just so there's no way to misinterpret what he means. And she will thank him and pretend that this isn't the end of a chapter.

'Thanks for meeting me today,' Sienna says. 'Anyway, drink up, I know you've got work to get to.'

She walks along the river before she gets the Tube home. She's always found strolling aimlessly gives her head the space it needs to order her thoughts. Just as she's suspected, everything points in the direction of Abby lying, but she still needs to get a feel for Holly's thoughts. It won't be a case of being direct, as she has been with Marty; the last thing she wants to do is cause her any offence.

And when she is convinced that Holly knows nothing about what Greg has supposedly done, it will be time to go to the police.

# THIRTY-SIX

*Abby*

Rob is away again – this time, on a business trip to Manchester. They barely speak during the day, and half the time he falls asleep on the sofa. She's tried to talk to him about Sienna, but he shuts the conversation down and tells her to leave it alone.

Sienna doesn't believe her; that much is clear. It's been a week now since they spoke on the day of the funeral and there's been no contact on Sienna's part. Abby has messaged her, telling her she's here if Sienna needs to talk, but all she gets in return is silence. It's not a peaceful silence, a symbol of moving on. Instead, it's laced with foreboding.

There is nothing Abby can say to make her believe that she didn't sleep with Greg, and it's only natural that Sienna won't trust what she's told her Greg admitted to. What worries her, though, is the possibility that Sienna knows what happened to Greg. It's been a rapidly expanding thought in her head, the only one that makes sense. Sienna is someone who had every reason to hate Greg.

She's scrolling through job vacancies when she gets the email. As soon as she sees the name, she knows she should delete it. Most of her wants to, but there's that tiny part – so much stronger – that won't allow her. It's always been this way.

Meet me. Please. I'm staying at the Marriott Hotel in Grosvenor Square. Room 231.

She closes the email. Now she wishes she'd had the strength to delete it.

All day she tries to ignore it, but it's there constantly, taunting her. They do need to talk, there is no doubt about that, but it will come at a cost. She takes her mobile upstairs, buries it under the duvet before going back down again. She uses the house phone to call Mel; she wants to tell her everything, plans to, until the words wither and die in her mouth.

At just after six p.m., she leaves the house, telling herself she needs to get out, that some fresh air will help clear her mind.

And then she is standing outside the hotel, walking towards it as if she's being pulled by a magnetic force. It's meant to be this way, she tells herself with each step she takes towards room 231.

–

'You came,' he says, reaching out and gently pulling her into the room. 'I didn't think you would.'

'It doesn't mean anything that I'm here.' She pulls away but still steps inside.

He smiles. 'Well, it has to mean something. Everything means *something*.' He's always so sure of himself; she remembers that about him. 'Come and sit with me,' he continues, and she notices the bottle of wine on the table. Two glasses ready to be filled.

'That's a bit presumptuous, isn't it?' She points to the table.

'How do you know I'm not expecting someone else?'

'Like your wife, you mean?' She regrets it as soon as the words leave her mouth.

'I've left her, Abby. It's over. I know I should have done it years ago—'

'I don't believe you,' she says. If he couldn't do it before – when she was waiting for him – then there's little chance he's done it now.

He sits on the edge of the king-size bed. 'It's true. I under-stand why you might not rush to believe me, but I've done it.'

'Does she know? Or have you just disappeared on her? You like doing that kind of thing, don't you?'

'I'm sorry I did that. I hate myself for hurting you like that.'

She folds her arms across her chest. 'I'm fine. I'm happy. Getting on with my life.' If she says it forcefully enough, she might just be able to believe it, even for a moment.

'Maybe you are,' he says, 'but you don't love Rob. I know you don't.'

Through the window, trees dance in the wind – it's breezy today, more like November than August. She focuses on their movements; if she narrows her eyes, she can almost believe they are human. 'You don't know anything about my marriage, Mark.'

'I know that you were leaving him, following your heart.'

And Mark trampled all over it – crushed it into a thousand tiny pieces. Left her fractured and broken. She continues staring out of the window, unable to meet his gaze. She's seconds away from breaking down; all the pain she's kept carefully bottled up is ready to explode from her body.

'Do you remember when we were at school?' he says when she doesn't respond. 'We used to spend every break time and every lunchtime together. Everyone thought we were crazy, that we'd never last the distance.'

'We didn't, did we?' she snorts. She knows what he's doing; he thinks taking her back there will soften her, break down the barrier she's spent years putting up.

He ignores her. 'We didn't need anyone else, did we? Only each other.'

He's right; that was exactly how she'd felt then. It was the two of them against the world. *With you by my side I can do anything*, Mark used to tell her. She'd felt the same. And even as they'd left school and grown older, become the adults they were turning into, nothing had changed. At least not until he had decided he needed a change. That they'd outgrown each other and both of them needed to experience a world separate from the one they occupied together.

'It wasn't healthy, was it?' Abby says, still unable to look at him. 'And look what happened. You wanted to know what it would be like to be with other people, to find out who you were without me.'

'It was intense,' he admits. 'And that's what scared me. We were so young, and it just didn't feel right to be in something so... heavy. I was afraid of what would happen to me if it crumbled away, so I tried to take control, to make sure I couldn't be hurt.'

'Don't, Mark. I don't want to hear all of this again.'

He stands and walks over to her, takes her arm. 'Nothing's changed, Abby. I've tried to move on and make my life work. I really have. But I love you and I can't stop. God knows I've tried.'

There are tears in her eyes now because she's realised something: they are both different people, changed in immeasurable ways, yet how she feels about him has remained the same. Timeless. Isn't that exactly what love is supposed to be?

Mark kneels before her and buries his head into her lap. His body is shaking, and she can tell he's also trying not to cry. It takes her a few moments, but eventually she places her hand on his shoulders. It should feel strange touching him after all this time, but it only feels right.

Her thoughts turn to Rob, and the mess of her life back at home. Sienna. Greg. What if she never had to go back and face it? Her mind battles with her heart. She needs to fight this, do the right thing. But isn't it already too late for that? She's gone so far beyond the line she doubts there is any coming back. This is what sways her, along with the fact that she has never stopped loving this man.

—

Afterwards, she nestles into him, breathing in his scent. Beneath the shower gel and aftershave is the essence of Mark, the smell that hasn't changed since school. It is comforting and familiar. Part of him that somehow also belongs to her. She should feel guilty, and it's there, somewhere, hidden, but all she feels is that, finally, she's where she's meant to be.

'I keep staring at you,' he says. 'I can't believe this is real.' He reaches for her hand, gently strokes it. 'I need to explain what happened that day. Why I never showed up.'

She's wanted to know this for years, but now the moment of revelation has come she's not sure she needs to. Abby wants to stay in this bubble, just the two of them, without letting the world back in. 'No,' she says. 'Don't explain. It's better if I don't know.'

'It was never about Cassie. I didn't love her.'

She hasn't heard her name for a long time and it's incongruous now, in this room. It doesn't belong. Mark's wife has always been a faceless person, an outline with no shading. She couldn't have functioned if it had been any other way. They'd met soon after Mark had left Abby, not long before she'd met Rob in that bar. And even when Mark had turned up on her doorstep, saying he'd made a mistake, she'd shut the door on him, knowing that he was involved with someone else, tears blinding her once he couldn't see her face.

'I was scared… You wouldn't go anywhere near me while I was with her, so I… maybe I didn't believe you really wanted me. Especially after the way I'd ended our relationship. And then Cassie told me she was pregnant. It was that same night. I was ready to tell her, I swear. But then she told me that.'

'You… you have a child?'

'No. No. Cassie had an early miscarriage, and then, well she wanted to try again, and we did, but it never happened. And I'm glad it didn't. It would have been the wrong thing for everyone.'

'Why didn't you tell me this before? When we met up after Mum died? You had every chance.' Until recently in the car that night, it was the last time she'd seen him. A time she's not proud of and wishes she could erase.

'Because you told me you loved Rob and that you didn't feel the same way about me any more. Remember that? There didn't seem any point. And it's not like we were doing much talking. Remember?'

She does. She'd just lost her mum and she felt angry with everyone, full of rage at the world. When Mark had messaged her begging to meet up, she'd almost done it to hurt herself, to inflict more pain to numb the wound her mum's death had left. 'I'm not proud of that,' she says.

'And this?' He lifts the sheet where they both lie naked underneath. 'What's this?'

'This is different.' And it is, because this time she knows her marriage is over, and that she needs to set Rob free, for his sake even more than hers.

Thinking of Rob now forces her to think of Greg, and Sienna too. The three of them are intertwined now, and there is no way to unravel one from the other.

She kisses Mark's chest, slides her hand along it. She is safe now.

And he will never need to know what she's done.

## THIRTY-SEVEN

### Sienna

'How are you *really* doing?' Holly asks. 'And don't give me any of that *I'm fine* stuff. It's okay not to be – it's only been three weeks.'

Sienna offers a smile. 'You're right. I'm not okay. But I'm managing. If that makes sense. I'm functioning. And that's got to count for something, hasn't it?'

'Of course.' She picks up her fork. 'And this is delicious. I can't believe you wouldn't let me treat you to a takeaway.'

Sienna needed to cook, to have her hands so busy that there was no place for intrusive thoughts. A break from her own mind. The meal she's made is a vegetarian ragu; since Greg's body was found Sienna can't stomach even the thought of meat. She doesn't tell Holly that she's been living on eggs and toast. Things that don't need a lot of commitment, and don't turn her stomach. 'How about you, Jackson? Do you like it?'

Across the table, he nods. 'Yes, thanks.' Yet his plate has hardly been touched.

'This is the most he's eaten for a while,' Holly says. 'Don't take it personally.'

Sienna assures her that she won't. 'How about I put the TV on?' she suggests. 'Your mum can help me clear up.'

Jackson's face brightens, and Sienna is relieved. She needs the chance to talk to Holly in private.

When she comes back from setting Jackson up in the living room, Holly is already clearing the kitchen. 'Sorry. Force of habit. I haven't forgotten this isn't my house, I promise.'

'No, it's fine. I appreciate the help.' She begins loading the dishwasher, all the time glancing at Holly, wondering how she will bring up what she needs to ask her. Sienna has always been outspoken, never shied away from confronting things that need to be said, yet now can't seem to begin.

'Can we talk?' she asks when they've finished. 'In here?'

'Of course. Actually, I thought there was something on your mind, but I didn't want to push you.'

'And there I was thinking I'm quite good at putting on a brave face.'

'Well, I'd say that's impossible at the moment, given everything that's happened.'

Sienna sits at the table, swipes a crumb away. 'I told you about Greg having an affair, didn't I?'

'Yes, and I told you it didn't seem like something he'd do. At least, not the Greg I knew.'

'I need to know if you meant that, or if maybe you were just trying to make me feel better? I just wonder if… he ever might have done it before?'

Holly frowns. 'Are you asking if he might have had an affair while we were married?'

'I'm sorry, but yes, that's exactly what I'm asking. Or if he'd ever mentioned he might have cheated on anyone in any relationship he'd had before you?'

'This is about your friend, isn't it? Did you get a chance to talk to her about it all?'

'Yes, we did. And she denied it again. I just find it hard to believe.'

'Why? Maybe you heard it wrong that day, or misunderstood? What makes you so convinced?'

She's not, though. Not any more. There are only two options: either Greg was sleeping with one of his patients and he killed her, or he slept with Abby. She wants to believe the latter, because she can't even begin to stomach the other alternative. It's not Greg, not the man she knew. So what does that say about their whole marriage?

'All I know is that she's lying about something.'

'Talk to her, Sienna. That's the only way you'll know. Anyway, in answer to your question, no, as far as I'm aware, Greg never did anything during our marriage. I'm not saying it's impossible, people can always find a way to cheat, can't they? But I'd be very surprised if he'd even had the time. He didn't even have time for me, let alone another woman.'

Holly's words echo what Marty has already said.

'I hope that can put your mind at ease?' Holly squeezes her arm.

It's not the proof that Sienna needs, but it's something. Holly was married to him; she would have sensed something, surely?

'There's something else I need to ask. Do you think there's any way Greg was hiding anything about his past from you?'

Holly's eyes widen. 'Like what?'

'An affair with a patient?'

Holly frowns. 'I don't think so. We were really close, especially in the beginning of our relationship. I told him all sorts of things about me, so I'm sure he would have told me something like that.'

Sienna makes a decision now; one she intends to see through until the end. Abby is lying, and there's only one reason she would make up this story about Greg: because she knows what happened to him.

Sienna makes coffee for them both and a hot chocolate for Jackson. She takes it to him in the living room, where he's watching television, and when he looks up at her, she can see his eyes are glassy with tears.

'How are you doing, Jax?' she asks. She's never shortened his name like this before, but it feels right.

He shrugs. 'I still miss Dad.'

She sits beside him on the sofa. 'I do too, every single day. I don't think that will ever go away, but we'll find a way to live with it. Together, okay?'

He nods, tries to smile, before turning back to the television.

'You're so good with him,' Holly says when Sienna's back in the kitchen. 'He really likes being here.'

A wave of sadness passes through her; it shouldn't have taken Greg's death for her to bond with his son. Was it her fault? She thought she'd always made an effort, but maybe it wasn't enough. Maybe she didn't feel like a mother figure to him until now. 'I enjoy having him here. I'm sorry that it's without Greg.'

Holly puts down her cup. 'That's not your fault. What happened to Greg is so awful, but don't ever blame yourself.'

She does, though, even if she hasn't been able to admit to it until now. She's directed so much anger towards Abby that she hasn't stopped to consider her own role. Greg went missing after they argued. The last words they shared together were venomous. She only has herself to blame for that.

'Can I ask you something, Holly?'

'I hope you know by now that you can. You don't need to watch what you say around me either because I'm Greg's ex-wife.'

'When you were still married to Greg, I saw you together once at the hospital when you came to see him. I didn't really know him well then, but there was something about the way you two were together that stayed with me. Even to this day I can picture you both so clearly. If two people ever seemed so right together then it was you two.'

Holly's eyes widen; Sienna has caught her off guard. 'I did go and meet him for lunch sometimes, when we could both get away for a couple of hours. It didn't happen often, but it was nice when we could make it work.' She sighs. 'Our timetables were so out of sync it's a wonder we lasted as long as we did.'

Seven years they were married, Sienna remembers. 'What was Greg like when you first got married?'

'Are you sure you want me to talk about that?'

Sienna nods. She wants to talk about Greg, to finally fill in the pieces his silence had never allowed her to. This is what she's wanted from the moment she let him into her life.

'He was a medical student when we met, and I worked part time in the bar they all used to go to in the evenings. I was always so tired – going to classes all day and then working in that place. I don't know how I did it, but I needed to support myself through uni, so I just got on with it. I guess I had a lot more energy in my twenties.' She smiles. 'I remember having a rule about never dating anyone I met in the bar and, until Greg walked in, I'd stuck to it, even though I'd been tempted a few times.'

Holly is a vivacious woman; Sienna has no doubt that she would have had her pick of the students who frequented that bar.

'He was a different person then,' Holly says. 'Not that confident. Some of the med students seemed arrogant, as if they were above students in any other fields, but he was different.' She pauses. 'Maybe arrogance is the wrong word, perhaps it was more about extreme confidence. Anyway, Greg was quite shy then, and I found it... charming?' She takes a sip of coffee. 'That's how we got together. But people change, and I think I just outgrew him. I'm sorry, that sounds so awful, doesn't it – as though I just discarded him.'

Sienna shakes her head. 'No, it doesn't. It sounds honest.' She likes hearing about Greg. Holly is bringing him back to life for her, and she can picture the young man that he was. 'I can see how he might have been shy,' she says. 'Even when I met him there was a quietness about him. I never guessed that's what it was, but now I see that it makes sense. We might change as people, but whoever we used to be must still exist somewhere, mustn't they?'

'I've never thought about that, but maybe you're right. I think his confidence grew as he progressed in his career. So how about the two of you? How did you get together?'

Sienna recounts the story: how she was resistant at first because she could tell how broken he was after Holly had left him, but that eventually she had fallen and there was no going

234

back. Does she regret this now? Sometimes she hates Greg in the same minute that she feels a huge surge of love for him. Sometimes she can't tell which emotion it is that she's feeling. There's a thin line.

They finish their coffee, and Holly says she should get Jackson home. 'He's hardly sleeping. I try to stay up with him, just so he doesn't feel so alone, but I end up drifting off. I feel terrible.'

Sienna knows all about lack of sleep; her mind begins to race as soon as darkness falls, and she can't shut out intrusive thoughts. Greg lying battered, blood leaking from his smashed head. Then his body being thrown in that canal.

'Jackson, we need to get home now,' Holly calls out. 'Thanks for dinner, and for your company,' she says to Sienna.

Jackson appears, his hands in his pockets, his cheeks swollen and red.

Perhaps it is this image – Jackson seeming shrunken and forlorn – which compels her to say what she says next. 'I've had an idea. Why don't you stay the night? Both of you? There's plenty of space and it will save you driving home so late.' Her offer is out there now, and she's glad it is, even though she hasn't planned this.

'Oh, thanks that's really sweet but I—'

'Please, Mum,' Jackson interrupts. 'Please.'

Holly looks at Jackson, then back at Sienna. 'Oh, I don't know. We can't impose on Sienna like this.'

'You wouldn't be,' Sienna says. 'You'd be doing me a favour – I could really do with the company.'

Holly smiles. 'Well, I guess Jackson could stay one night, but I've got an early meeting tomorrow, so I need to get home and prepare. Would that be okay?'

'Of course,' Sienna says. This will be the chance for her to truly bond with Jackson. It will do her some good to have someone else to focus on, someone to look after.

'Thanks, Mum,' Jackson says, smiling for the first time this evening. 'Thanks, Sienna.'

They're still up at eleven p.m., watching *Spiderman*. Jackson has told her that he loved watching it with Greg, that it reminds him of those evenings when they had movie nights. She'd rarely joined them, believing that it was their special time together and she should give them space to be alone.

The film is almost finished when there's a knock at the door. Her first reaction is panic; nobody she knows would have a good reason to come over this late, and there have been no messages on her phone from anyone. Jackson glances at her.

'I'll just get that,' she says. 'You carry on watching.'

There's no one there when she opens the front door, and no cars that don't belong on the street. Strange. She walks down the path to the end of the front garden, just to be sure, and all is calm and still.

Back in the house, she beings to wonder if she's imagined it. Whoever it was hadn't pressed the doorbell; it was only a knock she'd thought she'd heard. Paranoia, she thinks. She'd opened the door quickly, not leaving enough time for someone to have run off, out of sight.

'Jackson, did you hear someone knocking on the door just now?'

He shrugs. 'Don't know. Maybe. Who was it?'

'Oh, nothing important.'

In the kitchen, she sits down and buries her head in her hands. Wild and uncontrollable anxiety builds inside her, and she struggles to get a hold on it.

Jackson is here. How is she going to keep him safe?

# THIRTY-EIGHT

### Abby

On Monday evening, when she sees Rob for the first time since she was with Mark, she doesn't expect to feel such a surge of overwhelming sadness. It truly is over. They both seem to know it, although neither of them speaks this certainty aloud. She will have to, of course; she can't put it off any longer.

Even though Rob offers to cook dinner, she can't let him. If this is their last meal together, then she wants to be the one to prepare it. It will be the last thing she can do for him.

'Go on, then,' Rob says when they're halfway through dinner. So far, they've eaten in silence, both of them pretending to be so engrossed in the food that they forget to have a conversation.

'What?'

'I know you well enough to know that there's something you want to talk about, so what is it?'

Rob confronting her like this takes Abby by surprise – she's not sure she's ready to say it; her plan was to wait until they'd eaten.

'I think I should move out.' It's not how she wants to begin this conversation, yet it's the only way she can manage to start.

Rob stares at her, and she can't tell what he's thinking. He doesn't look surprised. Why doesn't he say something? Anything. His silence is suffocating.

'Did you hear me?'

Keeping his eyes on her, he nods and picks up his fork. 'If you want to move out, then I can't stop you.'

He hasn't asked why, hasn't demanded an explanation. He already knows, and Greg is the only person who could have told him. Even in death he still haunts her. It doesn't matter now, though – there is nothing to protect any more.

'You deserve more than me,' she continues.

When he doesn't answer, she turns away from his stare and begins clearing the table. 'I'll go and pack.'

'Wait,' he says.

Abby is relieved; she wants them to be able to talk properly. She puts the plates back on the table.

'You should stay here,' he says. 'You've got nowhere to go, and I can stay with Mum and Dad.'

Hearing this, tears form in her eyes. Even after what she's done Rob is still showing her kindness. 'No, that's not fair. I'll go.'

He stands. 'Stay. Please. You need to be around here to go to job interviews.' He doesn't give her a chance to stop him, but heads upstairs.

Despite his offer, everything's changed now, and she's not sure she wants to stay in London. From the minute they moved here, her whole life has been falling apart.

It's not long before Rob comes back down, clasping two large sports bags. She remembers them from their honeymoon – he's always hated suitcases and would rather lug about these two bags than wheel a case. 'I've got everything I need for now,' he says.

Everything about this is wrong – even if he's so easily accepted that it's over between them, he should at least have questions. Anxiety bubbles inside her. 'Don't you want to know why?'

He walks to the front door, fishes his keys from his pocket. 'I already know, Abby. This is about Greg, and clearly him being dead doesn't make any difference.'

She stares at him. 'How did you—'

'It doesn't matter. I'm not blind. I could tell the night of the dinner party there was something between you, some kind of attraction. But I fooled myself into believing I was being paranoid, that you'd never do anything like that to me.'

It takes a second for his words to register. 'You've got it wrong, I never slept with Greg.'

He turns to face her. 'Why lie now? What's the point? Can't you just be honest with me?'

'Please, Rob, just listen to me.' It's time to tell him the truth about Mark, that he is the man she's never been able to stop herself loving, even though she knows this will crush Rob above all else. He could handle it if he thought this was just about Greg – someone she only met recently – but Mark has been a shadow over them from the second they met in that bar. A shadow at their wedding, when they moved house... He's been there through everything Abby and Rob have shared together.

The pain on his face is visible as she explains how she and Mark had met at school and were inseparable for years, how she'd tried to stop loving Mark after he'd left her, to shut off everything she felt. How even when he'd married someone else, Abby couldn't shut him out. She explains to Rob that, in the end, though, it wasn't fair to anyone to keep up the pretence. And then she admits that she saw him at his hotel and gave into it on Saturday night.

She says all of this without being able to look at Rob. This isn't how she pictured telling him, as he's halfway out of the door, still holding his bags. But now that it's out she feels relieved, despite everything else weighing her down.

Rob shakes his head. 'No. I knew someone called Mark was your first boyfriend, but you never mentioned how serious it was. You're lying! It was Greg!'

'No, Rob. I never slept with Greg.'

But he's not listening, and is rushing from the house, slamming the door behind him.

She hurries to the window and watches him throw his bags into the boot of his car. She's never seen him like this before.

And that's when she realises there is so much more to this than even she knows.

239

# THIRTY-NINE

*Sienna*

'What's happened?' Sienna asks. 'You look dreadful.'

Drunk, she means. In the time it's taken her to get to this bar in Islington, it's clear that Rob has tried to drown his misery in alcohol. He wouldn't tell her anything on the phone, only begged her to meet him at this place. She tried everything to get him to come to her instead; she doesn't feel comfortable venturing out of her house. She's not sure why; it's just an irrational feeling she can't seem to control.

'I'm… not drunk,' he says. 'I've only had this one.' He holds up his glass. A beer this time, not wine.

Sienna glances at the table; there are no other glasses on the table, but they would have been cleared away. There's no way the one he's holding is his first. She slides into a chair. 'What's going on, Rob?'

'Abby and I are over.' He takes a large swig of his drink.

'What?'

He nods. 'Yep. Our marriage is over. Dead.'

Sienna instinctively reaches for his hand. She should have expected this, yet it still comes as a shock. 'I'm so sorry. What happened?'

He pulls his hand away to reach for his glass again. 'It's all wrong. I got it all wrong. Everything.' He downs the rest of his glass and stands. 'I need another one. You?'

'Just water,' she says. No alcohol has passed her lips since the dinner party. It hasn't been a conscious decision; she just can't bear to have any. 'Actually, let me go. You just sit down.'

When she comes back, he reaches for the drink and immediately takes a large sip.

'Okay, Rob. Talk to me. So you've moved out?'

He stares at the table, shaking his head. 'Yes. And you were wrong. We got it all wrong.'

'What do you mean? What was wrong?'

He slams his fist on the table. 'How could I have made such a terrible mistake!'

'Okay, Rob, you need to calm down and just tell me what's going on.'

He looks up at her. 'Abby didn't sleep with Greg. You were wrong.'

'No. I know what I heard. So Abby's convinced you that she didn't, is that it? Of course she's going to deny it – she wants to protect your marriage, cling on to it at all costs, she—'

'No,' he says. 'You don't understand. Do you realise what this means?' He's raising his voice, and a couple at the next table turn to stare. She doesn't care. She's quickly realising that what other people think doesn't matter, that it should never have been important.

'Abby didn't sleep with your husband,' he says, 'and I'm ashamed of myself that I believed she did. I should have known she's not that kind of person.'

'Rob, I heard her. She was telling someone on the phone.'

His face is red. 'But it wasn't Greg she was talking about!' he hisses. 'She was talking about the man she loves. The one she's never stopped bloody loving, and if it wasn't for you, she might have tried harder. She might have wanted to fight for us.'

Sienna turns cold. 'What do you mean? I don't understand what you're telling me.' She's also frightened; she's never witnessed Rob like this, even though she understands he's distraught. There's more to this, there has to be. 'Listen, why don't we go back to my place? We can talk properly there. Everyone's staring at us.'

'I don't care,' he mutters.

'I know.' And neither does she. 'But let's just go. If you want to drink yourself into oblivion, then that's fine – I've got plenty of wine. No beer, though, I'm afraid.' She makes this comment to lighten the mood, despite knowing nothing will work.

–

Rob apologises as soon as they get back to Sienna's. He seems to have sobered up, although he's been quiet all the way back. She makes him a strong black coffee and he silently takes it.

'Tell me what happened, Rob. Why are you so sure that I'm wrong about Abby and Greg?'

He leans back against the sofa, defeated. 'When I first met Abby, she'd just come out of a relationship with someone.' Sienna remembers him telling her this the night of the dinner party. 'Mark Holmes. They were... together at school. Star-crossed lovers. Like bloody Romeo and Juliet.' He shakes his head. 'I never stood a chance, did I? How could she ever love me when it was him she wanted all along?'

'You don't know that,' Sienna says, trying to offer some comfort. 'Plenty of people who were together from a young age don't last. Aren't meant to last. People come into our lives for a reason and they're not all meant to stay with us.'

Rob's not listening, she can tell. He's in his own bubble, drowning in his pain, and nothing she can say will help. 'She was brutally honest with me,' he replies. 'She told me everything – that just after her mum died, she bumped into him, and they ended up spending the evening together. And the night.' He looks away. 'That must be what you heard her talking about on the phone.'

'It can't be. She must be lying because Greg's dead now and she wants nothing to do with—'

'It's true, Sienna. And she met up with him again on Saturday. Here in London. They slept together again. She said she knew things were over between us, but she always planned to tell me straight away.'

242

Sienna struggles to digest this information. Has she been wrong after all? But she saw the draft email from Greg on his laptop, so there was definitely something going on. So many questions explode in her head. Why didn't Abby tell her about this Mark? If he was so important to her, how come it never came up? The two of them talked about everything, so why the silence on such a huge part of her life? Then she realises that she has been no different herself. There is so much she hasn't shared with Abby, even before the dinner party.

Does this mean Abby was telling the truth about what Greg had done? Abby was one of the last people to see him alive; if Greg was threatening her, if she exposed his past, it's possible she retaliated. Sienna is convinced Rob doesn't know any of this; if he did, he surely would have brought it up by now.

'So you believe Greg has nothing to do with Abby leaving you?' Sienna has to be sure; she's spent too much time already being buried in lies. It has to stop now.

'No. I believe Greg has a lot to do with it. Something changed that night of the swap. I know Mark had nothing to do with that, but it's when Abby changed. I think she was really trying to make a go of our marriage. Of our new life together here. She was never the same after that night.'

Of course she wasn't, because of what she'd learned about Greg, and what it did to her friendship with Sienna. That had to have taken its toll. 'But you don't believe they slept together?'

'No. Maybe being with Greg just made her see things differently. Or see *me* differently, at least. Maybe she talked to him about me, and he encouraged her to leave.' He buries his head in his hands. 'I'd do anything to take back that night. When you suggested it, I wish I'd said no. I wanted to. I didn't think for one second Abby would go for it, but then of course she wouldn't be jealous – even though you're an attractive woman – she didn't feel enough for me to worry. In fact, maybe she wanted something to happen between us. To ease her own guilt.'

'That's ridiculous, Rob. And if nothing else, Abby knows I'm not the kind of person who would do something like that.'

He stares at her. 'How do we know who we really are until we're pushed to the limit?'

–

Rob's asleep on the sofa downstairs. Sienna had no choice but to suggest it; there was no way she'd let him drive to his parents' after consuming so much alcohol.

Besides, she owes it to him. This is all her fault.

*PART FOUR*

# FORTY

*Abby*

October

Weeks have passed since she left Rob, and in that time, she's barely seen Mark and hasn't spent the night with him. Out of respect for Rob, she wants to leave some space before she jumps into something new. Their relationship isn't new, though, Mark insists, and he was there long before Rob, but Abby sticks to her guns. Besides, she still can't be sure that Mark means to see it through this time. It appears that he does; he's found a banking job in London and rented a flat in Fulham. It's the other side of London, but close enough. She's in no rush.

As time has progressed, she's finding it easier to leave Greg behind. The police still don't know who's responsible, and it seems the trail has run cold. It's no longer being reported, and she doesn't know whether this makes her feel uneasy or comforted.

Rob is keeping away from her, and she understands this. It's for the best. Out of everyone, though, it's Sienna her thoughts turn to the most. Abby hasn't contacted her – respecting Sienna's wishes – but she yearns to reach out in some way, to see how she's doing. She is the one who's suffered the most in this.

Despite this lull, this blanket of serenity that's wrapped itself around her, Abby should know better than to believe it's over.

It's soon after dinner time when someone rings the doorbell. She's just had a phone call offering her a teaching post she interviewed for that morning, and even though it's a step down, and she doesn't start until after Christmas, she's grateful for the chance to throw herself back into work. She's already started preparing lessons, can picture herself back in the classroom, surrounded by chaos, noise and laughter. The thing she's missed the most is the kids.

Mark is standing there when she opens the door, and she can't help feeling that surge of guilt, even though everything is now out in the open. Both she and Rob are free to do what they want. 'You shouldn't be here,' she says.

He smiles. 'Why should we hide away? Don't you think we've waited long enough?'

'Probably, but this is still Rob's house. You can't come in.'

'It's your house too, and we're not doing anything wrong.'

Abby remembers Mark rarely took no for an answer, even at school. He wasn't aggressive in his approach. He just always seemed to know how to get what he wanted subtly, almost undetectably. Half the time she wouldn't even realise he'd got his own way until much later. It was never important things, though, and she'd never have loved him if he'd been controlling. 'Come in for a minute then. But you're not staying the night. No way. Okay?'

Again, he smiles, offering a salute. 'Sure. Your wish is my command, Captain!'

As soon as they're inside, he pulls her towards him, his mouth hungrily searching for hers. She goes with it for a moment then gently pulls away. 'Not here, Mark.'

'I've missed you,' he says. 'These last few weeks have felt longer than the years we weren't together. Is that crazy?'

Abby's learned that nothing seems unusual any more. In fact, it's normality that she has begun to question the existence of.

They sit in the kitchen, the back doors fully open, and she tells him about her new job.

'That's great,' he says, kissing her. 'Things are really coming together, aren't they?'

She wants to believe this, and maybe she can allow herself to, but the only way to make this work is if she's honest with Mark. It's the chance for a new beginning, and she doesn't want to blow it.

'Do you feel like we really know each other?' she asks. 'We were so young when we met.'

He scratches his chin, and Abby notices stubble is beginning to shade his face. It makes him more attractive.

'Yes,' he says. 'I feel comfortable with you. One hundred per cent.'

'But we spent so many years apart and so much has happened – to both of us, I'm sure.'

'I don't need to know about that time,' he tells her, stroking her cheek. 'It's only now that matters.'

She needs some air. 'Can we go in the garden? Even with the door open it's stifling in here.'

He follows her out and they sit under the pergola. The climbing rose above their heads is beautiful, but it scatters leaves and petals all over the bench, and they fall as fast as she can clear them away. It was Sienna's suggestion to plant it, and it's the only idea of hers that Abby has kept.

She turns to face Mark. The short walk to the back of the garden has allowed her a moment to sort through how she's going to tell him, yet still she doesn't feel ready. She begins with the husband swap, and what Greg admitted he did. She explains all about Sienna and how their friendship crumbled, turning sour under the weight of a burden she couldn't share. It cleanses her to speak of it all, and now it's out there she feels lighter somehow.

All of this, though, is the easier part; it's what comes next that she struggles to say.

'He's dead, Mark. Somebody killed him, and the police still don't know who did it.' Abby searches his face, looking for any sign of mistrust, or horror, that his mind is playing over the question she herself would be wondering if this was the other way around. 'I don't know what happened to him, but it seems like I could have been the last person to see him before he went missing.'

Mark exhales and grips her hand, squeezing it tightly. 'Thank you for telling me. It can't be easy to talk about this.'

'Does it change anything? That I'm... tied up in it all?'

He frowns, then shakes his head. 'No. You didn't kill him. I know you aren't capable of hurting anyone.'

'The thing is, I'm sure Sienna thinks I had something to do with it.'

'Then you need to put her straight. Fight for your reputation. You're a schoolteacher, Abby — it's important.'

This is something she hasn't considered. If Sienna goes to the police and they start rooting around in her life, it won't look good. And then where will her career be? She shakes her head. Is this how Greg felt? That he had to do whatever he could to save himself? It terrifies her that she's even having these thoughts.

'You're right, I do need to talk to her. Everything's out in the open now, so I can be honest about you and what Greg was really buying my silence with. I'll try and see her tomorrow.'

'Do you want me to come with you?'

No, Abby doesn't. This is something she has to do alone. 'Thanks, but I'll be fine. I've got the truth on my side, haven't I? Surely that's the only thing that's important.'

But this is not what she has to fear about visiting Sienna: Abby wasn't the only person who was angry with Greg, and she knows she wasn't the only one with something to hide.

# FORTY-ONE

*Sienna*

She doesn't know how it's happened, but they seem to have formed a little family: Sienna, Rob and Jackson. Rob never went to stay with his parents after he stayed that first night at Sienna's, and when she offered him a roof over his head, at least until he and Abby sell their house, she could tell he wanted to stay as much as she needed him here. 'It will be easier for you to get to work,' she'd said. 'Reading is a long commute.' He hadn't needed convincing.

Then Holly had called, flustered, because she'd booked a week away for her, Jackson and Andrew, but now Jackson was refusing to go. 'He's so distraught and I don't want to force him,' she'd explained. 'I'm going to have to cancel.'

'No, you're not,' Sienna had told her. 'He can stay here with me.'

There's never a moment when she doesn't feel Greg's absence: heavy, like a pile of rocks weighing down on her, a crushing pain she doesn't think will ever lessen; but with Rob and Jackson here – two people she can look after and focus on – she is at least able to cope. She won't allow herself to think about when she will be alone again, and shuts it away somewhere in her mind, buries it with action.

Now the three of them sit down to breakfast, and she watches them both eat, glancing from one to the other as if they will both disappear if she doesn't keep checking they're still here. She's terrified of losing these moments. At first, she'd worried how Jackson would react to Rob staying here, but the two of them immediately hit it off, and Jackson knows Rob spends every night in the other spare room.

'So you're going to your friend's house today, Jax?' Rob asks.

'Yep. Josh. He's got a PlayStation 5.'

'That's cool.' Rob turns to Sienna. 'And what are your plans for today?'

She's got coursework to do, she tells him. This has been another lifesaver for her. That, and her regular phone calls with DC Roberts.

When Jackson heads off to get his bag ready, Rob asks her how it's going with the police. 'It's so hard to believe that in this world of technology they haven't been able to find out anything,' he whispers. 'No glimpses of him on CCTV. Nothing.'

'I know.'

'Sorry, you don't want to talk about this.'

She assures him it's fine. 'No, I need to. I don't want to bottle it up. Can I be honest about something? Soon after it happened, I felt that the police were looking at me, wondering if I had anything to do with it. And it made me feel guilty, even though I know I'm not.'

'Really? I had no idea they might think you could have—'

'I don't think they did, not really, but they have to cover all the bases, don't they? That's why they spoke to Abby too.'

Rob falls silent.

'You didn't know? I had to tell them I thought something had happened between them.'

'She never said they'd spoken to her.'

'It was when you were in Portugal. Anyway, nothing came of it. And I never told them about the night of the swap. They still don't know about that.'

'How come?'

'Because I was afraid of how it would make me look. That's terrible, isn't it? And now it's too late to tell them, because they'll wonder why I didn't mention it, and then they'll assume I'm covering things up. Do you think that's terrible? I've basically lied to the police.' And not just about that, but she doesn't tell Rob this.

'It's a bit of a mess,' he says. 'But I don't think it matters. What happened to Greg has nothing to do with any of us, it can't have. It's just a terrible thing that happened. A random attack. He could have got into an argument with someone on the street.'

She nods.

'I'd better get to work. See you later?' He pauses. 'Are you sure it's okay for me to be here? I'll be all right, you know. I'm not going to... do anything stupid. I'll get over Abby – I have to. There's nothing to fight for when she never loved me in the first place.'

Placing a hand on his arm is all Sienna can think of that might offer him any comfort. They're all members of a club, she thinks. She, Rob and Jackson. Victims in some people's eyes; the ones who have been left behind. But Sienna refuses to be labelled this way.

'I'm going to pop home after work,' Rob says. 'To sort out getting the house on the market.'

It surprises Sienna to hear this. 'Are you sure? It hasn't been that long; don't you want to give it time to see what might happen?'

'Do you mean in case Abby suddenly realises she actually does love me after all, and not her ex who she's been in love with since school?'

Before she has a chance to respond, Jackson appears, swinging his backpack onto his shoulder. 'I'm ready,' he says.

'How about I drive you?' Rob suggests. 'I'm heading out anyway, so it makes sense.'

'That's kind, but you don't have to do that,' Sienna replies. 'And wouldn't it make you late for work?' She's noticed over the last couple of weeks that Rob's usually prompt timekeeping has slackened. It's as though he no longer cares: all the passion he had for his job, for anything, has vanished. He's still good company, though, at least. He just needs time.

'It'll be fine,' Rob assures her. 'Come on, Jax, let's get going.'

–

It's an hour later when she gets the call from Abby. At first, seeing her name appear on her phone, she wants to ignore it. It's curiosity that compels her to accept the call, and as soon as Abby begins speaking, she knows she's done the right thing.

'I'm ready to tell you everything,' she says. 'All of it this time. If you're willing to listen.'

They arrange to meet in the park, the one she and Greg walked to the evening after the dinner party. She'd known then that something was wrong, but her imagination hadn't come anywhere close to how things panned out.

Abby walks towards her, a floaty white summer dress billowing around her legs as she moves. She looks different: somehow more feminine, more comfortable with herself. This should come as no surprise – her life has changed in the last few weeks. Sienna tries to work out how she feels about Abby as she gets closer – it's a zone somewhere between love and hate, not quite one or the other. She misses the friendship they had but realises she didn't know Abby at all. But above all else, it is fear she's feeling.

'Thanks for meeting me,' Abby says, sitting beside her on the bench.

Sienna shuts out the sound of her voice and focuses on the other noises. Children squealing. Birds. The hum of traffic. She wants to only hear these sounds. There is no place for Abby's voice in her world, even though she agreed to be here.

'You look well,' Sienna says. Now that Abby is right next to her, she can see she's had a haircut too – it's softer now, falling in feathers around her face. 'This must be what love does for you.'

'So you've been talking to Rob? I thought that would be the case.'

'There's nothing going on between us, Abby.'

'I didn't say that. I just know you were quite close before.'

'Before you left him?'

Abby looks uncomfortable. 'Yes. Look, this is really hard for me to say. I need to be honest with you, though.'

Sienna holds her breath, wonders if she'll ever be able to exhale.

'Everything I told you that Greg admitted to me was the truth. All of it. I swear to you. You'll make your own choices about whether or not to believe me, but I'm telling you now, he did it. He killed a woman he was involved with. A patient of his. It's... horrific.' She looks away. 'But I did lie to you about what he was blackmailing me over. Somehow, he'd hacked into my emails and found one from my ex, Mark. No doubt you know all about him.' She doesn't wait for a reply. 'Anyway, at the time it was well and truly over with Mark, but I did meet up with him soon after Mum died. And I cheated on Rob. I'm not proud of it; in fact, as long as I'm alive I'll regret it, not just because I did that to Rob but because it allowed Greg to silence me about what he'd told me.' She turns to Sienna now. 'I told Greg he had to tell you and I gave him a week to do it. He said he would, but then begged to meet up so he could talk it through with me just before he spoke to you. That was the last time I saw him, and then he went missing. He confronted me with the email and said he'd tell Rob.' There are tears in her eyes now. 'At the time that would have been my life over. I was really trying to make things work with Rob, I *wanted* them to work, but if Rob had found out I'd done that to him then there would have been no saving us.'

Sienna believes this. As much as she can see that Rob loves Abby, she's certain he's the kind of man who doesn't forgive easily. 'I'm sorry Greg did that to you,' she says.

'So you believe me now? You believe I didn't sleep with him?'

Maybe it's only in this moment that Sienna finally does. She nods.

'But… there's more I need to tell you.' Abby's chest contracts as she takes a deep breath. 'When we left the park, I followed Greg. I was so angry with him, and he was just walking off without a care in the world. He knew he'd got me.'

Sienna feels sick. She doesn't want to hear any more.

'He went home, and I followed him. I saw your car wasn't there, so I pounded on the door. I don't think I would have even cared if you had been. I wanted you to know, Sienna. You were my friend, and I wanted the truth to come out.'

But not enough to sacrifice yourself, Sienna thinks.

'He let me in. I didn't think he would, but he did. That's how confident he was. It shocked me, Sienna. And scared me. He was like a different person, doing whatever he could to save himself. His career. That must have been how it was when he was with that poor girl.'

'What are you telling me, Abby? What did you do?'

'We argued. I lashed out at him. It was like I wasn't really me, and I was watching myself from a distance, unable to control what I was doing.'

'Just tell me now!' Sienna screams. 'What the hell did you do to Greg?'

# FORTY-TWO

*Abby*

Sienna's scream pierces her eardrums. She's got this all wrong and Abby needs to help her understand. *Make* her understand. This has gone on long enough. 'No, wait, I didn't… he was fine when I left. He only had a cut on his face. That's it. It was just a cut. It wouldn't even have needed medical attention.'

Sienna falls silent. 'What are you saying? Tell me everything now.'

So Abby does. She tells Sienna that Greg refused to listen to her, no matter how much she pleaded with him. 'I'm ashamed to say I even told him that I wouldn't breathe a word to you, and I probably meant it. I'm sure I would have, but I just needed Greg to listen to me.'

He wouldn't, though, and in anger and desperation, Abby grabbed the nearest object she could find – a glass that still had water in it – and hurled it at Greg. It smashed into his cheek, and the sight of his blood appearing, trickling down his cheek, made her freeze. The image of him clutching his cheek then staring at his blood-soaked hand will never leave her.

'He was silent for a moment – in shock probably – but then he shouted at me to get out of his house. I ran, then, without looking back. But he was alive, Sienna. Greg was fine. I even turned around and saw him watching me from the window.'

Sienna is leaning forward, her arms folded defensively across her chest. She's shaking her head. 'You must have caused him an injury that he died from later. You did it, you must have. I've known all along.'

'Sienna, listen to me. That makes no sense. His body was found weeks later near Brighton in that canal. It had nothing to do with me. I only cut his face.' She holds up her hand. 'I know, that's awful, but it wasn't enough to... to kill him.'

'If this is true, then why haven't you told the police? I know they've spoken to you.'

'I can't tell them – they'd think I killed him. There might even be my DNA on him. Forensic experts can find anything, can't they? I didn't do this, Sienna. Look at me! I didn't kill Greg.'

Physically, Sienna is still, but Abby knows her mind will be in silent turmoil as she processes what she's just learned. For so many weeks now, Abby has wondered whether Sienna had something to do with Greg's death, but seeing her now, hearing her reaction to just the minor injury Abby inflicted upon him, she has trouble believing that. It needs to be addressed, though.

Abby needs to say something else. She can't bear the silence. 'There have been times when I thought... you had done it.'

Sienna's eyes widen, but surely this can't be news to her. Surely the police will have already looked at Sienna. Doesn't it often start close to home?

'I would never have hurt Greg,' she says, her voice soft and broken. 'That would be like hurting myself. No, worse than hurting myself. He was *everything* to me.'

Abby knows now that this is how strongly Sienna felt for Greg, although it's taken all this to show it to her. Sienna never wore her heart on her sleeve. She was too strong for that, too confident. She didn't want even Abby to see how much she needed Greg.

'Why did you suggest the swap that night?' she asks. 'I know we were all drunk, but what could you possibly have wanted to gain from it? I've tried to work it out and I can't understand it.'

There is no hesitation when Sienna answers. 'I wanted to prove something to myself. I needed to know that Greg wouldn't go for it. That he would never have wanted to spend a night with another woman and let me be with another man.'

Abby shakes her head. 'But it wasn't about sex, was it? So what would it have proved if he'd said no?'

'There's so much you don't understand,' Sienna says. She's watching a young couple walk past; hand in hand, they are oblivious to their surroundings, wrapped up only in each other. 'I bet they've only just met,' she says. 'There's no way they've been together long.'

Abby watches them too. 'Or maybe they're just with the right person.'

'Greg hardly touched me the last few months,' Sienna says.

Her declaration catches Abby off guard. 'Well, lots of couples go through a tricky phase. Maybe he was stressed at work.'

'No, it wasn't that. He was pulling away from me. Shutting me out. It's almost as if he didn't want to be around me.' She shakes her head. 'Maybe part of me wanted him to sleep with you.'

'What? But why? I would never have done that.'

'You're an attractive woman, Abby. Maybe I wanted him to try, at least, and then I could walk away from him, knowing he didn't deserve me. That would have been enough. It would have been all I needed to know.'

Abby is silent while she tries to make sense of this. Then it hits her. 'So you used me as some kind of experiment. All of us were just pawns to you.'

'No. I know it seems like that, but it wasn't a calculated move. I was just acting on impulse. Trying to push Greg. I'm sorry.'

'Well, look what happened because of that night.' As soon as she's said it, Abby wants to take it back. Whatever Sienna has done, her husband is dead; she needs no more punishment. Especially when it's clear that Greg wasn't the man she thought he was.

'We need to stop fighting, Abby,' Sienna says.

'That's what I want more than anything.'

She shakes her head. 'No. You don't understand. We're never going to be friends, not after everything, but we're in this together, aren't we? Because if neither of us did that to Greg, then who did? It's clear that you don't want to go to the police with the truth, and neither do I, so what the hell are we going to do? How will we feel safe until we know who did that to him?'

–

Sienna has been constantly on Abby's mind since their meeting in the park. It was hours ago, and she's at home alone now, yet she still feels her presence, as if she is still right by her side. Sienna has planted a seed in her head and no amount of reasoning with herself can make her feel better. This was supposed to be the end of her and Sienna; she's meant to be moving on, but now they are inexorably linked, tied by the secrets and lies they're both sinking in.

On the kitchen table, her phone vibrates. It's a message from Rob.

> I'm outside. Can we talk?

She's used to the flood of guilt that overwhelms her every time she thinks of Rob, or hears from him, but this time it's stronger. It shouldn't have been like this – Rob texting her from outside his own house as if he has no right to come in, to use his own key. Yet above all that, she knows she's done the right thing, even though she's gone about it the wrong way.

He smiles for a second when she opens the door, and for that brief moment they are the people they were before. The smile quickly fades; he's happy to see her, but he doesn't want to be.

'This is still your house,' she says. 'You can come in any time.'

'It doesn't feel like it,' he says, staring into the hall. He steps inside and brushes past her. His coldness chills her but she can't blame him. 'I need to pick up some more things.'

Abby watches him head upstairs; she's nervous but can't pinpoint why. All she knows is that Rob seems different, a stranger.

It's half an hour before he comes back down, carrying a black sports bag she hasn't seen before. He was empty-handed when he walked in, so it must be one from upstairs. Has she really paid so little attention over the years? That's not surprising when after losing her mum she couldn't focus on anything. The grief lingers on, though, always there, stopping her fully living. Now she vows to change that.

'You said you wanted to talk?' she asks.

He puts down his bag and gestures to the kitchen. 'I need a glass of water.'

While she fetches it for him, he pulls out a kitchen chair, staring at it without sitting. 'So are you and Mark together now, then?'

His question catches her off guard – she's assumed he would avoid talking about it, and she was never going to bring it up. 'Um. Not exactly. It's complicated.'

'How's that then? This is your great love story, isn't it? Shouldn't it be easy?'

'I don't think we should talk about this.' She places his glass on the table, sits down in the hope that he'll do the same.

'Does it make you uncomfortable?' He stays standing.

He's sneering at her, and it makes her defiant. 'No. It's just my own business, isn't it?' She realises how cruel this is as soon as it's out there.

Rob's eyes narrow and in them she sees something she's never seen before: hatred. 'We need to talk about the house,' he says.

'I know. At least sit down then.'

He does as she suggests and folds his arms, leaning back in his chair. 'Obviously, we need to sell it. I've arranged for the estate agent to come tomorrow morning. Ten thirty.'

'That doesn't give me much time to get it tidy.'

He looks around. 'It's fine as it is.'

She doesn't say anything. It's clear their separation will be acrimonious. What else did she expect?

'I've also got a solicitor to sort out a legal separation agreement. It shouldn't take too long.'

It stings to hear this, that he's gone ahead so quickly. 'Okay.'

'There's no point hanging around, is there?'

'No.'

She gets up and heads to the sink, stares out of the window.

'This place should sell quickly,' Rob is saying. She doesn't turn around. 'Then we can split the money and go our separate ways. The sooner the better.'

'I'm sorry.' Now she spins around to face him. 'You won't believe that – or care – but I am. This isn't how I wanted things to be.'

'You know, I do believe you mean that. But it doesn't matter. This isn't about *you*, Abby. You need me to forgive you, don't you? It will help you feel better about it all, won't it?'

'No, you're wrong. I'm just telling you that I'm sorry, and I mean it. I'm sorry for dragging you into my life when I was emotionally tied to someone else.'

'Mark.' Rob grunts his name, and she wonders if he's aware of how he sounds. 'Childhood sweethearts,' he continues. 'How... beautiful.' His tone is menacing, and it reminds her of the last time she saw Greg, how he seemed like a different person from the one she knew, however briefly.

'How are your parents?' she asks. He won't be happy that she's changing the topic.

'Probably fine,' he says. 'I haven't spoken to them for a few days now.'

'But I thought you were staying with them?'

'Nope. I found somewhere better to stay. Closer to work.'

'Oh, that's good.'

'I'm staying at Sienna's.'

Here it is again; no matter what, Sienna is everywhere, encroaching into every part of her life. Abby's known she and Rob have forged a friendship, but she's surprised that he's moved in to her house. Surprised and disturbed. Sienna mentioned nothing when Abby saw her earlier, yet she had been the one to say she wanted them both to stop fighting.

'How did that happen?' she asks.

Rob snickers. 'Just as you said earlier, that's my business.'

It occurs to her that Rob could be lying; if she's learned one thing it's that nobody is immune to deceit. 'You're right,' she says. 'It's none of my business what you do. In fact, I'm happy that you're moving on. It's what I want.'

Rob doesn't reply; choosing instead to stand and walk over to her. 'Do you know what the hardest part of all this is? It's not that our marriage was a sham – at least on your part. It's not even that you cheated on me. No, the worst part is that I got it so wrong. I got *you* so wrong.' He slowly places his hand on her shoulder.

'I know,' she says.

'No, you don't. I'm not talking about *Mark*. I'm talking about Greg.'

Abby feels sick hearing his name. 'What about him?'

Rob turns away and walks back to the table, grabbing his glass of water before he sits down. 'I knew that night I agreed to the swap that it was a mistake. But I kept silent, and there isn't a minute that goes by where I don't regret that. You were flirting with him that night. Oh, it was subtle, but I saw it. I *felt* it.'

He's not making sense; Abby was never interested in Greg. 'No, Rob, I wasn't. No way.'

'You were so drunk, you probably don't even remember. Maybe you didn't even realise you were doing it.'

'If you thought that, then why did you agree to it?'

'Because I trusted you, and at the time I thought it was harmless. It's only afterwards I looked back and saw it for what it was.'

She takes a deep breath. 'I've already said it to Sienna, and I'll say it again to you: nothing happened between me and Greg. Nothing at all.'

'That's just it. That's what makes it even worse.'

'Rob, you need to stop this. You're not making sense.'

'It doesn't matter if you actually did anything or not, don't you get that?' He's raising his voice now, his face flushed with rage. Again, she is shocked by how different the person standing before her is from the man she married.

'I think you should go now,' she says.

'What goes around, comes around, Abby. Just remember that.'

Once he's gone, she notices that she's shaking. She's not sure what just happened, but she knows it's something huge.

# FORTY-THREE

*Sienna*

Everyone deals with grief in their own way; Sienna knows this. And she doubts there are many who experience it in the way that she is now. The momentous pain of losing Greg is like a tightly zipped coat she can't take off, and that pain is multiplied by what he did. By the things he kept hidden from her. She believes Abby now; with no marriage for her to protect, there is no need for her to lie any more, nothing to lose and nothing to win either. Rob knows everything – it's all out in the open. Except for what happened to Greg, and why.

'I hope you don't mind me being here,' Sienna says to Rosa. 'There are some things I need to… know about Greg I suppose.'

Rosa smiles. She's a patient woman; something Sienna is grateful for in this moment. She pulls her glasses off and rubs the corners of her eyes. 'I'm happy to help, if I can. Like I said on the phone, I don't know what I can tell you that you don't already know. You were his wife; you knew him far better than the rest of us.'

Sienna sits, leans forward and lowers her voice; she doesn't want anyone to overhear them, and Rosa's door is open, just as it always is. 'That's what I used to think, but since he died, I've learned some things about him that I had no idea about, and I wondered if maybe you could help shed some light on them.'

'Oh? Are you sure it's me you want to talk to? I know I worked for Greg for a long time, but we didn't socialise or anything – he wouldn't have told me anything that was going on with him. In his personal life, I mean.'

'That's just it. This is kind of hospital related in a way. That's why I'm hoping you can help.' She needs to just say it aloud, get it out of the way. This hesitation is out of character for Sienna. 'He was seeing one of his patients. Years ago, before I met him.'

Rosa stares at her, shakes her head. 'Are you sure? I can't imagine Greg would do that. It's not appropriate, is it? Greg wasn't like that.'

'He did, Rosa, believe me. I've struggled to get my head around it too.'

'But when? Surely not when he was with Holly? She's a lovely woman; surely he wouldn't have done that to her—'

'It could have been before he was married – I'm not sure. But from what I know about Holly, I don't think she would have cared either way. I don't think her heart was in their marriage.'

Rosa is frowning. 'He was so distraught when she left him, though. If he'd been cheating on her, why would he have cared that their marriage was over?'

She can't tell Rosa what she believes: that if it was an affair while he was married to Holly, maybe he'd changed his mind, realised how much he'd loved her and put an end to it. Revealing this will lead to too many questions, though, and she only wants Rosa to help her identify any woman it could have been. Sienna ignores Rosa's question. 'I know it's a long shot, but if you think back, can you think of any time Greg seemed to take an extra interest in any of his patients? Maybe a woman who had a lot of appointments, even though they might not have been necessary?'

Rosa shakes her head. 'No, there's nothing like that.'

'Please, Rosa, I know I'm asking the impossible but please try and think back. You were there right from when he was made a consultant. You're the only person who can help me.'

She's still shaking her head. 'Greg was great with all his patients, Sienna. You must know that. He'd give up his time for anyone and nothing was too much trouble.'

Perfect Greg. Hadn't that always been how Sienna had seen him? At least before she was with him.

'I don't know what I can tell you,' Rosa says. 'Maybe you've got it all wrong?'

Sienna isn't getting anywhere. Rosa doesn't know anything, and it's clear that she doesn't believe Greg could have had an affair with a patient. That's not even the worst of it, but without a name then it's impossible for Sienna to find out exactly what Greg did.

'Thanks for your time,' she says, standing. 'I'll let you get on.'

'The police were here again,' Rosa says. 'I suppose they have to speak to everyone Greg knew again. Have they found anything out yet?'

This is no surprise to Sienna; DC Roberts told her they would be back speaking to everyone he worked with. She wants to ask what they said, but there is no way Rosa would tell her. She plays by the rules, no matter what. Which is exactly why Greg would have left her in the dark.

–

'Can I help you cook dinner?' Jackson asks.

Sienna smiles at him and ruffles his hair. She's still not sure whether he'd appreciate a hug from her, so she sticks to this small gesture. She has no idea what she can let him help with – is it safe to let him cut up peppers with a knife? Better if she doesn't, just in case. This is all new to Sienna, but she'll learn. It's what Greg would have wanted.

'How about you peel the potatoes?' she offers. That's got to be safe.

Jackson nods and takes the peeler from her. 'Where's Rob?' he asks. 'Is he eating with us?'

She glances at the clock on the kitchen wall. 'Yes, he's on his way home from work now.'

'Are you two, like, *together*?'

'No! Definitely not. I would never… it's only been a few weeks since…'

'He's nice, though, isn't he? I like him. He listens to me when I'm talking. Like Dad used to. Some kids at school say their dads never have time for them but... Dad always did. When I was here, I mean.'

Yes, Sienna thinks. She was the one who didn't. 'He was a good man,' she says. She still wants to believe this, is desperately clinging on to the possibility that she and Abby have got this all wrong. And if they have, maybe it's possible to be both a good man and a bad husband. Or any shade in between the black and white.

She's not prepared for the surge of love she feels when Jackson begins to cry, and she reaches across to hug him. 'Remember I told you we're going to miss him for the rest of our lives,' she whispers. 'But as time goes on it will get a little easier. It won't feel like that now, or even for months, but then one day you'll find you can think of him with a smile instead of sadness. Does that make sense?'

He nods. 'I... think so.'

'Good. Just remember that every time you feel sad.'

'I wish I could stay here forever,' he says. 'I love being with Mum, but when I'm here I feel like Dad's here too.'

'I get that,' Sienna says. She will have to face the reality of selling this house eventually. It's too big for just one person, was too big even for her and Greg together. Part of her wants to stay, though, for exactly the reason Jackson has mentioned. 'You know you're welcome here any time, Jackson. Your mum too.'

'Thanks. She likes you.'

Sienna's pleased to hear this. Before she met Abby, she often found it hard to bond with other women. It wasn't that she didn't want to. They just always misunderstood her, couldn't get past their assumptions about her. She must love herself, people assumed. Married to a doctor. Either that or they decided she must be cold and selfish for not wanting children. She'd long ago given up explaining to people that being happy without

268

children doesn't mean she isn't a caring person, capable of loving others – doing the best she can at being a good stepmother to Jackson is evidence of this.

Her phone rings – a number she doesn't recognise – and she wonders if it's the police.

'Hello?'

'Sienna? It's Rosa. I, um, after you left, I had a long think and… oh, well, it's probably nothing but I did remember something.'

Sienna's heart races. 'Hang on one second.' She turns to Jackson. 'I just need to take this call – I'll be back in a minute.' She leaves him and sits on the stairs, lowering her voice. 'Sorry. Rosa. What is it?'

'I don't think it's anything, and actually I feel a bit stupid mentioning it, but, well, if it helps you then…'

'Tell me.'

Rosa takes a deep breath. 'Okay, well, it was about seven or eight years ago now and Greg had a patient – a young woman. Really young actually, I think she was only twenty or twenty-one at the time. Anyway, she had a lot of appointments with him, but then so did a lot of people, so that's not unusual. What's strange was that she suddenly wanted to be seen as a private patient instead of through the NHS. It just made no sense to me.'

'Maybe she wanted to be seen quicker?'

'She was already his patient, though, so Greg would have been determining how often she needed to be seen. Going to his private clinic wouldn't have made any difference, would it?'

It had been a long time since Greg stopped working at the private clinic, before he and Sienna had got together; he'd always told her that he left because he needed to spend more time with Jackson, who was much younger at the time. His private work had been too consuming, he'd claimed. Sienna had bought into this reason, even though it had surprised her that it was the private work he'd give up. Now, though, she wonders if there was another reason.

'Anyway,' Rosa continues, 'one day I saw her downstairs in the coffee shop, sitting by herself. I thought it was strange as she didn't have an appointment, but I gave it no more attention until I saw you yesterday. Now, I'm not saying there was anything going on with her and Greg, and it's a huge leap to assume that, but... now I just don't know. She was always so dressed up for her appointments – that may have just been how she always liked to dress, but who knows? I just always had a strange feeling about her.'

There is something in what Rosa's telling her – there has to be. 'Can you tell me her name? What was she seeing him for?'

'I can't tell you that, Sienna. It's confidential, isn't it? Please don't ask me.'

'But Greg's dead,' she says, stunning herself with how she has just thrown this statement out so casually. 'He'll never know.'

'But his patient isn't.'

Sienna wishes she could explain to Rosa how wrong she is. That both of them are dead now, and perhaps what's happened to each of them might be tied together. 'Please, Rosa. We've known each other a long time, haven't we? I would never, ever put your job at risk. I just need to know her name.'

Silence. She won't do it; Rosa is kind but she's also stubborn.

'Please. I wouldn't ask if it wasn't important.'

A heavy sigh, but it's better than the silence. 'Her name was Leela Hall. That's all I can tell you.' She pauses. 'I'd better go. My daughter and grandson will be here soon, and I need to get dinner started.'

'Thank you, Rosa.' Sienna wishes she could express just how grateful she is.

When she goes back to the kitchen, Jackson is still peeling the potatoes. He looks up at her, smiling briefly before turning back to what he's doing.

Watching him now, Sienna vows that she will find out what Greg did, and if it's the reason he's dead.

# FORTY-FOUR

*Abby*

When the estate agent leaves on Tuesday morning, Abby feels numb. This is all happening too quickly, and it doesn't feel right. She can understand Rob wanting to move on, but he's pushing her faster than she'd expected him to. It's selfish of her, but she was hoping for things to move slowly, to give her time to adjust to everything, even though this has all been her choice. Rob wants her out of his life – she understands that – but still his behaviour feels off. Almost warped.

She tries to ignore it, spending the morning planning lessons for January, and she's grateful when Mark's call comes. 'Let's meet for lunch,' he suggests. 'In Covent Garden. I've heard there's a great tapas bar there. I'll message you the details.'

When she arrives, he's already there, standing outside, smiling at her. She likes the way he watches her, taking in every detail of her, consuming her. He really *sees* her.

'Did you talk to your friend?' Mark asks after they've ordered.

'I don't know if I can still call her that – so much has happened. But yes, we've talked it through.'

'And? What happened?'

'She told me she believes me. Finally. And she thinks she's found the name of the patient Greg was seeing.'

Mark raises his eyebrows. 'Oh.' He lifts his glass. 'And what's she hoping to achieve?'

'I think she just wants to know what he did. Part of her still probably believes it was an accident, and that maybe Greg

271

gave her the wrong medication or one of his procedures went wrong, which led to the woman's death, but I know that's not what happened. Greg told me he'd lost patients before and he'd learned to deal with it. He said this was different. Deliberate.'

She has never told Sienna Greg's exact words. 'Anyway, I'm going to go with her to find the family of this woman. Her name was Leela.'

Mark frowns. 'Abby, don't you think maybe it's time to let Sienna deal with this? You don't have to be part of it.'

'I already am, though. I still feel responsible.'

'You didn't suggest the partner swap, did you? And you didn't make Greg confess anything to you.'

On the surface this appears true, but Abby knows that by digging deeper, it's clear that she could have done something to stop things going as far as they did. If she hadn't been so consumed with protecting her marriage, then Greg might still be alive. When he refused to tell Sienna the truth, she should have done it herself, with no hesitation. How ironic that her marriage to Rob was beyond saving, with or without Greg's involvement. It always had been.

'I know that,' she tells Mark. 'I still need to be there for Sienna, though. She needs to know why Greg was killed… and so do I.'

'You can't think that it's got anything to do with what he told you? It sounds like it was a random attack.'

She's too tired to have this debate; it's been circling her head for too long already and she no longer knows what she believes. None of it seems real. 'Rob's put the house on the market,' she says.

This brings a smile to Mark's face. 'Really? Well, that's good. Are you okay about it?'

'It's all happening so quickly. I suppose it's a good thing, though. We can't put it off forever.' She lets out a deep breath. 'It means I'll have to start looking for a new house. Or flat rather. I doubt there's any house in London that I can afford on my own.'

Mark smiles. 'You don't have to. Why don't we move in together? I need somewhere to live too, so it makes sense, doesn't it? We don't even have to stay in London. We can go back to Ipswich. Or anywhere else.'

There's no hesitation when Abby answers. 'No. I can't do that. Not yet.' She sees the disappointment on his face. 'I love you, Mark – I always have – but I can't jump straight into anything. My life's already changed beyond recognition, and I just need time to get used to things.'

'Okay.'

'It doesn't mean I still want to be with Rob – I hope you know that. I have no regrets.'

He nods. 'Do you know what's strange? As much as I never stopped thinking about you or wanting you – I was never jealous of Rob. Even when you got married.'

'After you already were yourself,' she reminds him.

'Point taken. What I'm trying to say is that I knew you didn't love him, and I know your chemistry was nothing like ours, so I never felt threatened by him.'

She's not sure where he's going with this.

'But when you told me about that night you swapped husbands with your friend… well, I have to admit, it's been bothering me. Playing on my mind.'

'You know nothing happened. It was never about sex or attraction of any kind. And look how it ended!'

'I know, but at the time—'

The waiter appears and places their plates on the table. 'Is there anything else I can get you?'

'No, thank you,' Mark says. 'This is great, thanks.'

Abby waits for the waiter to walk away. 'What were you saying?'

He frowns. 'Nothing.'

'You were about to say something before the waiter came.'

'Was I? Oh… I was just saying that I suppose I felt a bit weird about you spending the night with another man. Someone other than Rob I mean.'

'You know that's ridiculous, don't you?'

He nods. 'Yeah. I do. But you must have felt excited by it, even if nothing was going to happen?'

Hearing this forces Abby to confront what she hasn't allowed herself to. 'I suppose. In a way. It felt... rebellious? Naughty? Even though sex was never on the table. Greg was... he was attractive and charismatic, I suppose. And yes, it was nice to be in the presence of someone other than Rob for a few hours. Greg was easy to talk to.' She catches a flicker in Mark's eyes. 'But that feeling didn't last. As soon as he'd told me what he'd done everything changed. It was like a light turning off.'

'But can you honestly say that if he hadn't confessed then you wouldn't have wanted him?'

'No! I would never have done that to Sienna. Or Rob.'

'You cheated with me,' he reminds her.

She grabs his hand. 'But that's *you*. I'm sure I don't need to explain why that was completely different.'

He smiles. Finally, she's appeased him.

'You weren't jealous like this when we were together before,' she says.

'People change, don't they?' He laughs, and she joins in, even though outside of this restaurant she has nothing to laugh about and everything to fear.

'I'll be back in a minute.' Mark stands and glances around for the toilets. He doesn't seem to notice, or mind, that he's left his phone on the table. He trusts her, and he's got nothing to hide. It's a comforting thought.

She still believes this when his phone rings and she sees Cassie's name light up the screen. This is fine. It's normal for them to still be in contact when they've got a house to sell and a divorce to sort out. Abby still talks to Rob, so she can't worry about Mark doing the same with his ex. This is it for them, this time; the feeling beats as strongly as a pulse.

The phone falls silent and seconds later an email noti-fication pings on the screen. Abby just has time to catch the name of the sender before the screen returns to black: *info@GrandBrighton.co.uk*.

Quickly, she grabs her own phone and googles the address. It's for the Grand Hotel in Brighton. Brighton is where Greg's debit card was supposedly used, although it now looks likely that it hadn't been him using it. It's also close to where his body was found. Why would Mark have an email from a hotel there?

The few minutes it takes for him to get back to the table feel like hours. Beads of sweat form on her forehead, she can feel them, and her whole body heats up. He's barely sat down before she asks him if he's ever been to Brighton.

Mark frowns. 'No, never. Why? We've got plenty of beaches near Ipswich, and I heard Brighton's only a pebble one anyway.'

'Just wondered.' Abby feels sick. 'By the way, Cassie just tried to call you.'

# FORTY-FIVE

*Sienna*

Leela Hall. It's a beautiful name, and the young woman whose picture Sienna is staring at suits it perfectly. She looks so young – she *was* so young – and she has to remind herself that Greg would have been younger too, not as youthful as Leela, but not the forty-two-year-old man he was when he died. This should be a comforting thought, but it isn't. Sienna already knows from comparing herself to Holly that Greg didn't have a type, and Leela is a contrast to both of them. It's hard to tell her ethnicity, but her coffee-coloured skin looks radiant in this photo. She was stunning. What did Greg do to her?

She doesn't know for sure that this is the patient Greg was seeing, but Sienna *feels* something. A connection to it? All she's found is a Facebook account she can't get into, but across the photo is written 'R.I.P.' She wonders why people don't close accounts down after someone dies; isn't it too painful to still have it out there, as if the person they've lost is somehow still communicating with them? Maybe it brings them comfort. All she knows is that if Greg had had any social media accounts, she would have deleted them all.

Sienna shuts down Facebook; she's already taken a screenshot of the photo, stored in her photos, easily accessible whenever she needs to see it. What she needs now is an address, and there is no way Rosa will get that for her.

But she knows someone who might.

'Well, this is a surprise,' Reuben says, joining her where she already sits by the bar. It's the same place they all met just before Greg went missing, although it's far quieter on an early Wednesday evening. He leans forward and kisses her cheek, lingering just a bit too long, leaving a trace of his saliva on her skin. Repulsed, she fights the urge to scrub her face, and almost pulls away. But she's expected this. 'What can I get you?' he asks.

She holds up her glass – still full with tonic water. 'Already got a gin,' she says. 'But thanks.'

He orders a whisky and turns to her. 'So how have you been?'

'I'd love to say great, but, you know.'

'I still can't believe it. I keep going to text him and then I realise.' He lowers his head, stares at the table.

'How's Nikki?' Sienna asks.

He looks up again. 'We're... she's fine.'

Sienna already knows from Marty that Reuben and Nikki are no longer together; it was inevitable, and perfect timing for what Sienna has to do now. She places her hand on his. 'It's okay. Reuben. I know. You can talk to me, you know.' It sickens her that she has to do this; but she feels how she used to, putting on this act. It's what she always did – playing a part – although never quite in this way.

He smiles. He's playing right into her hands. 'You'll have no trouble finding someone else,' she assures him, turning back to her tonic water. She takes a long sip.

'Watch it now – we wouldn't want you to get drunk, would we?'

She throws her head back and laughs. 'Let's go and sit somewhere more comfortable,' she says, pointing to the back of the bar, where padded leather sofas line the wall.

He watches her while they walk over. She can feel his eyes heavy on her, gluttonous. 'I have to say I'm surprised that you seem so... well, able to come out and enjoy a drink.'

'Greg was cheating on me,' she lies. 'So, sod it. I've done my grieving.'

Reuben's eyes widen. 'No. Are you sure?'

She nods, allowing her silence to tell him what he wants to hear.

'It wasn't with Nikki, was it? That wouldn't surprise me. The way she used to fawn over him.'

'She did, didn't she? But no, it wasn't with Nikki.'

'Not that it matters,' Reuben says. 'Our marriage is well and truly over. I'm not going back. No way.'

'What happened, Rueben? You've only been married a couple of years.' Not much longer than she and Greg. Still, it's better to know sooner rather than later.

'I always make the same mistake with women. And live to regret it. I seem to attract these... women who just want whatever they can get from me.'

She holds up her glass; she doesn't want him dwelling on any of this. Reuben will do it again soon enough, she has no doubt about that – he's a doctor, there'll be no shortage of women willing to become his third wife.

'You just need to enjoy yourself and not think about settling down,' she says, sliding closer to him so that their thighs are touching. A wave of nausea floods through her.

'You're right,' he says, leaning his head closer to hers.

It's an effort not to push him away and run from this place, but she's got to see this through, so she sits there without moving, for as long as she can stand it, while Rueben pours more and more alcohol down his throat. Then she strikes. 'I need a favour,' she says, lightly stroking his arm.

'Anything, just ask.' His smile turns her stomach.

She whispers into his ear. 'Let's go to your house. It's more private.'

Reuben doesn't hesitate, and grabs her hand, leading her outside, where he tries to flag down a taxi. There's a sharp chill in the air now; they are deep into autumn, with its longer, darker nights. She can't have this hanging over her any longer. She needs to lay it all to rest.

In the taxi he tries to kiss her, and she playfully pushes him away. 'No, Reuben,' she tells him, 'not here.' She laughs, and his eyes swallow her up. It's all she can do not to turn away and jump out of the cab.

Sienna's never set foot in Reuben's house in Chiswick before, has never even seen it, and this unnerves her. She reminds herself why she's doing this, how important it is that she sees it through. The fear remains with her though; this could all go horribly wrong.

'Here we are,' Reuben says as he opens the door. 'I don't think you've ever been here before, have you? How come you never came to any of Nikki's book club nights? Jo and Eva always did.'

'I was never invited,' Sienna says.

Reuben nods. 'Is that right? That's because they were intimidated by you.'

They're inside now, and Sienna's surprised by how much care has gone into maintaining the character of this Victorian house. 'What do you mean? Why would they be intimidated by me?'

'Because of your confidence. You don't care what anyone thinks of you, you're just free to be yourself. Something like that. Also, you're beautiful. Who wouldn't be intimidated?'

Sienna says nothing. She wants to shut him up. He's wrong about everything; he knows nothing about her.

'Let's have some wine.' Reuben leads her to the kitchen diner, where he heads straight to the wine rack. Pouring two glasses, he hands her one, and she takes it with a smile.

'I think you'll like this,' he says, stroking her hair.

'There's something I need to do first. Would you mind if I use your computer? It will only take a minute.'

Reuben frowns. 'What? Why?'

'I just need to check my email and my phone's died. I'm expecting something really important from a new client. Is that okay?' She places her hand on his chest. 'It won't take a moment.'

He doesn't want her to, she can tell, but he nods. 'Come with me, then. I'll log you in. Don't be long, though.'

He takes her to his office, where once again she's surprised by the effort that's gone into the layout and décor of the room. She hopes he doesn't hover around; but asking him to leave will only raise his suspicions. She has no choice but to log into her email and start typing a fake one. If she takes long enough, he's bound to get bored waiting and at least go back downstairs.

It's pure luck that after a couple of minutes his phone rings. 'I need to answer this,' he says. 'I'll just be downstairs.'

'Go ahead, I'm fine.'

The second the door shuts behind him, she exhales and begins. As she's expected, he hasn't bothered to log out, to keep his computer secure, and she now has access to everything she needs.

It's ten minutes before he comes back in: more than enough time. 'So, all done?' he asks.

'Yep.'

'Let's have that drink then. We can have them in the bedroom.'

She shoots up. 'Actually, I think I need to get home. Let's take a rain check. Actually, do you know what? I don't even know what a rain check is. It's something I hear all the time – maybe in films – but what does it actually mean? Anyway, it doesn't matter. I've changed my mind.'

He stares at her, his mouth hanging open.

'If Greg could see you now,' she says, making her way out of the room. 'Do you think he'd be proud to call you his friend?'

She doesn't wait for an answer.

Even though Reuben hasn't touched her, she showers the moment she gets home, needing to wash away everything about this evening. She feels better afterwards and focuses on the fact that she got Leela Hall's address.

Rob is downstairs. He's set up his PlayStation and is playing a game with Jackson, so they shouldn't disturb her up here. Rob was quiet when she got home, didn't even ask her where she'd been. She shouldn't expect him to – they're not a couple – but he normally does, so she can't help but question this change.

Still wrapped in her towel, she pulls out her phone and calls Abby. Listening to the ringtone, it feels as though they have come full circle. She doesn't know if she fully trusts her, but it feels as though they're in this together. She hasn't spoken of any of this to Rob; there's no way she can tell him what Greg did, and she doesn't think Abby has either. They are bonded by their silence.

'I've found her address,' she says the second Abby picks up.

'Whose?'

'Leela. The patient Greg was having an affair with. I know the address she lived at.'

'How did you find it?'

'It doesn't matter. There's somewhere to start now, isn't there?'

'But it was years ago. What are the chances of someone who knew her still living there?'

'She was young, Abby. Twenty-one. There's a good chance she still lived with her parents.'

'That is young. What was Greg thinking?'

'Remember he was younger then. And I'm not one hundred per cent sure it was this woman, but there's a good chance. I'm going there, Abby. Tomorrow. I need to know what Greg did. What if it's got something to do with his murder?'

'How?'

'I don't know. Revenge maybe? I don't know, but the police will be able to find out. I just need to give them a name, and I can't do that until I'm sure it was her.'

Abby falls silent. 'I understand why you need to go. And I'm coming with you.' There is a long pause before she speaks again. 'But, Sienna, what if it had nothing to do with what he did all those years ago, and everything to do with what we all did?'

# FORTY-SIX

### *Abby*

Waterloo station is crowded this morning. She watches people flocking to the escalators, rushing to work; it's like standing still in a hurricane. Sienna isn't here yet, nowhere Abby can see her, at least, but it's not yet the time they've arranged to meet. She tries not to think about Mark, and Brighton – she'll deal with that later. This morning is too important for her to lose focus, so she shoves it from her mind, keeps it at bay for now.

A hand on her shoulder startles her.

'Sorry,' Sienna says. 'You were miles away. Are you okay?'

Abby still can't get used to the change in their interactions. It appears that the animosity has gone from both sides, leaving behind a stifled courtesy. It's far from friendship and loaded with wariness, but it's something, at least.

'I'm okay,' she replies. 'As okay as I can be considering what we're about to do. How about you? This is huge, isn't it?' There's the strong possibility that Leela Hall's family no longer live at the address they have, but Abby doesn't mention this again. She's already been through every possibility with Sienna, including the one where they've got the wrong woman, or whoever answers refuses to talk to them.

'It's necessary,' Sienna reminds her. 'We both need to know what happened, don't we?' She doesn't wait for an answer. 'Let's go. We can get a cab from outside the station.'

Handy for Leela being so close to where Greg worked, Abby thinks but doesn't mention.

Both women are silent in the cab, and when they pull up outside the address they've given the driver, Abby is struck by how different this part of London is to where she lives. It feels claustrophobic, as if all the buildings have sucked in breath and are waiting to exhale. That's exactly how Abby herself feels.

The house they want has no front garden, and they're still standing on the street when they reach the door.

Sienna is the one who steps forward, pressing the doorbell then standing back with her arms folded. She looks defensive, as if she's ready for a battle, and Abby can't imagine how she's feeling in this moment; for Sienna, the stakes are so much higher.

A woman in her fifties answers the door. She's small and neatly dressed in a roll-neck jumper and long skirt. She looks at them and smiles.

'Hi,' Sienna says, full of confidence. 'I'm looking for Mrs Hall, but we're not sure she still lives here?'

The woman's brow furrows. 'I'm Mrs Hall. Kerry. Can I help you?'

Sienna is nodding. She appears calm, but Abby knows there will be a rush of adrenalin surging through her; that's how she feels too.

'I understand this might be a bit difficult for you, but my husband was your daughter Leela's doctor, and I just wondered if I could talk to you about a few things? I'm so sorry to have to ask this, but I think you'll realise why I am if you'll let me explain?' She reaches into her bag and pulls out her purse, searching through it until she finds what she's looking for. 'This is my driving licence. My husband was Greg Wells.'

Kerry stares at the card and nods. 'Oh, yes. A lovely man.' She hands it back. 'You said *was* your husband?'

'Yes, he died this summer.' Sienna's voice wobbles.

'I'm sorry to hear that.'

'Do you think you could talk to us? Please?'

A heavy silence falls. Kerry Hall is staring at them, digesting everything Sienna has said, making a difficult decision. She looks from one to the other. 'I... I suppose that's okay. Um, do you want to come in?'

Like Kerry, her house is neat and tidy; she's made the most of the space she has. It feels like a home. Lived in. Abby wonders how she's found the effort and motivation to keep it this way when she's lost her daughter.

'Sit down, won't you? Can I get you tea or coffee?'

'We're fine. Please don't go to any trouble. This is my friend, Abby, by the way. She knew Greg well.'

Abby shouldn't be surprised that Sienna's saying this; she'll be doing whatever she can to make Kerry Hall feel comfortable enough to open up about her daughter.

'I'm so sorry about Leela,' Sienna says. 'Is that her photo over there?' She gestures to the mantelpiece.

'Yes.'

'A beautiful girl.'

'I'm sorry, I'm a bit confused. It's been a few years, so I can't understand what Leela might have to do with your husband now?'

Sienna takes a deep breath. 'Mrs Hall... Kerry... My husband was murdered. I know how awful it is to have unanswered questions. It's impossible to move on when there are huge question marks hanging over your head.'

Kerry nods, even though what Sienna has said doesn't explain why they are here. 'Losing Leela was the hardest thing I've ever had to go through. I'm still going through it. She was my baby. An only child.' She wipes tears from her eyes. 'Do either of you have children?'

'No,' Abby says. 'But I imagine losing one is the worst thing anyone could possibly go through.'

Sienna leans towards Kerry Hall, speaks gently. 'You don't have to talk about this if you don't want to, but what was she like? In that photo she looks so happy, so content.'

'Actually, I like talking to people about her,' Kerry says. 'It keeps her alive for me. I don't want to stop talking about her

285

or thinking about her. I want to remember every detail of the person she was.' She stares at Sienna. 'Because it fades, you know. The memories you have of them. Soon enough you realise that what you're remembering isn't as clear.'

'I know what you mean,' Sienna says. She is already experiencing this.

'Time erases memories of the small things,' Kerry says, 'as much as you try to cling on to them.'

'That is exactly how I feel already,' Sienna says. 'I can't even picture Greg's smile in my head – it's only when I look at photos I remember.'

Kerry nods. 'I suppose that's our way of coping. If our memories didn't fade, then we'd be constantly in those first stages of grief and we'd never be able to continue living our lives.'

Abby likes this woman. She seems strong and rational, despite how her world has been torn to shreds.

'You will find a way to live with it,' Kerry says to Sienna. 'That's the only comfort I can give you.'

'Thank you.'

Kerry stands and walks over to the photo of Leela. 'She was only twenty-two. She had so many plans for herself, so much she wanted to do. That's what makes it even harder to get my head around. I can't even think of her as a woman – to me she was still a girl. She had her whole life in front of her, so it just didn't…' She chokes up, unable to continue for a moment.

Despite them being strangers, Abby goes over to her and puts her arm around her. 'I'm so sorry.'

'Well, this is strange. I can normally talk about her now without falling to pieces.'

'I think us being here is probably a bit of a shock,' Abby assures her.

'She wanted to be a nurse,' Kerry says, smiling. 'She would have made a brilliant one. She really cared about people. I'm a single mum, so life hasn't always been easy for us, but Leela and

I always looked after each other. I wasn't often ill, but if I ever had flu or anything, Leela would get me cups of tea and really take care of me. That's the kind of person she was.'

Kerry sits down again, and Abby does the same.

'Do you mind me asking why she was seeing a gynaecologist?' Sienna says.

'She had severe endometriosis. Needed lots of surgery to try and remove it, but it kept coming back, growing more. She was in pain at least once a month, but she just got on with it and rarely complained. Your husband was a remarkable surgeon.'

'Yes, he was,' Sienna agrees.

'Do the police know what happened to him?'

'Not yet. I'm sure they will soon, though.' She glances at Abby.

'Okay, so are you going to tell me why exactly you need to know about Leela?'

'Did she have a boyfriend that you know of? Anyone significant in her life?'

Kerry frowns. 'Nobody she talked about. She wasn't really interested – she was more concerned with what she wanted to do with her life. She'd done A levels but couldn't decide whether to go to university first then train to be a nurse or whether to just go straight into training. Why do you ask?'

Abby watches Sienna. She knows the plan is to reveal that she suspects Greg and Leela were having an affair, but now that they're here – face to face with the woman who's lost her daughter – she wonders if Sienna is finding this harder than she thought it would be.

'I have to be honest with you,' Sienna says. 'I think your daughter was having an affair with Greg. Years ago. Before I even met him. I'm his second wife, so I'm not here for any conflict – Greg was married to someone else at the time.'

'Oh God,' Kerry says, burying her face in her hands. 'I never thought this would come out.'

Abby holds her breath. This is more than they could have expected. 'What's that?' she asks.

287

'Leela never said anything, but I saw them once. It was really late one night, and I heard the front door shut. I rushed to the window, and I saw her getting into a car. Your husband was driving, and when she got in, they were... kissing each other.' She turns to Sienna. 'I'm sorry.'

'You have nothing to apologise for. Like I said, I wasn't with Greg back then.'

'Did he tell you about it?'

'Yes,' Abby says, even though it's Sienna who Kerry is addressing.

'Leela was his patient – that can't be allowed, can it?'

'It happens. Did you ask Leela about it?'

Kerry shakes her head. 'I wanted her to bring it up. She was a very private person, though, not one of these girls who plasters everything they're doing on social media. She never did that. We were close, though, so I thought that she would tell me in her own good time. Then she moved into her own flat and, well, it wasn't long after that she...'

'It's okay, you don't have to explain.' Sienna turns to the photo again. 'I know this is really difficult to talk about, but how exactly did she... die? It's so cruel and senseless that someone could do that to another person.'

'What do you mean?'

'The person who killed your beautiful daughter. I can't—'

'No, you've got it all wrong. Nobody did anything to Leela. She wasn't murdered. She did it to herself. She took her own life.'

# FORTY-SEVEN

*Sienna*

Again, they are silent in the cab back to Waterloo station, and as soon as they're dropped off, Sienna grabs Abby's arm, pulls her down so they're both sitting on the steps leading up to the entrance. It's beginning to drizzle, but she doesn't care; she relishes the cool sensation of the droplets on her skin.

'He didn't do it, Abby. Greg didn't kill her.'

Abby stares straight ahead. 'I don't understand. He told me, Sienna. He said he'd done it deliberately. Maybe it's someone else? Maybe it wasn't Leela he was seeing.'

'It was her, Abby. Her mother saw her with him. That's irrefutable.' Sienna is calm and rational; she hasn't felt like this for a long time now.

'It just doesn't make sense.'

'Maybe it does,' Sienna says. 'What if Greg ended the relationship, and Leela was so distraught that she felt she didn't want to live without him? She was so young – losing Greg must have felt like her whole world was coming to an end. Don't you remember what that first love is like? It's all-consuming, isn't it?'

'Yes, I get that. The same thing happened to me, but I would never have taken my life because of it. It's so sad.'

'This explains exactly why Greg would have felt responsible for her death. It's the only explanation.'

'I suppose so.' Abby doesn't sound convinced.

'And it looks like Greg's past has nothing to do with his death,' Sienna continues.

People continue walking past them, heading to wherever they need to be this morning. Nobody could have any idea of the enormity of what these two women are discussing.

Abby doesn't respond.

'That means it's got everything to do with the present. It can't have been a random attack.'

'Sienna, I was waiting to tell you this but yesterday I found out that Mark had an email from a hotel in Brighton, which must mean he's stayed there before. But when I asked him, he said he'd never been there and had no reason to go.'

Sienna stares at her. 'What are you saying?'

'I don't know. It's probably nothing. It can't be anything, can it? Mark didn't know Greg and he wasn't in my life that night of the dinner party.'

'The swap. It's difficult to call it that now, isn't it?'

'I need to confront him about it. I just wanted to tell you first, to see what you think.'

'I think that until the police find out who did this, we can't trust anyone.' Not even each other. She won't say this to Abby, though.

–

While Sienna clears up after dinner, she can hear Jackson and Rob in the lounge. They're playing on the PlayStation again, their animated exclamations filling up the house, filling the void. As good a father as he was, Sienna can't imagine Greg playing computer games with his son; it's good that Rob brings something different to Jackson's life. There are three more days until Holly gets back, and Sienna doesn't want this to end. She might suggest to Holly that Jackson stay here every weekend, but she's unsure how that offer might be received. This has been good for Rob too, and it's clear he's in no rush to leave. He eagerly agreed when Sienna suggested he stay here until his house is sold and he's bought somewhere new.

The only thing that troubles her about it is Rob's drinking. It's subtle, but it's there – the way he's constantly grabbing another bottle of beer as soon as he's finished one, the way the fridge is always stocked with more. She still hasn't touched any, and even the sight of it turns her stomach. Is she overreacting? Rob's going through a divorce. He's bound to need a crutch.

As soon as Jackson heads upstairs to bed, she asks Rob about his day. This was what she'd always used to do with Greg, until he became too distracted, or too rushed, to talk much. She thinks she understands. He had the burden of a young girl's suicide on his mind, and no amount of time passing was easing his guilt.

'I don't want to bore you with details of my day at work,' Rob says, opening the fridge and pulling out a beer.

'You're so good with Jackson,' she says.

He shrugs. 'He's a good kid.'

'Maybe while he's here, though, you could keep the alcohol hidden? Greg never used to drink in front of him and, well, it's clear that Jackson looks up to you. Kids are impressionable, aren't they? I just wouldn't want him deciding to try it for himself.'

Rob stares at her and she wonders if she's made a mistake bringing it up. 'Okay,' he says. 'But give the boy some credit. He's not about to turn into an alcoholic at thirteen just because his stepmother's friend enjoys a beer in the evenings.'

Sienna knows he's probably right, but the accusation in his tone sets her on edge, forces her to confront something she's been ignoring. Rob is changing and she hasn't wanted to see it. She's been so content living in this bubble, having something other than Greg's death to focus on, that she's been blinded to what's right in front of her. 'I know, but I'm just... well, worrying I suppose. I'm responsible for him while he's in this house.'

'Just relax, Sienna. It's all fine.'

This doesn't even sound like Rob, and she wonders how many beers he's already had. 'I just like having you both here,' she says. 'And I don't want anything to ruin that.'

Rob shakes his head. 'Are you surprised that I'm drinking in the evenings, Sienna? Am I not living up to this ideal you've made up in your head? You want everything to be perfect all the time, don't you?' He smirks, and again she's struck by how at odds his behaviour is with the man he always appeared to be. 'On the outside, at least,' he continues. 'You don't really care if it's real or not, just as long as it appears to be real.'

Even though she's thrown off guard by this verbal attack, Sienna is used to standing her ground, defending herself. 'No, you've got it wrong. Maybe I used to be like that but that's not who I am any more.'

'Then why am I here? Why is Jackson here? You're trying to play happy families so you don't have to face reality.'

His words sting, cutting into her, opening fresh wounds.

'Because you know, don't you?' he continues. 'You know that it's all your fault.'

# FORTY-EIGHT

## Abby

'Are you okay?' Mark asks. 'You've been quiet all evening.'

They're at his flat, and she's come here for answers. 'I'm exhausted,' Abby says. It's not a lie; the visit to Kerry Hall's home this morning has depleted her mental energy, which in turn has left her physically drained. As well as this, she's sick of not being able to trust anyone, and now she is forced to add Mark to that list. None of this is over – she feels it like a chill creeping over her bones, and she can't shake the feeling that worse is to come.

'You're going through a separation, and about to start a new job – it's no wonder you're feeling so tired.' He strokes her hand. 'You haven't been sleeping well, have you?'

'No.' Not for a long time.

'You'll get through it, you always do.'

She's adamant that she will. If all of this has taught her anything, it's that she can deal with whatever is thrown her way. Right now, though, she needs to know what's going on with Mark. Why he's lying to her. If it's got anything to do with Greg. The rational part of her brain tells her that's impossible – there's no way Mark could have any connection to Greg, but she needs to be sure.

'I'll go and get the food,' Mark says. 'It should be ready by the time I get there.' They've ordered Chinese food from the restaurant on the High Street; Abby knows they only do collections, that Mark would offer to collect it. 'I won't be long.'

Once he's gone, she stands in the middle of his living room, unsure where to begin. There's not much in Mark's flat yet; most of his things are still at his home in Ipswich, which is yet to be sold. Two buyers have already pulled out. Abby hopes she and Rob don't have this much trouble selling – she needs to put all of this behind her, including Rob and Sienna. Whether Mark comes with her or not depends on what she finds out tonight. It will be a shame to let the school down, especially at such short notice, but she's got to think about herself now. Her mental health. Her safety. Before it's too late.

She scans Mark's bookshelves, finding nothing out of the ordinary. His laptop is on the coffee table; he'd been working before she got here. Her steps towards it are tentative. This is wrong, an invasion of his privacy – but he's lied to her, and she needs to know why. This is what she keeps in her mind as she reaches down to it and taps the keyboard.

There's no password; she's straight in, staring at his desktop background – a desert scene which could be Las Vegas. It's too much to hope that Mark's left his email open, but she can have a root around and see if there's anything worrying on there. She needs to know what she's getting into before she throws herself deeper into this. Even though she's been in it with him since she was a teenager.

She doesn't find anything, and she's about to give up when she notices the photos tab. Somehow it feels worse to click on it, but she does – there are thousands of photos on there, most of them of him and Cassie. It doesn't upset Abby to see them, to be a witness to how happy they look in every photo, because she is the one he has chosen. She understands now what he meant about not being jealous of Rob.

A photo catches her eye. She stares at it, but it takes a moment to realise that she's staring at a picture of herself. She doesn't know where it was taken but it's recent. She's confused. It's not recent enough. And it's of her walking out of the fitness centre in Winchmore Hill, where she met Sienna. She checks the date: fifteenth of April this year. There are more. Candid photos of her she has no knowledge of him taking. And then she sees the one of her and Greg talking in the park the day he disappeared.

Abby's experienced so much in her life – grief, pain, every emotion it's possible to feel – yet she's never before felt like this, as if the core of her has been scraped away. Mark. The one person she thought she had an unbreakable connection with. Now the ground has crumbled beneath her and she's in freefall.

Using her phone, she takes photos of all the pictures of her then shuts down Mark's computer. She needs to get out of here before he comes back.

–

Abby never thought she'd find herself turning to Sienna again, yet here she is standing on her doorstep, texting her because it's too late to ring the bell:

> Can we talk? It's urgent.

'Why didn't you ring the bell?' Sienna asks when she opens the door. Her hair is damp, and she's wearing a white fluffy dressing gown; definitely not one of Greg's this time.

'I didn't want to wake Jackson if he's asleep.'

Sienna smiles. 'That boy could sleep through an earthquake.'

'Or Rob. I don't really want to see him.'

Sienna assures her that she doesn't need to worry about Rob. He's fallen asleep on the sofa, and she'd just been trying to figure out how she'd get him into bed. 'Drunk,' she explains. 'It's fine for you to come in.'

Outside the living room, Abby stands by the door staring at Rob. She feels a stab of pain to see him like this, and to know that she is the one who did this to him.

'He'll be okay,' Sienna assures her. 'He just needs to work through it all. It will take time, but he'll get there.'

Abby wants to ask Sienna how she can show such kindness towards her after everything that's happened, but she already knows the answer. Sienna is a better person than she is. 'Are you sure Jackson's asleep?'

She nods. 'Yes. Abby, what's going on? You're being weird.'

'Come in the kitchen.' Abby leads the way, even though this isn't her house and the woman who owns it is no longer a friend.

'I've just been with Mark,' Abby whispers. 'And I found these.' She taps on her phone and hands it to Sienna. 'These photos were on his laptop. He went out to get food and I... I had a look without him knowing.'

Sienna's eyes are wide circles as she stares at Abby's phone. 'These are of you and Greg. There are loads of them.'

'I know. It was when we met up in the park the day he blackmailed me.'

'The day he disappeared.'

Abby nods.

'Why the hell has your boyfriend got them?'

'I don't know. That's what I've been asking myself all the way here. It doesn't make any sense.'

'None of this ever has, has it? Did you ask him about them? And about Brighton?'

'No. I just left before he came back. I didn't tell him I was going, and I've been ignoring his phone calls. If I talk to him now, I don't trust what I'll say, and I want to be sure before I start accusing him of anything. I've done enough of that already and I've always been wrong. I thought you—'

'Don't say it,' Sienna warns. 'Please don't say those words.'

Abby stays silent.

'You need to go and confront him. Tell him you'll go to the police if he doesn't give you a good explanation for why he's taken all these photos of you, and why he denied ever going to Brighton. We should report him anyway.'

This is exactly what Abby needs to avoid. 'I can't let it all come out about me meeting Greg and him blackmailing me. Surely you can see that?'

Sienna bites her lip. 'I do. And I'm worried about that, too. I've kept things from them myself, and I could look just as guilty if they root around in my life. Maybe that doesn't matter any more. All that matters is justice for Greg. He deserves that, doesn't he? Especially as he didn't kill anyone.' She pauses. 'The police might want to question you about it, but they'll soon realise it wasn't you, just as I hope they'll realise it wasn't me.' She grabs Abby's arm. 'I think it's time to tell them, and we can do it together. I've been thinking about it a lot, and we're impeding their investigation by holding things back, aren't we? We need to tell them everything.'

Abby knows Sienna is right; it's the only way to put an end to this and lay Greg to rest. 'Let me talk to Mark first. I'll find out what he's got to do with it.' She shudders. It can't be possible that the man she's spent most of her life in love with has taken someone's life.

After a moment, Sienna agrees. 'Okay. But go now. And Abby?'

She turns to face Sienna.

'You need to be careful.'

–

The lights are off in Mark's flat, his Volvo not in its usual spot across the road. She scans the rest of the street in case, but there's no sign of it, not even a car of the same make or colour to give her a temporary flutter of hope.

She knocks on his door anyway. It's late now, so he could have gone to bed, although this theory doesn't explain his missing car. When there's no answer, she pulls her phone from her bag. There are seven missed calls from Mark and four text messages, but nothing since she left Sienna's house. His silence worries her more than him bombarding her with calls.

Abby needs to take control of this. She calls his mobile, pressing the phone to her ear. There's no answer, and she knows why; he's worked out why she left without a word.

A whole night alone in the house looms ahead of her, and that determines what she needs to do next. Mark doesn't know anyone in London well enough to be with them at this time of night, so that leaves only one place he could be.

# FORTY-NINE

*Abby*

Ordinarily, she'd be too tired to drive such a distance this late at night, but she's fuelled with adrenalin; she needs to find Mark now. She should have stayed at his flat, confronted him when she had the chance. She regrets this now.

It's nearly one a.m. by the time she arrives, and she heads straight to his house. Although she knows the name of the road – he'd told her when they spent the night together after her mum died – she's never seen the property. Many times, she's imagined what it looks like, and what he was doing behind its walls, what his life was like with Cassie. She'd thought about coming, just to look, but she never did. There's too thin a line between curiosity and obsession.

She sees it immediately – it's the only property with a *For Sale* board sprouting from the grass. Couples buy their houses, full of hopes and dreams for their futures, never thinking one day they'll be selling up, going their separate ways. She hasn't asked Mark how Cassie feels about their divorce; it's something she doubts she'll ever know now. And it's not important if Mark turns out to be worse than someone who's left her for another woman.

There's no way she can knock on the door now – she doesn't even know for sure that he's there – so she sends him a text.

> I'm in Ipswich, outside your house. Don't make me knock on the door.

It takes less than a minute for his reply to come.

> I'm coming. Don't do anything.

Her eyes remain fixed on the front door once she's read his text. He's in there, she knows it, and she's not going to give him a chance to say otherwise. She doesn't care that he's back in the home he shares with his ex-wife. She only wants to know what he's running away from.

For ten minutes she sits in her car waiting, seeing no sign of life in the house. Then the door opens and he's standing there, staring into the night. She rolls the window down but stays in the car, and it's not long before he sees her.

He's walking towards her now. She can't let him in her car. Throwing open the door she gets out, keeping her distance from him. It's reassuring that there are still lights on in a few of the houses on the street.

Mark stares at her, and she prepares herself to hear things her brain won't want to compute. 'What the hell, Abby? Why would you leave like that?'

'You really don't know?' She backs further away.

'No. I assumed you were just trying to get back at me for when I left you before.'

This is not what she's expected. 'What?'

'Can we sit in the car? I don't want Cassie seeing us.'

Abby glances towards the house, where only the hall light is visible. 'No. We'll talk out here.'

'Did you plan it all along? To make me feel secure about us before you just… disappear? I never had you down as being cruel. Heartless.'

She ignores him. 'What are you doing here, Mark?'

He takes a step towards her. 'Don't jump to conclusions. I'm here because Cassie called me when I went to get our food. She's been really depressed and was hysterical on the phone. I couldn't just leave her by herself. I would have told you I was coming here if you hadn't left.'

She stares at him. More lies. 'Really? You drove up here in the middle of the night to comfort your ex?'

He shakes his head. 'You really don't know me, do you?' Again, he steps closer to her. She fights every urge to back away; she needs to show him she's not afraid, that she's in control. It still feels as though she's shrinking.

'You're right, I don't,' Abby tells him. 'I'm beginning to learn, though, that we can never know anyone. Maybe not even ourselves.'

When he doesn't reply she pulls out her phone, finding one of the pictures of her and Greg and holding it in front of him. 'Recognise this?'

Mark moves closer and stares at her phone. Even in this darkness she can see his face drain of colour. 'How did you get that?'

'Stay there. Don't come any closer.'

'Abby, I can explain.'

'Go on then. Because for hours I've been wondering why the hell you've got hundreds of photos of me from months ago when we weren't even in each other's lives. And why you've got photos of Greg on the day he went missing. So go on, Mark, explain yourself.' Despite the force of her words, she feels as though she's seconds away from crumbling.

He glances back at the house. 'Please, can we at least sit in the car?'

'Sienna knows where I am. If anything happens to me, she'll know exactly what to tell the police.'

'The police? Abby, what are you talking about?'

She opens the passenger door. 'Get in then.'

'I don't know where to start,' Mark says as soon as they're both in the car, the doors shutting them off from the street outside.

Abby turns to him. 'Start with the truth. You need to know you've got no option now.'

'Okay. You're right.' He stares at his hands, clenching and unclenching them. 'I'm so sorry. I… I've been kind of following you a bit for months. Since you moved to London. I… I know it's wrong in every way, but I just needed to be near you. I know that's bad enough, and taking the photos makes it even worse. I can't explain why I did that – I think I just needed to have them so I could feel close to you when I was back in Ipswich.' He reaches for her hand, but she pulls away. 'If I'd known we'd be together again, I would never have done it. I just needed something to hold on to, and this was the next best thing to having you. I never thought for a second you'd take me back.'

Abby is incredulous. 'You stalked me. That's insane. At any point you could have just called and spoken to me. You were the one who said we couldn't be together.'

He hangs his head. 'I know. I'm not proud of any of this.'

'You followed me to the park that day I met Greg. You saw us together. You thought we were having an affair.'

He nods. 'That's what it looked like. I wasn't close enough to hear you or see your facial expressions clearly. It just looked like you were having a cosy chat. It's only when you told me he was blackmailing you I realised I'd been wrong.'

'You admitted you were jealous of him, because I'd spent the night with him.'

'I know.' He turns away, stares through the window.

'Did you kill him?'

His head shoots up, his eyes wide with horror. 'No! Of course not! Why would I do that? I didn't even know him.'

'You said you were jealous of him. You must have followed me when I went to his house after the park.'

'What? No, I didn't. I went back to Ipswich; I swear to you. So you went to his house afterwards?'

She ignores his question. 'I'm going to the police after this.' Her hand clutches her mobile phone. 'I just want you to tell me the truth. I'm sick of lies. Everyone's lying. You need to tell them what you did, and deal with the consequences.'

'You can't really believe that I'd take someone's life? Please, Abby, tell me this is some kind of test?'

'Brighton,' she says.

'What are you talking about?'

'When we went for lunch the other day, I saw an email notification on your phone from a hotel in Brighton. But when I asked you, you said you'd never been there before and had no reason to go. Brighton was where Greg's debit card was used. Where somebody wanted to make it look like he was still alive. You were there, Mark. You stayed in Brighton and there's no way that's a coincidence.'

She's backed him into a corner now; he'll have no choice but to admit to everything. So she's surprised when his shoulders drop, tension easing away from him.

He reaches into his pocket, and Abby backs towards the car door.

'Read the email,' he says, handing her his phone, placing it in her hand when she doesn't move. 'It was meant to be a surprise for you. That's why I denied all knowledge of the place.'

She reads the email from the Grand Hotel in Brighton. A booking for a penthouse suite next week.

He's shaking his head. 'I wanted to treat you to a weekend away before you start your new job. That's all I'm guilty of.'

Before Abby can respond, he grabs his phone from her and gets out of the car, slamming the door behind him.

# FIFTY

## *Sienna*

She's right back to square one – the police are no closer to finding out what happened to Greg, and it's clear now that Abby's boyfriend had nothing to do with it. All he's guilty of is being obsessive; something Abby will have to deal with herself. Her relationship is none of Sienna's business.

It's Saturday today, and she's already decided she will go to the police first thing on Monday morning. There's no way she can do it while she's still looking after Jackson, and Holly's not picking him up until Sunday evening, so she has no choice but to wait until then.

She will make the most of these last couple of days, because once she's spoken to DC Roberts, who knows what will happen to her? Lying to the police won't be taken lightly, and she's sure it won't just be a warning she'll get. It doesn't matter, though, she needs this to be behind her. She needs the truth, whatever she has to sacrifice to get it.

For Jackson's sake, she tries to maintain a sense of normality, making sandwiches for lunch, even though Rob hasn't surfaced from his room yet. She's called to him and even texted his phone to tell him she's made lunch, but silence is the only reply she gets.

Things are strained between them, and she's determined to clear the air, so she lets Jackson eat in front of the TV while she goes upstairs to speak to Rob.

He mumbles something when she knocks on the door. Although it's indecipherable, she's sure it's not a greeting, nor is it an invitation to come in. She steps inside the room anyway, pulling the door closed behind her. Rob looks different in the semi-darkness, his hair ruffled. The duvet only covers his lower half, so she can see that he's still wearing the T-shirt he wore yesterday. She needs to help this man; it's her fault he's unravelling. He didn't have to become this person.

She sits on the end of the bed. 'Rob, I think you might need to talk and, well, I'm quite a good listener. I know things are a bit weird between us right now, but please just talk to me.' She sounds like she's his wife, and she wonders if this annoys him.

Rob rolls over onto his back, looks at her with an expression she can't work out. 'Haven't we said enough?' he says. 'I have, at least.'

'I understand why you're angry with me, but can you see that not only am I looking out for Jackson, but I want you to be okay too? And... you're drinking all the time. You don't even seem to care about work any more.'

'I'm fine at work.'

'Just because you're going in every day, doesn't mean you're fine.'

'You're not my mother, Sienna. I have enough of this from her, so can you please just back off?'

She tries not to take his words personally. 'I'm just saying this because I care.'

He stares at her. 'You really do, don't you? Even though I've been an arsehole to you, blaming you for everything.'

'I understand that. I know your anger comes from a place of pain.'

Rob sits up in bed, swinging his legs out so he's sitting closer to her. She knows what he's about to do – it plays out like a film in her mind. He leans towards her and in less than a second his mouth is on hers, the weight of him leaning into her.

She pushes him off, so hard that he falls back against the headboard. 'No, Rob. That's not going to happen.'

He stares at her; there's no shame or regret scrawled on his face. He doesn't care that she's rejected him because it's not her he wants. 'I detest you, Sienna,' he says, calmly, reaching down to the floor for his trousers. 'You play people like pawns in a game of chess, and you don't even know you're doing it half the time. You and Greg were as bad as each other. I should never have listened to him when he told me Abby...' He stops. 'I need to get out of here.'

She freezes. 'What are you talking about?'

'I'm glad he's dead,' Rob says. 'He got exactly what he deserved.' She can't be sure, because he's speaking under his breath, but she's positive the next words out of his mouth are that he hopes she gets what she deserves too.

–

'Just hold on, Sienna – you need to slow down and tell me all this again.'

She repeats what Rob said to her, quoting every word precisely because they're firmly etched in her mind now and it will take more than time to remove them. 'I know it's not an admission of anything, but surely it's worth questioning him?'

'And this is because he knew his wife was having an affair with your husband?'

She hasn't corrected DC Roberts yet about Abby and Greg; that will only untangle the web they've woven. But she will do it soon. She just needs to know that they've thoroughly looked into Rob, and that they keep him away from the house while Jackson's here. She's tempted to call Holly and warn her that she should come and get Jackson, but she doesn't want to let her down. She just needs to keep him safe for one more night and then one more day.

'He admitted to me that he was jealous of Greg. I know that by itself it's not proof of anything, but it's important, isn't it? Motive?'

'We'll talk to him,' DC Roberts says. 'So he's not with you now?'

Sienna recalls Rob silently throwing things into his bags. 'No, he's gone. I don't know where. Maybe back to his house?'

Once she's off the phone, she grabs a bin liner and throws the rest of Rob's things into it. Downstairs, Jackson is sitting at the kitchen table, his schoolbooks spread out around him.

'Where's Rob gone?' he asks. 'He didn't even say goodbye.'

Sienna places Rob's things by the door and joins Jackson at the table. 'I'm sorry – he was in a bit of a rush.'

'How come he had all his stuff with him? Is he leaving?'

This is difficult for Sienna; she wants to tell Jackson what she knows about Rob – lies have already destroyed too many people – yet she's fully aware that he's only a child. And she's not his mother. It's Holly she needs to talk to first, then she'll be able to decide what's best to share with Jackson.

'He's got a lot of stuff to sort out. He's in the middle of a divorce, Jackson.' This reminds Sienna that she has to tell Abby what's happened. Warn her.

'Is that why he acts weird sometimes?'

Sienna frowns. 'What do you mean by weird? I thought you got on well with him.'

He shrugs. 'I do. But he's a bit... weird.'

'Can you tell me in what way?'

'I dunno. I tried to talk about Dad once and he just changed the subject. It's like he didn't want to talk about him. He kind of just cut me off.'

In light of Rob's recent behaviour, this shouldn't surprise her, yet it does. She always believed that Rob and Jackson were growing closer, that Rob was somehow filling the gap that Greg has left, as much as that's possible. 'Oh, Jackson, you should have told me.'

He shrugs. 'It was okay. We just carried on playing our game and I forgot about it.'

She's pleased by this; she's heard that kids are resilient, and Jackson is definitely living proof.

'Jackson, listen, I just need to make a quick phone call and then how about we go bowling? Would you like that?'

'Bowling? Yeah, okay.'

She goes upstairs to call Abby, relieved when she answers the phone.

It's difficult to start at the beginning when all she wants to do is tell Abby to lock her doors and call the police if she sees Rob. She needs to explain it from the beginning though; otherwise there's no way Abby will understand.

'He's like a different person,' Sienna says. 'And there have been odd comments he's made that really worry me. I know he's feeling low about you leaving him, but I really think there's more to it.'

'He has been acting differently,' Abby agrees, 'even before I left him. He hasn't really been the same since that night. But I don't think he could have hurt Greg. I've made this mistake before, thinking Mark had something to do with it, and I don't want to do that again.'

'You might be right, but it's better that the police know, isn't it?'

There's a moment of silence. 'You've told them?'

'Not everything. Not yet. But I told DC Roberts he might want to question Rob. I just wanted to warn you. If he turns up there, can you call the police? They're looking for him now.'

'Oh, Sienna, don't you think he's been through enough? There's no way it was him.'

'Why are you so sure? What aren't you telling me?'

'Nothing. No more secrets or lies, Sienna.'

But there are plenty more, she thinks.

# FIFTY-ONE

### Abby

It's easy not to be afraid when daylight streams though the windows, yet she knows darkness falls fast, and her confidence will wane as day merges into night. How could it possibly have been Rob all along? Her head can't wrap itself around this thought. Sienna had been convinced, though, and Abby knows only too well that when pushed, people can be capable of almost anything.

She's packing things into boxes, getting the house sorted so that she can leave for Ipswich as soon as possible; she doesn't want to be here any longer than she has to. Rob can have it until it's sold – unless he ends up in prison.

Abby is ashamed of the thoughts she's having: that she wants it to be Rob because then she will be free and this will all be behind her. There will be no more looking over her shoulder. She's doing that now, of course, heading to the window every few minutes to check nobody is outside the house. And she's lost count of the number of times she's checked the door is locked.

By eight o'clock there's been no sign of Rob, and Abby convinces herself that if he had any inkling that Sienna had called the police, this is the last place he would come. Still, she won't allow herself to be complacent – Rob despises her for what she's done, and that animosity has to be far stronger than any he would have felt towards Greg.

She's drifting off on the sofa when it happens. Someone banging on the door, jolting her awake. And that's when the enormity of the trouble she's in hits her. She rushes to the window and sees Lillian's car in the drive. Rob must have borrowed it. She needs to act normally, keep him outside the house so that she can call the police.

Keeping the chain on, she unlocks the door. When she pulls it open, she's surprised to find Lillian standing there, her eyes wide with a rage worse than Abby's ever witnessed on her before.

'Let me in, Abby,' she hisses. 'We need to talk right now.'

Abby owes this woman nothing. She should close the door on her; there is no need for Lillian to be in her life any more. Lillian despises her, always has done, so she should be happy that Abby has left Rob. Why, then, does she look like she wants to strangle her?

She's only partially aware of her motivation for opening the door: she wants validation. If Rob is guilty then it shows that Lillian was wrong all along: Abby is not the one who wasn't good enough for her son; it's the other way around if Rob is capable of taking someone's life.

'What do you want?' she says as Lillian brushes past her.

'This is low, even for you,' she says.

'I have no idea what you're talking about.' Abby stays calm. Everything has changed, and there is no way Lillian can get to her now.

'You've done this to get back at him, haven't you? I always knew you were evil. Well, it will all come out, and I'm on my way there right now to tell the police what a nasty piece of work you are.'

'Lillian, you've lost me. What am I supposed to have done?'

'You just can't let him be happy, can you? You're so bitter that he's left you and now you want to ruin his life. I—'

'Hold on a minute. You think Rob left me? Is that what he told you?'

For a second Lillian looks less sure of herself, but she quickly recovers. 'Yes, and Rob's not a liar. He's finally seen sense and left you, and now you're trying to—'

310

'Just stop talking. Please. Why don't you try listening for once in your life?' Only months ago, Abby would never have been able to remain calm in the face of Lillian's aggression and anger. Now, though, this woman is nothing to her, and she doesn't care what Lillian thinks of her. Slowly, she explains to her how mistaken she is, and that she wasn't the one who went to the police.

'You're lying.'

'No, I'm not. I left Rob. The funny thing is, in one way you've been right all along. Rob and I were never right for each other, but it was nothing to do with me not being good enough for him or living up to Tamara. Either way, it doesn't matter – you should be happy that we're no longer together. I certainly am.'

'It must have been you. Only you would tell the police Rob had... done such an awful thing. You were the one who was after that man.'

Abby rolls her eyes. 'Who? Greg? No, I wasn't. Is that what Rob told you?'

'No!' Lillian is flustered now, and it's the first time Abby has truly felt in control when dealing with her. Too little too late. 'He only told me that he'd finally left you, and that it had been a long time coming.'

Saving face, Abby thinks. She can't really blame him. He would have had to listen to years of hearing *I told you so* from Lillian if he'd admitted that Abby had left him for someone else. 'Then what are you talking about, Lillian?'

The smug smile on her face tells Abby that there is something Lillian can hold over her. 'His wife told me all about it. Lovely woman. Sienna. I think she was a friend of yours until you decided to try and go after her husband.'

'What are you talking about? I was never after Greg.'

'That's not what his wife said. In fact, I think the police will be very interested to know all about it. Especially as you've tried to blame Rob.'

'When did you speak to Sienna?' Abby needs to know this. Everything depends on Lillian's answer.

'It was months ago. She came to see me right after her husband went missing, and she said you knew where he was. I'll be telling all this to the police and then they'll know Rob had nothing to do with it.'

Now it all makes sense. Sienna went to Lillian right at the beginning to try and mess with Abby. At that time, she'd been convinced something had happened between her and Greg, and she would have done anything to find him.

'Okay, Lillian, please do go to the police. The man leading the investigation is DC Roberts.' Abby opens the front door. 'Give him my regards. I'm sure he'll remember me from the long discussion we've already had about Greg.'

Lillian shakes her head, moves towards the door and steps outside. 'It's a shame you didn't get that job you went for,' she says, a smug smile on her face.

It takes Abby a moment to realise what Lillian is referring to. So *she* was the one who sent that email to the school. And all this time she'd thought it had been Sienna's doing. There have been so many things Abby has been wrong about. 'Why would you do that?' she demands.

'Do what?' Lillian is smirking.

'You know what I'm talking about. You were the one who sent that email to the school withdrawing my application. Why, though? It doesn't make sense.'

'Clearly you're not as smart as Rob's given you credit for. It's simple: if you didn't have a job and were putting him under financial pressure, then it would be even more reason for Rob to realise he's with the wrong person.'

Momentarily, Abby is speechless. 'You're more bitter and twisted than I thought.' She's about to shut the door on Lillian when she remembers there's something else she needs to say. 'One more thing. Before you contact Rob, you might want to know that it was Sienna who called the police about him. Not me.'

She slams the door shut.

–

Two hours later, the house is finally packed up. Abby sits in the car, turning on the engine and glancing back at the house. She doesn't care about the furniture – it can all be given away – she's got everything she needs to take with her. Some people might say she's running away, but she knows it's not that. She's going home. Where she's supposed to be. Where the memories of Mum are and the shadow of all of this can't follow her. She will stay at Mel's until this house is sold or she's found a job and can get back on the property ladder.

Mark is still a big question mark hanging over her. He can't deal with the fact that she thought he might have been capable of killing someone. Maybe Abby understands this; it's the lowest you can ever think of another person.

She drives away, recalling that at one point she thought Sienna was responsible for Greg being missing. And as much as she tries, she can't pinpoint how or why that changed.

# FIFTY-TWO

*Sienna*

As far as she knows, Rob is still at the police station, being questioned by DC Roberts and his colleagues. Something will happen now. Justice for Greg. It's all too surreal for her to get to grips with. Rob. Kind, loving Rob. Did Greg die because of Rob's desperate love for Abby? Is that what loving someone can reduce us to? It doesn't bear thinking about.

'What time's Mum coming?' Jackson asks.

'Her flight lands at ten to four, so allowing for baggage reclaim, I reckon she'll get here just after dinner. Is that okay?'

He nods. 'Yeah. I like being here. But d'you mind if I go to my friend Luca's for a bit. He's got this new Xbox game.'

Sienna smiles. 'Of course.' This is progress. Other than at school, Jackson has barely seen any of his friends since Greg died. 'Do you want a lift?'

'It's okay – I've got my bike.'

'I'll have to call your friend's mum, though, to make sure she's expecting you. And just be back for dinner, okay?' Hearing her own words makes her smile. She sounds like a mother. She likes to think Greg would have been proud to see how much she's bonded with Jackson.

–

Once she's alone, guilt sets in. In her mind, she's convicted Rob without a trial. She knows that there's no firm evidence against him, and that sooner or later she might be back where she was, but this is the closest she's come to any kind of closure, and she wants to cling on to it as hard as she can. DC Roberts has already told her that the best they can hope for is a confession; all she can do is pray that Rob does the right thing.

Desperate for an update, she calls DC Roberts, only to be told that he's in an interview at the moment and she'll have to leave a message. 'If he could call me back when he's free,' she explains. 'My name's Sienna Wells.'

After that she plans what to make for dinner. Pasta is Jackson's favourite, and it doesn't take long to cook. She's already called his friend Luca's mother, and she kindly insisted that she'll drop Jackson back by six. 'His bike will easily fit in our boot,' she'd said.

It's difficult not to get anxious whenever Sienna hears any sound in the house. She's safe: nobody is coming for her; there's no reason for them to. She turns her attention to getting everything ready for Jackson leaving tomorrow. She should do his washing; prove to Holly that she can look after him so that she agrees to make this a regular arrangement. Sienna's sure it will help Holly out to have extra childcare.

Upstairs, she tidies his room, gathering all his clothes together. A scraping sound downstairs makes her freeze, her breath catching in her throat. She has nothing to defend herself with if someone's broken in. She waits to hear it again, but everything is silent. She needs to check downstairs. Scooping up the pile of Jackson's clothes she's collected, she spots a red T-shirt sticking out of his rucksack, which he's left on the floor by the bed. She pulls it out and something drops to the floor. Bending down to pick it up, she's puzzled when she sees what it is.

A bank debit card.

Dropping the clothes on the floor, she turns it over and stares at the name on it.

*Gregory Michael Wells.*

It takes a moment for the realisation of what this means to hit her, and when it does, Sienna drops to her knees.

–

It's minutes before she can pick herself up from the floor. In her hands is Greg's debit card, the one that was used in Brighton. The police have never believed it had actually been Greg who'd used it, but she had wanted to cling on to this hope. Until it hadn't been in his wallet when they'd found his body.

What she's struggling to comprehend is why it's in Jackson's possession. Did he see Greg before he disappeared? Does he know something? It doesn't make sense. All she knows is that somehow Jackson is right in the centre of this and she needs to confront him. He's still a kid, though; she needs to be careful.

It's nearly three p.m. and Sienna realises that Holly will be landing soon. Sienna will talk to her about this first and let her be the one to confront her son. Still, she searches through the rest of Jackson's belongings, rooting through every pocket without feeling a shred of guilt. She finds nothing else, and she abandons the idea of washing Jackson's clothes. It seems pointless now – trying to prove she's a good stepmother when she's about to approach Holly with something so awful.

A car pulls up outside, and Sienna rushes to the window. Part of her is hoping that it's Abby, even though she knows Abby is well on her way to Ipswich by now.

It's at least two hours too early but it's Holly's black Audi in the driveway.

Sienna rushes downstairs and opens the door before Holly reaches it, pulling her inside as soon as she's close enough. 'I really need to talk to you,' she says. 'Come upstairs. I need to show you something.'

The smile on Holly's face vanishes, quickly replaced with a frown. 'Sienna, what's happened? Is Jackson okay?'

'Sorry, yes, he's fine. He's at his friend's house. Luca.'

Holly lets out a deep breath. 'Okay. Thank goodness. So what's going on?'

'It's best if I show you.' Sienna leads the way upstairs, with every step she climbs hoping there'll be some sort of explanation, that Holly will pick up on something she herself has missed.

'What a mess,' Holly exclaims when she follows Sienna into the spare room. 'I'm so sorry. I'm always on at him to tidy things up, and actually he's usually good at home so I'm surprised—'

'Jackson didn't make this mess. I did.'

Holly stares at her. 'Oh. Why? What's going on, Sienna?'

Sienna sits on the edge of the bed. 'I was going to do Jackson's washing so all his clothes were clean before you picked him up. But then I found that in his rucksack.' She points to the debit card, which she's placed on the bed.

Holly frowns, takes a step towards it. 'What is it?'

'I think you should have a look.'

She picks up the card, turning it over just as Sienna did earlier. The colour drains from her face as she takes in the name on the card. 'I don't understand. What's one of Greg's cards doing in Jackson's things?' Her eyes widen. 'Oh no, please don't tell me he's been stealing money.'

Sienna shakes her head. 'That's the debit card that was used in Brighton. Only it wasn't Greg who used it. It was probably whoever...' She trails off, unable to close her sentence.

Holly stares at her, then back to the card. 'No, it can't be. I don't understand. What's it doing here?'

Sienna almost can't say the next part; how awful it will be for Holly to hear more. 'I found it in Jackson's rucksack. I was hoping you could help me work out how it got there.'

The frown remains on Holly's face and when she shakes her head, the sunglasses that have been perched on top of it topple to the floor. 'But... I don't understand. There's no way Jackson had that; he couldn't have.' She glances around the room as if the answer is written here somewhere. Sienna feels sorry for

317

her. 'He must have found it somewhere in the house,' Holly continues.

'No. No, he didn't. I promise you – I found it just now in his rucksack when I was pulling out that red T-shirt over there.'

Silence. 'That doesn't mean he didn't just find it and decide to keep it. It's possible, isn't it?'

'We have to tell the police, Holly. I've been going over it all and this is a key piece of evidence.' Sienna wishes she'd been more rational when she'd found it; now Holly's and her own fingerprints will be all over it.

'What exactly are you saying? That you think Jackson had something to do with Greg's death? That *he* did it?' It's clear that Holly's frightened now: all her usual composure has evaporated. She sinks to the bed, staring at the card she still clutches in her hand.

'I honestly don't know what to think, Holly. But it doesn't look good, does it? I think we need to tell the police.'

'No, please, Sienna. Can we just talk to Jackson first and see what he says? There must be a good explanation.' Holly reaches for her phone. 'Let me text him and tell him to come back right now.'

Sienna's about to agree when she hears footsteps in the hall. She spins around and there is Jackson, standing by the stairs, tears streaming down his blotched and swollen face.

'Please,' he says. 'Please don't call the police. I'll tell you everything, I swear. It was me. I killed Dad.' And then he sinks to the floor as if his bones can no longer support him.

# FIFTY-THREE

## Sienna

December

Sometimes, she likes to come to this park, even though she's never been here with Greg. It's one of the last places anyone other than Jackson saw him, and even though Abby might not agree, she finds it calming here. She'll never tell anyone this, but it's as though she can feel Greg's presence wrapping itself around her, comforting her, letting her know she'll be all right now. As okay as she can be, given that she can't shake the horrific image of a thirteen-year-old boy killing his own father from her mind.

She often goes through it all, hoping that the more she does, the greater the chance that she can try and make peace with it. *Jackson's just a child*, she constantly reminds herself.

It had been an accident, Jackson had claimed. They'd had an argument and he'd lashed out at Greg. And right after confessing this, Jackson had clammed up, withdrawing into himself as if neither she nor Holly were there in the room with him. The only thing that didn't stop were his tears. It was almost as if he had suddenly died, withered away, right there in front of them.

To this day, he still hasn't spoken a word.

As for him having Greg's debit card, the police can only assume that Jackson took it and went to Brighton to try and make everyone believe Greg was still alive, that he'd just walked out on his life. Sienna knows this just shows his desperation; at thirteen years old he didn't comprehend that this would only raise more questions.

She sees Abby walking towards her and gives a tentative wave. Things are much better now between them, given that neither of them is suspicious of the other, and Sienna still hopes that their friendship will withstand this.

When Abby reaches the bench Sienna sits on, she notices that Abby's changed her hairstyle yet again. This time it's shorter, highlighted with golden streaks. Perhaps she wanted to shed the person that she was. Have a new beginning. It always starts with a makeover, Sienna realises.

She stands up and hugs Abby. 'Thanks for meeting me here. I know it must be difficult.'

'Somehow it doesn't feel weird. Not now that we know what happened to him.'

'We may never know the full details, though,' Sienna reminds her, although perhaps this is better. She still can't make up her mind about that. She's sure that if Jackson does start talking, offering details of why he and Greg argued, and how it resulted in such a heinous attack, then Sienna may never get the images out of her head. This way, at least, she can remember Greg how he was.

'So he's still not talking?'

'No. They've got child psychiatrists working with him but nothing so far.'

'And how's Holly doing?'

'Not good. She blames herself for not seeing that there was something wrong, and for working so much that Jackson was able to keep this from her all that time.'

'It's all such a mess,' Abby says. 'But it's not your mess, remember.' Abby has spent the last couple of months trying to convince Sienna that she needs to step away from this, for her own well-being.

'Jackson's my stepson,' Sienna says. 'I owe it to him to try and help him.'

'I know that's what you want, but you can't help him. The doctors will do that. And the police. And his mother. Please don't forget that he was staying at your house, even though he knew what he'd done. It was so calculated, Sienna.'

'He's still just a child.'

'I know. There is no right thing to do, is there?'

Sienna tells her about the letter she's written to him, telling him that she forgives him and hopes that one day he can accept what he's done and take responsibility for it. She hasn't sent it to him yet, maybe she never will, but it's there, just in case.

'You're a good person, Sienna,' Abby says.

'Have you heard from Rob?' Sienna asks.

'Only by email. House sale stuff. It goes through tomorrow, so I can finally move on. I wanted to wait until it's sold and the money's in my account before I start looking for something. I want to take my time, make sure it's the right place for me. I think I'm driving Mel a bit mad, though. How about you? Have you heard from Rob?'

'Actually, he did email me the other day, apologising for his behaviour. And he said he understood why I called the police about him.'

'That sounds like the old Rob, doesn't it?' Abby says. 'Less anger, more compassion.'

Sienna smiles. 'Yes, it does.'

'What about *your* house?' Abby asks.

'I've just had an offer this morning, actually. It's a bit less than I wanted, but it's a cash buyer with no chain, so I'm going to go for it.'

'That's great news. You could be out before January.' She pauses. 'Have you had a chance to think about my idea?'

When Abby first suggested that Sienna relocate to Ipswich, she said no. She's never been there and wouldn't know anyone other than Abby.

'You'd meet people through me,' Abby had insisted. 'And you could set up your business there.'

Despite this being true, Sienna had resisted. Perhaps she and Abby needed to be out of each other's lives. Then, as she'd begun to see things more clearly, it occurred to her that what happened had nothing to do with their friendship, and if anything, it was their friendship that helped them both through this.

'I'm not sure,' Sienna says, 'I think I just need more time.'

Abby grabs her hand. 'Okay, I understand. But you'll love it there, I promise you.'

'Are you and Mark okay?'

'Time will tell. We're taking things very slowly.'

'Shall we go and get a coffee?' Sienna suggests. 'I think I want to say goodbye to this park now. It's time.'

Abby smiles. 'I can't say I'm sorry to hear that.'

They leave together, and Sienna listens while Abby talks about her new job. It's at the same school she worked at in Ipswich and, more remarkably, it's her old deputy head post. By some coincidence, the woman who took over went on maternity leave and decided she didn't want to go back to teaching.

This makes Sienna smile. People are always so focused on how good change is, and how we constantly need to make alterations in our lives, but maybe, sometimes, it's okay for things to remain the same.

# FIFTY-FOUR

*Holly*

Late April, Before

She still gets nervous when she has to drop off or pick up Jackson from Greg's. Mostly she stays in the car, keeping a safe distance from him because she doesn't want to feel those horrible flutters. The ones that tell her she's still not over what he did to her. Over him. What a joke. It's been years: time should have helped her, but it hasn't. It's only increased her anger towards him, because every passing day is another day where she's living a life she didn't want. She's a single mother now, and that's something she never saw coming.

Holly will never let Greg know this, of course, she will never surrender her power to him again. Those days are far behind her.

Something she's grateful for, though, is that Jackson is a good kid. When he's older, she'll make sure he doesn't turn out like his father, and she'll let him know too, exactly what his father did.

This evening Greg was supposed to be dropping Jackson off at home; instead, just because he's got dinner plans with Marty and the others, she has to now rush from her meeting to pick up their son. Sienna will be there, standing in the doorway, probably wondering why all she ever gets from Holly is a vague acknowledgement from the car. Holly has nothing against her – she's not the woman who destroyed her life.

Sometimes Holly wishes she could scream out to Sienna that she doesn't know the man she's married, that Greg isn't who she thinks he is. Holly always refrains from this, though. Greg has bought her silence. Literally. And without his regular deposits into her bank account, she wouldn't have this house, not on her own.

'Hi, Mum,' Jackson says, sliding into the back of the car, clicking on his seat belt. As she begins to drive away, she remembers the old days, having to put Jackson in a car seat, how awkward it was to strap him in. Those were shared moments with Greg, even though both of them were too busy with work to appreciate that those times would be over so quickly.

'No Dad today?'

'No.'

In the rear-view mirror Holly notices the disappointment etched on Jackson's face. His father is a saint to him, someone to idolise; it hurts him when things like this happen. She's had enough of it now; she's done with keeping Jackson in this bubble when it will only lead to disappointment, and probably do him more harm than good in the long run. He's nearly fourteen, it's about time he knew the truth.

'Well, it doesn't surprise me. Work always comes first.'

Jackson jumps to Greg's defence. 'Mum! Why are you attacking Dad? It's not his fault he had to work. He saves people's lives. It's important.'

Holly feels like a scolded child. She stays silent, concentrating on the road ahead. It's raining now, but so lightly that the wipers make that annoying squeaking sound as they scrape across the windscreen.

'None of this is his fault anyway – you're the one who left him.'

This isn't the first time Jackson has thrown something like this her way and, as much as it hurts, she always rises above it, telling herself that the choices she made were to protect him. But tonight, something snaps. She can't do it any more. None

324

of it is worth it and it's damaging her relationship with her son. She's dealing with those tricky teenage years now.

She swerves the car into a lay-by, ignoring the angry blasts of car horns behind her.

'We need to talk, Jackson, right now. Get in the front, please.'

Obediently, he climbs over and sits beside her. 'Mum, you're scaring me, what is it?'

She pauses, takes a moment to look at him and take in his features. Somehow, she knows that nothing will be the same once she's told him. 'You need to know the truth. I didn't leave your dad. He left me. He was... having an affair.' She turns to her son. 'Do you know what that means?'

He wrinkles his face. 'Yeah, I'm not stupid. But you said—'

'I know what I told you. What we both told you. It was wrong to lie to you, and I'm not proud of what I did, but I made your dad tell people I was the one who left him. I told him to tell everyone it was because I didn't love him any more.' She looks at him, tries to read what's going through his mind. Of course, that's impossible. 'He had no choice but to go along with this story.'

Jackson huddles against the car door, folding his arms around his body. 'I don't understand.'

'I wanted to wait until you were older to tell you all this because you're still so young, Jackson, but... the woman your dad was sleeping with was a patient of his. They would see each other at the hospital and doctors aren't supposed to do things like that. It's not right. So if people had found out, then your dad might have lost his job. It definitely would have affected his career. She was young, too. Twenty-one or twenty-two.'

Jackson screws up his face. 'That's disgusting. Why would he do that?'

'I don't know,' Holly says. She has often asked herself this question, but the truth is she doesn't know. She only knew about the affair when she got that call from Leela. She recalls the distraught voice telling her that he'd ended their relationship. She'd barely made sense to Holly.

Beside her, Jackson begins to cry. She doesn't tell him that Leela committed suicide that same night, and that it was most likely because of Greg. This is already enough for her son to cope with. He can never find out that Holly was blackmailing Greg, threatening to tell people about his involvement with Leela if he didn't pay her off every month. *Think of it as alimony*, she'd told him, even though the amount she'd demanded was far beyond what was reasonable.

'I was… in a lot of pain,' she continues. 'I loved him, and I didn't want our marriage to end. And I made him tell people that I was the one who'd left him because I couldn't handle being thought of as the woman who was left by her husband. I have too much pride, and that's my downfall.'

Jackson rubs his chin. 'Is this why you're always so sad?'

Holly is shocked; she hasn't realised that Jackson saw her this way. 'Maybe,' she says.

'Dad did this to you? He's the reason you're always on your own, and you didn't like Andrew?'

'Probably.' A tragic case, she thinks. Psychologists would have a field day with her.

Jackson leans forward and throws his arms around her. 'I'm so sorry, Mum. All this time I've been blaming you for leaving Dad when it was his fault all along.'

Holly holds on tightly to Jackson; he is the one good thing in her life, the only thing that makes everything Greg put her through worth it. 'You mustn't tell anyone, though, Jackson. Promise me? Your dad and I have an arrangement. He gives us a lot of money so that we can be in our lovely house. If people find out, then he'll stop paying so much and we'd have to move. Do you understand?' If Holly is honest with herself, she likes having this bond with Greg – until now, nobody knew about his affair other than her, and it's made her feel closer to him.

'Is that okay, then, Jax?' she says when there's no answer.

She thinks that she feels Jackson nodding his agreement.

After that, neither of them speak of Holly's revelation. On the phone, when Greg calls, Jackson is quiet, and he gives nothing away.

It feels good to have things out in the open – she's felt terrible keeping something so important from her son – until the evening she comes home and knows the second she steps through the door that something is wrong.

'Jackson? What is it? What's happened?'

He's sitting on the floor, clutching his knees, rocking backwards and forwards. He stares at her, his eyes wide with terror, but says nothing.

She rushes forward, sits with him on the floor and puts her arms around him. 'Are you hurt? Tell me what's happened.' She's trying to be calm, to steady her pounding heart. He doesn't look hurt, she assures herself. Whatever it is, Jackson is at least physically okay.

He shakes his head, continues rocking back and forth.

Holly strokes his hair. 'Okay, good. But what's happened?'

'It's... it's Dad.' He buries his head in her chest, clutching her so tightly she almost can't breathe.

'What about him? Did he call you?' She doesn't want to hear that Jackson has confronted him, but she knows that's what's coming. It couldn't be anything else.

'He's... de... dead.'

She takes his arms, peels him off her. 'What are you talking about?'

'Mum, I think I did something terrible.' He's sobbing, and she can barely make out what he's saying. 'I didn't mean to do it!' he cries.

What happens next is like living through a nightmare, only she knows she won't be waking up any time soon. She will remember it for as long as she's on this earth; she already knows this as Jackson stands, grabs her hand and pulls her towards the kitchen.

She sees the blood before she notices Greg. A deep, kidney-shaped crimson pool. She turns to Jackson, who is shaking and hysterical. He's trying to tell her what happened, but she can only grasp hold of certain phrases. She doesn't need to ask how Jackson did it – her solid marble fruit bowl is covered in blood next to his body.

She needs to be calm, for his sake. It's too late to help Greg, so now she needs to help her son and do whatever it takes to keep him safe. It's all so clear to her in these moments; there is no other option – she is a mother.

The words come out of her mouth before she's even thought them through, and she tells Jackson that everything will be okay. They will clean up, keep Greg's body somewhere – in the shed is the place that comes to mind – until she can work out what to do.

'What was he doing here?' she asks.

'I… called him and asked him to come. It was an accident! I didn't mean to hurt him! He kept telling me he didn't want to talk about it, but I needed to know why he did that to you! He just wouldn't talk and then he kept shouting at me!'

Holly holds him tightly, strokes his back to calm him down. All she can think about is how she can fix this mess. Does Sienna know he was here? There is a lot to think about and Holly needs to make sure she ties up every loose end; otherwise Jackson's life is over. And that means so too is hers.

'I'm sorry, Mum,' Jackson says, over and over.

And she is too. She's sorry for everything.

# EPILOGUE

## Greg

Seven Years Ago

He shouldn't go to her flat. She'll take it as a sign that he's changed his mind, that this – whatever it's been – isn't over after all. He doesn't need this grief. Plus, the girl knows how to weaken him, and that's the biggest problem – he's still attracted to her. It would be easier if he wasn't. But he needs to face up to his issues with Holly, without hiding behind this ridiculous affair. Is it a mid-life crisis? He doesn't know. All he knows is that it's not worth the consequences of anyone finding out.

Above anything else, he doesn't want to hurt his son.

He curses himself for giving in to Leela when she pushed herself against him in his office. Sure, they'd been flirting a little, and he'd probably crossed that doctor-patient line way before anything physical happened, but he should never have succumbed to his urges. He thought he was better than that.

Worse still, is the fact that he did it again. And again. Until it turned into something more; in Leela's eyes at least. He might have enjoyed being with her but it was never worth this.

Still, he's doing the right thing by giving her the chance to say what she's got to say in person. He owes her that much.

Just as he's expected, she answers the door wearing hardly any clothes – just a skimpy short pyjama set. Normally seeing her dressed like this would excite him, but now he just feels on edge. Like he wants to run.

'You came,' she says. 'I didn't think you would.'

There's something off about her. She's unsteady on her feet and her eyes are bloodshot. 'Have you been drinking?'

Leela smiles. Then she laughs. 'If only you knew what I've been doing, Greg.' She's trying to sound sexy, but it smacks of desperation.

He doesn't ask; he wants to keep this visit as brief as possible. He's still standing by the front door, doesn't want to venture any further. 'Leela, look, I'm sorry about everything. I'm very fond of you. I hope you know that.' He sounds ridiculous, even to his own ears. People are fond of animals; he's used a word that diminishes her.

'Fond of me?' She laughs, but it only lasts a moment. She tries to pull him inside, but her hand slips from his skin. 'Please?' she says. 'Just come in for a sec.'

Against his better judgement he steps inside, feeling as he always does when he's in this place. Like he doesn't belong and has no right to be here. It was easy to shove that aside, though, because it was an escape from his life before. From Holly.

'I called you hours ago,' she says. Her skin looks paler and she's breathless; it's clear to him that something is wrong.

'I had things to do. I shouldn't be here at all, Leela. I know you're hurt but you'll find someone else. Someone younger, better for you. I'm in my thirties and I have a son. You deserve better than that.'

She tries to grab his arm but gives up. 'I don't *want* better than that. I want *you*.'

'Right now, you do, yes, but in time—'

'Don't patronise me, Greg. I might be young but I'm not stupid.'

He knows this. He would never have been interested in her if there hadn't been something about her, something far deeper than her beauty. It still isn't enough, though. They were never meant to be together.

Her flat is a tiny studio flat, but he remembers how proud she was to show him it. It was the first time she'd lived away from home. What was he thinking? He's too far past that stage in his life to have got involved with her.

'Are you going to stay with your wife?' Leela asks, walking across to the sofa. He tries not to picture the times they've lain together on there, their bodies entwined.

'No. No, I'm not. My marriage hasn't been right for ages, so I'm going to do what I should have done a long time ago.' If there's one thing he's sure of it's this: he doesn't love Holly and he needs to set her free. It's something he should have done years ago. He's stayed for Jackson though; but he knows his son will be okay in time.

Leela stares at him. 'You're lying. You must be staying with your wife. Why would you be ending us otherwise?'

'Because this isn't right. That's it.' He glances at his watch. 'I really need to go, Leela.'

'Don't leave me.' Her voice is almost a whisper. It's like she's fading away. He needs to get out of here. Now. He turns to leave.

'I'm going to tell everyone what you've done. You were my doctor, and you kept on treating me long after we were seeing each other. Maybe you'll lose your job. I could have a case against you for abusing your authority. And your kid will find out. I'll tell him myself. He'll never see you in the same way again.' She laughs and clutches her stomach, wincing.

He won't ask Leela what she's done – he already knows, and this is confirmed when she vomits all over herself. It's the final part of her revenge.

As soon as he's turned away again, he hears the thud. Her body smacking against the wooden floor.

He walks over to her – she's still breathing; her breaths are shallow. Passing her, he walks to the bathroom, checks the cabinet above the sink. There's not much in there other than sanitary towels and some beauty products. He finds what he's looking for in the bin, reaches into it and pulls out the aspirin packets. Counts them. Ten of them, each with thirty empty blister packs.

He needs to help her, call the ambulance, at least, but then he remembers her threat. There is no way he can lose everything. He's worked too hard. And if Jackson ever knew... Greg can't bear to think about that.

He doesn't look at her as he walks to the front door, opens it and steps outside. He rushes to his car, keeping it together until he gets inside and slams the door shut.

That's when he breaks down, burying his head in his hands.

As he drives away, heading back to a life that is forever changed, he vows to do everything necessary to protect his son, and his career. Yet he can't escape the certainty that sooner or later he will get what he deserves.

## A Letter from Kathryn

Thank you so much for choosing to read *The Other Husband*. I hope you enjoyed it! Books should take us on a journey as well as entertaining us, and I really hope I've managed to achieve that with this book. I also hope it managed to take you by surprise!

If you'd like to keep up-to-date with news of my forthcoming releases, please do follow the link below to sign up for my newsletter. Your email will never be shared, and I promise I'll only contact you when I have news about a new release.

www.kathryncroft.com/mailing-list

Reviews are so important to authors, so if you liked the book, I'd be extremely grateful if you could spare a moment to leave me a short review on Amazon, Goodreads, or wherever you purchased it. I really do love hearing readers' thoughts, and your reviews help me to reach new readers. I'd also really appreciate any recommendations to friends or family who you think might enjoy the book.

Please also feel free to connect with me via my website, Facebook, Instagram, or Twitter. I'd love to hear from you!

Website: www.kathryncroft.com
Facebook: authorkathryncroft
Instagram: authorkathryncroft
Twitter: @katcroft

Thank you again for all your support – it is very much appreciated!

Kathryn xx

# Acknowledgements

This is my eighth book, and once again it wouldn't exist without the help of so many people. I'm hugely grateful to my editor Leodora Darlington. Your enthusiasm and vision have truly made this book the best it can be, and it's such a pleasure to work with you.

As always, to my agent Madeleine Milburn and the whole team – thank you for all the hard work you have put in to supporting me over the last nine years! Thank you to Liv Maidment for going above and beyond.

Special thanks to Stuart Gibbon at Gib Consultancy for answering all my questions and correcting any errors in police procedure. Any mistakes still present are all my own.

Thank you to Andrew Welch and Shilpy Welch for all your help with my medical questions; I really appreciate the fact that you never seem to get annoyed when I throw them into our conversations!

During lockdown I managed to complete two books, but I wouldn't have been able to do that without my husband Paul. Thank you for your constant support, and for never complaining when I lock myself away and write for hours on end!

I have to say a huge thank you to my children, Oliver and Amelie – you bring much needed balance to my life and make me laugh every single day. Everything I do is for you, and I hope one day you will be proud of Mummy.

To all my readers, I'm so grateful that you've picked up this book, and taken a chance on me. Time is precious, and the fact that you've given up some of yours to read my words means so much to me. I'm especially grateful to anyone who has ever reached out to me on social media to let me know you've enjoyed my books – it really does make my day to read your comments.